THUNDER GOD

Paul Watkins was born in 1964. He is the son of Welsh parents and was educated at the Dragon School, Eton and Yale. His previous novels are *Night Over Day Over Night*, *Calm at Sunset, Calm at Dawn*, *In the Blue Light of African Dreams*, *The Promise of Light*, *Archangel*, *The Story of My Disappearance* and *The Forger*. He has also written a book about his experiences at public school, *Stand Before Your God*.

PAUL WATKINS

Thunder God

ff

faber and faber

First published in 2004
by Faber and Faber Limited
3 Queen Square London WC1N 3AU

Typeset by Faber and Faber Limited
Printed in England by Mackays of Chatham plc,
Chatham, Kent

A CIP record for this book
is available from the British Library

ISBN 0–571–22311–7

2 4 6 8 10 9 7 5 3 1

Norway

975 AD

Wealth dies.
Friends die.
One day you too will die.
But the thing that never dies
is the judgement on how
you spent your life.

Havamal, *The Way of the Norseman*

PART I

'There are no ghosts,' my mother said, 'nor demons, or monsters, or devils.' Every night, kneeling by the bed, she whispered these words to my sister and me. Darkness pooled around us, held back only by the weak and greasy flame of a lamp.

The last thing I would see were her lips, pursed as if to kiss the fire, and ripples of shadow round her eyes. I would hear the rustle of her breath, the pop of the flame as it went out and the smell of smoke as it brushed past my face.

When she left, padding barefoot across the floor, I would take back what she had said. I made my nightly apology to the spirits I felt sure were hovering in the air around me, just beyond the grasp of human senses.

When daylight came, my friends and my sister and I would search the fields and rocks and streams above the town, which marked the border line between the world of gods and men.

There were four of us.

My sister Kari was tall and thin, with crow-black hair and eyes the mysterious blue of glacier ice. By the age of twelve, she had stirred in many boys the first confusions of love.

My best friend, a square-faced boy named Olaf, had no time

3

for such distractions. It was his certainty that we would find this hidden gateway to the other world which drove us out onto the fields, no matter what the weather. We followed his stocky frame, already the body of a man, topped by blonde and unkempt hair which stuck straight up on his head, as if he were hanging upside down. Often he would turn to make sure that we were not lagging behind, fierce eyes squinting, as if permanently blinded by the light of his own private sun.

Stumbling at the back, as usual, would be a boy named Ingolf, whose belly hung in a suspended avalanche of fat over his shapeless trousers, hiding bloated thighs which chafed so badly that he had to wipe them with butter before dressing every morning. Ingolf sniffled constantly from colds or pollen sickness. He did not like being up on the high ground and the relief on his face as we were heading home was clear to see. The tales Olaf told us – of blue-skinned ghosts and mountain hags who cut the veins from sleeping children and used them as thread to make their clothes – had frightened him beyond all curiosity.

Ingolf's father, who ran the alehouse, was ashamed of his son's weight and runny nose. Sometimes he chased his squealing boy around the garden, as if he were hunting a pig. Ingolf's mother was a sharp-faced woman named Tola, who made a living by travelling from house to house after dark, selling fortunes and good-luck trinkets made from bird bones. On moonlit nights, she drifted through the waist-deep mist that clogged the village streets. There were rumours that she left her legs behind when she went out, propping them against the door like walking sticks.

Stories of the land we sensed but could not see were like a labyrinth of tunnels running just beneath the mud streets of our town. Some of its inhabitants were named and shaped, reachable with offerings and prayers. Others could only be

4

guessed at, remaining distant as stars. None were harmless and many so dangerous that the adults would not even tell us what they were.

But this only fuelled our curiosity. Hoping to learn more, we followed the weekly procession to the temple, which lay at the far end of the fields. It was a long, low building, with a turf roof, on which dandelions gathered in the summer.

The people taking part in the ceremony moved in a solemn, shuffling procession, all of our fathers among them. The group was always led by the same two men. One was Olaf's foster-father, Tostig, with hands so old and frail they seemed like tiny, featherless birds. He leaned on the arm of his assistant, Guthrun, red-faced and barrel-chested, with long, unkempt hair and shaggy brows that sheltered eyes the same green as a cat's. When not assisting Tostig, Guthrun was a blacksmith. The smell of his forge hung over our houses in damp weather, and we were woken by the rhythmic clanging of hammer on anvil early in those foggy mornings.

Children were not allowed inside the temple, no matter how much we begged. So we would peer through the doorway at long benches where people took their places. At one end, draped in shadow, stood the trunks of two trees, stripped of their branches. A face had been cut into the top of each pillar, with bulging eyes and inlaid teeth from wolves. One pillar represented the male gods, like Thor, Odin and Frey. The other stood for female gods, such as Freya, Idunn and Hel.

For the first few minutes, while a fire was kindled to warm the temple, the door would be left open. During this time, Guthrun and Tostig would cut a circle in the dirt around the pillars, using the tip of an old sword. Then they laid an iron ring on the ground, on top of which they set a bowl, filling it with water from a jug. Into this water, they dipped bundles of hawthorn twigs and flicked the water around the base of the pillars. What happened after that we did not know, as the door would be shut in our faces. We would press our ears to the heavy slabs of wood, straining to hear what was said.

Afterwards, when the temple doors were opened and people made their way home, we would follow them back down the hill. Our fathers would carry us on their backs, happy to put aside solemnity now that the praying was done.

It was Olaf, rather than my own parents, who became the source of everything I knew about the gods to whom our fathers prayed.

He had coaxed his knowledge from Tostig, along with the old man's warnings not to dabble in a world he did not understand. But Olaf didn't care about the risks. He believed he led a charmed life, and often reminded us how he had already cheated death once.

He had been found one winter, washed up on the beach in a rowboat so sheathed with ice it seemed to have been made of glass. The man and woman whom they found on board, who must have been his parents, were frozen to death. They had been washed out to sea, or escaped from a larger ship that was sinking. From the condition of the boat, they must have been out on the water a while. The mother had died first and the father, with no other way to nourish the infant, had made cuts in his chest and let his son feed off his blood until the cold clamped down on his heart. When Tostig found them, Olaf himself was close to death. Tostig had to prise him from his father's frozen arms.

Tostig adopted the boy, having no children of his own. As keeper of the temple, Tostig raised his foster son on stories of the seven Norse worlds and all the living things which they contained.

Olaf proved a good pupil. It was from him we heard of the Nissen, tiny elves who lived around the house and for whom

6

bowls of grain were left at certain times of year. There were the Hulder – who could only be told apart from humans by the tails they hid beneath their clothes. From Olaf came the story of the timid Fossegrinnen, who lived behind waterfalls and could be tempted out with gifts of food, which they repaid with their beautiful songs. Where mountain lakes mirrored the sky, Olaf warned us to keep clear of the shape-shifting Nokka, who dragged people down beneath the milky-silted water. These creatures, Tostig had told him, were to be found all over the country, but the story which most captured our imagination belonged only to our town.

This was the legend of Sasser Greycloak, who had once been a man but lived now as a beast out on the fringes of our world. Searching would not find him, said Olaf. When the time came, Greycloak would find us.

Olaf also spoke of a great source, from which the whole Norse world had sprung. Tostig had mentioned this only in passing and could not be persuaded to say more about it. Olaf often spoke of what the source might be, what it looked like, and what powers it might bring to the person who knew its hiding place. More than anything else, this became the object of his searching, though he did not even know what he was looking for.

Sometimes I wondered if what Olaf really wanted to find were the spirits of his parents, to speak with them, and learn how he had come to be washed up on the beach, lips smeared with his dying father's blood.

None of Olaf's stories frightened Kari. Even though she was only one year older, I looked up to her as I would have done to an adult. She seemed, unlike myself, a perfect combination of our father's ability to be awed by the smallest of things and our mother's colder reasoning, which knew the difference between reality and what we conjured from imagination.

7

Kari was always stopping to examine things which others had walked past, in our rush to reach a certain tree or rock or stream rumoured to be the hiding place of some wish-granting creature. It was thanks to Kari that we made our only true discoveries – nests of ptarmigan, patches of whortleberries hidden beneath the purple-flowered heather and the branched white bones of reindeer antlers.

I had joined this group of wanderers with more recklessness than sense. When we were up there on the high ground, I did not care what monsters we might lure from their caves. I did not think about the risk. Only at night, when I relived the adventures of the day, did the dangers take shape in my mind. At first, I so unnerved myself that I could barely find the courage to go out on the following morning. But when search after search turned up nothing, I began to grow weary of the hunt, as Kari had done long before. These days, she only came along to keep me company.

Of the four of us, only Olaf never tired, even after months of wandering across the rocky slopes, where windblown trees grew hunchbacked and wind roared along the knife-edge of the glaciers. With Olaf in the lead, we searched in dripping caves, at sources of streams which bubbled from their beds of moss, and in the boulder-choked gulleys of the Grimsvoss mountains, which rose almost sheer from the ground.

If Ingolf came at all, he usually left early, the time of his departing always marked in advance by his mother, who told him to be back before the shadow of the Grimsvoss reached the alehouse roof.

Later, Kari and I would head for home, while Olaf stayed behind. There were times when I looked back and saw him watching Kari and me, disappointment clear on his face, but refusing to give up the search.

The routine of those days began to crumble. I was leaving

them behind. I knew that in the time ahead, some friendships would grow stronger, while others would vanish, like the twisting flame my mother kissed away when she wrapped my sleeping world in ghostless dark.

But that all changed one night, deep in the blind man's black, when I heard something scratching at the door. I also heard my name, whispered on the hissing wind of a storm coming down from the mountains.

Without a sound, I left my bed and crept past my dreaming family. When I lifted the latch and looked outside, I saw the storm riding out of the hills, bellowing thunder and walking on the crooked legs of lightning. I watched the rain approach, grey air seething like the crest of a wave. Just as the storm broke overhead, I stepped outside, looking for the one who called my name.

Rain thrashed against my body, pouring from my fingertips in silver threads. As a thunderclap split the sky, I caught sight of a figure striding out across the fields. He wore a pale shroud, which streamed behind him in the wind, and a pointed hood pulled down over his eyes.

I knew him.

It was Sasser Greycloak, heading for the Grimsvoss, shoulders braced against the roaring gale. Suddenly, all doubts about the spirit world were swept aside.

I set out to follow him, breathing through clenched teeth as the rain spat in my face. I ran as fast as I could, stumbling over the uneven ground and gaining on him with each step. Just as I breathed in, ready to call out his name, I realised that his shape was changing. His stride across the fields became the gait of some half-human thing, a flesh-twisted nightmare, conjured from the storm itself.

All my courage left me. Horror spread like black wings

9

behind my ribs. I skidded in the mud, ready to run the other way, but slipped and shouted as I fell.

The figure stopped. Slowly he turned.

I screamed but never saw his face.

In that moment, the air filled with greenish-yellow light. It closed about me, writhing like something in pain. I heard no sound. The earth fell away beneath my feet. A bolt of lightning crackled through the air. Its jagged spear punched through my chest, branching fire along the tunnels of my veins until sparks flew from my finger tips. My fingernails melted as if they were chips of ice. Skin fell away in blazing shreds. Bone-white light filled my eyes and my body rose into the sky, clutched in the wild storm's claw.

I woke up to a world of silence. My eyes slowly focused on a ribbon of smoke, as it rose from a smouldering log. It took me a moment to realise I was home, and that the smoke came from our fireplace. Through the open door I saw my mother in the garden, pruning herbs which grew against the wall, pocketed in morning sun and sheltered from the wind. The crossbeams of our house were hung with bunches of these herbs, drying in the smokey air. Peppermint, goat weed, tansy, feverfew, marigold. My mother moved carefully among them, snipping away with a scissors which she kept tied to her belt, along with the house key and a wooden box filled with three bone needles. Her grey-blonde hair fell across her neck.

Then Kari's face appeared above me. She blinked in astonishment. 'He is awake!' she shouted. Then she ran outside, grabbing my mother by the arm.

A moment later, my mother stepped inside the house, brushing the dirt from her palms. She came and knelt beside my bed and ran her pollen-dusty fingers through my hair. They smelled of lemon balm and rosemary.

'I do not understand why I am still alive,' I said.

'Neither do we,' she replied, and went on to say that when my father found me, my clothes had been torn to rags by the lightning but my body was untouched.

At first, I did not believe her. I held up my hand and looked at it, remembering what I had seen, but there was not a mark on me.

'Hakon?' asked my sister.

'Yes?' I replied.

'Why did you go out there in the middle of the night?'

'It was Greycloak,' I told her.

Kari looked pale and worried, but my mother was smiling, pale wrinkles on her sun-browned face. 'That man has been dead for years,' she said. 'It must have been a dream. Have you forgotten what I tell you every night? There are no gods, no demons . . .'

'It was him!' I shouted her back into silence.

Greycloak's real name was Sasser Geirson.

Thirty years before I was born, he had arrived in Altvik, claiming to be a priest sent to take the place of one who had just passed away. He wore a cloak whose undyed wool had been tarnished by the smoke of sacrificial fires into the dinginess that gave the man his name.

Tostig had been apprenticed to the town's old priest, but now he began working with Greycloak. They barely had a chance to learn each other's names before another priest arrived, claiming that Greycloak was a fraud and had robbed him of his possessions. He chased Greycloak into the mountains and out across a bridge of snow which collapsed, sending Greycloak down a crevasse. For a while, the priest could hear him calling out from far below, his voice growing fainter as the cold sucked out his life. The priest left him there to die and went back to where he had come from, saying there was nothing for him here and that Greycloak had got what he deserved – to be tombed in a glacier, along with the things he had stolen.

Tostig took over the running of the temple and had been there ever since.

In the years that followed, a great silence settled on those mountains where Greycloak had disappeared, as if it was a living thing, warning us to stay away.

By the time I came along, what truth remained of Greycloak's life had become so tangled in the legends, that no one knew anymore which was which. In our minds, he lived now in a great hall made of ice. High on the bared-rock skull of the Grimsvoss, he had found a way to go on living past all boundaries of age, shrugging the burden of time from his old flesh and bones. He came down only in the storms, riding the wind like a horse when it blew across the glacier's wrinkled skin. On those nights, while we hid ourselves away from the gasping thunder of the storms, he walked the streets and scraped his long-nailed hands across our doors, letting us know he was back. People said if you were brave enough to follow him, he might lead you to his treasure. And if you were quick, you might fill your pockets with silver and find your way back home. But no one yet had been that daring, no one that fast.

Olaf and I had sworn a secret pact that we would be the ones. When the storms blew in, we never slept, waiting for that scratching on the door, praying for courage and speed.

Was it just a dream I had? Was Greycloak no more than a skeleton, sleeping in the cradle of the glaciers? Or had he called me out into the storm? A hundred times I relived that moment. Each time I grew less sure of what I had seen. Only the lightning was certain. Only the fire, branching from the sky to stop my heart and set it beating once again.

*

In this way, my life began a second time.

By the end of the first week, my hair turned grey and fell out.

My father sat at the table, whose legs had been fashioned from the rib-bones of a whale. He stared helplessly while my sister swept the floor around his feet and my mother fed me bowls of orange cloudberries, salted goat's milk and smoked reindeer meat which made my jaw ache because it was so hard to chew.

My father's name was Magnus. He was a tall man, always stooping to leave or enter our house. He had a shyness that did not match his size and a moustache which my mother said made him look like a walrus. He worked by himself on a small fishing boat which rarely strayed far from the shore. I looked forward to the day when I would join him in his work.

On summer mornings, Kari and I used to sit on the stone wall of our garden, watching his boat out on the bay. Sunlight fell like embers through the pines which grew along the rocky shore, making tiny stars of every dandelion on the turfed roofs of the town. I would feel its warmth brush like a hand across my face and see the flicker of my father's net as he cast it out over a shoal of fish.

He had a gift for knowing when schools of fish came to the bay. He would be sitting at the table, in the middle of saying something, when suddenly he would tilt his head to one side, as if he were cricking his neck. 'The salmon are here,' he would whisper. Or it would be the herring, or the mackerel, and he was always right. He told me that he felt it like a rushing in his heart, as if the movement of a million fins deep in the black water of the bay had sent a ripple through the red tide of his blood.

Nobody seemed to find my father's premonitions strange, but a boy who had been struck by lightning, and survived, was too much to ignore. They said that those who have been struck are marked as outsiders by the gods themselves, granted sight beyond what human eyes can see.

In the days that followed, as my mother and father went about their usual business, Kari never left my side. She treated me the same as she had always done and was the only one who did.

I found this out when Olaf and Ingolf came to see me. They lifted the blanket from my egg-smooth head and gasped. When I tried to tell them that I was not sure what I had seen, Olaf said that there could be no doubt. He talked and talked, saying this was proof at last, and that all our searching had been worthwhile. While he spoke, Ingolf just stared at me, the way he would have looked at something dead.

My father, like Olaf, was also convinced that I had passed through a hidden gateway into the world beyond. What worried him was that I might not have returned as the same person. When he thought I was asleep, I heard him tell my mother of rumours he had heard in town, that I was some creature living inside the strapped-on flesh of the dead boy I had been, sent to spy on them from beyond the realm of dreams. I could tell from the tone of his voice that he believed these stories, and his suspicions only grew when my once-brown hair grew back a coppery red, like some reflection of the lightning's fire.

As soon as this news reached the ears of Ingolf's mother, Tola, she sneaked up to our house after dark. She impaled the head of a white-faced owl on a stick in our garden to ward off the evil spirit that she said I had become. My mother discovered Tola just as she was sprinkling flakes of dried owl blood on our doorstep. She grabbed the first thing she could lay hands on, which was a mackerel, and chased Tola down the hill, clubbing her over the head with the dead fish.

After that, Ingolf was no longer allowed to see me.

From Olaf, I heard nothing at all.

14

Eventually, even Kari had to go. Despite her protests, our parents sent her down into town every day, to begin an apprenticeship which had been arranged with the village tailor. Kari left home at dawn and returned home only in the evenings, too tired to do anything more than eat her meal and go to sleep. This work brought her new respect from my parents. A new sleeping bench was built for her, and she and I no longer shared the one which was left to me. Kari did not have to cook or clean, except one day a week. My parents spoke to her with a strange formality, as if to place a distance between themselves and her. They knew the time was drawing near when she would leave their house for good, and they had already begun their long goodbye.

I would also be leaving home more often. Or so I had been told. This was to be the year that I began work with my father on his boat, but suddenly my father changed his mind, believing I had now been chosen for a different path.

In preparation for this, instead of teaching me about his trade, he began to share what he knew of the world beyond our own.

Late in the afternoons, when he returned from his work, he would bring me out to the storage barn, where smoked hams dangled from the rafters and baskets of wrinkled apples were stacked in the corners. He would place two milking stools in the middle of the cramped space and motion for me to sit in front of him. My father spoke as much with his hands as he did with his mouth, long fingers trailing through the air and white palms appearing and disappearing as he clenched his sunburnt fists. 'Far below us,' he said, 'are the roots of Yggdrasil, the tree in whose branches the world hangs like a never-ripening fruit. These roots form the roof of a house, which belongs to three widows called the Norns. They spin the multi-coloured threads of life itself and weave the destinies of men.'

15

As he spoke, his fingers unravled an imaginary spool of yarn. 'Coiled beneath the house of the Norns' – he twisted his feet around the legs of my stool and dragged me close, until our knees were touching – 'is the Midgard serpent, which will wake on the day of Raggnarok and destroy the world in a storm of fire and ice.

'We, the Aesir, live along the rocky shores and in the gentle valleys of the north, but above us, in the foothills of the mountains, live the Trolls. They exist in many forms, some with more than one head.' With these words, my father's open hand became a second face beside his own. 'Some Trolls are the size of mice, others as tall as trees.' He stood and reached towards the ceiling, and then he began to pace around me, as if he had become the beast itself. 'They hide in caves whose entrances we cannot see, leaving only at night and returning before dawn, because the rays of the sun will turn them into stone.' My father sat down with a dusty thump on the three-legged stool. 'They are slow-thinking and bad-tempered but dangerous if you venture out at night into the hills.'

'What do they eat?' I asked, filling my lungs with the dry, sweet smell of the storage barn.

'They chew the moss from boulders.' He pretended to gnaw at his knuckles. 'At night, if you watch carefully, you can see sparks from their teeth as they bite on pieces of flint, or you might hear the scrape of their bristly tongues over the rocks.

'Higher still, up on the mountain tops, live the Jotun. They are giants; part ice, part flesh, part stone, whose hearts you can see beating in the frozen cages of their chests.' Rhythmically, he opened and closed his fist. 'They hate us, who live down in the warmth of the valleys, and will butcher' – he hacked at the air with the knife edge of his palm – 'anyone who wanders up into the snow. Afterwards, they use the victim's flesh like bloody bandages to fill the cracks across their hide.' And he slapped his arms and legs, as if patching his own frost-rotted skin.

My father believed the tales that Greycloak had not died but lived among these monsters and preyed upon the snow-blind people who trespassed into their world. He lured them with music from a flute made from the shin-bone of a man. Welcoming them into his house, whose ice walls glowed an eerie blue, he would serve them a meal of bone-marrow soup in a cup made from a human skull. The blinded guests would compliment him on the soup and would ask about that strange sound they could hear – that hollow thump which seemed to fill the halls – never guessing that it was Greycloak's heart beating in a fleshless ribcage made of wrist-thick icicles. After the meal, he would give them a bed whose shaggy blanket was sewn together out of human scalps. The guests, still blind, would say how warm it kept them. Then, while they slept, Greycloak would bring his face close to theirs, suck all the air from their lungs and use their bodies to restore his own. With the remains, he would prepare another meal for the next lost traveller to be summoned by the music of his flute.

The ocean, too, was filled with spirits. My father spoke of Ran, the mother of nine beautiful, red-haired daughters, who had names like 'She Who Is Glittering' and 'She Whose Hair Is Russet in the Evening Sun.' They lived together in a drifting fortress on the sea. Its walls were made from foam-topped tidal waves, and its roof was a cloud of shrieking sea-birds. Ran spent her time gathering treasure from ships that her daughters wrecked and sent below the waves. My father swore he had seen their fortress, sliding like an iceberg through winter sea. He swore, too, that he had glimpsed those beautiful daughters, long hair wet against their milky backs.

'I hear them calling me,' he whispered. 'Their laughter echoes in my sleep.'

And above us all, my father said, beyond the ceiling of the sky, lay Asgard. This was the land of the gods, who dabbled sometimes cruelly in the fates of men below.

'Those things are in your dreams,' my mother told him, if he was ever foolish enough to mention the subject in front of her.

But in my father's mind, the gods were not in our dreams. It was we who were in theirs.

At the centre of it all, he said, hidden someplace in the vastness of our northern world, was a secret that linked these worlds together. This was the very heart of our faith, whose source was kept so hidden that those who knew about it never revealed where it lay, or what its power was or even what it looked like.

One day, when my mother could stand it no longer, she stamped out to the storage shed, flung open the door and shouted, 'I forbid you to believe those lies! It was nothing more than bad luck that you were struck by lightning, but your father refuses to see it that way. He has spent too much time out on the water catching fish and now he is starting to think like one.'

'I am trying to explain the things he needs to know,' said my father, straining to remain calm.

'You are not explaining,' she replied, raising her voice even louder. 'You are just making noise. Fish noises. You are the one who needs to hear some explaining, but you are too stubborn to listen.'

He stood and faced her, clanging his head against one of the iron pots that hung on a hook from the crossbeam. 'Stubborn? Who is stubborn, woman? You or me? You are more stubborn in what you do not believe than I am stubborn in what I do. And that, believe it or not . . .' he paused for an unbearably long time, then breathed in deeply and shouted, 'is one of the reasons I love you!'

18

Then my mother could not help but smile.

My father had a way of saying things to make their arguments disappear. Of all the qualities he possessed, this one I most hoped to inherit.

Even if I did not believe every word my father said, it was not possible simply to do as my mother commanded and banish all his stories from my head. I began to wonder if perhaps I really had been chosen for a different path in life.

I grew restless. I was angry at my friends for leaving me, angry even at Kari, because it was her absence that I felt the most.

My mother's answer to this restlessness was just to keep me busy.

When she carried up from town the fish that my father had not sold, my job was to cut them into flat shapes like the clipped-off wings of birds. We hung them out on racks to dry. This was in summertime, when the setting sun would only brush against the horizon before climbing again through a sky streaked purple and pink.

Later, when the weather turned to rain, we carried the fish inside wooden sheds and smoked them over birch-wood fires. The smell of that fish was rubbed like salt into our skin, into the rafters of our house and the fibres of our clothes. Every evening, my mother brushed the dry-curled scales from her arms and shook them from her hair.

She tried to carry on as she had done before, still chanting her denial of all ghosts, monsters and devils, but it seemed to me that even she was not certain anymore.

On rare occasions when I could sneak away from the chores conjured up by my mother, I wandered aimlessly or sneaked inside the temple. I threw rocks at the pillars, bouncing them off those bulging, furious eyes.

One day, when I was walking in the fields, a stone hit me in the back, as if hurled in revenge by the pillars themselves.

I spun around but saw nothing. Then I noticed Olaf stand up from the heather where he'd been hiding, sunlight glowing in the shambles of his hair.

I was so pleased to see him that at first I could not even speak. Before I found the voice to call his name, he threw another rock.

I bent my knees and the stone flew over my head. 'What are you doing?' I shouted.

'I heard you could make stones stop in the air without touching them.'

Slowly, I straightened up. 'I do not know who told you that.'

He started walking towards me. 'Down there they say you can and plenty of other things besides.'

I laughed. 'But you know that none of it is true!'

He shook his head. 'No,' he said. 'I do not know. Tostig says you will never be the same again.'

For a long time, we stood there in silence.

'Then why are you here?' I asked.

The wind tousled Olaf's hair. 'I want you to show me where the spirits live. You can talk to them. You can make them appear. You can do all of that now. My foster-father says you are changed. That you have been chosen by the gods.'

'Olaf,' I said quietly. 'I cannot do what you want. I do not know how.'

He took a step back. 'That is a lie,' he said.

I breathed in and felt the air trail out again. 'Olaf . . . It is only me.'

'No!' he snapped. 'It is not you. Do you know what they are saying in town? They say you walk up here at night and that you are followed everywhere by a dog with the face of a man. They say you have the power to make water flow upstream.

That you can change the shapes of clouds.' He stepped forward and flicked at my chest with the tips of his fingers. 'They say a raven lives under your shirt and at night you send it flying down to Altvik to listen at people's doors and scrape its beak across their shutters. Then it flies back and tells you everything it has heard.'

'None of it is true,' I protested. 'Olaf, you are my friend.'

'You were my friend. All you are now is a liar.'

'I swear I am not lying to you,' I protested. But it made no difference. I could not convince him.

He stalked back down the hill, pausing now and then to throw stones at me.

Until now, I had been able to persuade myself that things would eventually return to normal. Now I realised that Olaf was right, even if his reasons for saying so were wrong. The truth no longer mattered. All that mattered was what people believed. I had never felt as lonely as I did then or as helpless to do anything about it.

The following day, my father left to dry his nets. Once a year, he had to dry out the twine or it would rot. The smell of those nets, weed-tangled and glittering with fish scales, was too strong to hang them near town, so he took them to an empty beach up the coast and laid them in the sun. He would be back the next morning.

Soon after he left, Guthrun the blacksmith climbed the hill to our house.

My mother stood in the doorway. 'What do you want?' she asked, with a voice she reserved for people who tried to sell her things she didn't need.

I stayed in the house, hidden among shadows.

'I have come to speak with Magnus,' said Guthrun, swaying on his feet from the exertion of the climb. The way his legs were planted on the ground made it seem as if the earth was rocking beneath him and he was the one standing still.

'He has gone to dry his nets,' said my mother. 'Whatever you have to say to him, you can say to me.'

'I think not,' said Guthrun. He turned to leave.

'Say it!' barked my mother.

This stopped Guthrun in his tracks. 'Very well,' he muttered and turned around. 'Tostig has chosen your son as his apprentice.'

'But he has you to help him,' said my mother. 'What need does he have of an apprentice?'

'I am only his assistant,' replied Guthrun. 'Your son will one day be a priest. What Tostig will teach him, only priests can know.'

'I will not let him get him mixed up in that.' She wagged her finger in his face. 'Why does he have to send you to deliver the message? What is he afraid of?'

'Tostig knows you dislike him.'

'Well, that is the first sign I have seen of his intelligence.'

Guthrun was not backing down. 'He felt it would be better for you to hear this from someone who cares about you, who would never do anything to hurt you or your family.'

She became quiet but continued to glare at him.

I was impressed.

Guthrun had reasoned my mother into silence.

I had never seen it done before.

'The path of your boy's life,' he explained, 'was laid out long before the lightning ever struck him, before you even knew you would have a son. Even if you do not want to believe that . . .'

'I have no intention of believing it.'

He looked down at the ground. 'Surely you can see that my offer is the only chance he will have to be accepted. Your daughter is making a future for herself down there in town, and if she grows up to be less stubborn than her mother, she will have a good life. But what is there for your son? He cannot follow in his father's footsteps now.' For the first time, he fixed me with his cat-green eyes. 'Besides, he is interested in what I am saying. I can tell.' Then he turned back to my mother. 'I did not climb this hill to get the better of you, which is what you always think the world is trying to do. Now take my offer and do not try to have the last word.'

'I will do it.' The words jumped out of my mouth. For the chance of being accepted again, I would have agreed to anything.

My mother looked as if she had been slapped in the face. 'If that is your choice, Hakon, you can go with him now.' The tone of her voice made it sound as if she were saying goodbye to me forever.

Guthrun smiled. 'Tomorrow is soon enough.' From his pocket, he pulled a cross cut from a kind of shiny black stone which I had never seen before. The ends of the cross were flared out and flattened at the tips. It was wrapped with an old leather cord, which Guthrun unravelled and then hung around my neck.

'What is it?' I asked.

'Mjolnir. Thor's hammer. That cross is like no other. Tostig wanted you to have it.' He nodded to my mother and started walking back to town.

'You took your time coming!' she called after him.

Guthrun did not turn around. He just shook his head. 'Always the last word!' he shouted.

That night, just as I was drifting off to sleep, I heard a noise outside the house.

'It should have been me,' said a voice.

I sat up in bed. My heart jumped into my throat.

'What was that sound?' asked my mother, sitting up in bed.

Kari stirred under her blankets, too lost in sleep to hear.

Then the voice came again. 'It should have been me.'

'Who is that?' asked my mother. She was afraid.

The voice was moving around the house, now at the door, now outside the shutters, now in the garden. 'It should have been me. It should have been me.'

My mother lit the oil lamp with an ember from the fire. Its feeble glow spread through the room. Her hair hung loose around her shoulders and her linen nightshirt was crumpled.

Kari pushed back her blanket. 'What is it?' she asked.

'Stay in bed,' my mother whispered.

But I did not stay in bed. I went to the door and flung it wide, because I had guessed who it was.

There stood Olaf, his face pale in the light of a cloud-veiled moon.

'He is drunk,' said Kari and pulled the blanket over her head again.

'What are you doing here in the middle of the night?' asked my mother.

Olaf nodded at me. 'He knows!'

'Can this not wait until morning?' asked my mother.

Olaf laughed. 'Until morning. Until the morning after. And the day after that. Until the day of Ragnarok, it can wait.'

'Go home,' said my mother.

'Home to what?' Olaf held open his hands. 'It should have been me. I cared more about it than you ever did. Everyone knows that. Tostig should have chosen me.'

'What was I supposed to do?' I asked.

'Turn it down!' he shouted. 'You should have turned it down!'

'And live up here by myself for the rest of my life?'

His eyes looked sleepy. He waved his hand in front of his

face, as if he had walked into a spider's web. 'I do not care,' he said. 'It should have been me.' He turned around and staggered away.

My mother closed the door.

From under her blanket came Kari's muffled voice. 'He will be sick in the morning, and it will serve him right.'

I pushed past my mother and out into the night, ignoring her orders to return. I tried to find Olaf, but he seemed to have vanished. I went up to the temple, looking for him, but the place was empty.

While I was there, it began to rain and then to thunder.

I left the doors open and sat down on one of the benches, waiting for the storm to pass, but it only seemed to grow stronger. The rain which fell in front of the door looked like a grey veil, and the smell of it sifted into the room.

Lightning flickered, and in its flash I saw Olaf.

He was standing in the middle of the fields. His arms were raised, as if to touch the fire branching from the sky.

I called to him, but either he did not hear me or the sound of thunder stole my voice away.

When the lightning flashed again, he was gone.

I woke up in the temple, amongst the charred bones of old sacrifices.

Sun was shining through the open doors, puddles from last
night's rain reflecting a clear blue sky.

As I started walking home, I saw flames rising from the
town. Houses were burning. Half hidden in the smoke were
two boats, moored in shallow water near the beach. Long and
thin with dirty square sails and curved prows, I recognised
them from my father's stories. They were Drakkar warships,
the greatest nightmare to come trampling through the sleep
and waking dreams of every person on this coast.

Raiders with long and braided hair were loading their ships
with everything they could find. They carried off goats and
sheep, some of the animals still alive, with their legs bound
together. Others were dead, broken necks lolling on the shoulders of the men. The raiders brought out trunks of clothing,
which they tipped into the street and began trying on to see
what fitted. I saw men from our town chased into the water
and killed with long-handled axes. One woman reached out
towards her attacker, as if to stop the sharpened steel with her
bare hands. Her screaming reached me on the wind.

While I stood there on the crest of the hill, too shocked to move, one of the raiders spotted me. He dumped the armful of rope he had been carrying and began running up the path towards me. His shirt was made of countless iron links, its sleeves reached down to his elbows and its skirt stopped just above his knees. The salt of dried sea-spray was etched around the metal like a frost. Under this he wore a bright red tunic and baggy trousers made of heavy brown wool, which were bound at the calves but left to billow about his thighs. He carried a sword and a large round shield slung across his back in a way that seemed to twist his shape out of its human form. He wore a helmet with a heavy plate running down the bridge of his nose. The salty iron seemed to grow like some deformity out of his weather-beaten face, from which sprouted a tangle of beard as red as my own hair.

Smoke spread above the town and twisted away over the sea, snuffing out the gleam of sun off the water. Down in the village, fire curled like a breaking wave from the doorway of Guthrun's forge. The roof of my father's boat shed collapsed in an upward-falling rain of sparks. The walls tumbled in after it, as if the whole structure were being sucked into the ground.

The sound of the cracking timbers brought me to my senses and I ran, muscles turned to fire under my sweating skin. I sprinted down the rows of drying fish, brushing past them so the husks of their fins rattled together, spinning light to dark to light again, like leaves in the breeze.

I glanced back to see the raider closing in on me and at last, when I could go no further, I stopped and turned towards him.

We faced each other, both gasping for air.

He reached out to the black stone hammer which hung around my neck and, with one tug, snapped the old leather. The cord trailed over the sides of his hand.

'Where did you get this?' he asked, in a language I half understood.

'It was given to me,' I replied.

Carefully, he wrapped the cord around the medallion and put it in his pocket. Then he closed his fist in the tangle of my hair and pulled me down to the town, past screaming children and women and men who lay bleeding in the mud.

I called out for my mother and Kari, but there was no reply. Both of them would have left for town soon after sun up; Kari to go to the tailor's and my mother to the market for bread and milk. But I did not see them now among the corpses in the street.

I noticed a horse lying dead in the traces of a cart it had been pulling. The cart had been flipped over and a face was peering out from under it. It was Olaf, his skin blackened with soot, staring wide-eyed at the man who dragged me along.

The raider and I reached the water's edge. Bodies rolled in the surf. The scudding foam was tinted pink with blood.

The raiders waded out to their boats, piling in what they had stolen. They muttered under their breath as their eyes passed over me and seemed to disapprove of my being brought on board.

The man still held me by my hair. We had just begun to wade out to his ship when a door slammed in one of the houses and we both turned to see Tostig emerge from the darkness of his hut. He must have hidden himself or else had been of so little interest that the raiders left him alone. He was carrying an old war axe, whose wide, grey blade showed a band of silver along the edge. Tostig raised the axe above his head, snake-veined hands knotted around the wooden shaft. Then he began, very slowly, to move towards us. Tostig's lips were pulled back from his gums with the effort of holding the axe.

The other raiders turned to watch. Some of them began to laugh.

Tostig stumbled forwards.

The raider let go of my hair.

I should have run then. Perhaps that was what Tostig had intended for me to do, but I was as stunned as everyone else to see this ancient man waving an axe that he could barely lift above his head.

The metal-shirted raider smiled as he unslung the shield from his back and held it close against his chest. He drew his sword and braced his legs in the shallow water.

The other raiders cheered at Tostig, as if he were winning a race.

Tostig took no notice of them. He moved like a man in a trance. With ten paces still to go, he suddenly tipped forward. At first it looked as if he had fallen, but then the axe left his hands and flashed through the air, end over end, and the gasp that went up from the raiders came at the same moment as the crash of the blade against my captor's shield. He staggered back as the axe blade cut clean through the metal strapping which held his shield together and jutted through the other side, a finger's width from his chest.

Tostig was on his hands and knees in the sand, head down, fighting for breath.

The raider threw aside his ruined shield and strode across to him.

I thought he would kill Tostig then, but instead he hooked his arm around the old man's body and lifted him up the way I had seen sheep hoisted from pens. He carried Tostig out to the boat, pushing me along in front of him.

When the warships left our bay a short while later, Tostig and I were on board, tied by our necks to the mast, side by side with our backs against the wood. On deck were bags of money from almost every family in town and chests filled with silver cups and amber beads. Clothes lay heaped upon the planks.

Despite its size, Altvik had been a wealthy town. The few

who had refused to give up their money were dead and burning in their houses or staring up through bloodied water from the bottom of the bay. The flames of Altvik reached into the sky. Above them, thick smoke gathered like some distorted shadow of the ships that had brought these men here. Then even that disappeared.

The second ship kept close behind us, following in our wake.

Soon after we lost sight of land, another boat appeared, coming towards us.

Instead of trying to get away, the raiders slackened sail and waited, curious who would be so bold as to come out to meet them.

It was my father. He stood at the tiller and his wild yelling reached me on the breeze. He must have returned to the town and found out what had happened.

Tostig's hand settled on my shoulder. 'It is no use,' he whispered.

I felt my muscles twitch, ready to hurl me into the water, but even if I could have untied the knot around my neck and jumped overboard, the cold would have dragged me down long before I closed the gap between us. I slumped back, as if the weight of Tostig's hand was too much for me to bear.

Across the foam-slicked waves, I heard my father call my name.

When the raiders saw that it was just a small fishing smack, nothing they could use, they tightened the sail lines, hauling them until their knuckles turned a bloodless white. The man at the steerboard arched his body like a bow, arm muscles taut under his skin. The Drakkar seemed to gasp as we lunged forward over the swells. My father's boat fell far behind, his shouting lost on the wind. His boat slipped behind the waves, then re-emerged and slid away again. Each time, I saw less of it, until the boat had disappeared for good.

A sudden, bone-hollowing emptiness spread through my body, as all the memories of my home, which until that moment had flickered through my head as if they were alive, like a flock of birds in the blue sky of my eyes, became still, their bright colours already fading.

Soon after, we ran into thick fog rolling off the land. It smelled of pine and mossy earth, mixing with the salt breath of the sea. The fog wrapped so thickly around us that we lost sight of the other Drakkar. Our boat hauled down its sail and waited. The crew lit torches, shot burning arrows out into the mist and called with hands cupped round their mouths, but the fog had swallowed up their friends.

As darkness settled on us, Tostig mumbled prayers to his wooden-faced gods.

The raiders discussed what to do. They were speaking in the Eastern Norse of the Danes and Swedes, not the Western Norse of my own people. They talked of the bad luck they'd seen this year, and how the haul at Altvik had made up for all of it. But now this. The quietest among them was the captain, a short, wide man named Kalf, with eyes almost hidden under a bony ledge of brow and calves that were thicker than my thighs. He covered a bald patch on the top of his head with a small round cap of blue wool and wore a brown cape with a hood. When the night grew cold, he pulled this up and peered from it like a badger from its burrow. He was a Christian and prayed to a brass cross nailed to the mast of his ship, but when the wind picked up, he prayed to Norse gods too. I heard him called an English Dane and learned through my eavesdropping that there were other Norsemen on the crew who had settled in England. They were heading back as soon as they sold off their cargo at a place called Hedeby, which lay further to the south. At Hedeby, the crew would split. Those who lived in the northlands would find their own ways home. The English Danes would take their ships and sail away. From the things they said, it seemed clear that Kalf had made a life's work of raiding. He came across the sea most years and recruited people from the coastal towns. Some of these men would wait every year for the sight of Kalf's sails on the horizon, then drop everything and go raiding with him.

Sitting among them, I felt the impossible frailty of my own life. Each time I raised my head, seeing only tar-black waves beyond the boat, I knew that Tostig and I were beyond all help except what we could pray for or could find inside ourselves.

I overheard that I was now the property of a man named Halfdan. Now and then, I caught him looking at me the way he might look at an animal, wondering if it could understand what he was saying.

Halfdan had few friends on the crew. Those he had, he didn't seem to want. It was clear that they respected him, but what he had done to earn their admiration I did not discover until later.

As the night wore on, Kalf's men grew quiet and peered suspiciously at Tostig, as if he might somehow be responsible for this fog.

I began to wonder as well, as I drifted from rage to tears to sleep. The faces of my friends and family seemed to hover in front of me, with the same flickering light as that which catches on the wings of insects when the sun is going down.

When morning came, the fog still lingered round us and there was no sign of the other ship. Kalf said they must have carried on to Hedeby, so we raised our sail and caught the wind, leaving the ghostly mist behind.

It would be many years before I found out what happened to those missing men. Until that time, I often saw them in my dreams. They sailed the red ocean of my sleep, caught in its currents, which steered them again and again to the shore of

32

Altvik. They burned it down a thousand times, as weary of the slaughter as the ghosts they came to kill. But in my dreams they were powerless to stop themselves, helplessly reliving the butchery they had begun.

The sun came out, and I slept with its warmth on my face, too exhausted even to think. I woke as Tostig's hand gripped my knee. He set a finger against his lips, motioning for me to be silent.

The raiders lay strewn across the deck, wrapped in heavy cloaks. They had rigged a cloth awning just forward of the mast, and it was under this that most of the men were sleeping. Halfdan stood at the tiller.

'You must get home again, no matter how long it takes,' whispered Tostig, his lips brushing against my ear and the warmth of his breath on my cheek. 'The purpose of your life has been made clear. You are to be a messenger between the gods and men. Yours is a gift beyond all the riches stolen from us today, even the black stone cross, which points towards the very source of our faith – the only thing to pass bodily from the land of the gods into ours and from which our world draws all its meaning and its strength.'

This was the source my father had spoken about, the greatest secret of the Norse religion.

'You children,' he continued, 'are brought up to believe that Sasser Greycloak was a thief, but he was the great protector of our people. His sacrifice is to be thought of as a monster, when everything he did was for the cause of our religion. To call him a beast is the only way to keep the truth hidden. He, like you, was struck by lightning and chosen as a messenger. That thing, which people say he stole, was the hammer you were given yesterday. It has been worn by every guardian of our temple since the source was sent down by the gods. I myself lifted that hammer from around the old priest's neck and gave it to Grey-

33

cloak to wear. Soon afterwards, a man arrived in Altvik. He claimed that the hammer was his and believed that it alone held all the power of our faith. When Greycloak saw the man coming, he fled into the hills, but not before he showed me that the hammer is only an illusion, hiding the truth from all but a few. Greycloak lured him up into the mountains, away from the true source. After Greycloak fell through the ice bridge, the man believed that hammer lost for good. But year after year I searched the ice caves until I found his frozen body and the cross which he still carried. That day the lightning struck you down, I knew you were chosen to wear it.'

'But if the source is not the hammer, then what is?'

'The answer to that is buried in the ground beneath the Altvik temple. The secret has been handed down for genera- tions, from one chosen priest to another. Only those who wear the black hammer ever learn the truth. Once these raiders have finished with me, you will be the only one who knows. That is why you must return to Altvik. Without you to protect it, the secret will be lost.' He took hold of my wrist and gripped it harder than I thought he could. 'Now swear to me you will go back, no matter how long it takes.'

I nodded, too afraid to speak.

Tostig sat back. He closed his eyes and nodded, satisfied.

Later that day, I overheard Kalf telling Halfdan to get rid of us.

'They have brought us bad luck,' he said. 'You must do it for your own sake, and for ours.'

Halfdan stared at the deck, frowning and saying nothing while he listened. Then suddenly he got up, drew his sword and cut the rope which fastened me and Tostig to the mast. The sword blade sank with a dry smack into the wood. He dragged us to the side and, without a moment's hesitation, heaved Tostig into the water.

Before the old man fell, I thought I saw him smile at me.

I cried out and tried to grab him, but Tostig drifted through my fingers like a shadow. He vanished under the waves.

As I watched the place where he had disappeared, I felt a thundering inside my head, so powerful that I began to lose consciousness. Pictures began to appear before me, blurred and thrashing and streaming through my eyes like dry sand blown across a beach. They poured into my head with such force that I felt sure my skull would shatter into gritty, powdered bone.

Then suddenly I was longer seeing through my own eyes. I was under the water, drowning, locked inside the flimsy cage of Tostig's body, drifting down into the freezing dark. Pressure stabbed into my ears. My lungs burned as the air in them grew stale. I clawed at the water, and with a last muffled shriek, my jaw locked open and the sea poured in. A stream of bubbles slipped from my mouth, like a broken string of pearls trailing towards the light. Blue sparks flashed behind my eyes. Then nothing. Not fear. Not life. Not even the knowledge that there was such a thing as life. I saw myself as I would be if I followed the old man – hollow-eyed and white with death in the blackness at the bottom of the sea.

As violently as I had been forced behind his eyes, I was thrown free. I looked down at Tostig's pale hands, which trailed upwards in the silty water as he sank away, clothes billowing around him. I watched until he vanished from sight, then climbed with the bubbles from his flooded lungs until I reached the rolling tundra of the waves.

I rose from the sea like a newborn drawn from the womb, returned into this house of blood and bone, screaming and thrashing and blind with the salt of my tears.

Halfdan held me by the neck, my face only an arm's length from the water rolling by. Halfdan was about to push me overboard when Kalf shouted at him to stop.

35

'Not that one! Wait until we get to Hedeby, then sell him to one of those Slav traders.' Kalf rubbed the tips of his fingers together in front of his face. 'Do not let him go to waste.'

Halfdan dragged me back to the mast and tied me up again.

I cried until I was hoarse, howling like a dog and struggling at the rope until it choked me into silence.

The remainder of the journey lasted three days, during which time I did not eat the food they put before me nor drank the water which they ladelled from a barrel with a wooden scoop and held against my mouth. I tucked my knees against my chest and did not speak, only slept or stared out at the sea. My mind went blank. I no longer cared what happened to me. Living or dying seeemed one and the same.

On the morning of the fourth day, we reached the port of Hedeby, a place many times the size of Altvik. Smells of smouldering peat, sour milk, roasting meat and human dirt fanned out to greet us. As we rode into the harbour, I saw two huge pillars silhouetted against the sky on a barren patch of land overlooking the water. Each was carved with a face, like the pillars in my village. Sacrificed animals hung from iron hooks embedded in the pillars. Fires smouldered on the shingle beach below and fur-clad figures hunched around them, shifting in the smoke.

The harbour was crowded with heavy-bellied trading ships.

Before we went ashore, Kalf divided the goods from Altvik. He carried out his work with a solemn face, selecting items from the jumble of property and laying them one by one at the feet of his men.

The raiders sat cross-legged and silent, never taking their eyes off the growing piles, most particularly the one that Kalf made for himself. He favoured the English Danes, which seemed to be expected by the Norsemen. But even the eyes of the English Danes grew dark as Kalf's hoard towered above their own.

By the time Kalf had finished, I felt sure the crew would kill him. But no one complained or lifted a finger against him. They gathered up their belongings and rowed into town in one of the many small boats which ferried people back and forth from their ships.

Kalf and his crew were not strangers in Hedeby. The arrival of their ship drew an assortment of cripples, some of them so torn from their natural shape that they barely looked human at all. Beside them stood owl-eyed merchants in gaudy fur-trimmed cloaks and long-toothed women with faces creased by scowls. They scattered when the rowboats began ferrying us ashore. The merchants looked down at their shoes as we walked by, and the cripples slunk back into the shadows, like snails retreating into their shells. Only the women held their ground, with the hard, unfocussed stares I had seen in the eyes of slaughtered sheep.

Everywhere around us, houses were being built. The blond glare of new wood stood out against the smoked timbers of the older buildings. Some structures were roofed with tent-cloth, others turf-capped like the buildings of my home. Everybody seemed to be shouting. Their words merged into a meaningless chant, while hands clawed the air with angry urgency. Women in mud-fringed dresses carried their shoes, walking barefoot with the cautious tread of herons in a pond. In the darkness of one building, I saw the glowing outline of a red hot sword and heard the coughing hiss as a blacksmith lowered it into a vat of water. Musty-smelling steam billowed out into the street. Down an alleyway, I glimpsed an old woman in the moment that she slapped a young girl in the face. The girl's nose immediately began to bleed.

Halfdan tied a rope around my neck and pulled me after

him, clearing a path through the crowds. I felt as if I were watching myself from a great distance in the sky. Beyond sadness. Beyond hope.

In the market square, standing among clumps of horse-shit seething with brown flies, I was put up for sale.

Men with dark skin and pointed beards gathered around me. Their clothes were long and draping and their breath carried a smell of smoke and sweat. They made me open my mouth. One man tapped my front teeth with a coin. They set their thumbs beneath my eyes, drawing down the skin to look under my eyelids. They made me take off my shirt and walked their fingers down my spine.

Three of these men began to bargain with Halfdan. They sat on a rug which one of them had laid on the ground. Onto the carpet in front of him, each man emptied a pile of coins, some of which were broken into pieces. As one added to his pile, the second increased his own. The third man, seeing the amounts laid out by his friends, began to sweat even though it was a cold day. He gathered up his coins, let them rattle back into the leather pouch that he kept around his neck, stood up and walked away.

The dealing continued. The men removed gold or silver rings from their fingers and threw them on their piles.

Halfdan kept glancing at me and then back at the men. He began muttering to himself.

The brown-skinned men looked at each other questioningly.

Suddenly Halfdan climbed to his feet. He held one hand flat at the level of his chest, then made a cutting motion outwards, to show that there would be no sale.

The other men began to protest. They babbled sharp and fast and raised their hands to Halfdan.

Halfdan folded his arms and looked at the ground, waiting for the noise to die down.

38

But the chattering only grew louder and angrier.

I worried they might draw the long, curved blades which they carried at their sides.

Before that could happen, Halfdan strode right through them, pushing the men aside and treading on the carpet, which upset the piles of coins. He walked over to where I stood, grabbed my arm and hauled me away.

The scattering of their coins distracted the brown-skinned men, who scrambled to gather up their money and immediately began to argue over which coins were whose.

As he led me away, Halfdan paused for a moment to watch the brown-skinned men. I saw his fist loosen around the rope.

I did not think about what I did next. The thought and the action came at the same time. I took hold of the rope and wrenched it out of his grasp. The cord slid between his palm and fingers, and Halfdan cried out as the rope burned his skin.

I ran, hearing angry voices as I barged down the narrow, crowded street. I ducked into an alley and then into another. I sprinted through a slaughter yard. Beheaded animals hung upside-down from wooden crossbeams, bleeding into the mud. Huge piles of entrails, kinked and twisted like the rope around my neck, were being shovelled into waiting carts. I crossed another street. Not knowing where I was headed. Only to get away. I could not tell if he was following. The rope scratched at my neck. I gathered the loose end against my chest.

A moment later, I slammed into a woman carrying a reed basket of green-and-black-backed mackerel. She was coming out of a house. The basket flew out of her hands, and the fish fell on the ground. Some of them were still twitching. The smell of freshly-caught fish, the colour of the woman's hair and the way she had braided it shoved before my eyes a vision of my mother. For a moment, everything that had happened to me since I left Altvik took on the substance of a dream. I felt myself sliding through veils of sleep towards the instant when my eyes would open. I expected to wake, and for my mother to be there beside me, having somehow trespassed into my imagination. But then the woman screamed a crow-like cawing shriek which drilled into my head and I knew then it was no dream. I dropped the rope and with my next footstep I tangled in the coils and fell.

When I looked up a moment later, Halfdan was standing over me.

'Get up,' he said. There was no fury in his voice, only a tired, fleeting patience.

The woman began shouting at him about the fish.

Slowly Halfdan brought his face close to hers. He whispered something in her ear.

The woman's eyes closed as he spoke. Her lips pressed tight together. Without another word, she picked up her empty basket and stepped back into the shadows of her house, leaving the fish where they had fallen.

Now that I had a chance to see where I was, I realised I had run so blindly that I had come around in a circle and ended up back where I started.

'Go on,' Halfdan told me. 'Run.' He held out his hand, as if to show me the way home.

I stared at him, and at the dirty faces which peered at me through half-closed doors, waiting to see what happened next, wide-eyed with the expectation of violence.

Halfdan bent down, hands on his knees. 'Where do you think you will go?' he asked.

I did not answer.

'How far do you think you will get?' he asked.

I saw the brown-skinned men watching me, their mud-spattered hands clutching gold coins.

Halfdan straightened up. 'Where you and I are bound, no

one will help you. No one will keeep you safe but me. Run again and I will not even do you the favour of killing you.' He reached down with his reddened palm, picked up the rope and coiled it back around his hand.

I had known before that I was lost, but I did not understand until that moment just how lost I was. I made no move to pull the rope away. Nor did he have to haul me to my feet. When he began to walk, I followed, treading in his footsteps, back towards the harbour.

'Why did you not sell me?' I asked.

'They saw the colour of our hair and accused me of selling my own son,' he replied. 'They thought I could not understand their language.'

Later that day, Halfdan fetched his belongings from Kalf's ship. Jokes were made about the fact that I had not been sold. Halfdan took to swatting me on the back of the head, as if this was all my fault.

We walked away through the muddy street. Halfdan had tied a rope around my neck. He kept the other end knotted in his fist.

'Kalf cheated you,' I said, as he dragged me along.

Haldan looked back at me and narrowed his eyes. 'Kalf steals it all twice,' he replied. 'First from places we raid and afterwards from us.' Then he swatted me again.

That night we jumped aboard a trading ship bound for the eastern Baltic and began the long journey to a city called Miklagard. It lay far to the south, down a river called the Dnieper. Five times we had to come ashore, while the boat was hauled across the ground over logs to avoid the rock-filled rapids, each one of which had a name – Always Fierce, Always Noisy, The Yeller, The Impassable, The Laugher. And worse than these rapids, I learned, were a people called the Petcheneg, who ambushed travellers here. When we passed through their country, rumours were still fresh of a prince named Svyatoslav, whose convoy had been attacked. After the Petchenegs had finished with him, Svyatoslav was placed on a raft, limbless, tongueless, blinded but still living, and sent downstream, where he eventually caught up with those of his caravan who had managed to flee the ambush.

Despite what had happened at Hedeby, I thought constantly about running away. But as the distance grew between myself and home, the prospects of getting back on my own grew smaller and smaller. Each chance of escape only guaranteed a fate even worse than being this man's slave. Any hope of fulfilling the promise I had made to Tostig now seemed beyond all possibility.

I learned, from dozens of smacks on the head, not to talk to Halfdan unless he spoke to me first. Even then I was not to answer unless he had actually asked for a reply. This did not mean that we travelled in silence. He often talked about his home in the north country, where he came from a people called the Svear. Upon the death of his father, his older brother had inherited the family land, leaving Halfdan to seek his own fortune. He had been moving from place to place for many years and no longer seemed to know what he was searching for.

Often Halfdan would take the black hammer from around his neck and examine it carefully. Again and again he asked me where I had found it.

I said I had been given it, and that was all I would say.

'There was another black hammer,' he said, 'sent down by the gods to be the anchor of our faith. But I heard that it was lost long ago.'

From then on, until the day he died, the hammer never left its resting place, tucked against the hollow of his throat.

Each day, wherever our boat put in to shore, Halfdan would find a secluded place to pray. The first time I saw him do this, we had come to a clearing in the vast and ghostly white birch forests south of Starya Ladoga. Sunlight filtered through the trees. Leaf shadows dappled the ground and shimmered in the branches above me. The smell of heated sap hung in the air. Halfdan's voice remained so quiet and steady that it did not stop the birds from singing in the nearby trees.

There were different prayers for whatever dangers faced him, as well as different gods to whom he prayed.

I saw an unexpected gracefulness to his gestures, as he drew his sword and carved a ring around himself in the dirt. He would empty from his leather prayer bag a linen bundle containing rock salt, a tiny fat lamp made of soapstone and a shallow grey-white bowl, which was the brain-pan of the first man he had ever killed. He faced north as he prayed, judging direction from the growth of old moss on the old trees. Holding his arm out straight, he would take up a handful of dirt and let it sift slowly through his fingers. Then he sprinkled some salt, only a few crystals, into the bone cup and added water from his drinking skin. If he had any fat for the lamp, he would light it and hold the cup over the tiny flame, dissolving the salt. He would lift the cup and pour the water over his head, then kneel with his hands on the hilt of his sword, sinking the blade into the earth.

This ritual marked the beginning of every prayer, which was always followed with these words:

> The boundaries of time are come undone.
> I stand in the gateway between two worlds.
> Hear me through the veil that hides you from my sight.
> Help me through this day.
> Watch me. Shelter me.
> Do not forget me.
> I am your child.

Sometimes our fellow travellers, draped in furs and weaponry, would come to watch. They kneeled at a respectful distance, swords laid out on the ground in front of them. Whatever words Halfdan had for his god, these others seemed to lack. They had no affection for Halfdan, but when it came time to ask for help in cruising the cataracts of the Dnieper, its banks strewn with wreckage and the rag-clothed bones of those whose luck ran out, these men would trust him with their lives.

To take his mind off the cataracts and the Petcheneg, Halfdan spent his time gambling. By the time we put ashore one night, he had lost half of what he owned, and took out his frustration by striking me for some imagined offence until my front teeth were loose and one of my eyes was swollen shut. Then he walked me out onto a treeless plain through which a river twisted sluggishly.

I wondered if he was going to kill me, and realised that I was less afraid of the beatings, or even of dying, than of the fact that I never knew what he was going to do next.

Halfdan pushed me far out through the rustling, knee deep grass.

'Here,' he said, suddenly, and pointed to the ground.

I understood then that he had only been looking for a place to pray.

A storm came down upon us while we prayed, twisting the gut of the sky into coils of greenish-grey. He took no notice of the first claps of thunder, but when the rumbling drew closer, stabbing the clouds with lightning, he grew afraid and lay flat in the middle of his sword-drawn ring. Storm clouds, veined with fire, tumbled across the plain.

'Get down!' shouted Halfdan. 'Get down!'

But I stayed on my feet. The only way to defy him was to sacrifice his property, which was what my life had become. The grass thrashed in sudden gusts of wind and soon it was raining so hard that I could barely stay on my feet. The bellowing of the storm was all around us, whipping past in a stampede of fire-legged beasts. The sky crackled like fat spitting from cooked meat. I breathed the burnt air and felt the pressure in my ears as the bolts cut through the sky above me. In all its wordless fury, the lightning raged but never hurt me, as if its only chance had failed, and I laughed as Halfdan cowered at my feet.

After the storm, sunlight blinded us with its sharp and twitching glare as we made our way back over the wet grass. A rainbow arced through the settling sky. Halfdan looked at me as if I might at any moment climb its colour-banded path and disappear into the clouds.

I had meant only to defy him, but in his mind, I had defied much more than that.

After that day, he addressed me in tones of respect, and put aside the beating of his slave. I became more of a student than a servant. There were times he even treated me like a son. The only way to keep his respect was to listen to his teaching, and in spite of myself, I could not help wanting to learn.

Soon I knew the names of all the Norse gods, not only Odin, Thor and Frey, about whom I had learned from my father, but Baldur, Bragi, Forseti, Heimdall, Njord, and Ull. He made me recite their names, and the names of the seasonal rites – The Feast of the Dead, Winter Solstice, Samhain, Walpurgisnacht, Imbolc, Spring Equinox, Sun's Turning, Lunasa, The Feast of Fallen Warriors and so on – until they merged in my head into one long barely-pronouncable incantation.

About each god, he would give only one or two details – Odin's single eye and frequent treachery to those who worshipped him; Thor's red hair, his stubborn loyalty and fearsome temper; war-god Tyr's one hand; Heimdall standing guard upon the rainbow bridge which spanned the gaps

45

beween the worlds. But any more than this, it seemed, was left to the mind of each one who prayed to them. In that way, the gods took on the faces of people who passed through our lives, broken down and reassembled in the workshops of our brains.

As well as different prayers, particular substances were used for invoking the various gods. For summoning Odin, Halfdan needed a gold coin, to be set inside a drawing of a raven, which he traced in the ground with a stick made from yew. For Thor, a piece of iron would be placed on the symbol of a double-headed axe, drawn with a sliver of oak. For Frey, it was the symbol of a boar marked out with a pine branch and fastened to the earth by a knuckle of brass.

It was expected, and seemed natural, that each person would pick a god in whom they confided the most.

For Halfdan, that was Tyr, a god not only of war but of sea-faring and of the persecuted. For prayers to Tyr, he used a hawthorn twig to draw the outline of a sword, in which he laid a lump of bronze.

It made sense for Halfdan to have chosen Tyr as his patron god, since although Halfdan had not been persecuted by any-one I ever saw, his mind was filled with notions of conspiracies against him. The fact that no one could be bothered to oblige him by actually persecuting Halfdan meant that he had, in the end, to persecute himself.

When ordered to choose, I picked Thor, who stood for order, strength in conflict and trust of instinct. This last quality spoke to me most clearly of all. Halfdan did not mind that my choice was different than his own. He saw it as correct that I would choose the Thunder God, especially after what he had wit-nessed in the storm and the hammer he had found around my neck.

As our journey toward Miklagard progressed, Halfdan sometimes asked me to choose the places where we would pray. At first, I had no idea how to go about this, and would just point to the nearest patch of flat, dry ground. Halfdan would move us on until we found a different place, and I could not deny that these locations did have a kind of balance absent from the spaces I had chosen. It was only when he explained to me that there was a gift to ground-choosing – a gift which he felt I possessed – that I began to understand.

Our world, he said, was made of layers, more than most people could perceive. Beyond the reach of untrained senses, the world of the gods swirled all around us, unchecked by the boundaries of space and time which fenced our tiny fraction of the earth.

Halfdan told me that each thing contained a kind of life beyond what anchored it inside its visible form. This life belonged not only to people and animals but to every tree and rock, to every cloud that drifted by. Even possessions which had seen many years of service took on a kind of life, burnished into them by the sweat of their owners. You could feel the faint vibration of it; in a sword or a shield, a set of carpenter's tools or even an old pair of shoes. It was everywhere, like the rumble of a river running deep beneath the ground. You could learn to sense the places where it was strongest, often around a particular tree, suspended in its leaves as raindrops are after a storm. Or it spread like a veil of fog across certain fields. It could be found near springs which bubbled from the soil. Halfdan said these marked the places where the veil between the worlds was thinnest, where the crossing could be made as easily as walking through a doorway, if only you knew how.

This ground-choosing was the first time the other world appeared truly alive to me, no longer a collection of names, and stories, and complicated prayers. At first, I could get no further than an understanding of how much it was that I had failed to understand. But even this, Halfdan said, was a necessary step towards the changes that would come. After many stages of transformation lay a voyage beyond the bone cage of the body, when people lay as if dead while their spirits ranged across the earth, sometimes inhabiting the forms of animals, sometimes disguised as breaths of wind.

Slowly, I began to see. New instincts appeared inside me, as if awakened from a hibernating sleep. When I walked through the forests to choose the ground on which we prayed, I felt the sharpening of those nameless senses which drew me to the sacred sites. Soon I could lead us to them as easily as Halfdan had done.

Just as this gift refused to be held within the flimsy clutches of our sight or touch or hearing, it also lay beyond the grasp of words, defying all who tried to measure it with speech. And yet it was there. When I prayed at Halfdan's side, the world around me seemed to shimmer with this life, reducing it to the grainy dream of an illusion, which my life back in Altvik, and the family and friends I left behind, had already begun to resemble.

Halfdan had come to Miklagard in order to offer his services to the Emperor Basil II who, at the age of eighteen, had just begun his rule over Byzantium.

Miklagard, its capital city, was a place so vast and crowded, steeped in the smell of unnameable spices and filth, that in all the time I spent there, I never felt truly at ease.

There were already a number of Norsemen working for the Emperor. In time, they became known as the Varangian Guard. They came from every corner of the Norseman's world, and in their meshing of the Eastern and the Western languages, as well as of words borrowed on their way across the Mediterranean or down the crooked path of the Dnieper, they had emerged with a language of their own. This suited them, because they were separated now, by much more than distance, from what they were before they left their pine-forested homes and the jade-coloured water of the fjords.

Any Norseman who could survive the voyage to Miklagard had already achieved a great deal, and if he passed the tests of swordsmanship and horseback riding, he would be welcome. Still, in those first weeks of their initiation, the sun often rose on empty beds, whose recent occupants had fled in the night for reasons they never gave or were expected to explain.

Among the ranks of the Varangian, I met the most hard-headed, sharp-instincted and pain-denying people that ever walked the earth. They had been drawn to this place like a migrating beast is drawn to its ancestral hunting ground.

The Varangian lived in a complex within the Emperor's palace walls. They were extravagantly paid, both for their loyalty and for their viciousness, the likes of which the Emperor could not find among his own people. They saw themselves as a kind of shifting brotherhood, with their own laws and traditions. It was in the torch-lit Varangian halls, that people like Halfdan found the first place they had ever thought of as home. These men took more pride in carrying the red-painted shield, which was the mark of the Varangian, than in anything they'd ever done before.

Like Halfdan, many Norsemen kept servants, who followed them everywhere, even into the fighting. I spent twelve years in Halfdan's shadow and lay each night like a dog at the foot of his bed.

The Varangian slept in long, stone rooms. There were thirteen beds in each, six against either wall and one in the centre at the back, reserved for whoever held the highest rank. Carpets were hung on the walls, and shuttered windows opened out onto walkways shaded by olive trees, reserved for the Varangian alone.

Training was carried out daily in high-walled gravel courtyards, where as Halfdan's sparring partner, I learned to handle weapons almost as well as he could. Soon, the skill of wielding them no longer required conscious thought. The movements of axe and spear and sword became so fluid that it was as if they had not been learned but remembered, from a time more distant than my birth.

Afterwards, in heated marble baths, we used sea sponges and olive oil soap to wash away the dust of Miklagard.

At long tables, we were served mutton and fish, flat bread and goat's cheese, black olives cured in oil. We ate dripping chunks of honeycomb and drank more wine than water.

Beneath these rooms, at the end of a passageway deep underground, was the temple of the Varangians. The pillars here were not made of wood but of stone and illuminated with fire pits fueled by olive branches. The wooden benches which lined the walls had been carved with flared crosses, sun wheels and dragon heads, all copied from Norse war-shields.

It was here that Halfdan went to pray each day. I would follow at his heels, the heat of the day fading as we travelled underground and the smell of olive wood fires gradually filling our lungs.

This was the only place where he and I were equals. It served to remind me that, as masters went, Halfdan treated me better than most.

I knew one boy whose master cut off his fingers one by one for such trivial mistakes as spilling food. When the boy had no fingers left, the man set him free. The last time I saw that boy, he was wandering away into the dust of a gathering sandstorm in the wastelands west of Itil.

For his part, Halfdan did not expect anything more from me than belligerent obedience. Anything else would have seemed to him insincere.

But no matter how well Halfdan treated me, I still hated him. No slave can love his master. His infrequent acts of grudging kindness, like the cast-off clothes he gave me and the food he sometimes shared, only made me hate him more. I watched him while he slept, when he would bark at all the demons in his head. I saw the blood pulse in his neck and thought about setting that blood free from its endless wanderings down the tunnels of his body.

In the end, I did not kill him, because it seemed more cruel to let him live. I even learned to pity Halfdan. He had been on the move most of his life and had travelled to places that could not be found on any maps, nor named, nor found again. He was as sick in the head from the things he had watched people do to each other as he was from the beauty of what he had seen but could not find the words to describe. As a result, he lived half in and half out of the past. It was Halfdan's curse that his thoughts did not live in the same world as his body.

My own thoughts swirled endlessly around the memories I kept of home. Slowly, these memories began to unravel. When the images faded, I tended to them as if repairing an old tapestry that hung against the inside of my skull. In the end, what remained was not really a picture of my home, only the idea of it. But it was an idea that made life bearable. Sometimes, the promise I had made to return there was the only thing keeping me alive.

Meanwhile, it seemed as if the only thing keeping the Emperor alive was the Varangian Guard. He was a short and stocky man, with pale blue eyes and a face as round as a coin. Unlike his courtiers, who swathed themselves in silk and gold brocade, the Emperor usually appeared in a simple purple tunic. Although he was physically frail compared to the average Varangian, the Emperor was strong in other ways. He was quietly and thoroughly aware of the vast complexities behind the workings of the empire he ruled. The wealth he commanded was almost unimaginable – rooms stacked with gold, sacks of jewels spilled across the floor – all the substance of fantastic rumour until you saw them for yourself. He stood like the hub of a wildly-spinning wheel, in which the Varangian were only one of a hundred spokes. He alone could navigate the canals of lies and bribery and blackmail which sluiced beneath the treasure rooms and incense-smoky halls of Miklagard. These backwaters were the Emperor's proving ground, from which he emerged unscathed time and again, while his enemies begged for mercy, found none and glimpsed the world for the final time through the veil of blood-dimmed eyes.

The codes by which a Varangian lived could not have contained a man like the Emperor, and yet it was because of him that the Varangian existed at all. The only thing we shared with him was a mutual loyalty, symbolised each month by the Emperor's inspection of his private army.

In the days leading up to the inspections, all the servants like myself busily polished shields, repaired clothes and sharpened swords.

It was the edge on a Norseman's sword which brought the Varangian into being, or so the story went. A group of Norsemen had been captured in a raid on Miklagard. The Emperor decided that their heads would be struck off with their own weapons. As the first man knelt before the executioner, he asked that his long hair not be cut by the blow of the sword. The Emperor granted the request. One of Emperor's men took the hair in his hand, wrapped it around his wrist and held it away from the raider's neck. As the sword came down, the raider jerked his head to one side, and the blade went through the arm of the man who held his hair, missing the raider's neck entirely. Impressed by the ingenuity of this, the Emperor offered to spare the man's life. The Norseman accepted, but only on condition that those who had been captured with him would be spared as well. A deal was struck, and they went on to become the Emperor's personal guard.

At the inspection, all Varangians would kneel in a line before the Emperor, hands on the hilts of swords balanced upright in front of them. Often, the Emperor reached out from the folds of his robes and touched our hair. The blonder it was, the greater his fascination, but red hair intrigued him most of all. This made Halfdan of interest to the Emperor, who sometimes stopped to brush his hand across the top of Halfdan's head.

Halfdan could barely contain his disgust. 'I may be on my knees before that man, but at least I know who I am. He and all his kind are lost in a maze and they cannot leave because they do not even know they are lost.'

'Why not?' I asked.

'Because they have grown more comfortable in dreams than in the waking world.'

I looked around at the bowed heads of the Varangian, heavy-knuckled hands resting on the hilts of their swords, eyes closed, peaceful in their reverence for the man who rented out their bravery from year to year. Suddenly, none of it seemed to have any substance. It all appeared to ripple, the way the surface of a pond moves in a breeze. And then, just as suddenly, I found myself again on solid ground, with the confusion of a sleep-walker shaken from his dreams.

Soon after our arrival, the Varangian had chosen Halfdan as their priest, to guarantee the favour of the gods. This role removed him from the lures of the outer world, in whose perfumed arms the others wrapped themselves from time to time. It was no rule which kept Halfdan away from women. Rather, it was the women who steered clear of him. They knew who he was, knew the powers he was said to have. He frightened them and the only kindness he could show was to keep his distance.

For the rest, caught up in Varangian life, the lack of natural balance between men and women made for its own frustrations.

Days would go by in Miklagard when I did not see a woman my own age. Most were old cleaning women brought in to wipe the floors and prepare food. They never spoke to Norsemen, nor did they look us in the eye. Others were children of the Emperor's men, who looked on us as monsters come to life from bed-time stories. Or they were concubines, who we almost never saw but only heard, laughing behind closed doors. Others were whores, the buying of whose temporary love had long ago become a fact of life among the Varangian, purchased without shame and openly discussed. The hardest working of these women, although they sold themselves to men, kept young girls as their lovers, often paying them as extravagantly as they themselves were paid. The whores of whores. Some were astonishingly beautiful, but carried in their eyes the emptiness of people in the twilight of their years.

Halfdan was as wary of women as he was of Christianity, the splendours of both being never far from view in Miklagard. This city was the centre of the Holy Roman church, and the vastness of its temples dwarfed the crude pillars of our Norse religion.

Halfdan pretended to have no knowledge of Christianity and no interest in it either, but secretly he hired a Christian to teach him about the religion. In this way, he believed, they might have less chance of taking advantage of him. We even attended a service in the great church of the Hagia Sofia, but Halfdan found it so dull that he spent the time carving his name in runes on the marble balustrade. Meanwhile, interminable chanting droned on down below, punctuated by puffs of sandalwood smoke. The lessons lasted two weeks, after which Halfdan sent the Christian away and decided he would never trust those people, though he had never trusted them in the first place. Halfdan could not understand why anyone would pray to only one god, or why someone should be expected to believe that only humans had souls. He wondered why people would spend their time here on earth worrying about what would happen to them in the next world, bribed into submission with the promise of heavenly rewards. Most worrisome to him was that Christians did not accept the gods

55

of others, sanctioning the death of those who would not follow their own faith.

To fight the Emperor's wars, we sailed aboard his Black Sea ships, and voyaged out across the burning blue Mediterranean. We travelled through the desert of the Abbasids and slept in the coppery sand, wrapped in our capes to ward off the night chill, waiting for the sky to turn the colour of our eyes.

In each new place, Halfdan would find something to mark his journey – sometimes a belt, sometimes a shield, once a helmet stolen from the dust-dry corpse of a Roman legionnaire, who we found buried under a shallow pile of stones at a dried-up oasis in the desert. His chest had caved in like the roof of an abandoned house. Some grey and pasty scraps of flesh remained upon the forehead and the hands, which lay folded on his chest. The hair had slid away from the top of the skull, leaving the chalkiness of bones on which a large black scorpion had made its nest.

The most prized of all Halfdan's possessions he acquired when we were campaigning against the Gotul tribesmen in the mountainous region of Arak, a fight which cost us almost half our number. Retreating across a frozen plateau, we came across a long-dead animal the likes of which none of us had seen before. It was a kind of elephant, but with long, matted hair and huge tusks that curved around in front of the animal's face. The creature must have been attacked but escaped to die with a spear still piercing its flank. The flesh had dried as hard as rock and the shaft of the spear had rotted away, but the bronze spear-head remained preserved inside. Its long point was shaped like a narrow tear-drop with strange circles carved into the metal. Halfdan gouged it out and named the weapon Gungnir, after Odin's own spear, which never missed its mark.

In that place, we had come to the edge of the world. Foul-smelling steam rose from open sores in the ground and yellow blooms of sulphur patched the earth, as on the mottled skin of corpses left unburied.

What lay beyond, in the endless emptiness of rolling hills and stunted trees, filled us all with wordless terror, because of what had happened to a group of Norsemen who had set out across these plains some years before. They were led by a Swede named Ingvar. Hundreds came along, sailing in a great fleet across the Baltic, down the Dnieper, across the Black and Caspian seas, rolling their ships on logs or hauling them overland on huge carts, even as far as the sea of Aral. From there, Ingvar and his men set out on foot. Somewhere in that emptiness, they disappeared. A few made it back. Barely a handful of men. One of the survivors was Halfdan. What had happened to them, and who or what had scythed them down, Halfdan either would not say or could not recall. The horror of it stood like a wall around his memories.

The mystery surrounding this disaster gave each Norseman room to shape his own worst nightmare in his head. This was why Halfdan had been favoured by Kalf and his crew, just as he was by the Varangians, as a man who had survived what they feared they could not. But, having reached this place a second time, Halfdan refused to go on, despite the Emperor's orders to continue.

Fear sifted through our ranks. It was as if some angry presence walked among us, breathing the dust of old graves in our faces and wanting to know our business here. This was the only time we ever retreated.

Months later, we returned to Miklagard. We rode through the streets, trailing the riderless horses of our dead. People came out of their houses and counted our losses on their fingers as we went by.

In many dreams to come, I would recall the precise balance of wonder and fear I felt at that moment, out on the wastelands

57

of Arak. It was as if a part of me would never leave that desolate ground and would always be standing there, trying to find the courage to go forward into the unknown.

My service to Halfdan ended when he was killed in a fight near Nicomedia.

We had been escorting the Emperor home after a month-long visit to Trebizond. We were halted in a steep and rocky gorge by about forty men, whose tribe was unknown to us, as was the reason for their attack. They blocked our passage and sent down a drizzle of arrows from their hiding places behind boulders and crooked trees which clung to the crumbling slope. The arrows whistled as they fell among us, now and then striking our shields with a clack of iron against wood. Turning, we saw that our exit from the gorge had now been blocked as well.

These strangers howled and swung their swords above their heads, sharpened edges gleaming in the sun. Others lined the exit from the pass, bent down on one knee and holding out double-bladed spears, one pointing forward and another pointing down. This would gut the horses if we galloped through their ranks. They assumed that we would have to try or face being whittled away by arrows in that cold-shadowed gorge.

The enemy looked surprised when we dismounted and began our advance on foot. No one had told them that the Varangian never fight on horseback.

I hung back in a second line with the other servants as well as one Varangian, a monstrous Celt named Cabal, whose wild hair and shaggy beard made him appear more beast than man. He came from the land of the Cymraig and stood taller than all but a few Varangian. His chest was banded in muscle, with a saddlebag of fat resting on each hip. Cabal had drunk bad wine the night before and was too sick to fight.

The Emperor also stayed behind with the horses. He was dressed as a servant, a precaution he always took when we travelled. He muttered curses at the strangers, while others tried to control the nervous animals.

My task was to keep Halfdan always in my sight. He carried his axe and shield and had left me with his sword, to bring to him if it was needed.

Ever since the first time I had taken part in a fight, I was surprised at how little fear I felt when things began to move. Later, I knew, I would suffer from dreams patched together out of near-misses and the sight of blood, the shrill screams of half-butchered men, the coughing of those with gut wounds, and the hopeless heavy breathing of men whose skulls were shattered. But now I had other things to think about as I ran forward through the dust, determined not to lose track of Halfdan.

I heard a shout from the rocks and watched a man stand up from his hiding place. His face was tattooed with two black horns, which hooked down under his chin. With a long spear raised above his head, he signalled his men to close in.

When they did not move, he shouted and waved the spear over his head. Silver bangles on his arm winked in the sunlight, which had begun to slide in a honey-coloured wave down the face of the gorge.

No matter what he shouted at them, his men would not advance. Rage and fear blurred on his painted face and he spat in their direction before stepping back into the shadows.

We moved slowly at first, then began a slow run and finally, raising axes and swords above our heads, rushed towards them with a howl that echoed through the gorge. The sound doubled and redoubled until it seemed as if a world of men were emptying their lungs.

The line of strangers toppled backwards, jolted by the sound of our shouts. They rose from their crouching, barbed spears clumsy in their sweating hands.

The Varangian line poured over them, swathed in dust. Armour crashed and bodies slammed the ground. Axes swung above the crowd, followed by the butchering thump as they struck home. One of their men ran from the cloud, empty-handed, eyes rolled round to white, blind in a seizure of fear. He was almost at our second line before he saw us through the sweat and dust which clouded his vision, and realised he was running the wrong way. Before he had even skidded to a stop, Cabal barged forward through our ranks. His skin was sunblotched and grey from fever-sweat, eyes narrowed almost shut. He swung his shield up in an arc, and the iron rim of the shield caught the running man just beneath his right ear. The blow lifted him off his feet and threw him back into the dust.

A blue-flighted arrow struck the ground in front of me, sending up a puff of powdery earth. Even though I had been looking at the place where it fell, I had not seen it strike. It just suddenly appeared. The arrow looked so harmless, with its little bundle of feathers neatly tied at the end, more like a toy than a weapon.

We moved through the bodies. Weapons were scattered on the ground. I stepped over a Varangian, who lay face down on top of the man he had killed. There was a thin line of red which ran exactly down the parting in his double-braided hair. I found myself staring at this peculiar symmetry and had just raised my head when I saw Halfdan walk back through the dust.

He was holding the broken handle of his axe, which he threw away when he caught sight of me. His shield was also missing, and I could see the bright lines of knife cuts across the dull chain-mail on his chest. He held out his hand for the sword.

I lunged forward and, as I ran, I saw a movement out of the

corner of my eye. I did not even have time to recognise it as the shape of a person. It seemed to be flying through the air towards me. Without thinking, I swung the sword out from under my left arm. The wood and metal scabbard flew off and struck what I now saw was a man who had crawled up from behind a boulder and was jumping down upon me. The scabbard caught him in the throat. His mouth locked open. He fell hard on his back and skidded to a stop in front of me.

The first thing I noticed about the man was that he was barefoot. The soles of his feet were black with dirt, as if he had been walking in ashes. He had earrings in both ears and his hair was dark and shaggy like the pelt of a bear. He wore a loose brown tunic, which had torn when he hit the ground, baring his chest.

I waited for him to get up, but he did not move. Dust swirled around me. The taste of it clung to the roof of my mouth and powdered my throat. Bodies shifted in the peppery air. All around me was the sour, leathery smell of the sweat of frightened men and animals.

It was then that I heard the high-pitched wail of a wounded horse and turned to see that one of them had been hit by an arrow. There were already two arrows embedded in its saddle, but this third arrow had struck the horse's neck. The other animals reared up and bolted towards the entrance of the gorge, leaving the Emperor and his servant standing in the open. The horse which had been hit went down on its front legs and then tipped sideways onto the ground.

Now I watched the tattooed man come scrambling down the slope, sword in hand, heading for the Emperor.

'Go!' shouted Halfdan, his bright blue eyes piercing the dust. He pointed at the man.

Obediently, I turned back, the weight of Halfdan's sword unbalancing me as I sprinted towards the Emperor, who had

61

begun to climb the steep slope at the other side of the gorge, along with one of his servants. They moved with unbearable slowness, pawing their way from boulder to boulder, grabbing at tufts of grass which came away in their hands.

In a few strides, the tattooed man crossed the flat space at the bottom of the gorge. He began climbing up the other side, where the Emperor and his servant were still struggling forward. Sunlight filled the valley now, blinking off the curved blade of his sword.

Over the swish of air through my burning lungs, I heard the soft swipes of my sandalled feet on the ground. Loose stones and earth tumbled down around me as I climbed after the tattooed man. My eyes filled with grit. The sword clanked awkwardly against stones as I moved, and the pain of climbing washed through my body like a tide.

The tattooed man caught up with the servant, grabbed him by the collar of his tunic and dragged him down.

The servant cried out only once, a piercing high-pitched sound like a rabbit makes when it is trapped in a snare.

Through the dust I saw the servant on his back with his arms raised towards the blade which came down on him again and again.

The man was lost in the rage of his killing and did not notice my approach until I stood almost beside him. Slowly, he raised his head and stared at me, eyes gone bleary with slaughter.

I looked down at the servant, an old Greek named Demetrios. He had been a fisherman but was taken as a slave after a storm washed him and his lemon-yellow rowboat out to sea. He said he had drifted for twenty days, mad with thirst and sucking the dew from his clothes, before reaching the shores of the Black Sea. Now I barely recognised him.

The tattooed man awoke from his frenzy. He bared his teeth and raised his sword to strike me but it clipped against a rock and the blade glanced off his knee, forcing his eyes closed with pain.

I did not have time to be angry about the dead Greek, or afraid for myself, or aware of anything except the movement of Halfdan's sword as I swung it up from my left side. Its own weight seemed to carry it forward. By the time the blade reached the man, it was moving so fast that I barely saw it connect with the flesh under his raised right arm, which held his own sword. The polished metal flowed through him as if it held no shape, no solidity. Like water. Like light. His sword flickered through the air. The arm which had held the sword spun in a slow arc, tracing a ragged circle of blood in the air, outstretched fingers turning at the centre of the wheel. When he tumbled to the ground, his body collapsing in upon itself, it gave the impression of two men struggling together inside one set of clothing. For a moment, his fingers twitched madly. Then they were still. The breath trailed from his lungs in one long heavy sigh. His silver armbands rolled down the slope, ringing like tiny bells as they bounced from rock to rock.

In the silence that followed, I looked out across the valley. Far below, the fight had all but ended. The men who had blocked our way were falling back, dragging their wounded whose heels carved snakes in the dirt. The Varangian let them go. With wounded to care for, they would not come after us again. Already, our horses had returned of their own accord. They snorted and stamped among the still, dust-shrouded bodies.

I heard a choking sigh and glanced up to see the Emperor, huddled in the shade of a boulder. Knowing that he was not badly hurt, and that it would be better for me not to see him this way, I turned and made my way down the slope until I reached the level ground.

I set off to help Halfdan, but I was too late.

He had been struck in the chest by one of the little toy arrows. When I found him, he was on his hands and knees, spitting bloody saliva at the ground. I knelt down next to him, and he patted his fingers against my face. 'Is that you, Hakon?' he asked. 'I cannot see. Is there blood in my eyes?' Halfdan dabbed his rough-padded fingertips against his cheeks, which showed no sign of any wound. 'Why am I blind?'

From the wheezy rattle in his voice, I knew Halfdan did not have long to live. But I could not imagine him dying. Only Halfdan could kill Halfdan, and even he did not know how.

I tried to draw out the arrow, but it was too deep and sent him into a fit of coughing and wretching. His arms and legs trembled, fingers dug into the dirt.

When I told him the arrow would not come out, he ordered me to push it through.

I did what he asked and it killed him.

Afterwards, seeing his lifeless body, I could not seem to get into my head the fact that his death had made me free. Now that freedom had arrived, I was afraid of it. In that moment, if I had been able, I would have returned to life the man who stole me from my home and would have given up my freedom once again.

Instead, I began gathering stones for a grave.

'You must not bury him like that,' said a voice behind me.

I turned to see Cabal. For the first time, I noticed that his eyes were the exact pale green of robin's eggs.

Cabal was a strange man, even to the strangest among us. Tied to the metal ringlets of his chain-mail vest were old coins and beads and small animal bones, which he had collected for luck. As if to prove the worth of these talismans, he had never gotten sick or been hurt in all his years among the Varangian. There were many who believed he was untouchable.

Cabal was said to be one of the last of a breed of Celts who had died out fighting the Romans. He seemed resigned to walk the earth as a shadow of his vanished tribe. He had left home to join the Varangian although in the five years it took him to reach Miklagard, he was not even certain they existed.

Now Cabal belonged to the brotherhood, but in many ways he also stood apart. He earned himself a reputation for brutality in battle even among the Varangian, who were considered by the inhabitants of Miklagard to be savage almost beyond comprehension. I had followed in the bloody path of Cabal's horse, as the heads he had taken in battle lolled wide-eyed and filmed with dust, tied by their hair to the pommel of his saddle. They said Cabal preserved these heads in pots of cedar oil, which he buried in a secret place.

When the fighting ended, Cabal would return to his old, gentle self, so unlike his other side that he seemed to be not one, but two people trapped inside a cage of flesh and bone. When asked why this was so, Cabal spoke of a thing called the Ail Gysgod, the Second Shadow, which the Celts had known and used in battle since long before his ancestors fought soldiers of the Roman Emperor Augustus. Arrayed before their enemies, the Celts had transformed themselves into a trance-like rage. The Romans saw the bodies of these men begin to ripple and shimmer, as if the boundaries of their skin had come undone and they were changing now into vast and terrifying creatures, which lived inside them and could be summoned with this pounding wordless chant.

The things Cabal knew about what horrors lurked inside him, the rest of us had never dared to dream of in ourselves.

'You must not bury him,' Cabal said again.

I knew the body should be burned instead, which was the Norse way, but there was barely enough wood to scorch a body here, let alone the great stacks of wood that it would take to turn him into ashes. As I looked at Halfdan's corpse, it occurred to me that the funeral was no concern of his. It made no difference now to Halfdan. It would be my own conscience that judged my actions now.

With Cabal's help, I gathered together every twisted, sun-bleached fragment of wood, every broken spear-shaft I could find and made a bed of them on which I laid Halfdan's body. We tore the clothes off the bodies of men we had killed, plugging them into empty spaces in the tangled wood. The sun thumped on our heads while we worked, and the heated blood pulsed in our temples like the beating of a drum.

Of Halfdan's belongings, I kept his red-painted shield which had grown so hot from lying in the sun that its iron rim branded my skin when I picked it up. I also kept the bronze-tipped spear and his sword, which had a fine double-edged blade made by the Saxon Ulfbert. On the blade, engraved in runes was 'Halfdan' and 'Varangian'. I kept his chain mail shirt, whose maker had built into the links over his heart one gold ring stamped with a crescent moon. Lastly, from around his neck, I pulled the black stone hammer, which Halfdan had kept all these years.

Cabal set the fire and soon the bed on which Halfdan lay was a climbing pillar of flames and black smoke. The last I saw of him, his skull was glowing red among the embers, smiling more in death than his fleshed face had ever done, as if the secret of his restless life had at last been revealed to him.

We threw the bodies of other dead Varangians into the blaze and they vanished in geysers of sparks.

Afterwards, we rested in the shade of the crumbling rocks. Our enemies we left out in the sun to rot and used their ornate lances for roasting the meat of our dead horse.

*

Later that same day, as a token of his thanks, the Emperor granted me my freedom. At the same time, he offered me Halfdan's place in the Varangian. By now, he had regained his composure. He sat straight-backed on his horse, which shifted uneasily from foot to foot as I knelt before both man and beast. When he made his offer, he looked hard at me, as if our deal would silence the memory of him cowering on that slope.

I had barely gathered his words into my mind, before the knowledge of my freedom spun me around and sent me running. I had no idea what I was doing. I only wanted to get away. The only constants in my life had been service to Halfdan and the thought that one day it would end. Now that I was free, my jumbled mind convinced me that if I did not start immediately for home, something might come along to take that freedom back again. I got ten paces before the laughter of the Varangian brought me to a halt. I had been running back into the valley, back to where dead men lay bloated by the sun and where Halfdan's bones still smouldered in the ashes of his funeral pyre.

Slowly, I turned back to face the Emperor.

He was smiling at me. The Varangian were smiling too, strong white teeth behind their sunburnt lips. They were not mocking smiles. Rather, they seemed sympathetic, as if any one of them, in my place, would have made the same mad dash to get away.

But it was hopeless. I saw that now. Being free meant only that I was at liberty to go off and get myself killed. Lacking the money to buy myself safe passage with some north-bound trading caravan, I stood no chance of reaching home again.

'What I offer you is an honour,' said the Emperor, tapping the air with one pointed finger. 'You should take it. Your time for leaving is not now. That day comes to all Varangian, and for each one the sign is different. You will know it when it comes.'

It was not until the Varangian asked me to carry on Half-dan's role as their priest, that I accepted the Emperor's offer. There was no time to mull over the decision. The Varangian didn't like the idea of being without a priest, even for a day. They would have given the place to someone else if I had not agreed at once.

I remained in the service of the Emperor another five years, slowly gathering the wealth that I would need to bring me home. Coin by coin by coin, I marked the days. In the meantime, there was nothing to do but be patient. While my body remained stranded down in Miklagard, I trained the spirit to rise from my body and to race out across the rooftops of the city, faster and faster, twisting beyond the clutches of the world into a realm where all familiar boundaries of time and space and distance disappeared. Out there, on the other side, I was surrounded by that same shuddering energy, whose faint echo I could feel back in the world. But here, it roared around me like an ocean, deafening me without sound, shaking apart that memory of my flesh and blood into fragments small as dust. I lingered there, oblivious to the passing of time. Then I felt myself begin to fall, the ashes of my thought-cremated body whirling together, spiralling down, taking shape and hurtling like a jagged spear of lightning back into the framework of my bones.

I would wake to see the frightened, staring faces of the Varangian who had come to pray. There were times when they ran from the underground chamber, telling stories of fire appearing around my body, of shadows unattached to solid forms which slithered up and down the walls, of inhuman voices which came from their own mouths.

It was no surprise that, because of these things, I had few

close friends. Even though the Varangian valued my presence, the job of priest was a solitary one. The stronger a priest's abilities, the more lonely his life. I had seen it happen to Halfdan. Now it was happening to me.

Only Cabal and I remained close.

He became my sparring partner, as I had once been Halfdan's. It was an important bond in the Varangian society and required a sharing of trust so intense that this loyalty became almost a tangible thing, like a separate living presence which accompanied us each morning into the training yard of the Varangian compound. Just after sunrise, the yard would be filled with pairs of men, each performing the intricate dance of sword practice. We would begin slowly, sword blades making barely any sound as they connected. Then we would move faster, until sparks jumped from the crashing iron and a single wrong move would have killed us both.

In the early afternoons, when most people slept through the heat of the day, Cabal and I would sit at the edge of a well from which the Varangians drew their water. A roof had been built over the well, shielding us from the sun, while cool air from the water drifted up its damp and mossy walls. Often, Cabal brought with him bundles of dried camomile flowers, which he carefully wrapped up in mint leaves and then chewed with the same absent-minded expression as a bull eating grass in a field, pausing only to spit green juice down into the blackness of the well.

Sometimes we just stared into space, lost in our own thinking.

Other times, I would wonder aloud whether my family were alive or dead. I had dwelt on these thoughts so often that they no longer overwhelmed me with sadness, as they did in the beginning. I always returned to that moment on the raider's boat and to the promise I had made to Tostig.

The more time passed, the more urgent my departure

became, but even though I saved almost every coin, it was still not enough to guarantee safe passage home.

To shake me from these wanderings in the labyrinth of my brain, Cabal told me about his life before joining the Varangian, when he had been apprenticed to a Christian monk, from whom he ran away, for reasons he kept to himself. The result of those experiences was that he had even less patience than Halfdan for the Christians and their ways. Cabal was forced to make an uneasy peace with himself, as a man with no love for the people he was paid to protect, but knowing that his place in life, at least for now, was to live among his enemies.

Now and then, he would tell stories of his own people; of Pwyll, Prince of Dyfed, and his meeting with Arawn, King of the Underworld, and his pack of white-furred, red-eyed hunting dogs. When he spoke of Lucan, God of Light, and Tiran, God of Thunder, I was surprised to find the faces of my gods in the descriptions of his own.

Despite the similarities, Cabal never took part in the Norse rituals. Neither did he seem to follow any outward signs of devotion to his gods. 'I do my praying in here,' he told me, and tapped a finger against his broad forehead.

In the evenings, we would walk down to the port, where fishermen grilled sardines over olive-wood fires. We sat cross-legged around the coals, eating the fish with our bare hands and throwing the remains in the air, where seagulls were always waiting to snatch them away. When we were finished, we clapped our hands, and a boy would come with a bucket of water mixed with lemon juice. We stirred our hands among the floating lemon rinds, breathing in the sharp, clean smell. It was expected that the boy be given some reward for his trouble, so Cabal would pull off one of the beads he had tied to his chain mail vest, like a tree picking some of its own fruit, and would hand it to the boy as a gift.

70

Once, as we walked back up the hill to the Varangian barracks, I asked him if he would tell me how to summon Ail Gysgod, the terrible Second Shadow.

'It is done with the pounding of shields,' he said vaguely.

'But how exactly?'

Cabal seemed reluctant to continue. 'With a certain rhythm of striking the hilt of the sword against the boss of the shield.'

'Will you not teach it to me?' I asked.

He turned his head slowly until he was facing me. 'If there was someone who could tell you the exact time and place that you were going to die, would you really want to know?'

I thought about this as we weaved our way along the narrow streets crowded with tiny market stalls that had spilled out into the passageways. Round, flat loaves of bread were stacked in precarious towers. Black olives in red earthenware pots glinted by the light of fish-oil lamps. Pots and pans, suspended from ropes in front of shops, clanged like prayer bells as people brushed by them. 'No,' I said at last. 'I would not want to know.'

'For the same reason, and because you are my friend, I will not teach it to you. Once you have seen that far inside yourself, you can never be the same again.'

We spoke no more about it, but I often wondered what that rhythm was. Sometimes, I would catch myself tapping the hilt of my sword against my shield, but nothing ever came of it except the denting of the metal.

As time went by, and the Emperor's wars against the Bulgars and Tsar Samuel of Ochrid seemed as if they might go on forever, he began to accept into our ranks Norsemen who had converted to Christianity. More and more these days, the Norsemen who arrived in Miklagard had abandoned their old gods. Christianity was spreading north, and these Christian

Norsemen swore that soon the old ways would be gone for good.

I thought of the great source, whatever it was, tombed in the earth below the Altvik temple. The secret lingered in me for so long that it became like a stone lodged in my chest, a sharp-edged twin of the one which hung around my neck.

'It does seem strange,' said Cabal, 'that we are here defending the Christians against their enemies when, back in our homelands, the Christians are the enemy. I have seen what they did to the old ways in my country, and I know what they can do to yours.'

Cabal's words reached me like a call for help from my own people, travelling on a cold wind from the north.

I could wait no longer. Even though I had not saved up enough to make the journey safely, the time had come for leaving.

That same day, I went to the Emperor and told him I was going.

'Going where?' he asked, as he twirled a finger in his long sideburns. He was ashamed of his delicate hands. There were rumours that he wore silk gloves when he slept, and that he soaked twice a day in a bath of olive oil.

'I am going home,' I said.

'To the north?' The Emperor leaned forward and spoke in a low voice. 'I once sent a man to your country. Actually I sent three, but only one came back. I sent them because I wanted to know what kind of land produced people like you. When one of them at last returned, the first thing he told me was that he would never go back there again, no matter how wealthy I made him. He said that the air became so cold in winter that his breath would turn into ice as it left his mouth and that it would fall at his feet like grains of sand. He said that in the coldest weather, a thick fog settles on the ground

and, when you walk through it, you leave a path that someone else can follow, just as one might follow a trail of muddy
footprints.'

'All that is true.' I recalled the precise rustling sound of the
ice crystals as they fell.

He shook his head in resignation. 'And you want to go back
and live in a world where you must remain embalmed in furs
or die from the cold?' He did not wait for my reply. 'How can
you go back after all you have learned among us? You speak
several languages. You can write both Rune and Arabic. I know
all these things because, you see, I have been watching you.
You are valued here, by me as well as by your own people.
Your place among us is assured. Why leave now?'

'Before I promised to serve you, I made another promise
which I now intend to fulfil.'

'That must have been a long time ago. You are probably the
only one who remembers making it.'

'The man I promised is dead, but the oath was made all the
same.'

'Then you are free to break it, if there is no punishment for
failing to keep your word.'

'The promise I made was also to myself. Excellency, it is time
for me to return home.'

He sighed, exasperated. 'Here is your home. Here among us.
It takes many years to train a useful member of the Varangian.
And it's often a long time before I know who is fit to be one and
who is not.' He levelled a finger at me. 'How long have you
been with us?'

'Most of my life.'

'And how long have you been away from this place you are
calling your home?'

'Most of my life.'

He bounced the heels of his palms off the padded leather

armrests of his chair. 'There is my point. What do you even remember about that place? What life do you truly know except the one that you have here? You have been away too long. They will not need you any more.'

I had thought about that almost as often as I had thought about going home. 'I will not know until I get there,' I replied.

'It does not matter,' snapped the Emperor, 'because the home you think you have does not exist. It is only a dream and you would do as well to dream it here down in the sun instead of in your land of ice.'

'And how do you know it is only a dream?'

He was laughing at me now. 'Because we all have the same dream. Even I do. It is a picture preserved, like an insect trapped in amber. As long as you remember that it is only a dream, you can live with it. But you don't ask yourself what you will do when you get there. How you will survive? What a stranger you will be to them because of the things you have seen. My friend, listen to me. You will find yourself one day at the end of the world, far from your Varangian brothers and from me who understands you. You will wake from your honey-coloured dream and find it is too late. What you do not see is that you are now, at this very moment, living the life you were meant to live. Look out there!' He pointed through a window and out across the city. 'That is your life!'

The vast city of Miklagard lay cradled in the hazy evening light. I watched the sleepy flight of seagulls riding up into the sky until they disappeared into the sun. I wanted to tell him that it was not the dream of a place which called me back. It was a dream of myself. It was as if, somewhere far to the north, time stood still. It waited for me to pick up where I had left off, in that very moment when I saw the Grimsvoss mountains disappear into the sea. In my mind, I had already departed. A shadow of myself had long since gone ahead, walking the

74

dusty roads north. The rest of me had to catch up, before the two halves became separated forever.

'Go, then,' said the Emperor, screwing up his full-moon face. 'Throw yourself away. Perhaps I was wrong. You never did learn to fit in. Look at you now in all your heavy clothes. That leather vest you wear in this heat. I am surprised you can even stand up.'

'In the north, this leather vest will not be nearly enough to keep me warm.'

He touched his fingers to his lips, as if to pull some congestion of words from his mouth. 'Once you leave you can never come back.'

He did not need to tell me. That was the law of the Varangians. Those people who had left we called 'ghosts'. Now and then over the years, men had returned, having squandered their fortunes or found it impossible to adjust to life outside. They returned as if to look for some possession they had left behind and always seemed surprised to find their old beds filled by those who had taken their places. Some asked, quietly and desperately, if we could bend the rules for old time's sake, and let them slip back in among our ranks. The answer would always be no, and they would smile and laugh and pretend that it was a joke or that it hadn't mattered much, or even that they had only been testing us. They would go on to tell us of their freedom and good fortune, to convince themselves more than to convince us. Then, when their stay was over, they would walk out through the gates. We would never see them again after that.

'You have held on to your own religion, with its beetle-eyed pillars and circles in the sand, when all around you are the glorious monuments to Christianity. This should have told me your mind was closed.' Then he sighed. 'But I suppose I did not pay you for your faith in Thor and Odin. I paid you for your faith in me.'

75

I smiled at him, which was not allowed.

He smiled back, and with that smile my service to him ended.

I climbed off my knees, picked up my sword and the leather bag which held all that I owned. As I straightened up, I felt a line of sweat run down the ridge of my spine. I turned and walked down the long hall from his chamber, rustling in my chain-mail shirt with its one gold ring at the heart, the hole still unrepaired where the arrow had punched out Halfdan's life.

'Take off that leather vest!' he commanded. 'It makes me sweat even to see you wearing it.'

But I was no longer his to command, and he knew it. What he did not know was that the vest was even heavier than it looked. I kept more than a hundred coins sewn into its lining, each one held in place by a spiderweb of red silk threads. The coins came from al-Andalus in the Emperorate of Cordoba, from Misr on the Nile, from Basra and Baghdad and from Bulgar on the banks of the Volga. There were coins from places I could not even name, but the names did not matter. Only the gold itself mattered. It was all that I had managed to save.

At the gates of the Varangian compound, I found Cabal waiting for me. At first, I thought he was there only to say goodbye, but then I saw that he had brought his sword and shield and the leather pack in which he carried a wooden spoon and bowl.

'I have decided to come with you,' he said. 'It is too late for my people, but perhaps it is not too late for yours. I am tired of serving my enemies and the time has come to show them the error of their ways.'

I was glad to have his company.

We painted our red shields white, as a sign that we had given up our days of soldiering for the Emperor. Then we slung our swords across our backs, picked up our spears and started walking.

It was said among the Varangian that you never truly knew until you left if leaving was the thing that would break you. And here I was, on the other side of the gates, quietly surprised to find myself unbroken still.

Bearing the white shields of the ghosts we had become, Cabal and I began our journey north.

Two months later, we had come as far as Novgorod on the banks of lake Ilmen in northern Russia, buying passage on boats or in carts from one village to the next. And when there was no one to take us, we wore out our shoes on rutted paths which twisted through the dark pine forests.

It was the beginning of a late summer day when we reached the outskirts of the town. We sat down to rest at the end of a wooden pier, looking down into the green-brown muddy water. We'd been told that a trading boat would dock here soon on its way to Hedeby in the Baltic. If we could catch a ride on this ship, it would take weeks off the journey. Otherwise we would have to travel by land up through Finland and across Sweden. That could take many months and would mean spending the winter in some cold and unfamiliar place.

We waited for three days. Each morning, passing traders told us that this would be the day. They said the man to look for was named Godfred and to watch for the yellow cross painted on his sail. Meanwhile, a seemingly endless procession of ox-drawn wagons had passed by on their way north, any one of which might have offered us a ride.

I wanted to be moving. My patience was worn thin.

Cabal seemed more resigned, as if he knew better than the

traders when Godfred would actually appear. He was in no hurry to see where this journey would take him in the end. We had spoken about the possibility that he might travel on to his own country after visiting my own, but he had not yet made up his mind. The journey itself, rather than its destination, seemed to be the purpose of his life.

Not wanting to miss Godfred's boat, we took turns wandering into Novgorod, to get food or a drink of the local sludgy brew called 'samahonka'. In the streets, I heard seven languages, three of which I could not name. It was never quiet in that city and never safe either. I preferred being out by the river, even though it smelled of rotting vegetation and its banks were thick with layers of black mud. We slept among the reeds beside a bullrush fire, which kept the mosquitoes away.

The smell of that fouled river water clung to my hair and my clothes. It woke me from my sleep with images of drowned men standing over me, dead men who did not know where they were or that they were dead, whispering their ghost words in my face, begging me for answers.

By the fourth day, I was beginning to wonder if Godfred's boat would ever appear. We sat on the dock, the sun bearing down upon our shoulder blades. The white paint on our shields forced our eyes shut with the glare. I took the last apple from my pack and rubbed it against the thigh of my trousers before taking a bite and offering it to Cabal. The air was still and swarming with insects. Among the bugs which visited me on their rounds were fat brown horseflies as large as the last joint of my thumb. The moment I gave up trying to shoo them away, one bit me on my calf.

The pain made me drop my apple, which rolled off the end of the pier and splashed into the river. I swore, got down on my knees and peered through the boards. My apple floated in the greasy water.

'We could go in and get it,' said Cabal.

I could tell from his voice he was hungry. I sat back on my haunches and sighed, trying to imagine what it would be like to wade out through the stinking mud to fetch the apple and what it would taste like after being in that filthy water.

At that moment, a voice called to us.

I looked up and saw a boat slide into view around the river bend. It was the trader, Godfred, with the yellow cross painted on his sail. On deck was an elderly man with an unkempt beard and flabby arms that jutted from a heavy blue cloak. He had dark rings under his eyes and his skin was olive in complexion. 'May I join you in worshipping our Holy Father?' he shouted.

'Our *what*?'

'Our Holy Father,' he repeated, smiling.

'He thinks you were praying like a Christian,' whispered Cabal.

'Have you been baptised yet, my brother?' asked the flabby man.

'No,' I replied, 'I have not.' I climbed to my feet. I was about to explain his mistake, when I heard him speak again.

'Can I offer you a place on my boat?'

His crew, which consisted of one pale-faced, spotty boy in an undyed linen tunic, was already throwing ropes over the pilings to tie up at the dock.

As soon as the ropes were fast, the man climbed onto the sun-bleached planks of the pier. He wore poorly-made sandals which revealed overgrown toenails. He walked straight over to us and rested one hand against each of our chests, in a form of greeting I had never seen before. 'I am Godfred. I see from your white shields that you are men of peace. You have had enough of the old ways. That is why you must accept the Lord into your life, so you can set out on the road of Christ!' He shouted

80

the last word of each sentence as if we were deaf. 'Bound for the Hedeby, by any chance?' he asked.

I nodded.

'Then you can ride with us.'

From Hedeby, it would only be a matter of days to Altvik. I decided he could think whatever he wanted about me kneeling on the dock. 'How much will it cost?' I asked.

He brushed away the thought of money with a sweep of his hand. 'Being future disciples of the Lord, you have already paid your way.'

As soon as the old man's back was turned, the servant rolled his eyes and grinned at us to show what he thought of his master. He led a small shaggy pony off the boat and harnessed it to a cart which he had also brought ashore. Many crucifixes were fixed to the sides of the cart. Some were carved from wood, others from bone, and still others were braided from reeds. They were nailed on haphazardly, some even hanging from the wheel hubs.

Cabal and I helped unload their cargo of fox pelts, iron buckles and wooden bowls, which had been carved from Russian birch and smoke-hardened so that the soot came away on our hands when we touched them.

While we stayed behind with the servant, Godfred rode the cart into Novgorod, where he had a regular space in an open air market called the Kubiak.

The servant lounged on a coil of rope, gnawing on a lump of dried meat and squinting at me suspiciously. He said his name was Yarl. 'Who tipped you boys off about old Godfred? You do not look like any Christians I have ever seen.' He nodded at Cabal. 'Especially you.'

I told him about the horsefly and the apple.

He sat up and laughed. 'He will try to baptise you, you know. Right here in this filthy water. That is his pastime. Bap-

81

tising people. He owns a book in which he writes all the names of people he has dunked in the name of his God.'

'He will not be dunking me,' I said.

'Nor me,' added Cabal. 'Maybe we should find a different boat.'

Yarl shrugged his bony shoulders. 'Why be in such a rush? You will not find a better ship to travel on. You might think him a bit of a fool, and he does have some strange ideas. But he is a good businessman and not the worst boss in the world.' Yarl wrestled with the piece of the dried meat, teeth clamped and head twisting until he tore loose a mouthful. He spoke as he chewed. 'So let him baptise you. There are others like him, you see. They run into each other now and then and compare notes. It is as if they are in competition, and when they die, the one who has converted the most pagans will get the house with the better view up in heaven. At least, I guess that is how it works.' Yarl was chewing while he talked. Now, having gnawed all the taste out of the lump in his mouth, he spat it over the side. The chewed clump of meat splashed in the water. Rainbows of oil spread around it. He kept talking. 'Let him think what he wants. Let him write your names in his little book so he can show it to his friends. You need not use your real names. You would not be the first who has travelled with us for the price of a bath with your clothes on. That is what you must do, you know. You have to go out into the water with your clothes on and then he shoves you under and pulls you up again and does a lot of praying. And if you could do him the favour of looking as if you have enjoyed the experience, he would be all the more grateful.'

I looked at the water slithering past and imagined how it would be – walking down through the reeds, feet sinking in the riverbank slime, grimacing as I allowed my face to be lowered towards the dingy water.

Cabal was thinking the same thing. 'I cannot do it,' he said.

'I wonder if you will still say that after six more months on the road.'

'We will let you know,' I said. I got up off the deck, feeling my knee joints complain.

Yarl motioned me to sit. 'Godfred has offered you the ride. He has set his mind on making you a Christian. He thinks it is a sign.'

'What kind of sign?' asked Cabal.

'He is always interpreting things, you see. Nothing is ever simply what it is. Everything he sees is some miracle or wonder. His God is always talking to him, or he is always talking to himself, depending on how you want to look at it.' Yarl held his hand up at the sky, to block the sun from his face. 'You might think it is madness that he should conjure up that story about your turning to Christianity after a life of soldiering in the name of some heathen god, but that is the way he sees it. He catches sight of you praying, or doing what he thinks is praying, and his mind just runs away with itself. He is quite harmless, and you will not go hungry. You will just have to listen to him going on about his church. You can just pretend you are listening. That is what I do. I am good at looking interested.' He set his jaw, narrowed his eyes and nodded slowly to demonstrate this talent.

'So you are not Christian, either,' I said.

'The only thing his God has done for me is to give me something to swear at. I am no Christian. I am just a boy who has a decent job and wants to keep it.'

'How long have you been with him?' asked Cabal.

Yarl breathed in deeply and let his breath trail out. 'Most of my life. We have travelled all over. Once, because of some bright idea of his, we went so far out into the ocean that I thought we would never come back.'

83

'But here you are,' said Cabal.

Yarl nodded. 'And perhaps I have his God to thank for that, but I think it was our bearing dial that saved us.'

'What is a bearing dial?' I asked.

'Godfred bought it off an Arab trader years ago. It can tell you which way your are headed if you know how to use it.'

Most sailors could only navigate on East/West lines, watching the movements of the sun or moon. Navigating North and South was always left to guesswork.

'I would like to see this bearing dial,' said Cabal.

Yarl nodded. 'So would many, but Godfred would pound my head flat with that big book of his if I brought it from its hiding place. He does not like people to know he has it. Godfred would prefer we all believed that God was his only tool for navigation.'

We let the matter drop.

Cabal and I eased ourselves back down onto the ropes and accepted the gnarled fist of dried meat which Yarl held out for us to taste.

'What were you looking for out there in the middle of the ocean?' I asked.

'Godfred had it in his head that if we just kept sailing, we would eventually reach another country and that there were sure to be people there. And then he could convert them all at the same time. He was dead set on it. I thought he was going to get us both killed.'

Cabal stopped gnawing at the meat long enough to ask, 'What did you find?'

'In two weeks of sailing all we found was more ocean.'

'But there is land out there,' I told him. 'The Faeroes. Iceland. Greenland.'

'We were well south of that.' He shook his head. 'I tell you I thought we were dead.'

84

'What made him change his mind about turning back?'

Yarl shrugged and looked uncomfortable. 'If you want to know the truth, I poisoned his food.' Then he added quickly, 'Just a little, mind. Just enough to make him think about saving the life he has now, instead of worrying about the next one, which is what he does most of the time. I had enough worry for the both of us, anyway, what with thinking we were going to sail off the end of the world. The funny thing is,' he continued, 'that once we started back, we found something floating in the water that made me think there might be people out there after all.' He went into the hold and returned with something wrapped in a piece of blanket. It was about half the length of his arm. When he unrolled the blanket, a heavy piece of wood, studded with old barnacles and drilled by worms, fell out onto the deck. It had been a long time in the water.

I could not see what was so special about the log, but then Yarl rolled it over with his foot and I found myself looking at the carved shape of a man, his knees drawn up and hands folded across his chest. The face was long, with deep-set eyes, a powerful, jutting nose and an unsmiling mouth. I picked it up. The hollow barnacles dug into the pads of my fingertips. 'This could have come from anywhere,' I said but did not manage to convince myself. There was a sullen anger in the crouching figure, as if it had been pitched into the sea on purpose, to take away some wretchedness from the people who had made it.

Cabal pushed it away with his foot.

'You see?' Yarl picked up the end of the blanket and tossed it over the wooden face. 'There is something wrong with it.' He bundled up the statue and carried it back to its place in the hold. When he reappeared, he was wiping his hands on his clothes. 'I don't even like to touch the thing.'

'If it troubles you so much, why not just burn it?' asked Cabal.

'Godfred will not let me. He does not like it any more than I do. He is afraid to keep it and afraid to throw it away. He worries that it will do something bad to him, and for once I agree with the old man.'

At that moment, we all paused to watch a dead sheep bobbing downstream, legs stiff and belly bloated.

'Baptised once too often,' said Cabal.

When Godfred returned from Novgorod that evening, his cart was empty. He carried money in two large leather purses around his neck, which made his chest bulge as if he had breasts. He immediately began lecturing us about the True Faith and how it would Welcome us and how he would be Pleased to act as our Spiritual Guide. Godfred set his arm around Cabal, or tried to since he could not reach the whole way around Cabal's back. 'Come,' he said. 'Let me baptise you now.'

'No,' said Cabal, with a voice of limited patience. 'I am no Christian.'

I bent down to pick up my gear. 'We had best be going.' The idea of reaching Hedeby in such a short space of time evaporated. In its place came thoughts of long days spent walking the mud-tracked forests of the north.

For a moment, Godfred seemed lost in thought. Then he smiled cheerfully. 'Come anyway,' he said . 'A Norseman and a Celt together. It would be my greatest triumph. At least allow me to try and convince you. If I cannot, what harm is done?'

That much we could live with, so we brought our gear on board.

It wasn't long before we reached the Baltic, making good progress towards Hedeby. The ship was faster than it looked.

Yarl turned out to be a good crewman. He tended to Godfred's fragile stomach, taking great care with his meals and bundling him in extra clothes when the old man did not dress himself warmly enough. To these attentions Godfred seemed mostly ignorant, convinced that he was sheltered by a greater power than his spotty-faced servant boy. Yarl cheerfully endured the man's ingratitude, as he was clearly fond of his master.

In spite of myself, I grew fond of him, too.

Godfred spent most of his energy on Cabal, whom he led up and down the deck, holding his arm like an old woman being led across a patch of stony ground. With his free hand, Godfred swatted the air as he made his case for Christianity.

Cabal tilted his head over and listened intently.

I wondered if Godfred might actually convert him, but then Cabal winked at me and I knew he was just wearing down the old man.

The only time of day in which I dreaded Godfred's company was the evening meal. He preached to us across the table, in a spray of holiness and breadcrumbs. Godfred was determined to convert us before we reached Hedeby. 'How can you not doubt your gods?' he asked. 'They are so crude, so change-able.'

'They are more like we who pray to them, perhaps,' said Cabal.

'Exactly!' he bounced his fleshy fist off the table. 'Why not have one perfect, faultless god? Why live in the shadow of doubt?'

I sat back and puffed my cheeks. 'I do not doubt my faith in them.'

'And what do you intend to do when you reach home? Do you think you can personally hold back the force of an entire religion?'

'I am not trying to hold back a new religion. I am only trying to do my duty to an older one.'

'But what good can one man do?'

'Jesus was only one person,' said Cabal, and left the table, rather than lose his temper with the old man.

Godfred wagged a stubby finger in my face. 'So you see yourself as prophets?'

'No. I am keeping a promise. That is all.'

The muscles in his back seemed to give way and he slumped in his blanket-draped chair. 'I cannot understand how anyone would choose a faith other than Christianity. What does your faith hold for you that Christianity does not offer in even greater measure?'

The question had never been put to me in that way before. Why choose one faith over another? Simply because I had grown up with it? Because I was too lazy or too frightened to change?

It was Cabal who gave him the answer. 'You have found magic in your one god,' he said.

Godfred raised his eyebrows, pursing his lips as he considered this. 'Yes,' he said, 'I suppose that is true.'

Cabal nodded. 'But we find it in everything around us.'

Godfred shook his head. 'What a distance lies between us.' Then his face brightened as a new thought bloomed in his head. 'Will you both do me the honour of signing your names in my book!'

'So you can tell your friends you baptised us?' I asked.

He seemed surprised, then glowered at Yarl, who sat at the far end of the table.

Yarl lowered his face to his bowl and hurriedly began ladelling soup into his mouth.

When Godfred turned back to me, he was smiling again. 'As my guest,' he said. 'Only that.' He opened the book, turned it around and and slid it across the table towards us. Then he mixed some ink from a leather bag of powder and gave Cabal a goosequill with which to sign.

When Cabal wrote his name in the Celtic form called Ogham, Godfred politely said that would not do and crossed it out and rewrote it in Latin.

Then I wrote my name in runes, and Godfred did not want that either. He held out his hand for the pen, to write my name in his own script.

Instead of handing back the pen, I wrote my name in Arabic, then Greek, then finally in Latin.

'Where did you learn that?' he asked suspiciously.

I explained where we had come from. It was all news to him since he had never asked, preferring instead to invent our past for himself.

'The Varangian Guard?' he asked. 'Both of you?'

We nodded.

'No wonder I am not getting anywhere!' Now Godfred stood, gripping the edge of the table with his age-crooked hands. 'All men are Christians in their hearts,' he announced solemnly, 'but there are some who do not know it yet.'

Although Godfred made no more attempts to convert us, his questions had left their mark in my brain. How much could one person accomplish? Was this secret source enough to hold back these Christians, who seemed as stubborn in their faith as we were in our own? The further north I travelled, the more overwhelming it all seemed. Added to this was the thought of seeing my parents again, if they were still alive. And Kari and Olaf and Ingolf. Would they be there to meet me, or had they moved on long ago?

We put ashore at Hedeby three days later. It was here, for the first time in as long as I could remember, that I saw the blonde hair and blue eyes of Norse people outnumbering any other race that walked the streets. I also saw the single-edged Scramasax swords and wide-bladed spears which were carried only by the western Norse – a sign that I was truly close to home.

But much had changed since Halfdan brought me through here. The town had grown to three times its former size, yet many of the houses were empty now and falling in upon themselves from neglect. Grass grew in disused alleyways and tatters of old woolen sail-cloth, which once served as doors and roofs, fluttered threadbare and rotten in the breeze. Only in the centre of town did I find the same shouting voices and stork-walking people, carrying their shoes while the greasy mud squelched between their toes.

The old market place had disappeared completely under houses. The new market was closer to the water and ringed with stalls selling swan-necked bottles made of glass and bloodless slabs of pork, which Yarl said were rumoured to be human flesh. One man with a leather blacksmith's apron offered to extract bad teeth with iron pincers. Neatly laid out on his bench were all the rotten teeth that he had pulled.

Christian preachers, standing on tables, drew crowds with their promises of unremitting pain for those who did not follow them.

On the outskirts, where the pillars had once stood, I saw a single cross. Its huge cross-beam was hung with the ragged flesh of animal sacrifices. Those converts to the new religion had not completely put away the ancient tokens of respect.

Cabal and I said our goodbyes to Godfred. He seemed preoccupied, as if his god had played a trick on him. He shook our hands and heaved out a sigh that popped against his fleshy lips. Then he turned to walk into the town. In that same instant, he seemed to forget us. A hopeful smile returned to his face, as he began another search for new converts.

Yarl followed his master. They disappeared among the crowds that tramped the busy streets.

Later that day, we heard of a ship bound for the Trondelag region on the western coast of Norway. We found it moored at an old jetty. It was an old Drakkar with a shallow reach, giving it plenty of speed but little room for cargo. To remedy this, the owner had tied a sheet of sailcloth rope from one side of the bow to the other, forming a canopy under which goods could be stored. There were many repaired boards, which stood out along its clinkered hull. Orderly coils of rope lay on the deck. Rawhide bindings laced the steerboard arm and more strips of leather had been used for tying the skull of a huge animal to the bowhead. The skull had two great tusks and enormous, salt-crusted eye sockets.

I went forward to speak to the owner, while Cabal slung his pack in the shade of a tree and lay down to rest.

'Walrus,' said the owner of the Trondelag boat, jerking his head toward the skull tied to the bow. He was a broad-shouldered man, with a beard the colour of straw. The hair that jutted from his head was like a shock of wheat. He sat on a bale of furs, a sheepskin wrapped around his shoulders, under which he wore a rough brown shirt and baggy trousers tucked into seal-fur boots. 'That is what you were wondering, isn't it?'

I remembered my father's long moustache and the jokes he had endured about looking like a walrus. I missed him suddenly, as sometimes happened when the returning memory of him caught me by surprise. The thought no longer brought me to tears, the way it used to do. These days, it was more a feeling of confusion, finding myself unable to make sense of how much time had passed.

'Everybody asks me about the walrus,' said the man.

'Where did you get it?'

'Off the Lapps. They say it is magic.'

'And is it?'

The man shrugged. 'I am still here, so it must be doing something right.'

That appeared to be all the explanation I was going to get. I turned my attention to the wooden chest, strapped with iron bands, which he had set out in front of him.

On the chest he had placed a lemon. It was slightly shrivelled, the bright gleaming yellow gone from its dimpled skin. But it was still a lemon, and I imagined not many of them made it this far north.

I thought about the basket-loads I saw every day down in Miklagard, the smell of them clean in my lungs as I walked by chanting vendors in the marketplace.

The man stared at this lemon for a long time. He seemed to have no idea what to do with it. Eventually, he drew a short knife from his boot and cut the fruit in half. Then he took a big bite out of it.

I winced.

He gagged and roared and spat the piece from his mouth. Then he slammed the lemon down, as if it had just bitten him and not the other way around. He stared at it some more. After a while, he sliced it in half again and took another bite. He cut the lemon into smaller and smaller pieces until the whole fruit lay in fragments on the chest. He sat back and muttered under his breath, scruffing his fingertips through his beard.

'It is better with honey,' I said, trying not to smile.

He glanced at me, one eyebrow cocked, fingers still wandering across his chin, the way I once saw a blind woman learning the shape of a child's face by touch. 'This is a lemon. Leee-mooon.' He dragged the word out of his mouth. 'You have not seen one before because they do not grow around here. And because you are an ignorant Norseman, you do not know what it is better with. Now I would like to eat my lemon in peace.'

'Suit yourself.' I turned to leave. Behind my back, I heard the man gagging on another sour bite.

'You!' croaked the man.

I turned again and waited.

'How did you know this would taste better with honey?' he asked, screwing up his face.

I shrugged.

He frowned at the wreckage of the lemon. 'I paid a lot of money for that. I bought it from a Moor. He said he had brought it all the way from Spain. He was keeping it in a box made from the wood of a lemon tree. It all looked,' he sighed, 'very impressive.' Then he stood up, squaring his shoulders. 'Now what is it you want from me?'

'A ride to a place called Altvik, if you happen to be passing through there on your way north. It is my home.'

The man raised his chin and squinted. He did not say anything. He just squinted.

I took that as a no, and turned to leave. I had not walked two paces before something hit me in the back.

Cabal was getting to his feet, a look of concern on his face as he tried to make out what had happened.

I spun around, just as the piece of lemon he had thrown bounced onto the boards of the dock. Anger sparked inside me. Is it not enough, I thought, to refuse me a place on your boat without even so much as a word, but to send me on my way like this? I stepped towards the man, ready to knock him into the harbour, or worse.

'Hakon!' he shouted.

That brought me to a halt. Suddenly I recognised him, his boy's face transported through time into the body of a man. 'Olaf?'

He bared his teeth, and smiled with the same narrowed eyes that I remembered from our childhood.

93

'Your aim is still good,' I said, too shocked to say anything else.

He was shaking his head in amazement. 'They are going to choke on their cheese when they see you again.'

For a long time, we just stood there, staring at each other across the crevasse of years. The worry I had felt about seeing him again, especially after the way we had left things, fell away to nothing.

Cabal came to a stop behind me. 'Do we have trouble here?' he asked.

'None at all,' I said.

Olaf spread his arms. 'Well, are you coming home or not?'

The Drakkar seemed to have a life of its own when it moved through the open ocean. The long strakes of its hull became like the skin of a snake, rippling as if it were alive when it answered the pull of the waves. The walrus skull unnerved me; the way its tusks reared up as the bow climbed into each wave. But this gave the boat a suitable look of stubbornness, which matched its many repairs and sun-faded planks.

Olaf seemed built for this work. His stocky legs kept him steady on the pitching deck, and his heavy calf muscles clenched in rhythm with the motion of the waves, as if an ocean current ran beneath his skin.

At first, he and I did not speak, not knowing where to start.

It was Cabal who made the conversation, asking about the markets and what goods Olaf was trading.

Olaf stared at him, barely able to reply, as if entranced by the beads and coins which shuddered on Cabal's chain mail vest.

Eventually, Olaf and I found the words to talk. He explained that my parents were dead. My father had been lost at sea two years after the raid. My mother lasted another ten years by herself. She raised a stone in front of our house, a rock as big as a man, and on it a stonecutter had carved in runes the story of how I disappeared.

It came as no surprise to hear that they had passed away. I had been gone so many years and they had not been young when I left, but hopeful doubt had always flickered in the corner of my mind, immune from all sensible thought. Now, with the acceptance of their deaths, that corner of my mind grew shadowy, folding into darkness like the closing of a butterfly's wings.

'And Kari?' I asked, afraid to hear what he might say.

'Alive and prospering,' he announced, 'despite the fact that she walked away from her job with the tailor only a few days after you left. Your parents tried everything to talk her out of it, but she is as stubborn as her mother and as much of a dreamer as your father ever was. It is a shame they never lived to see how she makes her living now.'

'And how is that?' I asked.

'With plants,' replied Olaf. 'Little weeds and flowers which she gathers from the woods and upland meadows. She brews them up or grinds them into powder, and uses them to cure the aches and pains of every grumbling sniffler in our town. At least one of us found what we were looking for up in those fields.'

'I would like to meet her,' said Cabal.

'I dare say you will meet everyone in town, whether you want to or not. It is a small place. We do not get many visitors, and none like yourself, I am sure.'

'Is she married?' I asked.

Olaf rolled his eyes. 'If she were not so set in her ways, she would be.'

'Did she turn you down?' asked Cabal.

He glanced up, and it seemed for a moment as if he might take offence. But then he smiled. 'I have not given her the opportunity.'

'And Ingolf?' I asked. 'How is he?'

Olaf held his hands out around his belly. 'Like a naked bear.'

The closer we came to Altvik, the more nervous I grew about seeing them again. I had been forced to imagine their lives in all the years I had been gone and did not know how far astray my mind had led me from the truth.

Before I could ask more about them, Olaf began speaking of how Altvik had never recovered from the raid. The old trading ships were not rebuilt or replaced. Now Olaf's was the only one. He also said that Guthrun, the blacksmith, had taken over from Tostig as priest.

'Who did he choose for an apprentice?' I asked, not doubting that the answer would be Olaf himself.

'Nobody,' he replied abruptly.

'Why not?' I asked.

'Because Guthrun is an idiot!' said Olaf, struggling to control his temper. 'Guthrun will be glad to tell you all about it, although I expect you have no interest in that business now.'

'In fact I do,' I said.

Olaf looked away. 'Well, it is no way to make a living, I can tell you.'

'It is not meant to make a living,' I explained. 'It is something I promised to do.'

Olaf grunted. 'Do you know what keeps its promise in this world?' Without waiting for my answer, he hauled out a heavy leather bag from under his tunic and tossed it into my lap.

I opened it and glimpsed inside old English sceattas and other coins from as far away as Samarkand and Damascus.

Cabal looked over my shoulder and whistled quietly. 'Even the Emperor would not turn up his nose at that pile.'

Olaf watched me closely while I sifted through the coins. He seemed torn between needing me to see his wealth and fearing that I might help myself to it.

When I handed it back, Olaf tucked the bag under his clothes

96

again. He patted his belly where it rested. The coins clinked musically, as if he had swallowed a sack of broken glass. 'I might not be against sharing some of this with you,' he said. 'Can either of you crew a boat?'

We told him we could, having both spent time on the Emperor's Black Sea ships.

He immediately offered us a job, and went on to explain that his old crewman, whose name was Ivar, had just deserted him, having fallen in love with a woman who danced for a living back in Hedeby. It made Olaf so irritated to recall this, that he could not get the story out of his mouth without spitting, and he spat so much that by the time he had finished his story, the dockboards around him were spattered with saliva.

'He has a shock coming, anyway,' said Olaf. 'That dancer is a man dressed up as a woman. So do you want the job, or are you both planning to starve to death in Altvik?'

Even though Cabal and I had saved some money by sharing the cost of our travels, we had spent most of our savings to get even this far. With no idea how long the rest would last, we accepted.

As we neared the region of the Trondelag, Olaf made detours up the fjords to remote trading posts, where houses hugged thin strips of land beneath the cliffs.

Cabal stood at the bow staring up in amazement at these vast walls of rock, and at waterfalls which painted white stripes down into the blue-green water.

It had been so long since I had seen this land myself, that I felt as if I were seeing it for the first time as well.

Olaf had no time for gawking at the fjords. At the trading posts, he did a brisk trade in belts woven from horse-hair, bone fish-hooks and glass beads, especially the red ones, glowering like plucked-out dragons' eyes from the leather bag in which he carried them.

He did some buying, too, especially of honey, which was sold in earthenware pots sealed with melted wax. The merchants who knew Olaf were dismayed to see him approaching. I watched some of them close up shop as soon as his ship came into view. It all had to do with the way he conducted his business. When buying goods, Olaf's tactic was to linger, politely but idiotically refusing to acknowledge the prices he had been told. He would keep mentioning a lower price, as if he had not heard the other number. At the moment when it seemed to me a fight was inevitable, he would suggest a slightly higher amount, but one still much lower than the asking price. The exasperated merchants always gave in.

It did not bother Olaf in the least to be thought of as a half-wit. His acting was always well thought-out and tailored to test the limits of whoever's patience he was trying to wear down. The game was not to go too far, only to exhaust them. He even brought in Cabal and me as accomplices. Our job was to wait until Olaf turned his back and then have a loud conversation about how difficult Olaf could be but that he was an honest man at heart. I never saw Olaf walk away from those dealings without getting what he wanted.

He seemed to be doing well for himself, and I was glad that his old bitterness towards me seemed forgotten. I hoped we could be friends again, as we had been in the old days.

It was twilight when we dropped anchor in the bay at Altvik. The glaciers of the Grimsvoss glimmered in the dusk. An ice-blade moon was rising from the snowy peaks. Silhouettes of buildings clustered by the water's edge, smoke drifting lazily above them.

'Olaf,' I said. 'My parents' house. Is it still standing?'

He shrugged. 'More or less.'

'Does Kari live there?'

He shook his head. 'Not in that draughty old hut. She had a new place built.'

'Nobody else has claimed the house?'

'No. Everyone thinks it is haunted.'

'By what?'

He grinned, teeth white in the dark. 'By you, of course!'

'And the temple?' I asked.

'It is a wreck. I would not even go inside if I were you. The roof might fall on your head.'

'But Guthrun . . .'

'Guthrun has done nothing!' he snapped. 'You might as well see for yourself.'

Olaf said he would sleep on the boat, so he could keep an eye on his goods. 'You can sleep here as well, if you want.'

But Cabal needed to walk the stiffness from his joints, and I was too restless to sleep. Fatigue from months of lying on the decks of ships or sitting in carts or walking in mosquito-humming forests had all been shaken from my bones by the sight of this place.

'Make sure you are back by sunrise,' said Olaf, 'to help me unload the cargo. Remember you work for me now.'

Borrowing a skiff that Olaf kept on board, we rowed ashore. As we moved through the quiet water, the only sound the creaking of our oars, I glanced back at the silhouette of the walrus skull tied up on the prow of Olaf's ship. In the gentle pulse of waves, the bone face tilted slowly back and forth. It looked like an old man, nodding himself to sleep.

Olaf stood at the bow, watching us make our way in.

'It is good to see you again,' I said to him across the bay, which lay so still that the sound carried without me having to raise my voice.

He raised his hand and nodded, then hawked and spat over the side.

99

Cabal and I jumped out into shin-deep water and dragged the boat above the high-tide line.

The houses hunched under their thick turf roofs. The sound of tiny waves slapping the beach echoed among the buildings. Here and there a sliver of light showed through a crack in a shutter. Two dogs wandered down to the beach and sniffed at Cabal. Then, exhausted by the effort, they flopped down in the dirt and closed their eyes.

We walked up through the main street, passing the alehouse. From inside came the sound of quiet laughter and the sour reek of ale.

As we moved on up the hill, it became clear to me that Olaf was right about the town never having recovered. Many of the buildings were in poor repair and the streets were ankle-deep in mud.

Cabal said nothing, but from his silence I could tell he was not impressed by what he saw.

I thought of the Emperor's palace of a hundred rooms, of the Hagia Sofia and the way its vaulted roof seemed to float on a cushion of sunlight. It all seemed like the substance of a dream, just as the Emperor had said it would be.

I stopped suddenly and turned to Cabal. 'I forgot to ask where Kari lives.'

'Tomorrow, my friend,' he said. 'You will frighten your poor sister to death if you show up on her doorstep now. Let her see you in the light of day.'

I had waited so long for this moment that now I had to stop myself from banging on every door until I found her. But I took Cabal's advice and forced myself to be patient.

When we reached my parents' house, I saw the stone Olaf had told me about. It looked like a tall man shrouded in a cloak, broad-shouldered underneath the folds of rock. Carved on the chest was a serpent with its tail in its mouth. Between the lines of the serpent's body were a line of runes, lichen-patched with age, which read: 'A mother set this stone in memory of her son, who vanished in a distant land.'

'How does it feel to be a ghost?' asked Cabal, running his thumbnail through the moss which had filled in the words.

I shook my head. 'We are both ghosts, you and I.'

'Are we going in?' He shivered in the night mist which was settling on the ground.

'Not yet,' I told him. 'There is a place I want you to see.' I had made up my mind to share with him the secret of what lay beneath the temple floor, whatever it turned out to be. He had put his life in my hands by travelling north with me, and I wanted to repay his trust.

As we walked out across the moonlit fields, I explained everything to Cabal.

'No wonder you were so anxious to get back here,' he said.

When we reached the temple, I was shocked to see the place almost in ruins. The doors were missing and much of the earth had come away from its walls, revealing the bare rock, like a skeleton showing through a body left to rot out in the open.

Inside the temple, the ground was pocked with the hoof-marks and droppings of sheep. The benches were either missing or broken, stamped apart by generations of boys released from the watchful eyes of their parents. The pillars still stood, fierce eyes defiant as ever. Moonlight shone through a hole in the roof. Its pale glow lay like frost across the wooden faces.

While Cabal gathered wood for a fire, I gave thanks for a safe journey home. I pressed my ear to the ground and lay there for a while, hearing the quiet thunder of the earth.

As the faint glow of Cabal's fire spread across the walls, I studied the ground, in case it might offer some clue as to where this thing might be buried. I used the blade of my sword to scrape away at the dirt in a few places, but turned up nothing.

'There is only one way to do this,' said Cabal. 'We must dig up the whole floor.'

He started at one end and I started at the other. Using pieces of broken bench as shovels, we heaved clods of earth against the walls, showering the rotten benches.

I was digging close by the pillars, making my way down through layers of ash and bone from years of sacrifices.

We kept working half the night, pausing only to wipe the sweat from our faces and to stoke up the fire.

'Are you sure this is the place?' asked Cabal.

I stopped my shovelling, then slowly straightened my sore back. I looked around the room. The ground was gouged with holes where we had started digging and then given up. Loose dirt lay piled against the walls. 'There is only one temple,' I said. 'It has to be here.'

'Maybe the old man was lying to you.'

I dropped my make-shift spade and pressed my blistered fingers against my closed eyelids. I was exhausted.

Cabal grunted, then returned to his digging.

A moment later, I heard his makeshift shovel glance off something which made a different sound than the stones we had unearthed so far.

'Look at this,' he said.

It was a piece of black rock, shiny like glass.

I reached for the black hammer around my neck and pulled it from the warmth between my body and my shirt. The hammer was made from the same kind of stone.

Cabal dug around the rock, trying to dislodge it, but it was bigger than he thought.

I didn't know what to make of it and went back to digging by the pillars. A short while later, I also hit a piece of the same black rock which Cabal had just uncovered.

Now Cabal and I began digging a trench towards each other. We began to realise that the rock stretched all the way across the room, an arm's length down under the earth. The whole temple was built upon this huge slab of black stone.

My breathing grew shallow and fast as the shock of our discovery set in.

I remembered what Tostig had said – that it was the only thing ever to pass bodily from the world of the gods into our own. It must have fallen from the sky. I tried to imagine it, cocooned in flames, shrieking with speed, and the tremor which must have shaken even the vastness of the mountains as it slammed into the earth. From that one terrifying moment, the Norse faith had been born.

'I know what this is,' said Cabal. 'It is a Thunder Stone. I have seen fragments of them before, like the one around your neck, but never one as large as this.' He set his hand upon its surface. 'My people say that Thunder Stones have the breath of life in them,' he said, 'and they have been alive longer than anything else on this earth. The first spark of our existence in our world came from these Thunder Stones, and life still streams from them like rays out of the sun.'

Cabal and I stood looking at each other. The black rock reflected the flames of our fire, as if it held its own flames deep inside.

I understood now why this needed to be hidden, having seen for myself what had happened to the places which other faiths had openly declared their holy ground. They became battlefields. The only way for their disciples to protect them was to turn them into fortresses, where the meaning of their sacredness was blurred by the blood shed in their defence.

In silence, Cabal and I scraped the dirt back into the hole, then trampled it flat so that there was almost no trace that the earth had been disturbed. We left the door ajar as we had found it, knowing that sheep would wander in and cover up the last signs of our digging.

At my parents' house, the door would not open. I gave it a push and the whole thing fell back into the building. A smell of damp wafted into my face. Inside, Cabal and I tripped on fallen beams and pieces of broken furniture until we reached the fireplace. Using a chair as kindling, we managed to light a fire there. Through the haze of rotten-wood smoke, I saw the place where my sleeping bench had been and where the iron hook that held the cooking pot still hung from the rafters like the curled tail of a cat. The roof had sagged in at the far end, spilling turf across the floor. Dandelions, huge and spindly, stretched up towards the gap in the roof, through which I saw the shattered glass of stars. From somewhere in the shadows came the cooing of a dove.

Cabal lay down beside the fire, using his shield as a pillow and hugging his leather pack against his chest. Almost at once, he began snoring.

As tired as I was, I could not sleep. I did feel like a ghost. A stranger even to the shadows of my parents, which still lingered in this place.

My mother had spent half her life in this room. An image returned to me of her sweeping the hearth with an alder-twig broom. Now her own restless spirit carried on as she had done – cleaning, mending, cooking, convinced of small conspiracies, unaware that her heart had stopped beating and that the dust she cleared away was her own.

I walked over to the broom and picked it up. Slowly and methodically, I began to sweep the floor.

PART II

I woke before dawn, curled beside the embers of the fire and with one of Cabal's feet for a pillow. Leaving him asleep, I went to the door and moved it aside, since it was no longer on its hinges and only propped in place.

Walking out into the morning fog, I looked down on the rooftops, which floated on the mist like upturned boats. I wondered which belonged to Kari, which to Guthrun, which to Ingolf.

When I walked back inside, Cabal was awake, rubbing the sleep from his eyes.

We washed in the stream behind the house, making our way through the overgrown garden, among the herbs my mother had planted. The thyme and rosemary, along with bearberries, gentian and mint, had all managed to survive. Cabal drew his hands through the mint, then touched the tips of his fingers to his nose, breathing in the dusty sweet smell.

We made our way down to the beach. Now that it was daylight, I could see even more clearly how run-down the town had become. The muddy streets, the saddle-backed roofs of the houses, carts which had been repaired too many times rather than being replaced, the tired-looking people in their worn-out shoes, all left me feeling ashamed that Cabal had to see it this way.

Either Cabal did not notice these things, or he was good enough not to mention them. This had once been a prosperous place, and I wished he could have seen it back then.

Olaf was there to meet us on the beach, having run his boat up on the sand. He was still half asleep and his hair stuck up in tufts, which made him look like an owl that had been knocked out of its nest. 'What do you think of our beautiful town?' he asked Cabal.

'I like it here.'

Olaf grinned. 'You ought to be a merchant. You certainly lie like one.'

'It is no lie,' replied Cabal.

When I asked Olaf where Kari lived, he told me I would see her soon enough.

'She will be down here before you could find your way to her house. I have brought some knives and bowls for her and she is coming to collect them. For now, I need your help setting up my tables.' He led us to his house, which stood close to the beach.

The place was a shambles. Two huge arcs of whale-rib formed the entrance. The door, which he had left open, was made of hide stretched over a wooden frame. The entranceway itself was so tilted over that to go through it a person would have to lean as if they were on the deck of a rolling ship. Inside, I glimpsed a tangled mess of boat parts, tools, rope, evil-smelling whale bones, broken pots and chairs which, when Olaf saw the look on my face, he announced he was planning to fix up some day. Then he went on to explain that, even if an object could no longer fulfil its original purpose, it might always be useful for doing something else. Because of this, he had never thrown anything out.

Olaf's shed leaned precariously against the side of the main house. This was where he kept his trading tables, which Cabal and I helped him carry to the water's edge. Then we unloaded the cargo, while Olaf busied himself laying out bolts of cloth and wooden crates containing glass, unfinished knives, soapstone bowls, and the pots of honey.

The first buyers were already gathering, women mostly, shawls pulled over their heads to guard against the morning chill. They were quickly followed by the remainder of the town, until it seemed that everyone who could walk or find someone to carry them had assembled on the beach.

A story-teller started up his act, and children gathered around him. Their grateful parents dropped a coin in his wooden bowl and wandered off to see what Olaf had brought. Nearby, an old woman squatted on a stone, telling fortunes with a handful of bones and glass beads.

With growing apprehension I watched the crowd, wondering if Kari would even recognise me, or if I had changed too much for her to know my face.

'Will Guthrun be here?' I asked, as I handed Olaf a crate of glassware padded with straw. Splinters from the flimsy wood hooked into my skin.

'You will not see him here this early,' replied Olaf. 'He is too lazy to get out of bed. Besides, he has no money. You will not need to find him. When he is ready, he will find you.' Olaf shook out a piece of red silk, which wafted in the air above the table. The silk shimmered and spread in the sunlight, like a drop of blood falling into a pool of water.

On the table lay Olaf's own sword, a handsome thing in the short Roman style with a leather-wrapped handle held by a twisted braid of gold. He used it for measuring cloth, which was always sold by the sword-length.

It was not long before news of my arrival began to spread. There was a great deal of muttering and pointing in my direction.

'You seem to be the main attraction today,' said Olaf. 'A shame I am not selling you.'

'I have been through that once already,' I replied, as I lifted a bale of cloth from the bow of the boat.

No one else spoke to me, which made me wish I could stand up on one of these tables and announce why I had returned, but my instincts steered me towards silence. I stole glances out across the crowd, searching for a familiar face.

Meanwhile, Olaf cut the strings that tied bales of cloth and prised off box lids, revealing pale green Frankish glassware in its packaging of straw. These were snatched up and then immediately put back after Olaf quoted the price.

The old fortune teller, her back bent like the arc of a drawn bow, offered to tell Olaf's fortune in exchange for a pot of honey.

Now that she was close, I thought I recognised her. 'Tola?'

She peered at me and smiled, gums pulled back from her peg teeth. 'You remember me, do you?'

'Of course I do.'

'We gave you up for dead long ago.'

'How is Ingolf?' I asked. 'Is he here?'

Tola nodded. 'He will be along to buy up some rubbish or other.' Then she went back to pestering Olaf about the pot of honey, until he took some of the straw packing, set it on her head, and pushed her away.

She scuttled back into the crowd, muttering insults and swatting the straw from her straggly hair.

Soon after, Ingolf appeared from inside the alehouse and strode towards the beach with a leg of lamb over each shoulder. He had grown almost as wide as he was tall, and his round, red face still showed the gentle nature which had marked him as a child. He wore a leather apron, which slapped against his knees with every step.

110

'He and his mother manage the alehouse now,' said Olaf as we watched him approach. 'His father died a few years back. He went out to slaughter the pig they fed on scraps left over from the alehouse meals, and the pig slaughtered him instead. Tola still runs Ingolf's life, same as she did when he was little. Or as little as he has ever been.'

Ingolf came straight over to me. 'Heard you were back,' he said, with a solemn look on his face. 'Thought you were dead.' He kept his arms wrapped around the legs of lamb.

I smiled and suddenly it was as if no time at all had passed.

Ingolf was grinning, too. 'I cannot stay,' he said. 'Have to get this lamb on the fire, and the alehouse will be open soon. I am in charge there now, you know.'

Olaf made a snorting sound and Ingolf scowled at him.

I introduced Ingolf to Cabal.

'I have a Celtic recipe for ale,' said Ingolf.

'I like you already,' replied Cabal.

Ingolf built a driftwood fire on the sand and began roasting the lamb on an iron spit. Soon, he had begun to sell slices of rare meat, which he laid dripping on top of thick slabs of bread. Cabal bought two of these, and held one in each hand, taking bites first from one and then the other. As he spoke to Ingolf, gesturing one way and then the other, juice from the meat flicked out over other people waiting for their turn to buy.

Nobody objected. They were too busy staring at the size of him.

My eyes drifted from Cabal to the beach, where I spotted a tall woman running out across the sand towards me. I knew immediately that it was Kari, from the black hair and bright blue eyes. Her skin was freckled and pale, and her high cheekbones, which had been the rounded cheeks of a child the last time I saw them, cut sharper angles now.

I tried to say her name but the breath caught in my throat.

111

Then Olaf was standing in front of me, tugging at the bolt of cloth in my hands. 'Let go!' he grumbled. 'What is the matter with you?'

I dropped the cloth and climbed over the table.

'Mind the merchandise!' shouted Olaf.

As I put my arms around her I knew I had prepared for anything but this. I had thought about it a thousand times, but I had not prepared for it. I had prepared for Olaf being the same person who could not see beyond the tasks he had set himself, whether it was hunting for the creatures of the underworld or selling pots of honey to old ladies. I had prepared for the stares of those who had, in their minds, already buried me long ago. For the deaths of my parents and the fact that the town had never recovered from the raid, I had prepared.

But to embrace Kari, and have her be my own flesh and blood and at the same time a total stranger, and what the sight of her would do to my mind and to my heart, I had not come close to understanding in the years I had been gone. Even now, I could not grasp it. The enormity of this could settle only slowly in my bones. Until then, there was nothing to do but get on with the uncountable small details of returning to life in this town.

We held each other for a long time. The bustle of the market swirled around us.

When she stood back, still holding onto my arms, the tears were running down her face. 'You have heard about our parents,' she said.

I nodded, blinking the tears from my own eyes. These were the first tears I had shed in as long as I could recall.

'Are you going to help at all?' Olaf shouted after Cabal, who had gone to buy himself some more to eat.

The women rummaged carelessly through bolts of wool that Olaf had stacked in neat piles on one table. They weighed the cloth in their hands, brought it close to their faces to smell the wool, then rubbed it between their fingers, even plucking a few strands to put in their mouths.

'Stop doing that!' shouted Olaf.

The women ignored him.

'You are working for Olaf?' asked Kari.

'For now.'

She laughed and wiped her eyes. 'Well, you are braver than most.'

'Will somebody help me get rid of these empty crates!' Olaf shouted.

Kari turned and pointed to a house about half way up the hill. 'That is where I live. Come and find me when you are done. We have waited this long. One morning longer will not matter.'

Reluctantly, I returned to the tables. The tears kept coming to my eyes.

Olaf thumped an empty crate down in front of me. 'Could you kindly tell your enormous friend that I am not paying him to talk to people who are not even customers. We have work to do!'

I could not find it in myself to be angry at his impatience. Olaf had not been patient as a child, and he was no different now. I reached across and patted him on the shoulder. 'It is good to see you have not changed. Now what do you want done with this crate?'

'Take them over to Ingolf and tell him to bring me a slice of lamb, which I do not expect to pay for since he is using my wood for his fire.'

I carried the splintery crates over to the fire.

Cabal was still talking to Ingolf. When he caught sight of me, he frowned. 'You did not introduce me to your sister.'

'I forgot. I am sorry.' I set the crates down on the sand.

'She is very beautiful,' he said, with a mouthful of food. 'Are you sure she is your sister?'

113

Ingolf wiped his greasy palms on his apron, leaving two burnished marks in the leather, like a pair of inverted horns that curved down the sides of his belly. He picked up the crates I had brought and threw them on the fire. 'I expect none of this is coming free,' he said.

'No,' I replied, and delivered Olaf's message.

'Well, that is no surprise,' he grumbled, and spat into the crackling flames.

The rest of the morning passed in a blur.

By midday, most of the dealing had been done. In twos and threes, the crowd made their way back up the beach. Some compared with each other the trinkets they had bought and the prices they had paid. Others strutted home with their goods tucked into woven-reed baskets, as if afraid they might be robbed by jealous neighbors. The only ones left were those who could not make up their minds what to buy. They slinked around the tables, tortured by their indecision as we packed our things away.

One of these was Ingolf. When nothing remained of the lamb, he tossed the bones into the fire and came over to inspect Olaf's tables. Ingolf pulled at his rubbery chin and ran his fingers frustratedly through his thinning hair, fussing over what to get, although in the end he bought nothing and eventually went home.

As Olaf and I packed up the things which had not sold, he told me some more about Ingolf and Tola. She made up for Ingolf's lack of business sense with a tightfistedness that was unnerving even to Olaf, whose own fists seemed tight enough. Under Tola's eye, no one could leave the alehouse without paying. There was no credit, even if you had been going there for years and only lived across the street. It was Tola who decided when the place should close each night, otherwise it might never have closed and Ingolf most likely would have slept on top of the bar, alongside his satisfied customers.

According to Olaf, the fact that Tola was not liked had less to do with her strictness than the way she treated her son. 'She makes sarcastic comments about him being timid, overweight and weak. She says these things in public, right in front of him. When arm-wrestling competitions start up at the alehouse, she asks him in a loud voice why he is not taking part. So, of course Ingolf joins in, and when he loses she makes fun of him. He hates her for never letting him grow up as much as he hates himself for never having the courage to move out on his own. Of course, he cannot bring himself to say any of that, but he is not as feeble as he seems. He uses that helplessness of his just as well as she uses her sharp tongue.'

Olaf went on to explain the way Ingolf had of getting back at his mother for her pestering, which was to buy useless objects from Olaf. These included gaudy arm rings, heavy bead necklaces, soapstone carvings of polar bears, anything in fact, that would annoy his frugal-minded mother. Ingolf's greatest triumph so far was a small bronze statue of a man with cat-like eyes and earrings, sitting cross legged and holding out one arm, from which the hand had broken off. Olaf had bought it in Birka from a trader who had found it someplace in the Caucasus. Neither of them had any idea who the statue was supposed to be, which made it completely useless. Of course, Olaf persuaded Ingolf to buy the thing as a present for Tola.

As word of this ridiculous purchase spread through the town, the only way for Tola to save face was to pretend she liked the statue. So she put it on display behind the counter at the alehouse, and Olaf never passed up the opportunity to tell Tola what a nice little sculpture it was.

*

Once Cabal and I had packed away the tables, Olaf pressed a few coins into our hands.

Both Cabal and I dropped them in our pockets without looking.

'You are not going to see how much I paid you?'

'We trust you,' said Cabal. It was easier than explaining that this was a habit from our days in Miklagard, when it would have been considered an insult to examine any money we were paid.

He raised his eyebrows. Then he handed us each another coin. 'I am not used to being trusted,' he said.

'Do you need us for work tomorrow?' I asked.

He shook his head. 'Soon,' he said, 'but not that soon.' With a quick nod, he set off up the hill towards his home, the bloated money bag clinking against his chest.

I brought Cabal to Kari's house. We knocked on the door and stood back.

'Should I comb my hair?' asked Cabal.

I looked at the tangle which hung down over his eyes. 'Too late now.'

Cabal raked his fingers through his hair and then got one of his fingers stuck in a knot. He was still trying to untangle it when Kari opened the door.

She stared at Cabal, whose hand was pinned to the side of his head like someone trying to remember something important.

With a grunt, Cabal wrenched his fingers loose, tearing out a small tuft of hair. 'I am your brother's friend,' he said, his voice too loud for the small space that separated him from Kari.

'Then you had better both come in,' said Kari, and stood aside to let us pass.

The house smelled sweet and dry inside. The ceiling beams were hung with bundles of drying plants. It looked like an upside down forest, flecked with the faded pinks and blues and yellows of meadow flowers. All along the walls were earthenware pots filled with crumbled herbs. Around them, the floor had been neatly swept, the sandy ground ridged by the twigs of her broom. Kindling lay stacked on the hearth. A pot filled with dried stockfish simmered above the smouldering fire, ready for dinner. On a table beside it, deep-green fronds of dill weed used for seasoning were heaped in a bowl.

An oil lamp illuminated a table by the fireplace, where Kari had been sitting before we arrived. Warm and watery light rippled across the walls.

For the rest of the day, Cabal and I sat around the table, telling of our years in the Varangian. To most of our descriptions, Kari only smiled and laughed, as if unsure whether to believe them.

Often I got up and walked about, forming with my outstretched fingers the great dome of the Hagia Sofia, or the smooth walls of the Emperor's palace, or the humped back of a camel.

'You remind me of your father,' she said, 'the way you talk with your hands.'

The person she brought to mind for me was not my mother or my father but myself. I saw my own face in the line of her brow, in her nose and in her lips. I had never cared about such things when I was young but now they seemed pricelessly important. To see this echo of my features made me realise that no matter how long I had been away from this place, and how little remained of my family, I did belong here after all.

When I told Kari of the promise I had made to Tostig, she only replied, 'This town has been without a priest for a long time.' She listened more than she spoke that day, having fewer stories to relate. But even in the little that she told – of rivalries and money made and lost, of unlikely marriages which

117

endured beyond all expectations, of children born and grown and moved away – I saw she understood even the subtlest ebb and flow of life inside this town. When I heard her talk, I would have traded all the unforgettable things that I had lived and seen for even half the quiet memories that she possessed.

By the afternoon, I had so exhausted myself that I fell asleep in front of the fire. When I woke, Cabal was pointing to the herbs and Kari was naming them, and telling him the use for each one.

I drifted in and out of sleep, waking now and then to see Kari and Cabal still talking.

A bowl of milk simmered by the fireplace.

More sleep.

Now Cabal was tapping his finger on the surface of the table to make a point, leaning towards her and speaking in an urgent whisper. Whatever he was saying, he had her full attention.

Then the warmth of the fire lulled me back into my dreams.

When my eyes opened again, Cabal was telling Kari about throwing the fish bones in the air at the market place in Mikla-gard. He flicked his wrist with the precise movement of send-ing the fish up to the waiting gulls.

Kari sat back and laughed, showing her strong, white teeth.

Cabal had lost his nervousness. The wide, innocent look on his face revealed the gentleness that had made him my friend all these years.

When they noticed I was awake, their conversation died away. Cabal walked over and handed me the milk, thumb hooked over the edge of the bowl. When I took the bowl, he wiped his hand on his trousers, which were so dirty that they had a black shine like old iron.

Soon it was time to go. The day was over. Kari offered to let us stay at her house, but we politely refused, as there was not enough room.

At the door, she embraced me and then, to Cabal's surprise, she hugged him too.

Hesitantly, he patted her back.

Cabal and I returned to the tumbledown remains of my parents' house. We lit a big fire and lay down beside it, but could not fall asleep. We talked long into the night, speaking of things we had not dared to tell Kari. Some were of the impossible cruelties we had both seen and done. Others were so tangled in the details of life among the Varangian as to make them indecipherable to anyone who was not there. With these stories, we reminded each other of the hard times we had shared, in the hopes that they all lay behind us now.

At sunrise the next morning, I was awakened by the sound of someone pounding on the door.

I had managed to clear off the old sleeping benches and spent the night lying on a ragged sheepskin which I had picked up in Starya Ladoga. The pelt had not been properly tanned and clumps of wool had started to come loose. It looked as if snow had fallen on me in the night.

Cabal still preferred the floor, where he was closer to the fire. Now, in his bare feet, he stepped across the cold flagstones and swung the door wide. He had forgotten that the door was not attached to its hinges and it fell back on top of him. He heaved it to the side and light poured in like water.

Guthrun stood in the doorway. Age had woven spiderwebs across his face. His pale grey eyes seemed out of place framed by such weatherbeaten skin. He looked at Cabal and muttered with astonishment. 'I was . . . I was looking . . .'

'He is here,' said Cabal.

I sat up from my bed. Flecks of sheepskin drifted to the ground. 'Guthrun,' I said.

'I knew you were not dead,' he replied, his voice so rough and deep it seemed to come from somewhere in his belly. He walked over to me, set his hands on my shoulders and squeezed the blood out of my arms. 'I knew you would come back.'

'I heard you might have use for an apprentice,' I told him.

He let go of my shoulders and stepped back. 'The truth is,' he said, 'I no longer need one.'

I felt my heart sink. In talking with Olaf, I had allowed my hopes to build too high. 'No. After all this time. Of course not. But surely there is some way I can make myself useful.'

'What I need,' he said, 'is for you to take over from me. Now. Today.'

My disappointment spun back upon itself with such a violent turn that for a moment, I lost my sense of balance. At the same time, as Guthrun's words sank in, I felt the loosening of muscles clenched so long I had mistaken them for bone.

He tapped a finger against my chest. 'You are still wearing the hammer that Tostig gave you.'

A picture of Halfdan's corpse splashed across my eyes. Blood had sealed a layer of dust against the dead man's face so that it appeared to be only the cast of a face, hollow and crumbling. I remembered how it felt to clasp the black hammer in my hand and the way the old cord came apart when I tugged at it, slithering from around his neck like a baby snake.

'I am on my way up to the temple now,' said Guthrun. 'Today we mark –'

'The Turning of the Sun,' I told him.

'I may have less to teach you than I thought,' he said.

Leaving Cabal to finish his sleep, Guthrun and I made our way up through the village and out across the field. The Grimsvoss rose above us in a wall of fractured rock and ice, and we narrowed our eyes at the glaring whiteness of the distant snowfields. At last, we came to the end of the fields, where the earth gave way to cracked stones cast down like crumbled sleep from the eyes of the mountains. Patches of dirty snow clung to hollows where the sun could not reach. Old ice hugged the mountainside, rippled hard like muscle and glimmering a deep mysterious blue, as if light were radiating from somewhere far beneath its skin. Above us, the frozen ground seemed to bulge out like the stomach of a sleeping giant, and wisps of powdered snow whirled across the blinding white. Above the jagged peaks, the sky was vivid blue, like salt thrown in a fire.

We stopped outside the temple. Wind moaned around the empty doorframe.

'I have not kept up with repairs,' he said quietly. 'After Tostig left, I tried to carry on as he had done, but Olaf spoke out against me. He said he should have been chosen to serve as Tostig's apprentice, and that since both you and Tostig were gone, and I was left to run the temple, he should be chosen in your place.'

'Why did you refuse?'

'For two reasons. Firstly because it was not in my power to question Tostig's choice, and, secondly, because I knew you would come back some day. I was sure of it. And you see I was right. I told Olaf, and the rest of the town as well, that the only way I would hand over the temple to him was if you came back and refused to run it yourself. That, you can be sure, is the only reason he offered you a ride back on his boat. He may have thrown all his energy into being a merchant, but what he most cares about is the one thing he has ever been denied, and that is to be a priest.'

'He has said nothing to me about it.'

'But he will. He is just waiting for the right moment to approach you. One thing I will say for Olaf, he never gives up. For years now, he has been ridiculing me, saying I have neither the strength nor the faith nor the favour of the gods that a priest requires. I tried to ignore him, but others did not. They stopped coming. One day, I found myself alone up here. Never in all my days with Tostig had we performed the rites by ourselves. After that, I no longer had the energy to maintain the place, and nobody else seemed to care what happened to it.'

As we stepped inside the temple, two startled sheep ran out, dirty shreds of wool hanging from their sides. Between their trampling and ours, and the building's general state of disrepair, Guthrun noticed no trace of our digging. At the far end of the room, the pillars glowered at us from the shadows. Stepping over the pellets of sheep droppings, Guthrun undid the strap of the leather bag he carried slung over his shoulder. From it, he took out a short knife with a reindeer bone handle. He did not ask me if I knew what should be done. Instead, he just held the knife out to me, handle first.

Bent double, I moved around the pillars in a wide circle, cutting a groove in the ground, following the path where countless grooves had been dug before. When the circle was complete, we would not move from it until the ceremony was over.

From his bag, Guthrun brought four bundles of twigs bound in scrolls of white birch bark and tied with dried grass. He also took out a wooden bowl and set it it on the ground. Into the bowl, from a cloth bag, he poured a handful of salt. With a sliver of glass, he cut a half-moon shaped slice into his palm, around the meat of his thumb. This place on both his hands was thickly scarred. He held his hand over the bowl, watching the red drops soaking into the crumbled salt. From a goat-skin bag, he poured some water into the bowl, stirred it with the blood and salt, and set it down on the ground.

Standing at the eastern edge of the circle, Guthrun walked around the rim, dipping his fingers into the water and flicking them at the groove cut in the earth.

We took the four bundles of twigs, set them burning with a piece of flint and a horse-shoe iron striker. Then we placed one at each of the four corners – first east, then south, then west, then north.

We knelt before the pillars, praying in silence while tongues of flame illuminated our faces. On this thin blanket of earth which covered the huge black thunder stone was the same shuddering energy as I had known in Miklagard. But here, it was even stronger, roaring around me. The words of the ritual seemed to be speaking themselves.

When the fires had died out, we gathered the charred twigs that remained; first east, then south, then west, then north, and threw them out of the circle. At the base of the pillars, we emptied the water from the bowl, then I took the short handled knife and ran it through the groove in the opposite direction, to open the circle again.

When all this was done, we stepped out of the circle and sat down against the pillars.

It began to rain outside.

'Guthrun,' I asked, 'was it only because of Olaf that people stopped coming to the temple?'

Guthrun was unwrapping a slab of dried reindeer meat from his pack. He softened it by tossing the meat between his hands. With a gentle slap, it bounced from palm to palm. Finally, he raised his head and blinked at me with wolf-pale eyes. 'It took me many years to admit that Olaf was right about one thing – that I was not fit to run the temple. With Tostig in charge, people walked out of this building certain that their prayers were being heard, but where Tostig travelled in his prayers, I never went myself. It was only a matter of time before people realised the truth about me. Who could blame them if they stopped coming? Even so, I refused to hand over the temple to Olaf. He may have been right that I could not handle the task, but he was wrong when he said he was the one who could. He might possess the strength. He might even have the faith. But he does not have the

123

favour of the gods, any more than I do. That belongs to you alone, as it belonged to Tostig before you The gods themselves made that decision.' Guthrun's voice was dry and choked.

I took the birchwood cup I carried in my leather pack, walked to the doorway and held it out into the rain where it quickly filled. A man in Starya Ladoga had made the cup for me one afternoon when I wandered into town, leaving Cabal behind to wait for Godfred. The maker's name was Herigar and he had one brown eye and one blue. He made a fist and told me to close my fingers around it and grip tightly. From the feel of my hand, he carved a cup which seemed to slide into each wrinkle of my palm. Silvery sinews in the wood glinted like tiny fish. I handed the water to Guthrun, who drank it all and gave me back the cup.

We looked out through the doorway towards the mountains, where glaciers stood like vast and tumbling waves, halted in the moment of their breaking.

'I have heard,' said Guthrun, 'that Trygvasson, the new king of Norway, is determined to wipe out the Norse religion. Trygvasson! Before he became king, people used to call him Crowbones because he had a gift for telling the future by emptying a pile of crowbones on a table and seeing how they fell. And now he wants us to be Christian? We will see about that.'

'But do you think he could succeed?'

Guthrun spat on the floor and wiped the back of his hand with his mouth. 'If he pushes this country in a way it does not want to go, he has about as much future as the crow whose bones he is reading.'

'You are not worried at all?'

'I am too old to worry. Besides, what happens to the temple now is up to you.'

I felt the burden of his words, but I needed to hear them. Now my work here could begin.

We made our way back across the wide and open field. The rain had stopped and the sky was powdered saffron yellow. Wolves howled in the mountains. We walked a little closer, side by side.

Olaf did not need Cabal or me for the next few days, since he was preparing for the mid-summer trading run, collecting whatever goods had been made here in town for sale down in Hedeby.

At my parents' place, Cabal and I hung our shields on the wall, then set our spears and swords across the rafter beams. We knocked down one side of the house and built it up again from scratch. We laid new turf over the roof and re-filled the gaps with moss. Against the wall I constructed two beds of wooden slats and padded them with reindeer pelts, while Cabal made a table and some chairs.

Kari brought me pots, wooden spoons and bowls, some of them left over from our parents. With her help, I gathered the trappings of a less restless life.

She and Cabal became so absorbed in hushed discussions that I had to find tasks which gave them time alone together or else risk being in the way. I wondered what they found to talk about, and there were moments when I was almost jealous, as much of Kari as of Cabal.

Kari's reasons for remaining unmarried were still a mystery to me, but what I had seen of the few eligible men in town left me convinced that she had made the right choice.

When she had gone, Cabal said nothing about her, thinking he had kept his emotions a secret.

I allowed Cabal to think so rather than embarrass him, but I found it hard to hide my curiosity about what had drawn them so quickly together.

*

125

In my mind, the past was grating against the present, like two pieces of broken glass, trying to fit back together.

As I moved around the house, moments from my childhood flickered to life in the same greenish glowing light that I had seen lingering in the air above old graves.

There was my father, hauling on his heavy cloak as he headed out to fish on a rainy day.

There were Kari and I, as children, sitting at the table with our arms folded, bowls of oats in front of us which we had refused to eat because my mother burned them and we could not stand the smoky, metal taste of burned oats. She always burned the oats and always denied it, and if my father was not there to agree with us, we would be made to sit at the table until her temper died down.

Images of my mother shimmered in many places at once, multiplying and overlapping. I could hear her voice, words twisted together and indecipherable, like someone speaking underwater.

Then suddenly, the voices would stop and the flickering pictures would scatter, like a flock of birds flushed from a tree.

At the temple, I scrubbed years of grime from the pillars, rebuilt benches, swept floors. Almost every day, I cut more coins out of my vest to buy materials for the following day's work.

Meanwhile, Guthrun fielded questions from those too shy to ask me in person. Would they be welcome at the temple? Would the rites of the seasons be observed? And the rites of the thirteen months? Wolf Moon. Snow Moon. Horn Moon. Plough Moon. Seed Moon. Hare Moon. Mead Moon. Fallow Moon. Grain Moon. Harvest Moon. Shedding Moon. Hunting Moon. Fog Moon. All of them. Yes.

Cabal and I knocked the wall stones into place and filled the cracks between with clay and moss. We refitted the beams which supported the old roof. As soon as I knew that the temple was not going to collapse in the next gust of wind, I began to carry out the rituals.

The first day, only one person besides Guthrun came to the temple, and it was Olaf. He sat stiff-backed on a bench by himself, closely watching everything I did. Afterwards, he left without saying a word.

'I have not felt so harshly judged in a long time,' I said to Guthrun, as Olaf trudged down the hill.

'The fact that he said nothing is the only sign of his approval you are ever likely to receive. Anyway, it is a beginning,' said Guthrun.

'Yes,' I said. 'It is.'

The next day, Olaf was back, silent as before. There were others, too, including Ingolf and Tola. Kari did not come, and I did not expect to see her there. Like Cabal, she had made her own balance of the world around her, in which the temple, and all that it stood for, did not play a part. For this, as I had learned from my years with Cabal, I did not love her any less, nor did I pity her or say a word about it.

Steadily, the numbers began to increase. The temple was never full but, as Guthrun had said, it was a start.

One evening, Cabal and I went down to Ingolf's alehouse, where we played chess with a set brought back from Miklagard. The pieces had been carved from soapstone the colour of honey. The board was of soft leather, which served as a bag to hold the pieces.

The struggle between the two faiths, which Cabal and I had expected to find here, seemed far away from this sleepy little town. With so little to occupy his time, I knew it would not be long before Cabal was on his way. He had taken to wandering after dark, usually when he thought I was asleep. His restlessness was growing. I wondered if, one of these nights, he would simply not come back, having found it easier to leave without saying goodbye.

I felt sorry for Kari and just as sorry for myself, but I knew that once he had made up his mind, neither love nor friendship would stand in his way.

On this evening, we had finished our game, and the pieces lay scattered on the leather board. The ale and the warmth of the fire had made us sleepy. Except for Ingolf, we were the last ones in the place. Any moment now, Tola would come in and tell us we had to go home.

'Do you miss our days in the Varangian?' asked Cabal.

At the mention of that name, the remembered scent of cloves and cardamon and the pollen-yellow mustiness of turmeric swirled dustily into my brain. 'I miss some things about it. I miss the taste of wine.'

'Yes,' he said dreamily. 'Wine.'

'I miss the taste of dates. I miss the heat of the sun.'

He smiled, and smoothed away the hard lines of his face. 'I have seen a little sun here too, you know.'

'I mean the midday heat, which snatches the air from your lungs. That is the sun I am talking about. And what about you? Do you often think back on our old life?' I asked.

Cabal stretched and yawned. 'When things remind me of it. Yes.'

'But what is there to remind you here? Not the buildings. Not the people. Not the food.'

'Little things,' he said. 'Like the light of this fire tonight. It brings to mind that time we stopped at the Oasis of Wadi Hamra, when we were escorting the Emperor home from Baghdad.'

I recalled it immediately. There were twenty of us Varangian, along with the Emperor, and we had been riding camels for eight days through the desert before reaching Wadi Hamra. This oasis was the only source of water for several days journey in any direction. A small village of stone huts had sprung up around the dirty green water and sloping palm trees.

From this speck of safety, Cabal had wandered out into the desert heat, still wearing the weight of his chain mail. Half buried in a dune, he found the skeletons of a man and a camel. Over the next two days, while the rest of us hid in the shade of our tents, gasping the oven-hot air, Cabal built a scaffold from the dried-out branches of old trees that jutted from the sand. From this scaffold, he hung the bones with hemp twine. The man and the animal were all mixed up. When the wind blew, hissing over the red ground, these bones clinked together with almost musical sounds. It was terrible and beautiful at the same time.

Seeing this, the Emperor would not go near Cabal again, convinced he was some kind of devil. He had similar suspicions about the Bedou tribesmen who passed through this oasis. They usually appeared out of the dunes at sunset, their faces and long robes powdered orange-red with dust. They hitched their camels to palm trees and made their way in among the houses, looking for a meal. We Varangian learned to eat where they ate, sitting on woven palm mats. We scooped food into our mouths with our right hands, hugging the bowls to our chests with our left hands, which was their way as well. We would sit against one wall and they against the opposite wall, staring at each other across a fire which burned in the centre of the room.

That same firelight, as it rippled on the walls of that stone hut, seemed to be dancing now across the heavy timbers of the alehouse wall.

'Have you been happy here?' I asked, speaking of it as a thing in the past, as I assumed it to be.

'From the sound of your voice, you seem to think I am leaving.'

I picked up one of the chess pieces, a glowering pawn with his teeth sunk into the top of his shield like a warrior gone mad. I spun it around on the table, rather than answer Cabal.

'Did you know,' he began, 'that your sister has found in the fields around this town over forty plants which can be used to cure any number of illnesses?' He began counting them off on his fingers. 'There is fennel for stomach and lungs. Juniper for sinuses and bladder. Licorice for colds and nausea. Hawthorn for sore throats and skin sores and lobelia for coughs and fevers . . .'

'She has taught you well,' I interrupted.

Slowly, his face creased into a smile. 'I taught myself, and long before I met your sister.'

'Taught yourself?'

Cabal seemed to hesitate, but then he reached down under the table and brought up the leather sack which he always kept slung across his back. He slid back the ring of bone which held its drawstring in place and emptied out onto the table dozens of small linen bags, each one marked along its edge with the strange Celtic writing called Ogham. 'Seeds,' he said, 'from every place I have ever been. I have gathered them over the years. Why do you think I never get ill? I know how to cure myself before I even become sick.'

I recalled the sight of Cabal chewing on leaves and flowers down in Miklagard. I had thought of that as one of his many strange habits, with no purpose to it other than his liking the taste. 'You know about plants?' I asked. 'Why did you never tell me?'

Cabal folded his arms across his chest and sighed. 'What would you and the other Varangian have said if you had found out I was walking around with bags of seeds?'

'I do not know,' I replied, 'but I do know what they said about your heads in cedar oil.'

He crumpled his lips, as if unwilling to recall. 'Those days are behind me now.'

'So that is what you and Kari have been whispering about.'

He touched his hand against his chest and slowly lowered it, opening his palm as he searched for the right words to say. 'Until now, your sister has only gathered her plants where they grew in the wild. Since the best time for collecting them is at night, when the flowers are closed, she has to go out into the fields by herself.'

'I think her time up in the fields has not been quite so lonely these past few nights.'

Cabal swallowed. 'I have suggested to her that these plants could be grown in gardens. I had always planned to have such a garden myself, in the place where I hung up my shield for good.' He spread his hand across the bags of seeds. 'Not all of these will grow here, but enough of them will.'

'For good?' I asked.

Cabal began to gather the bags, returning them to his pack. 'For Kari and me, the suddenness of things has caught us by surprise.'

I laughed. 'You are not the only ones who are surprised.'

He had been looking down, but now he glanced up and met my gaze. 'At first, seeing how quiet it was here, I had thought about moving on. But now I am thinking of staying.'

'Does Kari know this?'

He nodded. 'Nothing is certain, of course, but we seem to understand each other.'

It was quiet for a while. Burning wood crackled in the fireplace.

'It is more than Kari. More than you too, old friend. This place has spoken to me somehow. You do not always get to

131

choose what is sacred in your life. All you have to do is know it when you see it.' He slid the bone ring shut to close his pack. 'So here I will stay, if you do not object.'

I sat back and smiled. The past and present, which had scraped against each other in my head since the moment I set foot back in this town, were finally fitting together.

The alehouse door opened and Olaf walked in with a Finnish trader named Boe who had dropped anchor in the bay that afternoon. Olaf was softening him up for some business deal he had in mind.

Cabal nudged me. 'The master at work.'

We sat back in the shadows and listened.

Boe was a short man who wore a vest made from silver-fox pelts sewn together in horizontal lines. His conical hat was also made from fox fur and had a fox's head, squashed flat and eyes sewn shut, worn like an emblem on the front of the cap. When he took off this cap, he revealed a head of hair as fluffy as the fuzz on a dandelion seed. Boe was complaining that he had been up north looking for the Lapps but had not found them.

'I always find them,' bragged Olaf. 'They recognise my ship and light fires when they see me off the coast.'

'I always wondered how someone like you came by a ship like that,' said Boe.

Olaf launched into a long-winded explanation about how he had won the Drakkar gambling up in Nidarnes.

I did not believe that story. It seemed to me that Olaf valued what he owned too much to risk it on any game of chance.

'It will be coming up for sale soon,' said Olaf. 'You might be interested in a purchase.'

'So that is why you brought me here. Is there something wrong with the ship? Is that why you are selling it?'

'No, but I will not be travelling as much after I have taken over as priest at the temple here.'

I saw Cabal blink at me from the shadows.

I shrugged and shook my head.

Boe's look of sly suspicion was now replaced by one of curiosity. 'I did not know you had the makings of a priest.'

'Being made a priest,' said Olaf, leaning forward across the table, 'is like being given the key to a lock. You either have the key, or you do not. And when I have that key, as I soon will, this town will finally show me the respect I deserve.'

Ingolf was mopping the tables with a cloth rag, then wringing a stream of grey water into a bucket. He looked across at me and smiled.

But Olaf still hadn't noticed me and Cabal in the corner. 'My foster-father was a priest.' he continued. 'He was going to make me his apprentice, but things went wrong at the last moment . . .'

'What things?' asked Boe.

'Just things!' barked Olaf. 'Do you have to keep interrupting?'

Boe sighed and shook his head. 'I have to catch the tide,' he said, resting his knuckles on the table and raising himself to his feet.

'You had a good audience tonight,' said Ingolf, after Boe had disappeared into the night.

'It is not my fault he was the only one here,' muttered Olaf, 'and did you stop to wonder if that might have something to do with your latest batch of ale?'

'Ah, but he was not the only one here.' Ingolf nodded towards where I sat in the shadows, my face lit only by the pale embers of the fire.

Olaf peered into the dark. Then, seeing Cabal and me, he let his breath escape in a slow embarrassed hiss.

133

Ingolf laughed. 'What do you have to say now?'

Olaf scratched some sweat off his forehead with his thumb-nail. 'It was just talk.' Then he coughed up a laugh. 'Was that not obvious? I had to give him a reason for selling my boat. He needs to think he is taking advantage of me or he will never part with his money.' His eyes shone in the dark, like two coins resting in the sockets of his skull.

Cabal and I walked back up the hill in silence. Only when we were lying in our beds, Cabal by the fire as usual and me on my bench, half buried under sheepskins, did either of us speak.

'It was not just talk,' said Cabal, 'and that is not the only thing which was obvious.'

'I know,' I said.

'Was Olaf right when he said that being made a priest is like being given a key that opens a door and reveals everything?'

I had never tried to explain what he was asking. Now I answered slowly and carefully. 'Simply being declared a priest will bring him nothing. Nor will the black stone hammer, nor even the rock beneath the temple, grant him the knowledge he is seeking. It is not like a key. It is like trying to learn a language in which the words for things keep changing. You pass through veil after veil of complexity, until at last you realise that it is not a language of words. Only then do things become clear.'

Cabal sighed. 'Then he will never find what he is looking for. All that he has found is a way to blame you for his not becom-ing a priest, and he will find a way to blame you for his failure if he ever does become one. You had better change his thinking, before you have to scrape that white paint off your shield.'

The next morning, I told Cabal I was going to see Kari. I want-ed to talk to her about Olaf.

Cabal remained in bed, saying he would stop by later.

When Kari came to the door, she held a bowl of pea-pods

tucked in the crook of her arm. She split each pod by drawing her thumb down the centre, which sent the pale green balls bouncing softly into the wooden bowl.

'Is Cabal not with you?' she asked.

'He is coming soon,' I replied. 'He has not been sleeping well.' Then I raised my eyebrows and she swatted me.

Inside, I navigated past the hanging bundles of plants and sat down at the table. Kari poured some milk into an iron pot. Still with her back to me, she asked, 'Has Cabal spoken to you?'

'He has.'

'There is no telling how things will go,' she said. 'The longer you live alone, the harder it is to imagine not being alone. You learn to live without the uncertainty that comes from two people trying to make a life together.'

'Kari,' I said. 'I know.'

She turned, smiling with relief. 'Yes, you do.' She brought the milk to the table. From a basket woven of straw, she took a piece of honeycomb and placed it in the milk. The honeycomb bobbed in the steaming milk, sweetening the steam that rose from its ivory surface. 'It is strange,' she said. 'For the first time, I know how Olaf felt when we all walked across the fields together. How much he wanted to be sure. It is the same for me now. I wish I could be sure but, of course, it is beyond my grasp to know.'

'Olaf is still grasping,' I said, and told her about what I had heard in the alehouse the night before. 'He is going be disappointed if he thinks that is how things will go.'

Kari sighed. 'He has been repeating the same story for so long that he has made a mockery of himself in this town. You saw it with those women on the beach and how they treated him. His success as a merchant has brought him wealth but not respect. No one takes him seriously any more.'

'But he takes himself seriously.'

She slid the bowl across to me. 'That he does.'

We passed the warm bowl back and forth, sipping at the sweetened milk. 'Olaf,' she began with a sigh, 'has always felt that Tostig betrayed him. Seeing you again, he has allowed false hopes to grow inside that he might set things straight once and for all. It will take time for him to set those hopes aside.' She set the bowl gently before me and wiped a drip of milk from her chin. 'Do not forget that he was once your closest friend and what drove you apart was not the fault of either one of you. You will be friends again, if you can only remember what brought you together in the first place.'

When I returned to the house, I found Cabal sitting in a chair, holding a knife, surrounded by clumps of his own hair. What remained on his head was a strange and rumpled mass, which no amount of combing would undo. He had also trimmed his beard, with little more success.

'How does it look?' he asked, hopefully. Then, when I did not reply at once, he said, 'Oh, no.'

It was only then that I noticed he was wearing a new set of clothes. He had on a shirt of undyed linen, a vest of densely-woven dark-blue cloth with black horn buttons, and a pair of brown wool trousers, which were tight around his bulging calves.

'You could almost pass for a Norseman,' I said.

He gestured at his old garments, which lay in a heap in the corner. 'It was time for a change,' he said. Cabal's old gear had once been very fine, made for him in Miklagard by a Magyar named Berezanos. The old man had a long white beard, which he forked and tied behind his neck when he was taking measurements. Rolls of silk hung like veils inside his shop, filling the room with soft greens and reds and blues.

Like the clothing of all Varangians, Cabal's had been a mix of the old Norse style and the more colourful, baggier clothing of the Byzantines and Rus. At Cabal's request, Berezanos had fitted his tunic with extra pockets and quilted padding across the shoulders to take the rub of the sword slung on his back. But it was all in ruins now, stitching gone and padding bursting from its seams, which had made him look like a torn pillow.

'You could do with some new clothes yourself,' he said.

I glanced at the wreckage of my shoes. One of my toes was sticking out. The leather of my sweat-burnished vest had suffered in the salty breeze and the bone buttons were dried and cracked. 'Never mind the way I look,' I told him. 'Give me that knife.'

I took the blade from Cabal's hand and, carefully, I cut his hair to an even length. Although I had no more experience than he did, at least I could see what I was doing. My thoughts returned to a time when Kari had cut my own hair, right where Cabal and I were now. I remembered how carefully she worked, and the way I had closed my eyes when she brought her face so close to mine, eyes hard with concentration, that I could not focus on her. There was a moment when she picked up a piece of my hair and set it in my hand, and for a long time I studied the coppery threads. Afterwards, we had gathered the cut hair and burned it, as if sprinkling dried strands of fire on the flames.

'Next time,' I said, 'let Kari do this for you.'

He grunted in agreement.

When I had done all I could do, I set down the knife. 'It is ready,' I said.

Slowly, Cabal rose to his feet.

'Now go,' I told him, 'and make a good impression on my sister.'

'I plan to,' said Cabal and, squaring his shoulders, he strode out of the house.

Two days later, Olaf and I set sail on the mid-summer trading run.

Cabal stayed behind. He did not need to offer an excuse. It was no secret that Cabal and Olaf did not get along. Cabal preferred to spend his days with Kari now, although he continued to live with me in my parents' house. Word had already begun to spread that he was settling here. People were flattered that he had fallen in love with the place and with the woman who they thought would never fall in love herself. Like the Varangian, they believed he was lucky, possessing powers beyond those of ordinary people. His knowledge of plants, the news of which had also spread, seemed only to confirm that he and Kari were well-matched.

The mid-summer run was Olaf's biggest journey of the year, and every business in town depended on its success. The ship had been provisioned with water and food, then loaded with Altvik's carded wool, dried fish and sheepskins.

As we headed out towards the mouth of the bay, I manned the steerboard while Olaf trimmed the sail. The ocean beyond glittered like a field of broken glass.

Looking back, I saw Guthrun up on the roof of his house. He would take care of the temple while I was gone. When

Guthrun waved goodbye, I drew my rune-carved sword and held it above my head. Its bright blade flashed in the sun.

The pink flecks of raised hands, like cat tongues, dotted the beach as people waved goodbye.

It was then that I saw Kari and Cabal, standing on the wall behind her house, watching us leave the bay. Kari's long hair streamed in the wind.

'They wasted no time,' said Olaf.

'They have none to waste,' I replied. 'We are not children any more.'

Soon the rooftops of the town had vanished beneath the waves. All we could see was the buttercupped green of the grazing fields, dotted with white puffs of sheep. Above, snow on the Grimsvoss gleamed so purely in the sun that it was painful to my sight, branding the outline of the peaks onto the blindness of my closing eyes.

Olaf and I headed north as far as the Lofoten Islands, where there was a trader named Grim with whom Olaf liked to deal. Grim's family had been there for many years, each generation handing down that strange name to another boy. There had been eight or nine Grims in all, and Olaf had known three of them. According to Olaf, the one who lived there now was the last of the line. 'When you see him, you will know why,' he told me.

The island where Grim lived looked like the blade of a broken knife, rising sheer and jagged from the waves. At a distance, it seemed uninhabited, but Olaf steered us through a narrow fjord, which opened out onto a gently sloping field. There, a farmhouse nestled in the shadow of the cliffs. Neatly-made stone walls spread out around it, the lush grass dotted with sheep.

We sailed in to a small harbour. By the time we had dropped anchor, rowed ashore and dragged our boat clear of the tide-line, we were covered in sweat.

Then a small man appeared from a tangled grove of trees where the grass gave way to sand and rock. He set out across the beach towards us. Behind him galloped two huge hounds, the likes of which I had never seen before. Their pale brown fur was short and tightly curled, with legs that seemed borrowed from ponies.

'Whenever a ship comes in,' Olaf muttered from the corner of his mouth, 'Grim hides in those bushes until he knows it is safe to come out. He is a wealthy man, fabulously rich, but he trusts no one and prefers the company of dogs to men.'

As Grim approached, he seemed to be growing smaller. It was only when he stood in front of me that I realised how tiny he was. I wondered if this could even be the right person, since he did not appear to be a wealthy man. But, from the look on Olaf's face, painfully eager to please, I knew this must be him. Grim wore a cape made from old sail cloth, which was tied with a piece of string around his shoulders. The rest of his clothing, including his shoes, consisted of poorly-tanned seal fur. A combination of smoke, dirt and the wind-dug wrinkles on his face made his skin look like the bark of an old apple tree. Several teeth were missing. Those that remained were long in his drawn-back gums. He wore his hair short, with two small braids that stuck out to the sides, so that he resembled a goat with its horns upside down. He had not cut his hair but instead had burned it to the length he desired. The ends were brittle and crumbly.

With great solemnity Olaf introduced me to Grim.

He jerked his head forward in a little bow.

I was so much taller than this man that I felt I ought to get down on one knee and speak to him as if he were a child.

The hounds sniffed at us and growled.

'They'll eat you if I tell them to,' he told me.

He led us up to his house. The place was set into a hummock

in the earth, built to stand the winds and winter storms. The door was made of driftwood held between two iron cross bars set on rusted hinges. To keep out the wind, hides plated the other side of the door.

Inside, the stone-paved floor was dry and warm, thanks to a peat fire he had burning. The whole place smelled of soot and sweat and mutton.

We sat down at a table made of one large piece of slate with gnarled driftwood for legs, while Grim heated up some lamb stew in an iron pot. The lamb bones rattled around the bottom as he stirred it. He picked one out and sucked at the marrow until it was hollow, then tossed it to the hounds, who cracked the bones to splinters in their jaws.

Grim set one bowl of stew in front of us and brought out three wooden spoons from a box made of birch bark. We each took turns ladelling up the hot and greasy liquid, washing it down with a bucket of peat-tinted water brought in from a stream behind his house.

Grim told me his people had come from the mainland. 'I forget how many years ago,' he said. 'We used to keep count, but then we stopped.' He glanced up at one of the cross beams of the roof, where neat rows of lines had been cut into the wood.

Grim's wife had been gone for many years. That was the way he said it. Gone.

As if suddenly shy to have made this confession, he looked down and wiggled his toes in his worn-out sealskin boots. This movement made the boots look like two small furry animals trying to crawl up his filthy trouser legs.

I did not know if this meant his wife was dead or if she had left him. Grim kept what he called a picture of her propped up in the corner. It was no more than the outline of a face, scratched onto a piece of slate. But to Grim it was the mirror image of his wife, and he gazed at it with softening eyes.

There was no talk of business that night, which seemed to be the way of doing things with Grim.

Olaf and I slept on his table, while Grim curled up with his dogs beside the fire. The next morning, Grim led us out to his storage sheds, which were crammed with walrus tusks, cord made from seal leather and feathers from arctic birds, all of which Grim had bought from the Lapps. From Olaf's ship, we brought in wool and sheepkins, and I sat with the hounds while Olaf and Grim bargained back and forth for the remainder of the day.

By the time we were finished, it was evening. Olaf said we should be going and Grim did not invite us to stay.

He walked us down to the beach. The tide was going out and he stopped to look in rockpools, stooping over now and then to pick out a mussel, which he cracked on the rocks and ate raw.

As we rowed out to the Drakkar, Grim raised his hand once, showing the pale web of his palm. Then he turned and headed back to his house, moving with the same stride as the hounds which followed him.

We sailed towards the mainland, hoping to find the Lapps, so we might trade with them ourselves. As Grim's island faded into the mist Olaf spoke with great admiration for the old man. He seemed to find nobility in the wretched state in which Grim was prepared to live, despite the wealth he possessed.

Olaf profited greatly from his visits with Grim, but whenever he could he liked to trade directly with the Lapps. This was not easy, he said. The Lapps were hard to find. They came to the coast only in the summer months. In the winter, they travelled inland, following the reindeer far from any trading route.

Olaf had arranged to meet the Lapps each year on a certain beach north-west of the Lofotens. In the years before they came to this arrangement, he had only managed to find the Lapps by accident, sailing up and down the coast, searching for signs of their camps.

The Lapps spotted us first and made signal fires piled with lichen, which gave off plumes of thick, white smoke.

These Lapps were the most mysterious people I had ever come across. They were stocky, with wide faces, dark hair and deep, untrusting eyes. They smelled of smoke and sweat and their lives revolved around the movements of the reindeer, which they followed back and forth across the tundra. The Lapps worshipped the reindeer, ate their meat, lived in reindeer-skin tents and made clothes of their leather and fur.

They were a very superstitious people with their own gods, about whom they spoke very little. To chase away the demons whom they believed were always among them, they used rings of different materials and sizes, squinting through them with one eye in whatever direction they thought the demons would appear. The rings were on the scabbards of their belts, around poles that held up their skin tents, and looped through the headboards of wooden-slat cribs in which they bundled their infants.

The Lapps believed strongly in the power of their priests. Their shaman was an old man who wore a cap made from the top of a reindeer's skull, complete with horns, and tied under his chin with a leather cord.

They liked to hear Olaf tell stories, although I doubted if they understood more than one word in five. They sat in a circle about him, passing round a knot of smoked reindeer meat, from which each man would cut a red sliver and slide it from the blade onto his tongue. Now and then, they hawked blood-tinted spit into the fire.

Olaf told the story of how he came by his boat in a betting match. Olaf's success at gambling impressed the Lapps greatly. They believed in luck as a skill more than a matter of chance.

Around the Lapp camp were many reindeer, which ate the crusty black blooms of rock-tripe lichen off stones that lay in the woods just back from the beach. The reindeer drifted like shadows in amongst the trees, hooves clicking together as they moved. The pelts of slaughtered animals were stretched on nearby racks to dry. Huge cuts of meat dangled over the smouldering fires, tended by women who otherwise stayed inside their tents.

Olaf had brought the Lapps crude knife blades, combs made of bone, cheap silver pendants and small wood-working tools for which they traded antlers and whalebone. After the dealing and a meal of yellow-orange cloudberries, smoked salmon and reindeer meat, the Lapps shared with us some of the secrets of how they survived in their part of the world.

In the course of one long night, they taught us many skills, allowing us to watch as they prepared three sleds for a journey across a glacier. Over a fire, they boiled a cauldron of blood gathered from the hanging carcasses of slaughtered reindeer. Then they flipped the sleds over and painted this blood on the undersides, using brushes made from bundled twigs.

At the same time, they chipped out lumps of ice with an axe from the foot of the glacier, trimming it into sections as long as a hand and twice as thick. They laid the ice slats one by one along the bottom of the sled, pressing them down hard with the heels of their palms, until the blood stuck this ice to their sleds. With a knife blade heated in the fire, they shaped the slats to fit the curved belly of the hull.

The Lapps said this had to be done once a day for as long as they stayed out on the snow fields, but there was no better way to make a sled run smoothly over ice and snow. They showed us the eye-coverings worn to shield against the blinding glare of sun off the snow. The coverings were made from two strips of antler bone with slits carved into them and joined in the middle with leather lacing. A second lace fastened the bones around our heads. Olaf and I tried them on, peering at each other through the slits while the Lapps made fun of our bewilderment.

This knowledge was their treasure and made our gifts of beads and honeycomb seem worthless. They accepted what we offered with a dignified indifference that made our blood run cold.

Having agreed to meet at the same place again next year, we left on the evening tide, heading south with our cargo. We would go all the way down past Altvik to Hedeby, where these Lapp goods would fetch much more than our original cargo of wool and sheepskins.

As we moved out to sea, a dusty-orange moon rose from the tundra.

It was cold out on the water. I buttoned my old vest, feeling the last of my coins from Miklagard pressing against my ribs. Then I huddled on a stool, knees drawn up to my chest. The stool was actually a block of a whale's spine, two fins of bone stretching out on either side. I had traded it off the Lapp shaman for one red bead, which he tied onto a leather cord and wore in the hollow of his throat. He said it would protect him from bears.

All around us was the hiss of water as our bow pushed through the waves, trailing blue-green sparkles in its wake.

Olaf sat on a block of driftwood, his eyes narrowed against the wind. 'My business is a success,' he said, as much to himself as to me.

'It certainly is,' I replied.

'Perhaps,' he said, and then paused. 'Perhaps you would like to be my partner. Make a living for yourself. You cannot do well earning the odd handful of coins from me, and how long will it be before the money you have saved runs out?'

'I have nothing to bring to a partnership, Olaf.' I raked my nails down my face and studied the black lines of campfire soot under my nails. 'How can I be your partner if all I have to offer is my sweat?'

He leaned forward and grasped at the air in front of him. 'You have more than you know. You have the temple, after all.'

'Olaf,' I said, as calmly as I could, 'what you want I cannot give you. What is done is done, and what more can be said about it?'

'What can be said?' he stamped his foot on the deck. 'That the world has played a trick on us! Our fortunes were reversed. I know what people think of me in town. If I could be the one to wear that black stone hammer which hangs around your neck, I would prove them all wrong. It should have been me . . .' and then he choked, as both of us recalled those words, hissed through the shutters of my house, the night before the raiders wrecked our town. 'I was always the one who stayed behind, after you and Kari had gone home, and long after Ingolf had left. I was the one who never gave up.'

'I don't deny that, but it is over! Decisions were reached long ago, and they were not ours to make.'

For a long time, he only stared at me, half hidden by the misty air.

'Olaf,' I said, 'we were friends once and I hope we may be friends again.'

'I hope it, too,' he said.

But we both knew that until this matter was resolved, it would always come between us.

Silence settled on the boat. Sea spray clung to our clothes like tiny beads of glass.

I pulled my cloak around me, smelling the smoke of a hundred campfires steeped into the wool. 'That story you told to

Boe and the Lapps,' I said. 'The one about your winning this boat in a gambling match.'

'What of it?'

'Is it true?'

He stared at me down the length of his nose. 'You risk offending me,' he said.

'You risk taking me for a fool,' I replied.

Slowly a smile worked its way across his stubbled face. 'In that case, you had better know the truth. You have seen this boat before, you know.'

'Seen it before?' I stared at his silhouette in the dark. 'When?'

'When the raiders came to Altvik.' He bounced his heel off the deck. 'This was one of their ships!'

I remembered how we had lost the other Drakkar in the fog. I recalled the anxious faces of the raiders while they waited in the mist and the way they looked at Tostig and me, as if we had somehow brought it down upon them. 'But how did you come by it? And what happened to the crew?'

'When the raiders left, Guthrun sent me running along the coast after them. He said they were probably tired and might not go far before stopping to rest. If they were close enough, we might be able to hit back at them and rescue you and Tostig.

'The fog forced them in close to shore. Sometimes I could see them. Other times I could only hear their voices carried on the water. After a while, the two ships split up. One of them stayed near land. The other disappeared.

'I had been tracking that one ship for several hours already. I was thinking that maybe I ought to turn around. Then I came around a headland to a small inlet and saw the carcass of a whale that had washed ashore. And there were bears all around it. They had eaten a hole in the side of the whale and were walking into the hole and coming out of the whale's mouth. Their skin was matted with blood. There were baby

147

bears clambering up the side of the whale and then sliding down, raking their claws through the blubber and leaving deep white cuts. The whale could not have been dead long. It must have swum into the inlet and been grounded when the tide went out.

'The raiders saw that dead whale too, and they must have wanted some for themselves. They set fire to a few arrows and shot at the bears to scare them away. I hid behind some rocks and watched as the raiders rowed their skiff ashore and began hacking out chunks of the whale's meat. They were laughing and throwing chunks of blubber at each other and splashing around in the gore. Then they gathered up driftwood for a fire to cook the meat right there. I counted eight men in all.

'That was when the bears came back out of the forest. The men yelled and threw rocks. It looked as if that might work, but then some of the baby bears came out onto the beach and the men chased them around.

'Suddenly one huge bear raced out of the woods. It reared up on its hind legs and knocked a man dead with a swipe of its paw. Then more bears appeared, ten or twelve of them I counted. If there had not been so much to eat, you would never have seen so many bears gathered in one place. The bears chased men into the belly of the whale and killed them or drove them out into the water and mauled them in the shallows. One man reached the boat and was fending off a bear with an oar when a second bear climbed into the boat from the other side, knocked him down and tore him to pieces. It was a slaughter. Not a single man survived.

'I waited until night, when the bears went back into the forest. It was summer then, you remember, and still light. I walked among the dead. I took whatever valuables I could find, their purses full of silver which they had stolen from our village, arm bands, armour, helmets and shields. I carried it all back into the woods and dumped it in a pile. Then I dragged the dead men back into the forest. As much as I could anyway. I used ropes from the ship to tie it up on the beach and make sure it wouldn't drift away. Then I headed back towards the village, because I thought the bears might come for me if I spent the night out on my own.

'I was running as fast as I could. The fog was still around me. I could feel it right down to my bones. I was getting ready to tell everyone about the whale and the bears and the men and their boat. But after a while, I had a different idea. That boat could be mine. Why did it have to belong to anyone else? There would never be another chance for me. That beautiful ship would be squabbled over and before long it would become some used-up hulk on the beach. I knew that was how it would go. So I decided that boat would belong to me, and I would run it as a trading ship.'

'But you were only twelve years old!' I said.

'I knew I would have to be patient. The hard part was hiding the boat and keeping it safe until I was old enough that it wouldn't just get taken away from me. So when I got back to Altvik, I told Guthrun the raiders had sailed out to sea. Tostig was gone, and in those first few days, nobody knew what to do with me. They were too busy trying to put things back together after the raid. I took advantage of the confusion and brought three of Tostig's horses to the boat. I cut down some trees to make rollers, then had the horses drag the boat up off the beach and into the woods. Over the next few weeks, I sneaked back to the boat and built a shed around it with stones, a bank of earth and timber. I even built a roof. I rolled the sail up, stashed the oars and ropes. There was a wooden chest on board, a huge thing in which, to judge from the smell of it, they had kept dried fish and meat. It was covered with leather which had

149

been draped wet across the wooden frame and then dried and hammered down with brass nails. I loaded it with as many of the swords and shields and as much of the silver as it would hold. Near the boat, I found a hollow made from the roots of a fallen tree. I shoved the trunk as far back in the hollow as it would go. Then I walled it in with stones and threw earth on the stones to hide it. Once in a while, I checked on things to make sure they were safe.'

While Olaf spoke, my thoughts drifted back to that morning in Hedeby, when the raiders watched the harbour entrance for each boat that came through, certain every time it was the one, then sighed and swore under their breath when they knew it was not. By then, their friends lay in a reeking pile of bones, skin sagging from their skulls and flesh sliding off their hands like too-loose gloves.

'And so you left the boat there,' I said.

Olaf nodded. 'Until I was twenty. Yes. By that time, I was running a fishing smack around the bay, catching herring mostly, sometimes mackerel. I told people I was fed up with fishing, which was the truth, and that I wanted to start a trading route with Grim in the Lofoten islands. They told me I was crazy for trying it in such a small boat.

'When I left, they were betting at the alehouse as to whether I would come back at all. I sailed out of the bay and even tacked to the north a way before I doubled back to the south and reached the raider's boat. I dropped anchor in the little inlet and stayed there for three days. Even after all that time, you could still find the odd piece of whalebone washed up by a storm above the high tide line. I spent those days taking apart the shed I had built around the boat. Using logs from the shed and some pulley ropes, I rolled it down to the water's edge, unfolded the sail and strung it up. When the tide came in, the ship floated free. I spent three days bailing it out while the boards swelled shut, then I sailed north, towing my old fishing smack behind me.

'I do not know how many actually believed my story of what had happened. But what else were they to think? And what did I care anyway? I used the silver I had found on the boat to buy goods in Trondheim for my first trading run. Since then, I have been in business for myself.' He gestured at my feet. 'You can still see the marks where the bear killed that man on the deck. It is right where you are sitting.'

I lifted my heel and saw the old gouges of the bear's claws. I had noticed them before, but assumed it was just some heavy cargo that had scraped the wood. When I set my heel down again, I moved it to a different place.

Just after dawn, we spotted another ship heading down from the north. The comfort of seeing another boat, out here so far from land, was soon replaced by a tremor of worry as to who these people might be.

It was a large vessel, whose rough sides showed no signs of the neatly clinkered planking of a Norseman's ship. It glimmered dull grey and white and its crew took no notice of us, even though we seemed to be following the same course.

Neither Olaf nor I had seen anything like it before.

That evening, just as suddenly as it had appeared, the ship turned away to the west and vanished.

This encounter troubled us deeply. Even though we did not say the name, both of us had been thinking the same thing. It was the Nagelfar, the ship of the dead, whose sides were hulled with the nail clippings taken from corpses. It was for this reason that the finger and toenails of the deceased were trimmed before their bodies were burned, so that the Nagelfar would not grow bigger, not grow stronger. So that it would stay away.

151

Back on land, with the reassurance of the earth beneath our feet, we might have been able to persuade ourselves that we had only imagined it. But out here, the world made a different kind of sense. It reminded us that we were not welcome, not built for this place, kept alive only by chance.

We did not linger there, but filled our sail with wind, gathering speed across the sunset sea of blood.

Two days later, we dropped anchor at the settlement of Ytre Moa which lay at the far end of the Sognefjord.

Ytre Moa was a strange and melancholy village, set on a barren, windswept spit of land. Sheep wandered among the houses, which nested in a grove of stunted birch trees. These houses had been built with the old Norse technique of upending boats and gradually raising it by building walls underneath. The old, salt-cured boat planks were buckled and painted with mould. Empty drying racks for fish cast spindly shadows on the ground.

I pitied the people of Ytre Moa, who tried to make a life out of this dreary place, especially during the long winters, with the wind trying to knife through the walls. A kind of madness seemed to hang over the foggy ground and Olaf said most of the families had at least one child not right in the head.

The sheep scattered as we walked ashore, dragging their dirt-stained wool behind them like the capes of beggars.

A feeling of loneliness swept through me, chilling my bones. Out in the bay, half-hidden by the drizzle, our ship rested on the calm and dimpled water. The fjord swelled with lazy waves, grey air meeting grey water and the grey of the land, as if the world was fading away and everything it contained was only a compression of this greyness. I shivered and drew my cloak around me.

Olaf did not like it here any more than I did. He wasted no

time, but began the trading at once, giving them poor-quality linen in exchange for beautifully carved sword handles made of antler bone. These were engraved with interlocking snakes and dragons, then rubbed with verdigris to make the carvings stand out against the brownish-white of the bone.

Although I gritted my teeth at the unfairness of Olaf's dealings, it seemed that the people of Ytre Moa valued our visits more than our goods. Few traders ever put in to Ytre Moa, and the sight of Olaf's ship appearing in the fjord was a sign that they had not been forgotten by the world.

I knew we might sail in here one day and find the settlement deserted, just as it was when the people who lived there now had arrived. What they found was an empty farmstead, beside which four graves had been dug. One of the graves had not been filled, and in this they discovered the bones of a man. He must have buried his whole family and known that he was dying, too. Or else some other nightmare overtook them, whose story would never be told nor could be guessed.

The Ytre Moa people lived in quiet fear of that same vanishing. They spoke of these nameless ones who had gone before as having failed somehow, leaving no monuments to themselves, no signs of great prosperity.

But I wondered if it really was a failure. Perhaps those people had not cared to make their mark. Maybe they were not like us, who felt the need to prove to the world that our lives had been well spent. I thought if they could return and see who had taken their places, they might pity us in our struggle to be remembered.

Olaf and I spent that night on the dirt floor of a disused house in the village. I heard no talk from the other houses, no laughter, no singing, not even the lowered voices of argument. When at last I fell asleep, I was plagued by dreams of murder and starvation which did not seem to have come from me, but

153

rather from the ghosts that drifted back and forth through the silent houses and the rustling birch trees.

When we left Ytre Moa the next morning, its people lined up the beach to see us off, strained smiles on their faces. Wind blew the heavy skirts of the women around their legs. As we raised our sail, they turned and trudged back to their houses. They disappeared in the mist rolling down from the mountains, as if we had just spent our time among a tribe of spirits.

The remainder of our trip took three days. A cold wind from the north sped us on, speckling our sail with frost. We wrapped ourselves in cloaks and held on while the Drakkar seemed to skim the surface of the water, carrying us south towards Hedeby.

Before long, we saw the smoke which always clogged the sky above that town. We joined a line of ships preparing to enter the port. The harbour was already so crowded that we had to wait beyond it, moving in one at a time, the place of each departing ship claimed by one coming in. It was a hard process of lowering the sail, dropping anchor, raising the anchor again, then moving ahead so as not to lose our place in line.

When we finally dropped anchor in the port, we scouted the broad field which stretched down to the beach, looking among the shelters there for one that might be empty. That was how it went at Hedeby. There were longhouses that had been built and added to over the years, but which belonged to no one. Traders coming in by ship were welcome to move into a longhouse, fix it up if they wanted, and use it as a place of business. Rarely did anyone stay long enough to make any improvements, so most of these shelters were in poor repair.

Craftspeople in the town would come down to the field to buy antler-bone for making jewellery or knife handles. They also came looking for amber, tiny insects marooned inside its honey-coloured stone, gathered on the wind-raked beaches of Jutland. Blacksmiths bought iron ore, particularly the kind called 'lake ore' which came mostly from Sweden, since the local variety was of poor quality. They took any silver as payment, even pieces of coins or bracelets which we called 'hacksilver'. The form of it didn't matter, only the weight and purity, which was judged by its colour.

Olaf and I left our cargo on the boat, having hired someone to watch it. As we rowed into the shallows, our bow skimmed through pale green weeds slithering in the currents. They reminded me of snakes charmed from baskets by men with flutes in the marketplace at Miklagard.

On the beach, I exchanged dull stares with the crippled men and women whose hands, noses or ears were missing because of some offence for which such cutting was the punishment. They had drifted into Hedeby like the wood of ships wrecked out at sea. Now they loaded boats in exchange for food.

'Look around,' said Olaf. 'They call this place the anvil of the north.' We made our way through the crowded, muddy streets, looking for an alehouse where Olaf thought he might find a Bulgar with whom he liked to trade. Looking around at the clusters of whispering people who crowded every doorway, it seemed to me that everyone at Hedeby was dealing in one thing or another.

In the town square, a Christian church was under construction. It towered above the smaller, dingy houses that surrounded it. The walls were made from heavy logs caulked with tar, and its steep-sloped roof was already in place. Dragon-headed rain gutters jutted from the corners and interlaced Nordic and Christian signs had been intricately carved around its door. From inside came the raspy panting of saws.

I felt a muddle of anger and helplessness at seeing the

155

church. The last time I had passed through here, the Norse pillars had already been taken down and replaced with a Christian cross. Now here was one more sign that the Christians were settling in for good.

Olaf found his alehouse. 'Coming in?' he asked.

I told him I was going to pray.

'Please yourself,' he said, 'but I have no idea where a Norseman prays in Hedeby these days.'

After asking around, I was told that two pillars remained standing, somewhere on the outskirts of the town.

Eventually, I found them on a patch of marshy ground. A walkway made from the branches of a fallen oak tree led to a hump of land, which rose above the level of the swamp. Exposed to the northern breeze, a skim of ice had formed across the murky water, despite the summer sun. In the middle of this little island stood the pillars, with faces carved at the top just like the ones at Altvik and like a hundred others I had seen in the world of the Norsemen. Iron spikes had been driven into the posts at different levels and on these hung offerings of birds, rabbits, flanks of deer. The pillars had not been kept clean. Wind gusted in from the ocean, cutting around my face and ruffling the fur of these dead animals. At least it blew away the smell of rotting meat. Red icicles hung from the offerings. Some of these had broken and lay scattered on the ground in patterns which seemed to spell out words in runes. I thought of the story of Odin, how he had hung himself from the tree of life, sacrificing himself to himself as the highest of the gods. He hung nine days from his noose, twisting in agony but unable to die. His thrashing loosened branches from the tree. They fell on the ground in shapes which formed the alphabet of runes. It was in exchange for his sacrifice that Odin learned the secrets of that language. This was how the icicles seemed to me now, spelling out some message I would never understand.

Standing there, in that backwater of my faith, I wondered what satisfaction the gods could draw from these ragged strips of feathers, blood and fur.

Using a sliver of oak from the branches of the walkway, I traced a double-headed axe in the ground, then tugged loose one of the iron spikes and laid it in the centre of the drawing. Lying down flat on the ground before it, face against the trampled soil, I spread my arms, closed my eyes and prayed to Thor for luck in selling our cargo and for a safe journey home. I could not hide from myself a feeling of hopelessness, as if this place had truly been abandoned, not only by the people who prayed there but also by the gods to whom we prayed.

But I was not completely alone. While I lay there, a few others came to worship, clumping and squelching along the half-sunken walkway.

One man hung an offering of a dead seagull on an iron spike and walked off without saying anything. I watched a woman walk in circles around the pillars, holding a soapstone bowl filled with boiled blood, sipping from the steaming drink as she muttered out her prayers. Another man ran up to the base of the pillars, a cloth pressed to his face to avoid the stench. He pressed two silver coins into the earth, then ran away again.

By the time I stood to leave, the sun had set, bannering the sky red and purple. Strange lights scratched across the evening sky.

A lanky, black-haired dog appeared from the marshes. It sniffed at me, then tore down the remains of a rabbit from one of the spikes and carried the dead thing back amongst the swaying bullrushes.

I set the loose spike back where I had found it and walked away.

When I reached the end of the walkway, my feet stained by the black swamp water that had welled up between the branches, I turned to stare at the pillars. The ball of the moon seemed to balance between their heads, fragile and precarious. The pillars looked so sad and shamed, half-forgotten on their muddy little island. A terrible emptiness surrounded this place.

I shuddered and turned away, then headed quickly to the alehouse. It was only a shack, roofed with an old sail. Strips of frayed cloth hung in the doorway. Through them, illuminated by the fire inside, I saw the misshapen shadows of people moving back and forth. There was laughter and the hum of conversation. Stepping inside, I breathed in the sour smell of old ale and unwashed bodies. A jumble of people sat at long wooden tables, playing games on boards carved into the table tops and using painted bone chips as markers. There were Arabs with silver-bangled arms and thick, embroidered robes who drank goat's milk instead of ale. I saw Slavs, horses and dragons tattooed on their faces, elbow to elbow with people from the north, long hair braided down their backs and blue eyes bright in weather-beaten faces. In one corner stood a blind boy, his eyes like two peeled eggs. With wooden spoons in each hand, he stirred a tub of ale on one side and a vat of mead on the other. There had been no mead in Miklagard, and by the time I reached the north again, I had no taste for its musty sweetness.

'There you are!' shouted Olaf. He waved to me from a table in the corner, where he sat drinking ale with a short man, whose belly flopped over obscenely tight breeches. Untidy grey hair seemed to float around his skull like smoke. He wore a tunic of brown sacking cloth, fastened by green glass buttons and patched with squares of purple silk.

I sat down and reached for one of the overturned ale bowls. They were attached to the table by nails and lengths of tarnished copper chain. I turned the bowl right-side up, which was the sign that I wanted to be served.

'This is the Bulgar,' said Olaf. 'He is heading down to Itil on the Volga, with a dozen slaves to sell. And we will not ask how you came by them.'

'No, you had better not ask, and I do have a name, by the way.'

'Yes,' said Olaf, 'but I keep forgetting what it is.'

'Oleg,' said the Bulgar. 'My name is Oleg.'

'You would do better to call yourself Bulgar,' said Olaf.

I could tell from the way they swapped insults that they knew each other well.

The alehouse owner saw my upturned bowl and came over, lugging a bucket and ladel. He was clearly the father of the blind boy. They looked almost the same, except for the father's eyes, which were a shining brown mockery of the boy's pasty white irises. 'What have you got?' he asked.

I lifted the leather money bag from around my neck, slid back the bone ring which kept it closed, and poured out some chips of hack-silver. I chose half an Arabic coin and pushed it towards him across the table .

'I can fill it three times for this,' he said. 'That should be enough to chase the spirits from your head.'

'How much to chase them back again?' I asked.

'I am not in that business,' said the man. He dropped the coin in his apron, then sank the ladel into the bucket and filled my bowl with ale.

I took a sip and winced. It was a hard brew, sharp and metallic in the corners of my mouth. It reminded me of slave days, to drink with the sound of a chain rattling close to my face.

Olaf and the Bulgar continued to trade insults.

'I fail to see what is so special about that Lapp stuff you bring to market.' The Bulgar sipped from his bowl, clutching its sides with short-fingered, powerful hands. The copper chain was wrapped around his wrist. 'I cannot understand why people buy it.'

159

'Every time you say that,' replied Olaf, 'and every time you buy it anyway.'

'There is a man down at the water's edge tells everyone he is a Lapp,' said the ale man, who had been listening. 'He can sell you good weather for the journey home.'

'What do you mean, "sell good weather"?' demanded the Bulgar. 'How can you sell good weather? That makes no sense.'

'Not to you, maybe,' said the ale man.

Olaf and the Bulgar agreed to do some business. The Bulgar needed to inspect what we had brought, so Olaf swept back the sailcloth door and we stepped out into the dark. Back in the alehouse, fat lamps sputtered as the night wind snaked its way inside.

The Bulgar had unloaded his slaves on the beach. Each one had a heavy iron ring around his neck. The iron was wrapped with old rawhide to stop it from gouging their skin. The slaves were joined one to the other with a length of chain the thickness of a finger but so short that they all had to walk in step. Most of them looked so shocked at what had become of them that they stood as if entranced, patiently waiting for sunlight to wake them from this terrible dream. The week before they might have been traders themselves. If only they had reached Hedeby, they might have been safe. There were laws governing conduct within the limits of the town, but what happened beyond it had no laws. Men killed in arguments were dumped in the bay and left to drift or sink. From the look of the Bulgar, those slaves were lucky to have made it even this far. I doubted whether half of them would reach Itil alive.

'I have no need of slaves,' said Olaf. 'What I need is silver.'

'Calm down,' drawled the Bulgar. 'These are not for you. I am just letting them stretch their legs before I set off down the river.'

As soon as I could row our cargo ashore, Olaf and the Bulgar got down to business. The Bulgar was paying in bars of silver, each bar the double Ore weight. He rummaged through the pelts and sacks of feathers, clucking and shaking his head. The sound you heard more than any other at Hedeby was the clicking of tongues to show disrespect for what another person had to sell. Despite the confusion of different languages, that one sound was common to them all.

I glanced at the slaves again and this time I was shocked to see a familiar face among them. It was Yarl, Godfred's servant. He had a broken nose and a black eye. He carried a small canvas bag slung over his front, whose flap he dabbed against the dried and crusted blood in his nostrils. Next to him stood Godfred, dazed and miserable, his hair all blown about. Neither one had noticed me yet.

Without thinking, I walked over to the Bulgar. 'How much for the old man and the scrawny one with the busted nose?'

Olaf glared at me. 'What? Have you gone mad?'

The Bulgar realised that if he was going to make a deal for those slaves, it had better be before Olaf found the words to talk me out of it. 'I might sell them. What are you offering?'

'Gold.'

'Gold?' asked Olaf. 'I am not handing over any gold!'

'You will not have to.' I pressed my hands against the sides of my vest, trying to remember how many coins I had left. 'Ten coins a piece,' I said.

Olaf stared at me. 'Where are you going to get twenty gold coins?'

'Not enough,' said the Bulgar.

'Look,' I told him, 'The old one will not last a month. You will have to unload him in the first port you come to and even then he will have eaten more than he is worth.'

'Not if I can help it,' said the Bulgar.

Godfred saw me now. His eyes grew big. He opened his mouth to speak.

At that moment, Yarl elbowed him in the ribs. He had already seen me and had guessed what I was doing. Yarl knew what it would do to any deal if the Bulgar saw we knew each other.

Godfred seemed to understand. He lowered his head and stared at the ground, lips moving as he mumbled out a prayer.

The Bulgar slapped his hands together. 'Even if the old man dies, which I grant you he probably will, the bony one is worth more than twenty coins by himself.'

My mind was racing. I drew out my sword.

The Bulgar stepped back in alarm.

I flipped the blade around and handed it to him hilt first.

The Bulgar laughed nervously as he took hold of the sword. 'What is this engraving?' he asked. 'I cannot read runes.'

'That is the name of the Saxon swordsmith, Ulfbehrt.'

The Bulgar was trying to show no expression, but by the twitching of his lips it was clear he knew the value of this blade. It was pattern-welded from many thin layers of iron pounded together by several men working in shifts, with fine steel welded on the cutting edge. The red-hot blade had then been quenched in a vat filled with honey and blood, to harden the metal. I had watched it being made for Halfdan, one sultry afternoon in Miklagard. I recalled the sweet smell of the honey and the blood rising in a cloud of vapour when the burning sword was plunged into the vat. This technique produced wavy lines which seemed to ripple like water on the surface of the metal. 'It might be worth something,' he said. 'Maybe this and the gold, providing the coins are not hacked.'

'Done,' I said quietly.

'Done!' echoed the Bulgar. He slapped one palm across another, which was a sign that the transaction was complete.

While I cut the last coins from my vest, the Bulgar slid the sword into his belt. The pale flesh of his belly pressed against the blade.

In silence, Olaf watched me unfastening the coins.

The Bulgar put the coins one by one into his mouth and rolled each one around, clicking it against his teeth. Then he spat the coin out into his palm, sliming the gold with spit, and announced, 'Pure.' When he had finished sucking his money, the Bulgar grinned at me. 'I cannot see what you want with those slaves. They are just a couple of mangey Christians. They are everywhere these days. Infesting the place!'

I walked down to the water's edge where Yarl and Godfred were being unchained.

Godfred walked towards me with his arms held out. 'God has sent you to rescue us!'

The Bulgar heard this and laughed. 'That is what you get for buying Christians! The fat one never shuts up.' He waved at his own servants, who hauled the remaining slaves to their feet and sent them shuffling down to the water where the Bulgar's ramshackle boat was waiting to take them away.

One of the Bulgar's servants carried a lump of wood tucked under his arm. The Bulgar took it from him and tossed it in the air. With the sunlight behind him, his ears glowed poppy red. The piece of wood turned lazily above his head.

I recognised it then as the strange statue Godfred and Yarl had found drifting out in the middle of the ocean. As the Bulgar threw it high again, I saw the statue's angry face, twisting in the air. This time, the Bulgar dropped the statue. He kicked it along for a few paces. Then picked it up, stuck it under his arm and headed down to the beach, where Olaf had gone to unload his cargo.

'How did you lose your ship?' I asked Yarl.

'We were on our way here with a cargo of soapstone. Raiders

caught up with us. Took everything. Food. Clothes. The lot. Then they set the boat on fire. After that, the raiders sold us to that wretched Bulgar.'

'I see he has the little statue.'

Yarl made a ratty smile. One of his teeth had been knocked out. 'Yes, he does. And he has been dropping it and kicking it around ever since he got his greedy hands on it.'

Godfred raised his head. His eyes were wild. 'I hope it rots his balls off!'

We both turned to stare at him.

Godfred put his hands over his face and moaned.

I turned back to Yarl. 'Do you have some place to go?'

'We will get by all right.'

I reached into the lining of my vest and tore out one more coin, realising as I did that it was my last one. I pressed it into his hand, still trailing the red thread which had bound it to the vest.

Yarl folded the coin into his hand. 'I thank you.' He jerked his chin at Godfred. 'He thanks you, too. Or he will thank you when he gets his wits back. Here,' Yarl took a frayed linen bag from around his shoulder. 'I think Godfred would want you to have this. I convinced the Bulgar it was just a toy.'

In the bag was a circular piece of wood about the size of my outstretched hand, with a hole in the middle. The bag also contained a wooden spike, which fitted into the hole in the plate. Around the edge of the circle, thirty-two small triangles were carved into the wood. Branching down from one of these triangles was a line of horizontal cuts, like the rungs of a ladder. Across the top of the hole was a straight line and below that, arcing around the hole, was another line which formed the inside of the crescent.

'What is it?' I asked.

'This,' he replied solemnly, 'is the bearing dial I told you about.'

It took Yarl only a few moments to teach me that these triangles were direction markers, that the ladder signified north and that the crescent line showed the path of the sun during the summer solstice, wheras the straight line indicated the sun's path during the equinox. Depending on what time of year I was travelling, I would either take my bearings off the straight line or the curved line. If I held the dial out in front of me, the shadow of the spike would touch on the point of north/south alignment. If I took a measurement before I left land, I could use the bearing dial to show whether I was north or south of that place.

I had heard stories that the Arabs had learned how to navigate with the use of specially-marked sticks, and that they had learned this technique from a people far to the East, but this was the first time I had seen such a thing for myself.

I thanked Yarl as he set off towards town, leading Godfred by the arm.

'Rots his balls off!' shouted Godfred, still lost in his raging.

When they were gone, I went back to find Olaf, who had finished his dealings with the Bulgar. 'Will you explain to me what you just did?' he asked. 'I should have thought you would be pleased to see a Christian locked in chains.'

I explained how I had met them and the kindness they had shown me.

Olaf shook his head sadly. 'That was a nice sword you just gave away.'

I nodded. For such a fine blade to have gone to a man like that Bulgar left me feeling sick to my stomach.

What the Bulgar had not bought from Olaf, we sold to people who made their way across the sand to us, hacksilver coins pinched between their thumbs and forefingers. Then, carrying their purchases, they filtered away into the night.

The weather-selling Lapp crawled from the hole where he

lived, offering to trade us a good breeze for a coin. In each hand, he carried a paddle, like a shortened oar, on the blades of which he had carved swirling rings. It was by waving these, he said, that he could change the direction of the wind. When I told him I had been up to his country, he confided in me that he was tired of selling weather and would soon be heading home, past the great forests and the mountains, until he was once more out on the wind-sheared tundra.

After picking up a few things for people in Altvik, we ran up our sails and headed out with the night tide. The boat slipped silently by crews sleeping on their decks, huddled together under the dingy blankets of their sails. As we left the port, I saw the Christian cross which had taken the place of the Norse pillars. Four bodies hung from the crossbeam, two at each end, dangling from short lengths of rope. Out in the marshes, dogs howled by the blood-soaked pillars of the Norsemen. The smell of rotting food and filth and the skeletons of men who talked too much, all jellied in the mud beneath our keel, soon gave way to the hollowing wind of the sea.

We rode towards the moon, as if we were caught in its spell, pulling tighter on the sail lines to gather more speed, until it seemed we must collide with it or sail straight through into another world. The walrus skull seemed to charge ahead, refusing to give up the chase. At the last minute, as if tired of the game, the moon rose above the water, leaving us alone out on the silver-crested waves.

Five days later, we dropped anchor in the bay at Altvik. It was evening when we rowed ashore, working the oars through the still water. The air was filled with soft, pink light, like the lining of a mussel shell.

We went straight to the alehouse to pay off the people who had given us goods to sell.

Olaf sat himself down at his usual table in the corner and began sifting through the pile of coins. People thought of this table as lucky because of all the gold and silver which had rattled over its old planks.

The news soon spread that we had returned, and it wasn't long before the alehouse bustled with laughter and warm bodies. It had been a successful trip. No one would go hungry this winter. As the night wore on, Ingolf rolled in more barrels from his storage shed outside. Old men sat on the benches outside, sucking their teeth and drinking watered-down ale from wooden mugs.

I could still feel the movement of the ocean in my head, like a mother rocking a child.

Cabal appeared. He was immediately surrounded by people who questioned him about a batch of wine he had begun, using blueberries, bearberries and whortleberries gathered in the fields. 'It is not ready yet,' he kept saying. 'I will tell you when it is done, I promise.' He looked above the heads of those who were pestering him and waved at Olaf and me.

'Cabal and my mother are going in business together,' Ingolf called across. 'Soon they will have no need of me!' He laughed when he said this, but there was a paleness in his face, as if that just might be the truth.

'If that Celt can brew wine,' said Olaf, 'he will do all right in this town.'

Olaf and I were sitting with the owner of a trading ship that had come in the day before. He was a rat-faced man called Anskar, nicknamed Anskar Berry-Face, since he once lost a bet and had to stick his head into a vat of purple dye. He and Olaf passed a mug of ale back and forth, their upper lips slicked with foam.

Anskar Berry-Face handed me the bowl and gave me a stern look. 'I heard talk of *you* further down the coast. The one who got struck by *lightning* and who runs the temple now.' He had a way of talking that rose up and down like the motion of a boat in heavy seas. 'What are you going to tell the Christians when they get here?'

At that moment, I could not imagine the Christians ever coming to Altvik. The dangers I had pictured down in Miklagard, of the old faith being overwhelmed, had not appeared. I felt safe. This was not Hedeby, Kaupang or Nidarnes, just a small place hardly worth their attention. 'I expect I will not have to tell them anything,' I said.

'Indeed you *will*,' he barked, 'because they will be here by tomorrow.'

'Tomorrow?' I was sure I had misunderstood him.

Anskar shrugged. 'They are sailing up the coast.'

'Are they traders who happen to be Christians,' I asked, 'or just Christians?'

168

'Traders they *are*,' said Anskar, 'but not trading in the goods that you and I would bring to *sell*. They want your *souls*, as soon as they can persuade you that you *have* them. *Those* are their goods. And they make enough noise about it and do enough of their Christian *magic*, that if they were selling what I am selling, they would put me out of business in a *week*.'

'What magic are you talking about, Berry-Face?' I asked.

'You will see that for yourself.' Anskar took back the bowl in his long and spindly fingers. 'This man who's making his way up the coast is named Brand. He is English. Brought in specially by the king of Norway to deal with hard cases like yourselves. I heard he is *already* a saint. And before you go asking me, no, I do not know what that is except that they say he can talk to his god, just as you can talk to yours.'

'Let them make Christians of those who want to be,' I said, 'and leave the rest of us alone.'

'Ah, that's how *you* think,' Anskar shook a finger in my face. 'But that is not how *they* think. They *only* want you praying to their Jesus. And if you do not' – he brought his face close to mine, breath sour from his drinking – 'you know what they *do*? They tie you *up*,' said Anskar, making an imaginary knot in the air. 'Then they jam a hollow bull's horn down your throat. Then they put a poisonous snake through the horn, *right* down your throat. And it bites you and you are *dead*.'

'Are you a Christian?' I asked him.

Anskar shrugged. 'I *am* when it suits me.' He pulled a silver ornament from around his neck, where it was held fast with a sweat-waxed leather cord. 'This is a crucifix. They used to nail people up on these big wooden frames and leave them to *die* in the *sun*. I'm a Christian when I go among Christians. But when I am with *you* . . .' He let the ornament hang upside down.

I recognised Thor's hammer now.

'You *see*?' said Anskar. 'I can be whichever one I want.'

169

'But you will always be a Berry-Face,' said Ingolf from across the room, 'and you can take comfort in that.'

Anskar shrugged again. 'Christians, Norsemen, Muslims. I have run into people whose gods have names I cannot even *pronounce*. I know a *lot* about religions. *That*, for example,' he pointed at the statue of the cat-eyed man behind the counter, 'is called a *Buddha*. They pray to him out in the east. That little man is a *long* way from home, I can tell you. People are already starting wars over which one to believe in. How much *good* is that for merchants like us?'

'No good at all,' said Olaf. 'Business and religion have to ride the same horse.'

'Business rides everybody's horse.' Anskar rummaged in his pocket. He pulled out a few silver coins, looked at them and sighed. 'I did not sell much in this town, and what I made I have spent drinking. If you ask me, those Christians will be *wasting* their time in Altvik.'

'Stop talking, Anskar,' said Ingolf. 'You are making me sea-sick.'

Anskar shrugged. 'If you do not want to listen, then I have got nothing to say.' He sprinkled the coins back into his pocket and headed for the door.

I looked around at the laughing crowd, each of them lost for now in the blur of their drinking. A tremor passed through me, as if the ground beneath my feet had suddenly quaked. I realised then that the safety I had felt here was only an illusion, and that the fight I had persuaded myself would never happen would have to be fought after all.

Late in the night, as I lay in bed, watching the last of the firelight fade across the sleeping face of Cabal, I looked at our old Varangian shields hanging on the wall, white paint chipped, showing the blood red beneath. Cobwebs, layered with dust, hung from the rim and swayed in some faintness of breeze I could not feel. I stared at our rusted chain-mail vests, draped on two nails by the door. They were the same two nails my father had used to hang his winter cloak and seal-fur mittens. In the corner was Halfdan's spear, untouched since I set foot inside this house.

Muscles clenched inside my chest, robbing me of sleep, preparing for what was to come.

The next day, late in the afternoon, a hollow moaning reached us on the wind, like the sad song of whales I had heard out on the open sea.

The whole town gathered by the water's edge as a ship entered the bay. At the bow stood a man wearing a brown cloak tied with a black cord and a small red cap perched on the top of his head. He seemed to be alone on the boat and was blowing into a huge trumpet made from the twisted horn of a ram. The sound filled the bay, scattering the gulls.

Dogs began to howl.

The ship dropped anchor fifty paces from shore. When this was done, the man held his arms wide, heavy rings knuckling his fingers, and shouted in a voice even louder than the trumpet, 'Do you know the power of the Lord?'

There was a murmur from the crowd.

'Which of you' – his voice echoed through the empty streets – 'will join me this day on the road to Paradise?'

This time only silence drifted back across the water.

But this man was not discouraged.

'Look at yourselves,' he shouted. 'Look at this place! Your old gods have forgotten you. No true god would let his people suffer the way you suffer now.'

The huge man heaved a rowboat over the side and stepped into it, bringing the rim dangerously close to the waterline. I expected his bulk to take him straight through the hull, like

171

Thor in the story of the Midgard serpent, when he hooked the monster and pulled so hard on the line to draw it to the surface that his legs punched through the bottom of the boat. The bow rode up precariously as the man began to row for shore, the bony arms of his oars tracing slow arcs in the still air.

Now the murmur on the beach rose to a babbling of excited voices.

As his rowboat ground against the shingle beach, the huge man climbed out into the shrugging waves. His long cloak trailed in the water. His gaze passed over us, then he smiled and showed his teeth. With one hand, he dragged his rowboat up onto the beach. His big feet crunched the empty mussel shells and dried-up seaweed. 'Do any of you know my name?' he asked.

'You are Jesus Christ,' called Tola, 'and I can tell your fortune for a price!' She stood at the back of the crowd, holding up her leather bag of glass beads, animal bones and sea-smoothed pebbles with which she predicted the future. 'Make way!' She pushed forward, jabbing with her crooked little feet, in which the blue veins twisted and doubled back on each other like the meanderings of an old stream.

'No,' said the man, his voice deep and patient. 'I am not the Lord and Saviour Jesus Christ. My name is Brand. I have carried the word of the Lord to the farthest reaches of the earth. I am his loyal servant. I stand before you now, ready to do his work and bring you all into his flock.' One arm flew up, the sleeve of the robe fell and his hand emerged, gripping a small wooden cross. 'Which of you are Christians already?'

Nobody moved.

'Who will come forward, then,' he shouted, 'and receive the blessing of the cross?'

'Does it hurt?' asked Tola, emerging from the front rank of the crowd.

172

'Hurt?' shouted Brand, peering down at the old woman as if he could not understand how such sagging skin could hold her bones together. 'No, it will not hurt. What will hurt is if you do not accept the offer of Christ's mercy. Then you will live in hell on earth.' He spun about, the robe dragging after him. Small waves broke around his bare feet. His broad toes gripped the sand. 'It is here, all around you, the endless nightmare. Can you not see it, consuming your lives in its eternal flames? Have you not suffered enough?'

There were some who craned their necks around, as if to find themselves enveloped in the blaze.

'You doubt me?' shouted Brand. 'You *do* doubt me!' he cried in well-rehearsed amazement. 'Do you need proof? Is that it?' Even though no one replied, he began to nod and look from one side to the other, as if we were all talking to him now, demanding that he show us his proof. 'Very well,' he said. 'You will have it! This afternoon, in the town square.'

'We do not have a town square,' said Olaf.

'No town square?' Brand's smooth forehead crumpled and he seemed for a moment to be having second thoughts about this place. But then the confidence returned to his face. 'On this beach then! Tonight. And when you have had proof, I will lead you one by one into the water to be baptised in the name of the Christ our saviour, and this forgotten outpost will become the house of the Lord until the end of time.' Then Brand pulled from his rowboat a large object wrapped in a piece of sailcloth dappled with what looked like blood. He dumped it on the ground and kicked back the edges of the cloth, revealing a whole leg of beef. 'A gift!' he said. 'And who is the aleman here?'

Ingolf stepped forward, nervously wiping his hands on his leather apron.

Brand pressed some coins into his hand. 'For a barrel, so you

173

can wash down your meal, all thanks to the church.' Then he stopped forward and I was close enough to hear him say to Ingolf in a quieter voice, 'Make it the good stuff. No cheap brew, or you and I will have words about it afterwards. Can you cook this meat?'

'I can,' said Ingolf.

'Then get to it,' said Brand. He stepped back and beamed at the crowd. 'I will see you all later this evening!' he shouted, as he dragged the rowboat back into the surf and returned to his ship.

Ingolf set about making a fire. Then he skewered the beef on a spit, turning it slowly while fat dripped into the hissing flames.

Several smaller fires were kindled up and down the beach, which gave the place a festive look. Flames threw their light across the water, and fish gathered in the shallows, drawn by the glow. Children scooped up the fish with nets made from sacking cloth and roasted them on sharpened sticks.

Ingolf rolled a keg down from the alehouse, meaty hands slapping the iron fetters of the barrel as he pushed it out across the sand.

I stood with Cabal by the water.

'So they have come after all,' he said. 'Well, they will not have this place. I promise you that.'

I glanced at him, realising that his hatred of the Christians had only grown stronger since our days in the Varangian. 'Let him say his piece. People will decide for themselves.'

'He can talk all he wants,' snapped Cabal.

A fire had been lit in a brazier on the ship's deck. It burned brightly, throwing off sparks. Brand was walking back and forth, barechested and rocking his arms in front of his chest, like a man getting ready for a fight. Then he knelt down by the brazier, holding up a wooden cross, eyes closed and lips moving in prayer.

'What is that smell?' asked Cabal.

'The roasting meat, I think.'

'No,' he said. 'Something else. Like tar.'

Now that Cabal mentioned it I did smell something which was not the smoke of the beach fires or the meat. 'Must be incense,' I said, remembering the dusty fragrance of sandalwood twisting in the still air of the Haga Sofia. 'They burn it when they pray.'

When the outer layer of meat was cooked, Ingolf carved off slices and distributed them. Slowly, as each layer of meat was cut away, Ingolf made his way down to the bone. The keg was opened and the ale passed out in bowls from person to person until each one was empty. Then the person with the empty bowl walked back to the keg and filled it once again.

I watched Guthrun sink an entire bowlful by himself. He had no money to come to the alehouse and refused what I had offered. But free ale he would not refuse, no matter who was paying. He sat on the sand and beamed, ale foam frosting his beard.

Tola ate so much that she looked like a cormorant with a fish stuck in its gullet.

Cabal sat himself down on a flat stone to watch, refusing the food that was offered to him.

It was the first time I had seen him do that.

Twilight crowded in around us. Grey clouds over the bay still caught sunlight from beyond the hills, which streaked their undersides crimson.

The beef was soon eaten up. To feed himself, Ingolf cut scraps from the bone and ate them off the blade, teeth scraping over the iron.

At last, just as people were getting sleepy and talking about heading back to their houses, Brand set out in his rowboat and soon arrived at the shore.

175

He had changed his light cloak for a heavier one with a hood, made from a tightly-woven fabric. 'Your bellies are full,' Brand announced, 'thanks to the generosity of the church.'

Then he took off his red cap and began to walk among the crowd with the cap held out. 'Thank you for repaying the church's kindness with the greater kindness of your own.'

'So we are paying for this after all,' said Cabal. 'That is a fine trick. I bet he makes a fortune this way.'

'He has not met the people of Altvik yet,' I told him.

And it was true that Brand's red cap stayed mostly empty.

When Brand approached Cabal and me, he was stopped in his tracks by Cabal's palm raised towards his face. 'I had none of your bribe,' said Cabal.

'Are you a Celt?' asked Brand, noticing his accent.

'I am that,' he replied, 'and I know what you people are.'

'Well, this bribe as you call it was not meant for you,' he said. His face was hard with contempt. He turned away, jingling the few coins he had gathered.

Cabal's eyes were glazed with rage. Slowly, he leaned forward. His fingers slid into the sand and closed around a stone.

'Cabal,' I said softly. If he killed this man now, the whole town would turn against us.

Cabal glanced at me.

I did not speak again, but only met his gaze with mine.

He understood. His fingers uncurled from the stone and he sat back. The strange fire which had glimmered in his eyes died away.

It was then that I noticed Kari, standing a short distance away. She had seen what passed between Cabal and me. Her face was pale with fear.

Brand still made his way among the crowd. His teeth-clenched smile sputtered on and off his face like a failing candle flame. He returned to the edge of the water. With a wave of his hands, he gathered the crowd around him.' How often did you eat so well under the rule of your old gods?' he asked. 'And where are these gods? Who can come forward and show me the power of these giants? Who speaks for them?'

I saw a few heads turn towards me.

Brand followed their gaze until his eyes fastened on mine. 'You!' he called. 'You are a priest?'

'I am,' I replied, feeling the blood run to my face.

'He got struck by lightning,' said Guthrun, whose eyes were foggy from drink. 'He was chosen by the gods!'

I wished Guthrun would be quiet and let me speak for myself.

Brand walked over until he stood too close to me. His massive chin was dimpled and his short, flattened-out nose looked as if it had been broken several times. 'I have heard about you. The man from Miklagard. Too hot for you down there?' When I gave him no answer, he stepped back and boomed at the crowd. 'To be struck by lightning is indeed to be chosen. But not by god. By the devil!' His breath swept past me, smelling of sour milk. 'This has been foretold by our scriptures, in which it is written, "I beheld Satan as lightning fall from heaven!"'

I wondered how many times he had done this, on how many beaches and in how many village squares, the air thick with the smell of roasted meat and greasy-fingered people drowsy from heavy drink.

'I will show this devil the way of love and compassion,' he shouted. 'The power of Christ will compel him.'

I caught sight of Olaf, standing by himself at the edge of the fire's light. The flames glowed on his face.

'In a town I visited last year,' Brand told the crowd, 'I heard a story of a man who was killed when he stepped outside his house one night. He had been awakened by a dream of nine

177

women, clad only in black, riding black horses down from the north. And then from the south, he saw nine women clad only in white and riding white horses. But when he stepped outside to shake the dreaming from his head, he saw these nine women in black gathered right in front of him. They were no dream after all and neither were the knives they used to cut him down. They fled when the women in white appeared. The man's family rushed out to help him but it was too late. All they found was a dying man and the ground trampled with hoof prints. He lived long enough to tell them his story, then he died. It was a mystery to the people there, but I knew its meaning at once. This man had allowed himself to be brought into the fold of the true church, but at the last moment, when salvation and protection were within his grasp, he refused to be baptised. This was the price he paid! Those black witches were the servants of the old god, come to take one last sacrifice before they fled before the white angels of the Christian church. That man need not have died, not then or ever after. And your lives and your souls could also be saved. Let me be your guide! Let me save you from the black witches who ride down from the hills in the dead of night.' He aimed a finger at the Grimsvoss, as if the witches were already on their way.

Tola stepped forward from the line of murmuring people. The story had snagged deep in some wrinkle in her brain, waking a nightmare perhaps even older than the ancient woman herself. 'What do you want us to do?' she asked.

'Let me baptise you!' Brand took her hand, which vanished under his massive furry knuckles. 'Come down to the water with me.'

'Why should we believe a word you say?' It was Guthrun, who had stepped forward from the crescent-shaped line of people. He was weaving, and Ingolf stepped forward to steady the old man.

Brand dropped Tola's hand and turned to face this new threat. 'Yes. Why should you? Words are never enough, are they?'

'No, they are not,' muttered Cabal.

'Do you need me,' Brand called out, 'to show you the proof?'

'Yes!' shouted Guthrun. 'Let us see some proof.'

Everyone was shouting now: *Yes! Yes! Show us the proof!*

'So few of you?' asked Brand, as if their voices barely reached his ears.

'All of us!' they screamed. 'Show us the proof!'

Brand held up his arms for silence. Then he dropped to his knees and clapped his hands together in front of his face. He stayed this way for some time.

Ingolf heaved the bone from the leg of beef into the fire, sending up a flurry of sparks. Then he began stirring a heavy stick in the embers.

At last, Brand rose to his feet. He went over to Ingolf and held out his hand for the burning stick.

Ingolf threw it to him.

The stick turned in the air and Brand caught it. He held out the burning end towards the faces of those who were watching. This stick was as thick and as long as his own arm. He swept it back and forth, trailing smoke and sparks, which sent the front row of the crowd squawking backwards. It made a whooshing sound as it travelled through the air. Then he turned to me. 'Will your gods protect you once more from the fire?' He moved towards me, holding out the burning stick. 'I want to see your gods shield you from the heat of these flames, just as my God will shield me.'

It was only stubbornness that made me hold my ground.

He brought the sputtering, crackling end of the stick close to my face.

The heat pinched my skin. The smoke was painful in my

179

nostrils. I could smell the bitter reek of my own burning hair.

'Will they save you?' he asked. 'Ask them to save you. Go on. Ask them.'

For a moment longer, the burning stick wavered in front of my face.

'No,' I said quietly, tasting the smoke in my mouth. The heat stabbed at my eyes. The moment I closed them, I felt a blow to my chest from the stick. I toppled over backwards onto the sea-weed-crusted sand.

Brand stood over me, swinging the burning stick slowly back and forth, just above the ground. 'They would not save him!' he told the crowd, 'and my God is too kind to let me hurt this man.' He wheeled away.

My shirt was smouldering in the place where he had hit me. I could feel the scorch mark on my chest. I climbed to my feet, not thinking. Anger like a black-red fluid swam inside my brain. I took a step towards him.

Brand spun about. He brought his face close to mine and spoke through gritted teeth in a voice too low for the others to hear. 'Years ago, before I joined the Christian faith, I killed a priest here in this town. If you are not careful, I may finish off another here tonight.'

I realised he was the one who had chased Greycloak into the mountains and left him there to die. It seemed to me that what-ever was about to happen had already taken place long ago, woven by the widow Norns into the fabric of our lives.

'By this time tomorrow,' he murmured, 'I can have the peo-ple of this town building a Christian church over the ruins of your house. What do you think of that?'

'I can build another house,' I told him.

'That is not the point. The point is that your former congre-gation is ready to convert. Your people have no unity. You are like a wheel with no hub. How do you expect to stand up to the

180

Christian church, which organises its people into one voice, one thought? What is it that unites you?'

'There is a hub to our wheel,' I said.

'Yes,' he said dismissively. 'The black hammer, lost here in the hills above your town. It is no use to you now.'

Even as he spoke, I felt its weight around my neck, hidden from his view by the ash-blackened cloth of my shirt.

'Walk with me,' said Brand. 'Let us try to solve this without bloodshed.'

We moved away from the fires and into the gathering shadows.

With each step, Brand dug his heels deep in the sand, as if he did not trust the earth to hold still beneath his feet. 'I have brought you away from the long ears of your friends in order to make you an offer, because we are sensible men.' He held out his hand, as if some evidence of our good sense was balanced on the great creased slab of his palm. 'We understand that religion is more than just a pathway to a life beyond this life. More than just discussions with our various gods. It is the binding that holds a community together. Let us set aside for now the idea of your conversion to the Christian faith. All I ask is that I may baptise you and that you kneel for the Prima Signatio.'

'The first sign? What is that?'

'You kneel before me. I make the sign of the cross over your head. That is all. It does not mean you are Christian. It means you are setting out on the road to becoming a Christian. What it means is only that you are thinking about becoming Christian.'

I shook my head. 'I am not thinking about it.'

'You have not heard the rest of my offer. Trygvasson has declared himself a Christian and requires that the people of this land should also become Christians. What is more, they will be taxed. King Trygvasson's men are travelling all over the country now, collecting what is owed. They will be here in this town in a matter of days.'

'We do not have much to give,' I said.

'That makes no difference to Trygvasson. You had best hand over what they ask from you, or they will leave this town in ruins, as I have seen them do to other places on this coast. On that, you have no choice but to do as you are told. But you' – he aimed a baubled finger at me – 'can take a share of the profits if you are intelligent about it. If you will allow yourself to be baptised here today and will oversee the building of a Christian church, you will receive a third of the taxes that come due each year. I will say that God himself, the Christian God, has chosen you to be the leader of his church here, even if you have not yet chosen him.' A faint smile passed across his broad, flat face. 'From then on, if they go against you, they go against God, for which the penalty is death. Come now. Let me baptise you now before these people start heading for home.' He turned to walk back down the beach.

As soon as he realised that I was not following, he turned and looked at me, his face a mix of anger and bewilderment. 'A *third* of the taxes!' he snapped. 'For the rest of your life. How is it going to feel ten years from now, knowing you have turned me down, when your bones ache in the winter and you have no means to survive except to gnaw the bones of sacrifice in your dreary temple on the hill? I will not make this offer twice. Do you think you can stand in the path of the inevitable?'

When I breathed, the air felt hot on my lips, as if I were drawing in the embers of a fire. 'You have misunderstood us,' I said quietly.

He dismissed my words with a wave of his hand. 'You have misunderstood yourselves. The fire of the Norse gods has burned out and you are living in the ashes.' He strode away down the beach. When he reached the fire, he jammed in the stick and twisted it in the embers. Then he raised the stick above his head. 'His god would not save him,' cried Brand, 'but my God will save me!' He tipped his head back, as if he meant to ram the burning end down his throat, but instead he touched it to his chest. When the smoking stick brushed against the fabric, the whole cloak seemed to shudder as it erupted into fire.

The crowd shrieked but made no move to help him.

From where I stood, I watched as Brand turned his back to the crowd. He was hidden from them by the boil of flames and smoke. He pulled the cape up over his head and hunched over, while the fire ran in fierce, bright liquid from the ends of his cape.

I understood then what I had smelled earlier. It was the scent of wax, which Brand had used to paint his cloak and over which he had splashed some kind of alcohol to feed the fire. But under the wax-coated barrier, the flames would not reach him. I wondered how many times Brand had pulled this trick, how many people it had caused to be converted, and how many would be joining him tonight.

On the other side of the blaze, standing level with me, I saw Cabal. He, too, could see the way Brand had hidden under his cape. He was watching me. The reflection of the fire flickered in his eyes.

Soon, the flames died away, leaving a huge plume of smoke which curled in the air like fingers closing into a fist. As Brand turned to face the crowd, he pulled away the cape and let it drop at his feet. He held open his arms to show he was not burned.

The open-mouthed silence of the watchers gave way to cheering.

Guthrun dropped to his knees. He stared open-mouthed at the smouldering cloak.

Now the crowd converged on Brand and would have lifted him up off the ground if he had not been too huge to lift. 'One at a time!' he was laughing. 'One at a time, my brothers and sisters!'

'Do it again!' shouted Cabal, standing at the edge of the fire-light.

Faces turned to look at him.

For a moment, the sound of the cheering died down.

'Do it again,' he repeated.

'Stay away from this, Celt,' said Brand.

'You are the one who should have stayed away,' growled Cabal.

'I want to see it again,' said Ingolf.

'One miracle is enough for today!' Brand turned to him and smiled.

Smoky air poured into Ingolf's mouth as he breathed in. 'If your God is so strong, he can protect you.'

'Of course he can protect me,' replied Brand, 'but you have seen all the proof you need.'

Now Guthrun appeared, pushing his way to the front. 'We decide when we have seen enough!'

There were mutterings. People stepped back.

'My friends,' Brand held up his arms for silence.

But suddenly the mood had changed. It was as if they had all been asleep and woke to realise that we were not his brothers, nor his sisters, nor his friends. The space around him grew. 'You will see the miracle again,' he told them in his deep show-man's voice, 'first thing in the morning.'

'Now!' shouted Cabal.

'What trickery are you selling?' demanded Ingolf.

'All right,' said Brand, 'but first I will return to my ship and pray for guidance.' He turned towards the rowboat. Then his face grew suddenly pale.

The oars were gone.

Guthrun had carried them off. He was making his way over the barnacled rocks at the end of the beach, one oar tucked under each arm, leaving two trails into the sand.

'What kind of gratitude is this?' asked Brand.

'Why should we show you gratitude?' asked Cabal. 'You give us something we did not ask for and then expect to be paid for it. Now you say we are in your debt.'

'I told you to stay out of this, Celt!' Brand's voice cracked. 'This is none of your concern.'

'This is my home now,' replied Cabal, 'and these people are my people. We are all each other's concern.'

There were noises of agreement from the crowd.

'Do you not understand,' said Brand, still trying to force authority into his words, 'that when you offend me, you offend God himself?'

'He is not as offended as we are!' shouted Tola, shaking her bird-claw fist at the priest.

It was then that Brand noticed the black hammer around my neck. One of the buttons had fallen off my shirt when he struck me. Now the front of the shirt had come open, revealing the stone against my chest.

Brand stared in disbelief. He opened his mouth to ask a question, but the shouting of the crowd drowned out his voice.

Brand looked at the faces which had closed in around him, searching for one that might show him some pity. But they were blind to him now.

Slowly, Brand put on the cape, sliding his body into it with the same look of distaste as a man getting dressed in wet clothes. He tightened it around him, knotting the charred black cord. Then he reached for the stick, which only smouldered

185

now. He touched it against the hem of the cape and quickly pulled it away again. 'You see?' he said. Then his eyes grew bright with defiance. 'It will not burn!'

But even as his voice rose up in triumph, the cloak began to smoulder. Suddenly, the flames jumped up, enveloping him. His voice kept rising, past words, past screaming, to a terrible wail which none of us had ever heard before. Brand flailed his arms, splashes of fire arcing out into the night sky. The cape clung to him now. He could not shake it loose. For a long time, he stood facing us, painted with flames. The wailing continued, beyond what any one breath could spend. Slowly he raised his arms. He seemed to be looking at his hands. Smoke slithered from his fingertips. Then he staggered back into the water and a rush of steam hid everything. A great silence followed, broken only by a rustle of the incoming tide over the sand.

When the crowds had sifted away into the night, Cabal and I dragged Brand's body from the surf and brought it out to his boat.

Once on board, we lit torches and moved cautiously around the deck, almost tripping over a wooden cage of snakes, whose tiny heart-shaped heads and skin decorated with dark red lozenges told me they were poisonous. They were hidden under a blanket and writhed when I pulled it away, as if the light of our torches caused them pain.

Cabal found a bucket of wax and a thick horsehair brush for painting it on Brand's cape. The smell of it was in everything on the boat.

I opened a trunk and discovered it was filled with animal bones. Another trunk held hundreds of small wooden crosses, each one the same. There were many dried and salted hams hanging from hooks below deck, and at the head of Brand's bed.

We set Brand's body on his bed, which was strewn with feather-stuffed pillows, a silk-brocaded tapestry which he had been using as a blanket, and many crumbs of food. For a moment, we both looked down on the charred remains of what had once been a man, and then we left him where he lay.

After hauling up the anchor, which was a huge piece of white stone bound with ropes, we moved the boat out onto the open sea, towing the rowboat behind us. We ran up the sail and roped the steerboard in place.

Then Cabal and I pitched our torches into the water and climbed down into the rowboat, taking nothing with us. We did not speak as we rowed back to shore, nor had we said a single word when we were aboard Brand's ship.

We left Brand's ship to sail away into the night, rather than burn it in the bay and risk having pieces of it wash up on the beach, where they might be recognised by traders passing through.

The last I saw of the boat, it was riding a calm ocean towards the north. The blind man's eye of a full moon glared down through the tumbling clouds.

Back in my house that night, as I lay down to sleep, a single, overwhelming thought came rolling through my mind, like a boulder come loose from the sheer cliffs of the mountains. It was a realisation that the war in which Brand and I had found ourselves was no longer a struggle for faith but a war over property, whether it was taxes, land or the black rock for which I had sworn my life away.

I could not get out of my head what Brand had said about the fire of the Norse gods burning out and how we were living in the ashes. What if the prophecy of Ragnarok, the great war between the gods, had already been fought? Did their world lie in ruins far above us, strewn with the dead to whom we were still praying? Had one new god survived to rise above them all? Was I simply blind? Doubt perched like some great raven in the rafters of my mind, clacking its iron-hard beak, claws hooked into the softness of my brain.

But it was too late for doubt. The war had already begun, and the death of this man had not silenced his message. It had only killed the messenger.

PART III

I was in the temple, sweeping the floor and stacking firewood. My mind was taken up by thoughts of the King's tax men. Word had spread through the village that they would soon be here. Some favoured gathering our money now, to pay them as soon as they arrived, but since we did not know how much they would demand, the decision had been made to wait. I wondered how we would be able to pay them anything at all, since we had so little already. I had become so preoccupied that I did not hear someone approach until a rustling in the doorway brought me to my senses.

It was Kari. 'I came to talk with you,' she said.

'About what?' I asked, wiping the sweat from my forehead onto my sleeve.

She came inside and sat down on one of the benches which lined the walls. With the expanse of empty seats stretching out on either side of her, she looked small and pale and lost. 'About Cabal,' she said.

I went and sat beside her.

'I am frightened,' she said. 'What I saw in him last night, I had not known was there.'

'He has a hatred for the Christians,' I told her.

'But he will not tell me why.' Now she set her hand upon

my arm. 'You must know. You were with him all those years.'

I shook my head. 'He has told no one. Not even me.'

'I love him,' she sighed, as if she had made some terrible and irreversible mistake, 'but last night he seemed to be a different person than the one I thought I knew.'

I remembered the second shadow, the Ail Gysgod which Cabal said lived inside him. I turned to her and took her hands in mine. 'When we spoke to you of our days in the Varangian, we did not tell you all of it. Nor could we. He and I have seen terrible things and have done terrible things, the memories of which we cannot lose, no matter how deeply we bury them inside our brains. They will always be there, and sometimes they will claw their way back to the surface. But who we were, Cabal and I, we do not want to be again. What you saw in him last night was his old self, the one he is trying to forget. I have trusted him so many times with my own life that I know I can trust him with yours.'

She brushed the hair from her tear-stained eyes. 'Thank you,' she said.

At that moment, Cabal appeared in the doorway. 'I wondered where you had gone,' he said to Kari.

Kari rose and walked across to him. Standing on the tips of her toes, she set her hands on either side of his face and kissed him.

As they left, heading down the path into town, I climbed to my feet and slapped the dirt from the seat of my trousers. I stood in the doorway and filled my lungs with the cold air coming down from the mountains.

Cabal and Kari spoke softly to each other as they walked. Cabal reached across and took her hand.

I realised suddenly how Olaf must have felt to be left up here alone.

Wind sifted through the tall grass in the field. Soon the sun would dip beneath the waves.

I turned back to my work, stacking wood under the unblinking gaze of the faces on the pillars, their wolf-toothed jaws cracked wide in a endless silent scream.

The next morning, I awoke before dawn to find myself standing outside my house, wearing my old battle gear, everything from the chain-mail vest to the shield and helmet. I had no idea how I had come to be there. I had never walked in my sleep before.

I looked down at the bay, expecting to see the tax collector's ship riding into the harbour on the incoming tide. But there was no ship, so I went back inside.

It seemed as if I had only just fallen asleep when Cabal shook me awake. I sat up. The door was open. The clouds had been swept away like cobwebs from the corners of the sky. It was a sunny, windy day. By the quality of light, I could tell I had slept away most of the morning.

I smiled at Cabal, but he did not smile back.

Then I knew they had arrived.

The King's men had come in two large, deep-hulled traders. The first ship stayed out in the bay. There was a large crew on board and many warshields hung against the side. The second ship had anchored closer to the beach and ferried ashore a tall and dignified-looking man. He wore a dark-blue cloak trimmed with wolf's fur. Held to his chest was a large, leather-bound book.

With him came four men wearing tunics made from the same dark-blue cloth. Their swords were too large and ornate to be of much practical use. Behind their rowboat, they towed a second skiff, which was covered with a piece of dirty sail cloth.

Word of their arrival spread, hissed through half-open shutters from house to house.

193

I went down to meet them, as no one else had volunteered.

When the men reached shore, they set up a table on the sand, attaching the legs with wooden pegs which they hammered into place. In front of the table, they rigged a set of scales, which hung from an iron scaffold. Brass block weights with lead-filled centres had been stacked beside it. Each weight had a ring for lifting it, like rings I had seen in the noses of bulls.

The dignified man sat on a stool beside the table. From a small leather bag, he brought a silver bowl and two small stoppered glass jars. One was filled with black liquid and the other with a syrupy, clear liquid. He mixed some of each in the silver bowl, then brought out a feather, which he sliced at the end to make a writing point. The four men watched this with reverent fascination, as if he were about to perform some kind of magic.

The guards watched me approach, eyes narrowed and arms folded, muttering to each other. They looked like hard people, more used to breaking the law than enforcing it.

The man at the table had been writing in his book. Now he looked up, blinking me into focus after the concentration of his writing. His eyes were brown and he was bald except for a few strands of grey hair above his ears. 'Who are you?' he asked.

'Hakon Magnusson. I am the priest here.'

'You represent the town?'

'Only because no one else wants to talk to you.'

His eyebrows rose slightly, then settled back again. 'I am Egil Arneson,' he said as he climbed to his feet, 'tax collector for the King. He has charged me to deliver to him 150 pounds of silver from the town of Altvik, unless you have begun construction of a Christian church, in which case the amount is set at 100 pounds. But I see no church here. Only a temple of the old faith, up there on the hill.'

I stared at him in shock. 'We have nothing like 150 pounds of silver, nor even 100.'

'You are the priest, you say?' A breeze blew off the water, twitching the fur on his cloak.

'I am.'

'And you have met with Brand? He should have passed through here some days ago.'

'He was here,' I said.

Arneson looked confused. 'Did he not explain that you were to receive a portion of this amount, provided that you became the guardian of Christianity in this town?'

'He did explain that.'

Arneson scratched at his chin. 'You are either very stubborn or very foolish.'

'We are very poor,' I told him.

Arneson breathed in sharply. 'You are also short of time. I will give you until the end of the day to raise 150 pounds of silver. After that, I must turn matters over to the soldiers who are travelling with me.' He gestured out to the second ship at anchor in the bay. 'I assume it is not necessary to explain what they will do to this town.'

'It is not,' I said. I set off from door to door, in the hopes of raising the money before the end of the day. There was no doubt in my mind that I would fail. If we could not come up with 150 pounds, there seemed to be no choice except to settle for 100 pounds, for me to be baptised, and to begin construction of a church, whether anyone prayed there or not. In the end, it did not matter, as I collected only one bucket full of silver. The people with whom I spoke had no doubts about the job that Trygvasson's soldiers had come to do. If there had been silver, they would have handed it over. Memories of the day the raiders sacked this town were still clear in the minds of many. But the money simply was not here.

I went back to the water's edge, carrying the bucket.

Arneson had not left the beach. Now and then, I saw him

pacing back and forth, hood pulled over his head, hands tucked in the deep pockets of his cloak.

By now, the guards had realised that there would not be any resistance, at least none that would prevent them from doing what now appeared inevitable. They took off their surly faces and stacked their swords with the hilts locked together and the scabbard tips dug into the sand. Then they sat down beside a driftwood fire. They looked disgruntled, as if humiliated by their matching tunics and their ornamental swords. To make a living by menacing peaceful villages with their war-scarred faces and long blades slung across their backs was beneath them and they knew it.

I set the bucket on the table.

'This will not do,' said Arneson, his voice cold and clipped.

'Perhaps we can offer you some things in trade,' I began.

But he cut me short. 'I do not have room for all the goats and blunted swords I have been offered since I began this wretched task. Let me show you something,' he said, and led me over to the boat which had been covered by the sailcloth. He swept back the cloth revealing dozens of torches, their heads wrapped in strips of tar-soaked wool. 'If I give the order, my men will fire every house in this town. Do not think I am play-ing games. That is a mistake the people of Ytre Moa made three days ago.'

I thought of their village in ruins, abandoned just as they had found it, and its people fading into the hills, to join the ghosts of those who had gone before them.

On the scales, Arneson weighed out the silver. It came to 30 pounds. He wrote the number down in his book.

'There was a time,' I said, 'when we might have been able to pay you.'

'And how is that?' he asked, without looking up from his writing.

I told him about the raid, but he did not seem to be listening.

Arneson spun the book around and held out the pen. 'Make your mark there,' he said, and pointed to the place where he had written Altvik, and the amount of money he had gathered.

I wrote my name in the same Latin script he was using and slid the book back to him.

He raised one eyebrow. 'How is it that you read Latin?'

I told him I had learned it down in Miklagard, during my time among the Varangian.

When I said this last word, his eyes lit up. He actually smiled.

I had never seen a face changed so completely by a smile.

He told me that his younger brother had served with the Varangian. 'Perhaps you knew him.'

'Perhaps,' I replied.

'His name was Halfdan.'

I had been leaning slightly over the desk, but now I stood up straight. 'Halfdan!' I described him to Arneson, wondering if it was another man by the same name, although I had known of no other..

'But that is him!' Arneson set his palms down hard on the table. His eyes opened wide and his lips trembled as questions massed in his brain, clamouring to be spoken. 'I have had no news of him for many years.'

I told him the whole story.

Arneson sat at his table, refusing to move even as the tide came in and lapped against our feet.

The guards watched all this with tolerant confusion, knowing it was none of their business to question Arneson, and if he wanted to sit there while the bay washed him and his table away, that was his right. They moved up to the high-tide line and rested on a cushion of dried weeds.

When I told Arneson of Halfdan's death and his funeral

pyre out in the wastelands, he lowered his head and wept in silence.

The guards stared at the strange sight of this man crying at his half-submerged table.

Arneson wiped the cuff of his cloak across his face. His eyes were red and his lips were drawn tight over his teeth. 'I feel I owe you an apology.'

'For what?'

'That it was my own brother who took you away from here. I am grateful that you saw to his funeral in the way he would have thought correct.' He stood and the ends of his cloak sagged in the shin-deep water. 'I do not intend for such a gesture to go unnoticed.' He paused for several moments in silence, then leaned forward across the table. 'I will make you a gift of time.'

'Time?'

He nodded. 'I am sailing up the coast to the city of Nidarnes. In one month, when I return south, you must have the remaining 120 pounds owed to the king. I suggest you also build yourself a Christian church and find a Christian priest to baptise you, so that you will only owe me 70.'

'Even if I do as you say, I still do not know where we will find the money.'

Arneson closed his book. 'Then I hope when I return that I do not find you here.' He summoned his guards with a sharp wave of his hand.

Before the Dog Star winked from of the twilight sky their ship had vanished out to sea, leaving behind only the remains of a fire and some footprints in the sand.

That night, the whole village met at the temple, to discuss what should be done.

Men stood in groups, picking their nails and talking in

hushed voices. Women lined the benches or paced back and forth with restless children on their hips. Old people sat by the fire, poking the embers with their walking sticks and leaning into each other as they spoke, like white-topped tufts of cotton grass swaying in a breeze. Guthrun sat among them. He leaned forward over the fire, his hands twisting and turning in front of him as he held court.

I stood before the pillars and asked for silence. When the room had quieted down, I explained what Arneson had told me.

There was silence, as some tried and failed to conjure from their minds a picture of what 120 pounds of silver looked like, or even 70. For the rest, who had seen enough coins measured out in their lives to imagine the mass of so much money, it was as if the weight of that silver had been hooked into their skin like brutal ornaments, dragging them down to the ground.

'The choice is yours,' I said. 'The King's men will be back in a month. By then, if we have not begun the building of a Christian church, there will be no choice to make.'

'Seventy or 120,' said Ingolf, his voice gone suddenly hoarse. 'It might as well be 1000 pounds because we will never be able to get it.'

I caught sight of Olaf standing at the back. He was studying the faces in the room, as if trying to guess which way the vote would go.

I looked around for Cabal, expecting to see his shaggy head towering above the rest, but he was not there. I wondered why he had stayed away.

Now Guthrun stood, and cast his gaze about the room, seeming to stare at each person in turn. 'We cannot surrender to blackmail, no matter how much they want. What will be left of this town if we give in?'

'Its people,' said Kari.

The crowd turned to look at her. They seemed surprised to hear Kari's voice.

'And its houses,' she continued, 'and its animals and everything else we can see with our eyes and touch with our hands. Perhaps it is the will of the old gods that we no longer hold them sacred anymore. Maybe we are not supposed to survive. Not as we are now.'

As her words cleaved into my head, I glimpsed us long into the future, so far beyond the boundaries of our lives that the only thing left of us was the dust of our cremated flesh, pitted swords and rotten shields, just silhouettes of rust and bone. We would live on only in stories, like Sasser Greycloak, the truth so patched with lies as to make us strangers even to ourselves.

'It is about more than just the old faith and the new,' I said. 'Without that money, Trygvasson will take everything, and he will become the god we pray to, the one we beg to go on living. Is that the life you want?' As I spoke, I felt an utter helplessness, knowing the decision did not rest with me.

So I kept silent, hearing the tide of argument ebb back and forth.

Then a voice boomed out, 'So you have given up already.'

The room grew suddenly quiet, as everyone in it turned to see Cabal filling up the doorway. He must have been standing outside the whole time. He looked dishevelled, as if he had not slept in a long time. He stepped into the room and shut the door behind him. 'Trygvasson knows you cannot find the money. He wants only to break you, so that you have no choice but to do what he says. And do you think that when he has finished building churches all across this country that he will simply leave you in peace? Give in now, and you will never stop giving in.'

'So what would you have us do?' asked Ingolf.

'I know how you can get that silver,' he replied, 'and plenty more besides.'

'You're talking about a raid,' said Olaf. They were the first words he had said.

'More like a robbery,' replied Cabal, 'and if it is done right, no one will be hurt.'

Now Olaf pushed his way forward, until he stood in the centre of the room. 'A raid? A robbery? Call it whatever you want. How is it to be done? With one ship which happens to be mine? With our host of *warriors*?' He swept his arm around the room. 'There are barely enough weapons in this town for one person to commit suicide, let alone start a fight.'

'We may not be warriors,' said Ingolf, in a rare moment of defiance, 'but we could try to get the job done.'

'You could take along that little statue of yours,' hissed Tola, 'and throw it at whoever gets in your way.'

Ingolf turned to her. For a moment it looked as if he might say something, but then he just shook his head and fell silent.

'Are you saying that we go on a raid every time we have to pay these taxes?' asked Kari.

'No. All we need is a fair chance,' said Cabal, 'to put the past behind us and begin again.'

In that moment, I knew he was talking only to her, and the past he wished to put behind him was his own.

Now Cabal looked around the room. 'Have you never dreamed of streets paved with stones instead of mud? What about a ship-building yard, a decent foundry and herds to graze the meadow, instead of the few straying cows and goats and sheep you own right now? *That* is the kind of place that can pay 120 pounds of silver and not be turned into a village of beggars at the same time. If you bring wealth to Trygvasson, he will not meddle in your affairs. No farmer will slaughter a cow that is producing milk. As you are now, you have nothing to

201

bargain with. You live at the mercy of whatever thug comes walking into town to take whatever he wants. Why will you not fight for what you have?'

'This is not some warring outpost at the end of the world,' said Olaf. 'We will fight, just as most people will fight, but only as a last resort.'

'This *is* your last resort! If you wait any longer, it will be too late, because of what these Christians are doing to you, and you do not even know it.'

'What are they doing?' asked Ingolf.

'They are writing,' said Cabal, pinching the air in front of him and raking his hand madly back and forth. 'Scribbling the history of their time, in which they call you a scourge sent down by their own God to punish them for their sins. You are not even real to them! You are a figment of their God's imagination. But the silver I can get for you is real. It is ten days sailing from here, maybe less, and stored in a church, a *Christian* church, in a little village on the coast of my old country. You have two choices now. You can all leave, just pack up and go, so that when those tax collectors return all they find are ruined and abandoned houses. Or you can stay,' he continued, 'and get on with your lives, and even make them better than before. If you want that, you come talk to me.'

Then he was gone. The slammed door boxed our ears.

I followed Cabal out into the dark. 'If this is such a simple task,' I asked, 'why has another raiding ship not made off with the silver already?'

'They do not know it is there,' he replied. 'Most of the churches that have been raided are those whose spires can be seen from the water. This church is in a village called St David's. It is impossible to spot the church from the sea, because it was built without a spire, to hide it from the raiding ships that come across from the Norse colonies in Ireland. I know because I was apprenticed to a monk in that place.'

'And that is where you learned to hate them.'

'It is,' he replied.

'And still you will not tell me why.'

'Some secrets are meant to be kept,' he said. 'You know that much yourself. And the secret those Christians have kept at St David's is that they have a tunnel beneath the church for hiding their money. I saw them carry chests of money down into that tunnel, even helped to carry them myself. It was all done at night, so that even the townspeople would not know what was hidden there. The village lies upstream from a narrow river which feeds into the sea. I can guide us there. If we go into the town at night, I can lead you straight to the church. I can get us into the tunnel and we will be gone again by sunrise. The two of us alone could do it, if we had someone to bring us there and back.'

'We would need Olaf's boat, and I do not know if he will agree.'

'I thought as much myself, and whether Olaf agrees or not, his boat is the one we will use.'

'But he will have to sail it. No one else has the skill.'

Cabal kneaded the muscles of his neck, setting the bones straight with dull clicks under the skin. 'You speak to Olaf. Tell him if he refuses, I will see to it that he never sails his boat again, or walks without a stick.'

'It is a long time since you last saw that church,' I said. 'What makes you sure the money is still there?'

'If the money was safe, why would they move it? Unless you have a better plan, this is our only chance.'

When I walked back inside, all faces turned towards me.

Guthrun stood out in front. 'We have decided,' he said. 'We trust you to do whatever is best for the town.'

I nodded. 'Cabal and I will leave as soon as we can.'

In twos and threes, the crowd stepped out into the night, the restless children sleeping now on the shoulders of their fathers and the old ones plodding arm in arm along the stony path.

I asked Olaf to stay behind.

When he and I were the only ones left, I closed the door behind us. While I threw some more logs on the fire, Olaf walked over to the pillars. He rapped his knuckles against each one, as if to summon out whatever lived inside. Then he turned and smiled at me. 'I wonder if I can guess what you want.'

'I expect you can,' I sat down by the fire and warmed my hands before the crackling wood.

He knotted his hands behind his back and began to pace in front of me. 'It seems to me you are out of luck.'

'Are we?' I asked.

He spun around to face me. 'Yes, you are. You, in particular, are out of luck.'

'Are you going to sail the boat for us or not?'

'Gladly. I will take you there and bring you safely back again. Is that what you want to hear?'

'Yes,' I said cautiously, watching him over the tops of the flames.

'What I have to say next, you might not want to hear, but you had better listen anyway.'

'Think carefully before you speak, Olaf. At this moment, we might not be the friends we used to be, but we are not enemies, either. Do not alter that if you can help it.'

'At this moment, whether we are friends or enemies is of no consequence to me,' he said. 'As soon as I have brought you back, you will hand over the temple, saying only that you have had a change of heart.'

I breathed out, shifting the smoke. 'And if I refuse?'

'Then you will watch everything you have done for this

town, and everything you dreamed of doing, vanish under the floorboards of a Christian church. I told you this was not over, and I told you I would not give up. I have endured a life of ridicule from the people of Altvik because I have never stopped believing that I deserved what I am now going to get. I have waited too long for this chance, and I am not going to wait for another.'

A darkness was moving across my mind, like the shadow of a cloud across a field. 'Olaf,' I said, 'What you want, you will not find by doing this.'

'From now on, I decide what I want!' he shouted. 'Now leave! You do not belong here any more.'

I found Cabal waiting for me halfway down the hill.

He was standing on a rock, wrapped in his cloak, which whipped around his legs with a sound like the beating of wings.

It took me a moment to chase from my mind the image of Greycloak. Time and again over the years, I had returned to the memory of myself as I ran out after him, into the crashing jaws of the storm. I would wake from a dead sleep, calling out to myself to stop, to turn back before it was too late, but my old self never heard. It scrambled on until it disappeared into the lightning's roaring fire.

'What did he say?' asked Cabal.

I told him what had happened.

Cabal stared up at the temple, where a sliver of orange firelight flickered through the half-open door. The rest of the temple was hidden in such darkness that the fire seemed to be standing by itself, an almost human shape.

'Tell him we have agreed,' said Cabal.

I knew what he was thinking. Olaf would bring us there and back, but he would never live to set foot in this town again.

Cabal would snap Olaf's neck like a piece of kindling wood. Then Cabal would feed him to the fish.

'You hesitate,' said Cabal.

'Of course I hesitate,' I replied. 'I have known him since we were children, and even if I despise what he is doing, I cannot help but understand his reasons.'

'The time for reasoning is past,' snapped Cabal. 'From this point onwards, we owe him nothing, not even his life.' He jumped down from the rock and set one huge, blunt finger against my chest. 'The man I knew in Miklagard would not have hesitated even for a moment.'

'I am not that same man, anymore.'

'Even so, the purpose of your voyage home is still the same. You can no more let him steal from you what is yours by right than we can let these Christians steal what little wealth these peope here possess. Even if you try to forget who we were in the Varangian, you cannot forget the codes by which we lived. Those belong to the present as much as they do to the past.'

I stared at the ground, wrapped in silence. Then I raised my head and looked him in the eye. 'Why would you lead us in a raid against your own people?' I asked.

Cabal gave no answer. All he said was, 'Think no more about it. This is as good as done.' Then he set off down the hill.

I stood there, alone in the dark. I though about Olaf. In my mind, he was already dead. I imagined his pale and lifeless face, sinking to the bottom of the sea.

Morning fog drifted across the beach, smelling of seaweed and rain.

Olaf, Cabal and I loaded water barrels into the rowboat.

Cabal made no sign that he knew about the deal Olaf had made. There was almost a gentleness in the way Cabal spoke with him now, the way a condemned man is spoken to, with old grudges set aside as he prepares for the last journey of his life.

Olaf himself was quick to smile as he lifted the barrels from the sand and set them in the boat.

We realised that there were not enough weapons even for the three of us. My sword now belonged to that Bulgar trader. Olaf had no shield and his sword was better suited to measuring cloth than swinging in a fight. Only Cabal was fully armed, with an axe, sword, spear and his round, white-painted shield.

Olaf brushed aside our concerns. 'Hakon will come with me this afternoon, and I will return with all the weaponry we need.'

The first sign of anyone stirring in the town was the creak and thump of the alehouse door as it opened and closed. I knew it was Ingolf without even turning to look, as the door had such a particular sound, like that of a weary person trying to get up out of a chair. Then came Ingolf's heavy footsteps and the slap of the leather apron against his knees. He carried an old sword in a wooden scabbard, one of his purchases from Olaf. 'Here I am,' he said.

'What of it?' Cabal sat against the rowboat, one heavy leather bag in each hand. The bags were filled with salt, for seasoning food on the trip.

'I will come with you.' Ingolf patted the scabbard. 'I am ready to go.'

'And you have been training?' Cabal nodded at the flimsy sword.

'I know enough,' said Ingolf.

'Draw it then,' said Cabal.

'What?' he asked, his face turning pale. 'The sword? Now?'

'Now,' whispered Cabal.

Ingolf set his hand on the hilt and began to draw the blade.

But the sword had not left its scabbard before Cabal swung one of the salt bags into the left side of Ingolf's head.

Ingolf tilted over, the sword wobbling out of his grip. He was on his way down when the other salt bag thumped into his right cheek. For a moment it looked as if Ingolf had steadied himself again. But then he collapsed and lay at Cabal's feet.

We all stared down at Ingolf in wordless disappointment.

Ingolf groaned and sat up. He lifted his apron and pressed his face against it, and when he let it drop again, the soggy imprint of his cheeks and forehead were smudged into the leather. 'What happened?' he asked.

'You fell over,' said Cabal. 'Eventually.'

Ingolf climbed slowly to his feet. 'Let me come along. What do I have to look forward to for the rest of my life except making ale and wiping those wretched tables fifty times a day? I cannot stay here doing nothing.'

'What do you have to look forward to?' Cabal slung the salt

208

bags into the bow of the boat. 'Old age! To throw away your life proves nothing. Take some advice and stay home.'

'Ingolf,' I said, 'Cabal is right. Give up the alehouse if you cannot stand it anymore, but do not give up your life.'

Ingolf rubbed the side of his head, where the salt bags had slapped against his temples. 'I told her I was coming,' he said.

We did not need to ask who he was talking about.

Ingolf sighed heavily. 'At least promise me you will talk about it.'

'We will talk,' said Olaf, and patted him gently on the back.

When Ingolf had gone, Olaf turned to Cabal and me. 'Is there anything to say?'

We shook our heads.

'Then here he stays, but that old witch who calls herself his mother will never let him hear the end of this,' said Olaf. The muscles of his jaw flinched with anger as he spoke.

Olaf and Cabal shoved the skiff out into the bay and rowed towards the Drakkar. All that could be seen of them above the fog was their heads. Their muttering voices reached across the morning mist.

While they were out at the Drakkar, Tola came down to the beach.

I was coiling a length of walrus-hide rope. 'What is it, Tola?'

'The things I said . . .' She pressed her hand against her mouth and slid her fingers down over her lips. 'I never thought he would ask to come along. He is not a brave man. You cannot let him go.'

I straightened up. 'Why not?'

'He will get himself killed.' Her voice was weak and hoarse.

'There is that possibility.' It was all I could do not to spit in her face.

She moaned. 'You would risk the life of a friend just to spite me?'

'There are several lives at risk.'

'I love him. I know it does not always show –'

I cut her off. 'No, it does not show.'

She jabbed her finger at me, sudden anger in place of her sadness. 'If he goes, you will be responsible for him! I will hold you to it.'

I stepped forward, crowding her space. 'But you are responsible for his asking to come with us, and I will hold you to that.'

She walked away sobbing.

I was not going to say anything else to her, but then I changed my mind and called her back. 'If I tell him to stay,' I began.

'Please!' She held her clawed and begging hands beside her face. 'Please do not bring him with you.'

'You will never mention it,' I said.

Slowly, she lowered her hands. 'Never,' she said quietly.

'Nor will you humiliate him again in front of the whole town,' I said in a low voice. 'Do you not see? He would rather die than go on living like that. Can you not understand how much he loves you and how much he hates you as well?'

'Yes,' she whispered.

'Promise me, Tola.'

She nodded, then she sniffed and swallowed.

I began to coil the rope again.

She opened her mouth to speak.

'Go now,' I said, and turned away.

Later that morning, Olaf and I sailed out of the bay, then turned south, hugging the shore.

He did not say where we were going, but there was no need for me to ask. We soon sighted the cove in which he had watched the raiders land all those years ago. Then we lowered our sail, dropped anchor and rowed ashore.

Olaf was nervous as we walked up the shingle beach. At the

high-tide line, dried seaweed, crumpled and black, lay tangled in amongst old sea shells, twisted driftwood and the empty armor of dead crabs. 'This is where it happened,' he said, almost whispering, as if afraid someone would overhear us.

I wondered how many nights the grey faces of the dead had lunged at him from the darkness of his sleep, stalking him across the years.

Under the canopy of pines, the bones of the raiders were still lying on the ground. Even though they were green with mould and cracked from age, I had not imagined they would be so well-preserved. There were even fragments of clothing and curled and brittle shreds of leather from their shoes. In silence, we walked among the slender ribs, the scattered dice of spine and hooped bones of pelvises.

I thought about the bears that had done this. I wondered if they still lived here. There were bears in these hills, but they were rarely seen these days. Sometimes, in the early summer, older males would chase the younger ones down from the high ground. I had seen them lumbering across the grazing fields, their fur dark brown or silvery or black, rarely the same colour twice. Sometimes they would rise up on their hind legs and sniff the wind. That was when you could see how big they really were.

In the gloomy green light which sifted down through the trees, Olaf found the place where he had stashed the weapons. We pulled aside the rocks and uncovered the swords and armour sheathed in spiders' webs. We sorted out the things we could still use, smearing our hands with decades of grime.

The wooden shields had rotted, as had the leather-wrapped wood of the sword scabbards, but the sword blades inside them were in fair shape. The helmets and chain-mail vests seemed usable once we had shaken them out, showering our feet with flecks of rust.

As I lifted the swords and handed them to Olaf, I realised my hands were shaking. A memory had returned, of myself on that other raider's ship. I felt a sudden rage take hold of me. In the madness that it brought, I wanted to conjure these men back to life, to bind their rotten skeletons with ribbons of vein and slippery knots of muscle, to jam new eyes into their hollow heads and pour the blood back down their throats until their hearts gasped into motion. Then I would kill them all over again, for what they had done to Olaf's childhood and to mine.

When we returned to Altvik, we handed over the gear to Guthrun, who made no comment about where we had found these things. Either he already knew, or he was wise enough not to ask. He resharpened each sword blade, scrubbed off the rust with a mixture of oil and sand, then removed the old leather and wire wrapping from around the handle, replacing it with simple leather cord.

Olaf chose a sword with a winding pattern of serpents and vines on the hilt.

I took one of simpler but more sturdy construction. Then I brought down my chain-mail vest from its hook by the door, as well as my old shield and spear. After tipping out a bat who had been living in the hollow of the boss, I wiped off the dust and painted over the white paint with red.

Cabal did the same with his.

We looked at the shields, the paint still shining wet, drops of it stretching from the rims, then breaking and splashing on the ground in tiny bloody sunbursts.

'It is no good painting those things white,' said Cabal. 'They always end up red again.'

Later in the day, I headed down towards the beach, carrying Cabal's gear as well as my own. We would leave on the outgoing tide. On the way, I stopped off at Kari's house, knowing that Cabal would be there.

I found them standing on the doorstep, arms wrapped around each other.

'It is time to go,' I told Cabal.

Slowly, he released her and stepped back.

I handed Cabal his weapons and his shield.

'Look at you now,' she said to us. 'I thought you had left your pasts behind you.'

'We thought so, too,' I said, 'but they caught up with us again.'

'None of this will have been worth it if a single life is lost,' she pleaded.

'And if we do not take the risk,' replied Cabal, 'how many lives will we lose later in the name of Jesus Christ?'

Kari saw that it was no use arguing. 'Promise me you will look after each other. I have already lost you once,' she told me. Then, turning to Cabal, she said, 'And you I could not stand to lose at all.'

Despite what she said, there was a blankness in her her expression, a sadness beyond tears which told me that she did not expect to see either of us again. The happiness, which had only just begun to seem permanent, now took on the blur of an illusion. Even as she implored us to take care and to come home, we were already freezing in her mind into a thing which belonged in the past and only and forever in the past.

It was evening when we left town. We ran up the sail. Its belly filled with the breeze and ropes creaked as they drew taut. The walrus at our bow nudged out into the open ocean. Soon I felt the familiar yielding of the boards under my feet as the deep-sea waves slid by beneath us.

Our shields hung along the outside, strapped to the oar ports. Sea spray cut across them, beading on the new paint.

I checked the bearing dial, while Olaf stood beside me at the tiller.

Cabal watched the land vanish slowly into the water, colour draining from his face as he lost sight of the Grimsvoss mountains. He turned to me and smiled weakly, lips pinched bloodlessly together. A few minutes later, with the motion of the water churning in his stomach, he roared his guts into the waves, hands white-knuckled on the rim of the boat.

Olaf and I shook our heads. The ocean had already set its rhythm in our bodies.

We sailed hard with a leading wind, south by south west as Cabal had told us. At night, we hauled the spare sail over the bow to make a canopy, then took turns sleeping beneath it.

For two days, Cabal lay curled up under sea-sprayed blankets, hungry but too sick to eat. Now and then, he lolled his head over the side and streaked the warshields with his retching.

When it was time for a meal, I would join Olaf at the steerboard, handing him slabs of bread with dried meat and cheese on them. We drank rain that poured in rivulets from the steerboard arm, or scooped our wooden mugs into the casks we had brought on board.

Olaf could not hide his happiness at the reward which he thought was waiting for him once we reached Altvik again. 'I only want to show you, and everyone else, that Tostig made a mistake. The opportunity was not given to me, so I was forced to take it. I will see to it that you are provided for. You will be welcome to work for me once things are settled.' He slapped me on the shoulder. 'You will not go hungry, I promise!'

I played along and smiled, but inside I felt so cold it was as if every vein in my body had turned into branches of red glass.

On the morning of the third day, Cabal announced that he was well again. He more than made up for the food he had

missed with the huge portions he devoured now. Then he
stood at the bow, riding the waves, as if to smell the English
coast approaching.

'We are coming to a stormy sea,' he told us. He had many
names for the wind which I had never heard before. The damp
and gentle breeze which came in from the east he called the
Cigfran. If it blew from the west, he called it Heligog. A southern wind was Morfran.

I found myself trying to memorise these new words, as if
knowing their names might help me to control them.

The wind to fear, Cabal said, was from the north, the Arador,
which ploughed the sea into a frenzy so relentless that you
could not sail into it, nor reef your sail and ride it out. The only
thing you could do was to slacken sail and run with it as far as
it would take you, then hope you could find your way home
when the wind let up. 'The Arador is alive,' he said.

'What do you mean?' I asked.

'I mean it is alive, like you and me. It has a voice. I have
heard it.' Cabal looked around, as if he heard it still, like the
beating of wings above our heads.

Olaf and I looked at each other and shuddered.

The clouds thinned out. A vault of palest blue enclosed us.
The waves looked soupy green. Clouds gathered on the horizon, flattened on the bottom and rising to a great height in
huge bubbling plumes, showing that land was near.

A nervousness spread through us. Even the Drakkar seemed
to wake from its years of sleepy trading runs to the purpose for
which it had been built.

In the distance to the west, we saw pale cliffs of chalk rising
from the water. We rounded these cliffs, staying as far out to
sea as we could while still keeping them in sight, and headed
west along the southern flank of England.

For another three days, we cruised along the English coast,

then headed north into the stormy seas about which Cabal had spoken. We were close now, passing long beaches with high grey cliffs, beyond which stretched fields of heather and bracken.

Cabal prepared his weapons. The grating sound of a blade over a sharpening stone cast me back into the Varangian compound during the long afternoons of preparing for the Emperor's inspection.

At first light of the following morning, we came in sight of Cabal's country, which he called Cymru. It seemed to hover on a plateau of haze, as if the land had come loose of its anchor to the world and was riding towards us faster than we were moving towards it.

Close to shore we jibed and dropped the sail. There were no houses on this stretch of coast. Broad beaches ended in waves of dunes and rock. The land beyond rose gently, dotted with yellow buds of gorse.

Cabal turned to me. 'We will wait until dark,' he said. 'Then you and I can go in and look around.'

It took forever for the sun to run its course.

When the first stars pocked the sky, we lowered our rowboat over the side. I climbed in and took the oars, while Cabal sat in the stern. The shield slung across his back made him look like a giant turtle.

Olaf pushed us off with his heel. 'Come back safely,' he said. And then he added, 'Both of you.'

I started towards land, digging the oarblades deep and watching the whirlpools of my strokes spin away into the grey-green sea. Ahead, the rumble of the surf was deafening.

On the Drakkar, Olaf's face blurred in the mist. The walrus skull nodded with the rising, falling waves. It seemed to be laughing at us.

'It is a shame,' said Cabal.

216

'What is?' I asked.

'That I have begun to see his better side.'

As we neared the breakers, I turned the boat broadside, so that I could watch how the waves were going in. When I stowed the oars, cold water ran down the wooden handles until it reached my hands. Through the spray I could make out the grey-white collar of surf along the shore and, beyond it, dunes patched with tall grass. Having studied the waves, I set the oars again and spun the boat around. I rowed hard, coasting in on a breaker which brought us up onto the beach.

We jumped out and hauled the heavy boat into the dunes. By the time we had the boat clear of the water, our feet were caked in sand and we were sweating hard.

We agreed that Cabal would go inland alone, and I would wait here with the boat. A Celt would not arouse suspicion, but news of a Norseman would spread quickly. There were plenty of Norsemen in Ireland, both Danes and Norwegians, and even a few settlements on this coast, said Cabal. The sight of them was rarely good news for Cabal's people, who were known as the Cymry.

I handed him his sword.

'Better off without it,' he said, and scrambled up over the dunes, running across the open ground towards the woods. He reached the wall of trees, then ducked into the shadows and disappeared.

I wondered if I would ever see him again.

While waiting, I gathered driftwood and dune grass, laying it across the rowboat to hide the shape. The incoming tide swept away our footsteps and the keel line of our boat. It was a cloudy day, the air warm and damp. I took my spear from the boat, walked down the beach, and found myself a hollow in the dunes which was sheltered from the wind. I could stick my head up from time to time and see if anyone was coming.

217

I found it hard work just sitting there all day, wandering in and out of my past like a man lost in a house with too many rooms.

There was no sunset, only a faint but steady dimming of the light. The white slicks of breaking waves glowed strangely in the dusk. Mist rolled in from the sea. The colours bled away to grey and then to black. I wrapped my cloak around me and drew my knees up to my chest.

When night fell, I saw a figure moving without sound through the woods a short distance away, hunched over as if the darkness were a weight upon its back. Every few paces it stopped and raised its head, sniffing the wind like an animal hunting for a scent.

I could not tell if it was Cabal and it was too much of a risk to call out his name. I stared back into the darkness, to see if he was being followed, but could only make out the silhouettes of wind-blown trees shifting in the woods.

The figure was at the dunes now. He vanished over the humped sand and was gone.

I moved towards him, creeping through the grass. As I reached the crest of a dune, something suddenly rose up in front of me.

It was Cabal, leaping through the air, trailing sand from his heels as if his feet were burning. His fingers were spread like claws, ready to choke the life out of me. For a moment, it was as if he had forgotten who I was, but then he smiled and lowered his hands.

'Did you find out anything?' I slapped the damp sand off my shoulders.

'St. David's is just up the coast, less than a day's sailing.'

There was nothing to do now but wait for Olaf to return. We huddled in our damp clothes, back to back in a pocket in the dunes. The wind picked up and blew a steady hiss of sand off the lip of the dune, until it powdered every wrinkle of our bodies.

'There is a cross in that church,' said Cabal. His face was a mask of sand, as if he were a stone which had been conjured into life. 'A gold cross. I want it.'

'To melt it down?' I asked.

Cabal shook his head, then closed his eyes. In that moment, he became a stone again.

I wanted to ask him what was so special about this cross, but it was too cold for talk. I pulled my cloak more tightly around me and clenched my jaw to stop my teeth from clattering together.

Our huddled forms reminded me of an old man we once found frozen in the mountains of Askhazi. He was kneeling beside a dead horse, one hand held against his forehead and the other still gripping the horse's bridle. He must have lost his way in the mountains and ridden the horse too hard trying to find his way down. He wore a look of concentration on his ice-hard face, as if he were still trying to remember the way home. If someone had stumbled across us now, half-buried in the sand, they would have thought us just as lost as that old man, and just as dead.

At dawn, we spotted the Drakkar. It rolled in the swells beyond the breakers. Immediately, we dragged our boat down to the water and rowed out to join Olaf.

In the Drakkar, we tacked north along the coast, keeping close to shore. Through the spray and breaking waves, we saw sheep grazing in fields which had been cleared down to the water.

Blue sky appeared through the clouds, like the glimmer of old ice deep in the heart of a glacier.

It was close to midday when Cabal spotted the river mouth. Its course was well hidden, unfolding almost imperceptibly from trees and mudflats on the banks. The safest plan would have been to wait until dark, but Cabal told us it would not be possible to navigate from the ocean into the river at night, because we would never find the channel. The only way was to head in now and hide along the bank, waiting for darkness before we made our way into the town on foot. At dawn the following day, we would move out to sea again before the Cymry noticed anything was missing.

We hauled in the salt-crusted shields and laid our weapons on the deck.

Now, if we were spotted, we could pretend to be traders who

had lost our way. Then we would leave for open water as quickly as we could.

Cabal and I took up the oars and rowed with the incoming tide into the estuary. Even in daylight, we were lucky to find the channel. The route was so narrow that Olaf had to keep lashing the tiller in place, running to the bow, so he could tell which way to turn, then running back to the tiller. Several times, the steerboard dragged in the mud and threatened to strand us, but each time the force of our momentum carried us through.

The first trees slid by as the roar of the ocean faded behind us. The round leaves of poplars flickered in the breeze and willows trailed their sinewy branches in the water. A few houses stood on the high ground. Their roofs were thatched instead of turfed, like the houses of the Norse. It was still very early in the morning, and so far there was no sign of people.

Soon after that, just as we were growing confident, our luck ran out for good.

Olaf spotted a bearded man on a horse, silhouetted on a rise. The rider sat straight-backed and dignified, watching us drift by.

'Wave to him,' whispered Cabal.

Rowing-reddened palms were raised in greeting.

The man held up one hand, then tugged at the horse's reins and rode down the field towards us. He did not look afraid, but held the reins loose, letting his body sway with the motion of the horse's steps. It was a big, heavy-shouldered animal, not like the short-legged and long-maned ponies that we knew. I had seen horses like this down in Miklagard, plated with armour and hideous in their battle-masks.

When he reached the bank, the man reined in his horse, cupped his hands to his mouth and called to us.

Cabal hauled in his oar and began a shouted conversation.

221

While we drifted with the current, the man rode his horse lazily, keeping pace with us. With only one ship and such a small crew, not to mention one that spoke his language, it was clear he saw no danger in our presence.

The conversation finished and the bearded man rode off, his horse's hooves digging up clumps of the soft grass as it galloped up the hill.

'If we start now,' I said, 'we can be out to sea before they realise we are gone.'

'No!' barked Cabal. 'I told him we had come to trade, and he wanted to know what cargo we were carrying. I said we had amber and whale oil and Frankish cloth, all things they want to get their hands on. That is the reason for his haste. The merchants of the village will turn out to meet us when we arrive.' He was sweating and his eyes were wild again, as they had been on the night Brand died. 'We can tie up the boat here and go in on foot. They will be expecting us to come up the river, but I can get us to the church along a back road. By the time they figure out why we are here, we can be back at the boat and on our way again. We will not be able to hide ourselves, but we will not have to if we go in now.'

'What about the silver?' asked Olaf. 'That is a heavy load to carry, and it would be easy to spot us in daylight.'

'We can steal some horses if we have to,' said Cabal. 'It will take them time to collect their weapons and launch an attack. By then we will be out to sea again.'

I glanced at Olaf, uncertain how we should proceed.

'If Cabal says we can do it,' he told me, 'then I think we should keep going.' Despite what Olaf had said, his face was grey with worry.

'So it is settled,' murmured Cabal.

Olaf and I nodded, to show that we agreed.

Around the next bend, we pulled in and tied up to the wil-

222

lows. Mosquitoes whined drunkenly around us. Watery green light filtered through the branches overhead. We picked up our weapons and climbed onto the bank.

'Olaf,' I said. 'You stay with the boat.'

He was staring at a puddle, where a water beetle scudded jerkily across the surface, its legs making minute dimples in the muddy water. He looked as if he might collapse under the weight of his chain mail vest.

'Olaf,' I said again.

His head jerked up. 'I am ready,' he croaked.

'Stay with the boat,' I told him.

He was silent for a moment, as the words sank in, but then he breathed in suddenly. 'Do you think I cannot pull my weight?'

'Someone has to stay with the boat,' said Cabal. 'You are the one who knows best how to sail it.'

Now Olaf understood that there was no shame in remaining behind. He nodded and, without another word, stepped back onto the Drakkar.

Cabal and I agreed to meet back here in case we were split up. Without the dark to hide us, there could be no stopping until we were on our way out to sea again. We set off through the trees, heading uphill towards a ridge where the ground levelled out.

Cabal raced ahead, muscles jolting in his calves and his chain mail shirt swishing as he moved. He was making for a white, dusty-looking road which ran along the top of the ridge.

My heart was sloshing and my face burned as I ran up the slope. I heard a shout, then saw the horse and rider galloping from the direction of the town. It was the same black-bearded man. He called to us with friendly urgency, no doubt to let us know that we had moored our boat in the wrong place and thinking we must have misunderstood him. He left the road, ducking low against the horse's neck to avoid the tree branches. Leaves brushed across his back.

He was just raising himself back up in the saddle when he caught sight of our warshields and drawn swords. He cried out and tried to rein in the horse, clanking the bit against the animal's teeth, but the horse had gathered too much speed. On the soft grass of this downhill slope, it could not stop. Fear had spread across the rider's face, like a shadow from beneath the skin. He never even saw Cabal's axe, which looped once and struck him square in the forehead. The man was lifted from his horse and landed hard on his back, already dead by the time he hit the ground.

The horse galloped away along the riverbank.

Without breaking stride, Cabal's arms swung down, grabbed the handle of his axe and prised it loose.

At the top of the ridge, we spilled from the shadows into the chalky light which glared up from the road. The shallow ditches were speckled with white elderflowers and pink foxgloves. Sculpted clouds marched past above us, frosting the deep-blue sky.

We carried on towards the town, hard going with the shields and chain mail vests, which chafed across our chests and shoulderblades. A short while later, we came to a dip in the road, beyond which lay the village of St David's, the slate-scaled roof of the spireless church clearly visible above the other houses.

Just then, a donkey and cart driven by an old man appeared over the rise. Pale green cabbages jostled in the back of the cart as it rolled across the uneven road. The old man was so shocked to see us that he dropped the reins. The donkey slowed and came to a stop at the bottom of the slope. The old man bent over, struggling to reach the reins where they dangled down to the ground. At last he had hold of them and sat upright, but by then we were almost on top of him. There was nothing he could do. He closed his eyes, clasped his hands together and held the reins against his chest.

I ran past the cart on one side. Cabal went on the other. The donkey watched us, sad and patient.

From the corner of my eye, I saw Cabal's body disapppear in a blur. At first, I thought he had been hit by something. But when I turned my head to look, I understood that Cabal had drawn his sword and spun himself about, even as he was running, moving with such force and speed that I only glimpsed a single frozen picture. The blade of Cabal's sword had passed through the neck of the old man, and his head, suspended in the air above his body, had flipped completely upside down. The old man's hands still clasped the reins against his chest.

As soon as we were past the cart, I grabbed Cabal's arm and wheeled him around to face me. 'What harm would he have done us?' I shoved Cabal backwards with the boss of my shield. 'You said no one would be hurt, but now you are killing everyone in your path!'

'If they had not been there,' snarled Cabal, 'they would not have been hurt.'

'What did they do to you, Cabal? Why do you hate them so much?'

He gave me no answer, but pushed past me and charged onwards, footsteps kicking up pale dust as he sprinted up the hill.

From now until the fighting ended, I knew there could be no reasoning with Cabal, because he was not Cabal any more. Instead he was that creature summoned from the shadows in himself.

For a moment, I stood there in the road, watching as the donkey set off to wherever it was going, hauling its load of cabbages with a headless man holding the reins.

It was the sound of a woman's scream which brought me to my senses. Then dogs began to bark. I knew that Cabal had reached the outskirts of the village. I sprinted to catch up with him, and we moved along the narrow, dirt-paved streets. Houses loomed on either side. We passed women with baskets and a cluster of boys gathered around some game drawn in the dust. They scattered as soon as they saw us. Dogs barked from the safety of the side streets. Their dirty hackles stood on end, bodies trembling with rage, but they did not come out to attack us.

We reached a graveyard of cross-topped stones, which was enclosed by a low stone wall. Beyond that lay the church and village square. Through sweat which trickled into my eyes, I saw men and women setting up tables and laying out trade goods for the arrival of our boat. A few had paused and looked in our direction, but so far, none of them seemed to have understood what was happening.

'There it is,' said Cabal, nodding at the arched doors of the church, whose heavy wooden planks were strapped with iron.

While I crouched behind the churchyard wall, Cabal ran up the stone steps of the church. They were worn down like the back of an old horse from years of use. Cabal tugged at the latch ring, which rattled heavily but would not budge. The doors were locked. Shielding his eyes from the sun, he peered into the gap between the two doors, then turned and walked back down the steps.

'Hurry!' I whispered. 'Hurry!'

It wouldn't be long before this whole village went mad.

Cabal faced the door. He raised his arm, swinging his axe high above his head. He bared his teeth and jumped forward, sprinting up the steps, and swung the axe at the gap between the two rings of the door. The axe head disappeared in a spray of sparks and the clank of iron on iron. The shaft of the axe snapped off the head. It seemed to have done no good at all, but then Cabal rammed his shoulder against the doors. This time, they swung wide, dumping him onto his knees in the doorway of the church. The doors banged loudly as they crashed against the stone walls inside. A moment later, the faint odour of sandalwood incense drifted past.

I heard a rumbling noise and turned to see a man rolling an ale barrel down an alleyway towards the market square. The man saw us and stopped. He stared, trying to fathom what was going on. Then, as the truth began to dawn on him, his eyes grew wide. He turned and ran, leaving the barrel to roll on by itself, across the cobble-stone square and past it, down a stretch of grass which sloped towards the river.

The merchants stood, arms filled with pots and bundles of cloth, watching the barrel as it picked up speed, then bounced and split. Ale fanned out in a bubbling hiss over the grass.

The merchants turned to stare at Cabal, who stood at the entrance to the church.

The only sound was the faint rustle of the ale as it sifted away into the ground.

Then Cabal raised his shield and sword, as if he meant to fly. He howled at the merchants in one long bellowing scream until his lungs were empty.

The whole village was suddenly filled with the crash of dropped crockery and pots. People ran in all directions, some of them right past us, as if they had forgotten we were there. Others headed down towards the river. They ran the way people sometimes run from thunder, with no idea where to go, running only to get away.

Cabal shouted for me to follow him.

As I ducked out from behind the wall towards the steps, shield held close against my chest, one man ran straight into me. He knocked his head against the boss of the shield and fell back unconscious.

When I reached the doorway to the church, I glanced out across the square and down towards the river. People were swimming across it. The long dresses of women billowed in the murky water. Bright green weeds were tangled in their hair. One woman already stood on the far bank, wet clothes moulded to her body and limp hair snaking across her shoulders. Against the dark undergrowth, her white form seemed to glow as if she was on fire.

I ducked into the church and my eyes struggled to adjust to the dark. It was damp and cold inside. Rows of benches trailed away into the gloom. The altar table stood on a raised stone platform at the end of the room. The table had been pushed aside, revealing a heavy wooden trap-door in the stone floor. The trap door was open.

'There!' shouted Cabal, 'There it is!'

Just then, I saw a figure clad in a brown robe. It was a priest. The top of his head was shaved, leaving a ring of hair round the edge of his skull. He popped up from the hole, glanced at us, then grabbed the trapdoor handle and pulled it down over him. Wood clanked against stone as it slammed shut.

We ran to the altar platform and clawed our fingers around the edges of the door, but the fit was tight and there were no handles.

'The tunnel is down there.' Cabal drew his sword and worked the blade into the crack between the wood and stone. A moment later the sword snapped with a strange musical clank and Cabal fell back cursing.

I heard a noise behind us and turned to see a movement back among the benches. I ran down the aisle and found another priest, cowering behind the seats.

I hauled him up by the scruff of his thick robe and dragged him over to the altar.

Cabal barked a question in his face.

The man shook his head.

Now Cabal grabbed him by the neck and forced him down to his knees, bending his head over the trap door. Again he shouted the question and once more the priest shook his head. Cabal slammed the priest's face against the trap door, then wrenched him to his feet and shouted in his ear.

The priest moaned and held one hand against his nose, blood pouring between his fingers. With the other hand, he pointed to a gap in the stone where the floor of the platform met the wall.

Cabal went over to the gap and drew out a long metal rod, almost as long as my arm, with a loop at the end. He dropped it in front of the priest, who slowly picked it up and pointed the end of the rod at a tiny hole in the stone at the base of the platform. He was crying now, as he tapped the iron rod weakly around the edge of the hole.

Cabal snatched the rod out of the priest's hands and slid it into the hole until we heard a clunk. One end of the door popped up just enough that we could get our fingers under it.

I lifted the door and looked down a flight of narrow steps, lit by a torch placed in a metal holder. I went down first, grabbed the torch and waited for Cabal to follow. But there was no sign of him. I called his name, and when he still did not appear, I climbed back up the steps to see what had happened to him.

Cabal was talking to the priest in a low voice, his fist bunched in the priest's heavy brown robe. I thought he was going to let the man go, but then Cabal picked him up and with a roaring bellow heaved him through one of the stained-glass windows. The panes smashed out around the frail, cloaked figure of the priest, filling the room with glittering greens and browns and reds as the sun flickered through the flying glass. Then came the thump of the priest's body when it struck the

229

ground. After a pause, I was surprised to hear the sound of his footsteps running away among the gravestones.

We clambered down the staircase into the tunnel and Cabal followed me as I ran into the darkness, carrying the torch. In the sandy ground were imprints of sandalled footsteps and the drag marks of what must have been the chest. The ceiling of the tunnel was low and the walls were narrow. We ran hunched over and the rustling chorus of our breathing returned to us from the walls of rock and earth which passed by as if they were moving and not us. In places, the walls were wet and sparkling with crystals, which looked like the eyes of thousands of insects. The rest of the passage was dry and dusty, marked by the tools which had carved it out. Flakes of ash, thrown down by the torch, singed my hair.

Suddenly, from down the tunnel came the glow of another torch.

We skidded to a stop.

My heart was beating in my throat.

Cabal leaned over my shoulder and brought his face close to mine. When he spoke, his voice was soft, like the voice of a lover. 'Kill them all,' he said.

We ran through the tunnel. Our torch scraped along the tunnel roof, sending down a rain of dirt and sparks.

The walls seemed to be narrowing. Ice-white crystals blistered on the walls. Darkness rushed behind us like a silent wave, and I felt panic closing in on me. The tunnel veered to the left and when I rounded the corner, I saw something that even my worst nightmares could not have invented.

It was a wall of human skulls.

I cried out and Cabal skidded into the back of me.

By the light of the torch, we stared at the dozens of black-gaping eye-sockets, the hundreds of bared teeth and lightning-jagged cracks which snaked across the craniums. The skulls were placed in careful rows, one beside the other, filling an alcove carved into the wall of the tunnel.

There was no time to stop, or even to wonder what kind of people would do this and why. We kept moving. Oily darkness swallowed the grotesquely sorted dead.

A little further on, we reached the source of the light we had seen earlier. A priest was trying to drag a heavy chest along the passageway. Lying on top of the chest was a large cross made of gold, studded with rubies and emeralds. With one hand, the priest gripped the leather side-strap of the chest. With the other, he held up a torch, whose light winked off the jewels which were set into the cross. The old man was exhausted. Sweat darkened his robe and gleamed on his face.

We bore down on him along the gullet of the tunnel in an avalanche of chain-mail armour, shields and knives.

When the priest saw us, he dropped his torch and knelt before us, holding up his empty hands. 'Brothers!' he called to us in Norse.

We stopped before him, gasping for breath, caught off-guard by the fact that he could speak my language.

The man rose cautiously to his feet. Grey hair, like iron filings, flecked the darker strands around the edge of his half-shaved head. 'I am your firned,' he said. 'I have lived among you as a missionary to the court of Harald Bluetooth. I converted many hundreds of your countrymen who had been blind to the mercy of God before I reached their shores.' He pointed at the trunk. 'The contents of this chest belong to God. Only to God.'

'It belongs to us now.' Cabal's voice bounced off the walls, where crystals frothed like frog-spawn from the rock. 'Do you not remember me, Ethelred?'

The priest stared at Cabal. Slowly, he narrowed his eyes. 'How do you know my name? And remember you? From where?'

'From the ground above our heads!' snarled Cabal. 'You do not remember me, who carried this cross for you so many times? The one you taught about your Christian hell and then forced him to live in it?'

'Cabal?' The man reached out, fingers pale and twitching.

Cabal slapped them aside. 'That same hand beat me senseless more times than I can count. And worse! The things you did to me and called it love.'

Now I began to understand the source of Cabal's hate, so terrible to him he could not even speak its name.

'You ran away,' said the priest.

'Of course I ran away! A dog would have run away. And what do you have to say now?'

With careful movements, the old priest moved around to the other side of the trunk, fingers trailing over the cross. 'Take the chest,' he whispered, shrinking from the torch's flame. 'Take everything. It is yours.' He turned and staggered away into the shadows.

Cabal walked after the old man. He did not need to run.

The priest shrieked when he heard the footsteps behind him. The sound sank into the walls.

After only a few paces, Cabal grabbed hold of the priest's hood and hauled it back, knocking the old man off his feet. Then he bent down and set his knee on the man's chest.

'Let me live,' the old man choked. 'God will forgive you.'

'It does not matter if he forgives me,' said Cabal. 'I do not forgive him.'

The old man clawed at Cabal, tearing at his clothes.

Cabal set his hands on either side of the priest's head.

I turned away.

The darkness filled with screams.

When I looked back, Cabal was already on his feet, staring at the dead man. His whole body was trembling. Then he unhooked the latches of the trunk and swung it open.

I expected to be dazzled by the flash of coins, as I had been when I walked into the Emperor's treasure room, so clumped with glittering wealth, heaped to overflowing from chests and strewn about so carelessly that the mosaics on the floor could hardly be seen. Instead, here, deep in the crystal-sweating earth, I saw only the dull brown lumps of leather bags.

Cabal fished one up, untied the leather lace which held the

233

mouth closed and poured out a clattering stream of silver and gold coins onto the other bags. 'Now we have what we came for.'

We dragged the chest back to the entrance of the tunnel. I climbed the steps and stuck my head up. The church was empty. I went to the doorway and looked out across the square, which was deserted except for copper pots, broken crockery and the up-ended tables of the merchants. I heard no voices, no footsteps, not even the barking of dogs. The whole town seemed deserted, but it would not be long now before they organised themselves and began to hunt us down.

I could see from the direction of the distant river weeds that the tide was turning. We had to hurry or we would be rowing against the current. Then the Cymry could stop us before we reached the sea.

An overturned cart blocked the alley that led to the square. I jumped down off the wall and turned the cart back onto its wheels. Picking up the two wooden arms for fastening the horse into its traces, I pulled the cart to the foot of the church steps. Cabal and I slid the chest down the steps and heaved it onto the cart. From the weight, we could tell that it contained much more than 120 pounds of silver.

We hauled the cart along the same road we had used to reach the town, its iron-strapped wheels clattering noisily over the hard-packed earth.

We had not gone far when Cabal stopped.

'What is it?' I asked, looking around in case he had seen someone approaching.

'We forgot the cross,' he said.

It was true. I remembered seeing it by the door. 'Too late now,' I told him, wiping the sweat from my face.

'I am not leaving without it,' he said.

'Cabal,' I began, but then I fell silent, knowing it was useless to reason with him. He had waited too long for this day. All that he had endured, and the pain of memories he had carried for so long in silence, were somehow contained in that cross.

'I will catch up in a moment,' he said. 'You go on down the road.'

When I did not move, he gave me a gentle shove. 'Go!' Then he smiled. It was the smile of his old self. 'I am untouchable. Remember?'

Then he ran back towards the town, and I kept moving in the other direction. Going down the slope, I found I could not stop the cart. It was all I could do to keep pace with it, and I was halfway up the other side before I felt again the drag of the cart's weight on my arms.

It was hard to spot the turn-off down to the boat. Just when I was convinced I had passed it, I saw where our footprints had disturbed the tall grass. I ran the cart off the road and into the shade of the trees, then stopped to catch my breath. A warm breeze blew in off a field of barley, just across the road, cooling the sweat on my face. The barley swayed and changed colour, like the sea when clouds are passing overhead.

I pulled the cart down from the ridge, twisting it this way and that around the trees, until I reached the riverbank.

At first, I could not see the boat. Then I noticed it half-hidden by leafy branches which had been cut and thrown across the deck. There was no one on board. I was just about to call out Olaf's name, when he rose from the weeds where he had been hiding up to his neck in the water, with river grass draped over his head.

'What happened to Cabal?' he asked, wiping the mud from his eyes as he climbed up onto the bank.

'He went back for something,' I said. 'A cross.'

'A cross?' His jaw was shaking with cold.

'Just help me get this silver on board.'

'Is there enough?' he asked.

'More than enough.'

Olaf and I set to work loading the silver. Without Cabal, we were unable to lift the trunk from the cart, so we had to move the bags of silver one by one. After throwing them onto the deck of the boat, we moved the empty chest on board, refilled it with the coins and then wedged the chest under one of the rowing benches.

Afterwards, we decided to move the boat to the other side of the river, where it would be safer. We untied the ropes which held us to the willows and drifted across to the other bank, a short distance downstream. We cut some branches and laid them over the deck to hide us. From the shelter of the leafy shadows, I stared at the water sluicing past, dappled with pale green pollen dust. Already the current was growing slack. Soon the tide would ebb and turn against us.

The birds had begun to sing again. A river rat plopped into the water and swam to the other bank, pink paws scrabbling through the weeds. Far above, I saw a flock of small birds, thousands of them, swaying in one dappled mass in the sky.

Suddenly I caught sight of a movement in the trees on the other side. It was no more than a flickering of the leaves, but I knew something was there. I rose to my feet and peered through the screen of branches. The leaves shook again and then I heard a branch crack.

Olaf and I remained motionless, staring dry-eyed at the shadows on the opposite bank.

A shape was weaving its way down towards the water. A bird screeched.

I took up the spear that lay beside me.

Then the shape stepped into view and we realised it was the

236

bearded man's horse. Its bridle trailed on the ground as it pulled up clumps of grass, grinding its teeth together.

We sat back and sighed, fists unclenching from weapons.

A breeze blew in from the ocean, rustling the willow branches.

'The tide is changing. We cannot wait any longer,' said Olaf. His soaked clothes clung to his shivering body. Water dripped from his sleeves.

'He should be here by now,' I replied. 'I had better go and find him.'

'That is too much of a risk,' he said.

I took off my chain-mail vest and laid it in a rustling heap on the deck. My shirt was checkered with the dirty imprint of old iron. 'We cannot leave him here,' I said.

'Then let me go.'

I looked at him in surprise.

'If we do not stick together now,' he said, 'then we deserve whatever fate these people have in mind for us.'

'If you have to,' I told him, 'you can sail home by yourself. That is why you have to stay with the boat. Wait as long as you can, but if we are not back by the time the tide has changed, then you will leave. Do you understand?'

Olaf nodded, his face pale with cold and fear.

I lowered myself into the water and struck out for the opposite bank. It was warm at the top but down below I felt the cool undercurrent, like a second river running underneath the first.

When I reached the muddy bank, I hauled myself up and looked back. The Drakkar was well hidden. Overhanging willow branches swayed in front of the boat. I set off along the river bank, heading for the town. The ground was carpeted with thick grass, glowing emerald in the shady light.

I began to run along the river bank, keeping in the shadow of the willows. Just ahead lay the body of the horseman. A fox was licking the blood from his face. As I passed by, it streaked away in a blur of black and dusty orange.

Through the trees ahead, I saw the rooftops of the town. When I reached the muddy place where people had crossed the river, I began to move up the slope, remaining hidden in the trees until I reached the wall of a house. There, I lay down and crawled to the edge of the building.

Peering around the corner, I saw that a crowd had gathered outside the church. The men in the group were armed, some with longbows taller than themselves and quivers stuffed with arrows. Others carried broadswords. One man carried a huge wooden mallet. It looked as if they were preparing to set out after us.

At the top of the church steps, a priest was shouting at the people who had gathered. I recognised him as the man Cabal had thrown through the window. He was shaking a hammer in the air. In amongst his own language, I heard him say a few words in Latin. 'Libera nos, Domine, furore Normanorum!' Deliver us, O Lord, he was saying, from the fury of the Northman.

Then I saw him lift a torn red blanket up to the door of the church. He held onto a nail and hammered the blanket into place. After several more nails, he stepped back so that the crowd could all see what he had done.

It was then, as the people moved forward, that I saw Cabal's body lying at the base of the steps. He had been stripped and was lying face down. His back was a cloak of blood. He had been flayed, exposing the bones of his ribs and spine. The blanket on the door was his skin.

I crawled behind the wall again. My head was spinning. I had to force myself not to cry out. I pressed my hand against my mouth, muffling the moans which rose from deep inside my lungs.

Looking once more around the corner of the house, I saw that the crowd had begun to disperse. The armed men moved off down the road we had used to enter the village.

Two women took hold of Cabal's feet and together they dragged his body across the square. His face raked on the gravel. Straining, they hauled him down towards the river. Cabal's fingers seemed to claw at the grass, as if trying to stop them from what they were about to do.

They rolled Cabal's body into the water, where it sank but then rose up again.

The women turned to walk back up the hill. Their dresses were splattered with blood.

Before they could spot me, I darted into the trees. Cutting down through the woods until I reached the river, I could hear the men as they advanced along the top of the ridge.

When I saw the boat, I dove into the water and swam across.

Olaf reached out to help me on board.

We glanced at each other. There was nothing to say.

Olaf lashed the tiller in place. It was no use to us now because we were, in effect, moving backwards. He took his place beside me at the rowing benches and we pulled out into the stream. Once we reached the estuary, we could bring the boat around, but there was not enough room here on the narrow river. We rowed hard through the slackening tide on our way towards the open sea.

Shadows of the trees passed over us. As we drew near to the river mouth, the water ran more swiftly. The smell of salt air reached our lungs.

I heard a dull clapping sound and looked up to see an arrow embedded in the mast. Then two more arrows landed in the water, just short of the boat. They sliced under us, trailing chains of silver bubbles.

Above us, on the ridge, men were silhouetted against the

sky. Others appeared on the river bank. I saw the men on the ridge draw their bows, leaning back to give the arrows height, then jerk their bodies forward as they loosed the strings. The arrows seemed to wobble as they climbed, almost pausing as they reached the crest of their flight. Then I lost sight of them against the trees. The next thing I heard was a crack as one of the arrows smacked into my shield, scattering red chips of paint off the wood.

The men drew their bows again. A flock of arrows sailed above the water. With a loud clatter, three of them struck the deck. Others sliced into the water, passing under the boat before rising to the surface again.

The man with a huge wooden mallet emerged from the forest and stood on the bank, waving the strange weapon wildly over his head and bellowing insults.

We were moving quickly now. The men could not keep up with us. We slid around a bend and they fell out of sight. Now there was no sound except the grinding of the oars in the oarlocks.

As I turned my head to wipe the sweat from my face on my sleeve, I saw an arrow sticking out of Olaf's back. But Olaf was still rowing as if nothing had happened to him.

'Olaf,' I said.

He turned to me, bleary-eyed.

'You are hurt,' I said.

He set his oar, then reached over his shoulder and broke off the arrow shaft, leaving a short stump protruding. He looked at the arrow, then flung it away over the side and began to row again.

We reached the muddy estuary, which had become a field of choppy surf now that the tide was changing. Quickly, we brought the ship about, so that Olaf would be steering from the stern again. Meanwhile, I struggled to raise the sail.

240

As I was doing this, I heard Olaf call to me. When I turned my head, I saw a boat beyond the line of surf. It was just lowering its sail, as if preparing to go up the same river we had just come down. At first, I was relieved to see the familiar dirty wool of the square sail and the overlapping planks which swooped down from the bow into the water and then rose again towards the stern. It was a Norse Drakkar and on board were a full crew, sixteen at the oars, one at the steerboard and another who stood at the bow, pointing towards us. This man's face was broad and red and his long hair blew in the wind. Around his shoulders, he wore a cloak made from the shaggy brown pelt of a bear and, underneath it, a leather vest with perforated iron squares laced across his chest.

Their shields hung over the side. One was painted black with a blue star in the centre, another yellow with a red sun and rays spreading out to the corners of the shield. And closest to the stern, hung a red shield, flecked with white paint, the mark of a former Varangian.

The crew lowered their sail, since the wind was against them. They set their oars and began to row towards us.

Now my relief turned to fear. I had no doubt what they would do to us if they found out what we were carrying.

Olaf jibed the boat and our own sail filled with the wind. We began to move across the angry surf. Waves broke against our bow, sending arcs of spray across the deck.

The men in the other Drakkar had cleared the line of breakers. They were in the estuary now. The one at the bow shouted at us to draw alongside them.

He spoke the southern Norse of Danes. They had probably come from one of the Danish settlements across the water in Ireland, and were raiding the coast, as Cabal had said they did.

I tightened the sail lines to gather more speed as we made our way towards the open water.

241

The Danes brought their boat around, oar blades hacking the murky water. The bear-cloaked man stayed at the bow, chanting to keep them in time.

Olaf cried out in frustration. We were not moving fast enough. Between us and the sea, the current surged against itself, waves rolling under each other. On either side of the river mouth, white-bearded rollers crashed against the dunes.

The Danes changed course to cut us off and run our boat aground. Any moment now, they would pull in front. There was nothing to do but keep on towards the jagged surf.

The bear-skinned man swept back his cloak and took a long-handled war-axe from his belt. Its sharpened edge shone silver like a crescent moon. He moved the axe slowly back and forth in front of his face, staring past the blade, which was an old trick for setting the range.

We were so close that I could see his pock-marked skin, his rotten teeth and hawk-beak nose.

My palms were bloody from gripping the sail lines.

The Danes were about to overtake us. The strain of rowing showed in their windburned faces and clenched teeth. The man at the steerboard arched his body to hold the boat on course.

The patterns of their shields weaved before my sweat-stung eyes. With a shout from the bear-cloaked man, the Danes on the starboard side hauled in their square-tipped oars. Then they took up their shields and swords.

We were moving straight towards them. All the Danes had to do was to guide their boat onwards, propelled by the force of the current, and they would be able to walk from the deck of their boat onto ours.

I tied the sail line in place and grabbed my red shield. Snapping off the arrow which had struck it, I threw the feathered stick into the waves. My whole body was shaking. Energy for the fight thrashed inside me. Without thinking, I crashed the hilt of my sword against the boss of my shield. And then again. And again.

Olaf lashed the tiller and came to stand beside me, shield in one hand and sword in the other. After a moment's hesitation, he began to strike his shield as well.

I had not grasped at first what was happening. But when Olaf took up the strange metallic chant and the sound began to multiply, I understood. Already I could feel the shadow taking shape beneath my skin, climbing to the surface like a face rising up through murky water, moulding its features to my own. It stretched into my fingers, stealing my senses, drawing my flesh around itself. A murmuring fury filled my head, changing my blood. All fear gone. The hammering thunder was everywhere. I felt my lips pull back around my teeth and a horrible, shrieking howl tore out of me. In that moment I no longer knew who I was.

The bear-cloaked Dane roared his hate at us. Sea spray matted his hair and the shaggy ruff of his fur cloak.

I raised my shield to my chest and steadied my legs for the collision of our boats.

As their boat slid between us and the wind, it caused the waves to slacken. Our boat began to turn with the current. Now it seemed as if the two boats might not collide after all. The Danes on the port side struggled with their oars, but they could not make their boat move sideways. The steerman pushed the heavy tiller back and forth, trying to scull their Drakkar back on course.

The bear-cloaked Dane cursed and hurled his axe at us. It flew end over end and thudded against our mast. Chips of wood spat into the air. Then the Dane hurled his shield, which spun flat and would have taken off Olaf's head if he had not dropped to his knees and let the shield fly past above him.

Now the Dane stepped up onto the prow of his boat. He balanced there uncertainly. One of his crew shouted and held out his hand, ready to help the man back into the safety of the boat. But the man was too crazed now to understand. His cloak billowed around him and the tendons in his arms were taut from his grip on the prow.

As he perched there, ready to leap across onto our boat, a pale and ghostly thing rose from the murky water. The Dane narrowed his eyes, struggling to make out what it was. In the moment of his realisation, he gasped so loudly that I heard it even over the rumble of the churning water.

It was Cabal, this bloodless thing. He floated face down, torn flesh shivering in the current. His body swung back and forth in the slack water between the Danes' boat and our own. It seemed to hover there, arms outstretched and fingers twitching in the cold grey water, as if there was still life in them.

All of us stared. A great silence descended upon us. We who were about to butcher one another had been bound together in horror.

With movements as slow as in a dream, I took up my spear, which had been lying on the deck. I raised the shaft to the level of my shoulder, drew back my arm and sent the bronze point flying. The spear was only in the air for a moment. It crossed the space between us so quickly that its blade had cracked through the Dane's chest before the expression could change on his face.

He fell back among his crew, who caught him in their arms and held him while he thrashed out the last of his life.

The silence which had fallen on us tore away and the sounds of wind and water roared back into my ears.

Quickly, Olaf returned to the tiller, while I went back to the sail. We steered towards the breakers, gathering speed.

The Danes struggled to bring their boat around. Some of the

crew remained around the body of their fallen leader, while Cabal's body, pitched by the waves, threw itself again and again at their hull.

We ploughed through the surf, heaved up by the breakers and slammed back down again. The steerboard raked across the sand, sending a shudder down the spine of the Drakkar. I thought we might founder, but then we passed into the open water. The wind swept us out to sea.

I looked back at that estuary, as it faded away in the mist, and it seemed to me that years from now, perhaps centuries into the future, people might come to this place and feel the savagery still hanging in the air. It would remain here like a shadow brought to life, howling in their dreams, the echo of our pounded shields calling through the silence of their sleep.

Then I saw the Danes clear the mouth of the estuary, their sail bellied out with the wind and heading right towards us.

I knew then that they would follow Olaf and me off the end of the earth rather than give up the chase. We had killed one of their own. Now they would make us pay.

As long as the wind kept up, we stood a chance of outrunning them, but only if we went with the wind, wherever it took us.

The land drowned in the sea. Deep swells moved against the hull. Our ship sailed on into gathering darkness. The Danes were still visible in the distance, now falling behind, now gaining, their curved prow riding up on the crests of the waves.

There was no moon, only the black cloak of the night sky, flecked with countless silver droplets like the sea spray on our clothes.

Olaf manned the steerboard, his gaze fixed beyond the bow. 'If there is a fog,' he said, 'we can come about and tack to the east. Then we might lose them, if they do not decide to do the same thing.'

245

'Your wound,' I said. 'Are you in pain?'

He shook his head. 'I have no feeling at all in my shoulder.'

While he stood there at the tiller, I cut away his blood-soaked shirt and looked at where the arrow had gone into his shoulder blade. The flesh was mounded up around the splintered arrow shaft.

'I am going to try and pull it out,' I said. Setting my left hand on his shoulder, I gripped the shaft with my right hand and tugged at it hard.

Olaf groaned and struggled to stay on his feet.

The arrow would not come out, nor could it be pushed through, since it was lodged in bone. The point would have to be cut away, and such a thing could not be done on the deck of this pitching boat.

'No luck?' he gasped.

I patted him on the head. 'No, but I have seen much worse than this in men who lived to tell about it.'

He tried to smile. His face was covered in sweat.

'Rest,' I said. 'I can manage the tiller.'

'I will tell you when I need to rest,' he replied stubbornly.

So I sat down beside him on my whale bone seat, put my face in my hands and felt the warmth of my fingertips against my closed eyelids. Exhaustion clouded my mind. When I thought back on the day, I could not recall when the pounding of the shields had ceased. I could still hear it and felt the black self still inside me, drifting in the river of my blood.

I could not get into my head the fact that Cabal was gone. I kept thinking that I saw him from the corner of my eye. I seemed to hear fragments of his voice. Along with the rest of the Varangians who knew him, I had convinced myself that Cabal was only partly of this earth, and the sufferings of mortal men would not be his. I had not believed that he would ever die.

It seemed to me as if the gods had abandoned us, not only ours but the Christian god as well. They had started this fight and then left us to slaughter each other, while they remained distant and beyond harm, unlike the once-untouchable Cabal.

As the hours went by, the truth began to sink in, I flinched in sudden, uncontrollable shudders. I stared out at the black waves, which looked to me like an endless, glinting plain of thunderstone. Our movement on the water seemed to carve a path through time itself, away from my old friend and all the years we spent together.

The wind blew hard that night, as the Danes pursued us out along the whale-road's trackless path.

PART IV

Five days we ran south with the wind, sliding over the hunch-backed waves.

The Danes did not give up. They seemed not to care about their own lives, governed only by the rage of vengeance. At times, they came close enough that we could see their faces and the patterns on their shields. Other times, we were convinced we had outrun the Danes, only to climb the mast and see them out there still, trailing in our wake.

Something besides the Danes was following me. It came in those moments of half-consciousness as my exhausted mind trailed away towards sleep, like a ball of yarn unravelling across the floor.

I found myself again in that wave-churned estuary. But I was not on Olaf's boat. I was among the Danes. I stood at their prow as the man in the bear cloak had done. I was him now, feeling the great weight of the spray-soaked fur cloak and the metal plates across my chest. And in this vision I could see the bronze spearhead glimmering pale and dusty green as it flew through the air towards me. For a moment, the spear seemed to pause in front of my body, hovering as if it were a humming-bird. I looked around me and saw everything frozen in place – the glassy waves and pregnant sail, men's hair blown by the

wind and even the tiny droplets of spray off our bow, suspended in space. Then I turned to face the spear again and felt
the tearing jolt as it ripped through the cage of my chest. I felt
myself falling, arms thrown out, eyes already growing dim.
The force of these images jarred me so violently that I would sit
up and find myself staring at the horizon, where the blue of the
night met the black of the sea and stars shuddered in the great
silence of the sky.

As often as I could, I bathed Olaf's wound with salt water
and patted it dry. The skin around the arrow shaft was red and
sore, but the swelling had gone down. He was in constant
pain, however, as the feeling had returned to his shoulder, and
for this I could do nothing. He refused to rest any more than I
rested myself. Olaf knew as well as I did that if I cut out the
arrow now, he would grow worse before he grew better. I
could not sail this boat alone and keep up the speed we needed to stay ahead of the Danes.

On the sixth day, thunderhead clouds filled the northern sky.
The wind picked up out of the north-east and we heard a
strange moaning sound around the ship, as if invisible creatures were crying out in pain. It was the breeze, slipping
through the rigging lines.

I checked the ropes around the tiller, fastened the waterbarrels shut and battened the spare sail cloth over the bags of food,
which by now were nearly empty.

'Look!' said Olaf, and jerked his chin in the direction of the
approaching storm. His left arm had stiffened so that it hung
almost useless at his side.

The Danes had turned about. They were tacking away to the
east. They had seen the storm too, and the size of it crowding
the sky, like some vast creature rising from the water.

We felt no relief. If we came about as well, it would only put
us within reach of the Danes again. The threat of the storm

seemed almost as bad. Both were determined to send our life-less bodies to the bottom of the sea, but we stood a better chance against the wind and waves.

The moaning of the gale continued, surrounding our ship. I wondered if this could be the voice of the wind, which Cabal had spoken of. I found myself listening for words inside its droning chorus.

The sun disappeared, smudged out by smoky blue-grey clouds. Hard gusts ploughed the water. The boat heaved up on swells and sail lines groaned with the strain.

We heard the drums of thunder. Lightning clawed at the sky. This was no small storm. We shortened sail and tacked as the Drakkar rolled from one wave trough to another. The first rain drops darkened the sail cloth and sank into the scuffed deck planks. Soon, the rain fell harder, roaring out of the low-hanging clouds. Before long, it was pelting so viciously that I had to start bailing, while Olaf shortened sail even further. The wind cut straight from the north.

It was the Arador.

'We cannot tack through this,' said Olaf. 'It will tear us to pieces if we try. We will have to loosen the sail and run with the wind until it blows itself out.'

A tremor of fear passed through us. We were already far out to sea, and this storm would only push us further from land.

I staggered around the deck, making sure the cargo was lashed down. Then I made my way back to the steerboard. 'Ready,' I told him.

We loosened the lines, and the storm wind surged into the sail, hurling us forward over the waves.

The rest of that day and into the night, I sat with my arms on the steerboard, guiding the Drakkar down one foam-slicked valley of water, up the gasping wall of the next wave and down again. I could not tell where the waves ended and where the sky

began except from the white line of foam of the next approaching wave. Clouds crackled with the fire in their bellies. Rain
pounded the sail. We opened the rain barrels and they soon
filled to overflowing. It was the darkest night I had ever seen.

Olaf was stooped over, using one hand to bail with an old
wooden bucket, when a wave jumped the deck and the force of
it almost carried him overboard. Afterwards, we tied ropes
around our waists and lashed them to the mast, in case the next
wave washed us away. As the hours went by, we grew used to
these strange umbilical cords.

Olaf was growing weaker. He complained of feeling hot
when the air was almost freezing. A fever had begun to burn
inside him.

'Are you hungry?' I asked. 'There is still a little food.'

Olaf spat over the side. 'I have no appetite,' he said.

Morning spread a dove grey light over the waves. The rain
was still falling and the wind had not slackened. My joints felt
stiff from the cold and wet.

There had been no chance to think how far this storm had
taken us, nor time to be afraid, nor to eat, nor sleep, nor to mull
over past grievances, which seemed now to belong to another
life.

Whenever we tried to tack into the wind, a gust much harder than the rest would barge into the Drakkar and send us skid-
ding down the bank of another wave. I had to use all my
strength to hold the steerboard straight.

Another day passed, and then another. The moaning wind
carried us south and west.

I grew so tired that sometimes I fell asleep at the steerboard.
My mind grew blank, sluiced of dreams. Darkness crowded
my skull.

Olaf's skin turned grey, with a haziness of green under the
flesh.

254

I fed him water from my wooden cup and pressed flakes of dried fish into his mouth. 'I could try to cut away the arrow now,' I said.

He raised his bloodshot eyes to meet my own. 'And how many days would it take for me to recover?'

I shrugged. 'I don't know. It depends on how things go. Maybe three or four if we are lucky.'

'By then we would be drowned. You cannot sail alone across a sea like this. When the storm is over, then you can try out your swordsmanship on me. Until then, I am going to sail this ship.'

Three days.

Five.

We fought an endless war against the storm, having no idea where we were headed since the bearing dial could not be read without the shadow of the sun.

I woke to find Olaf sprawled on the deck beside the steer-board. He had fainted.

I cradled his head in my hands.

'There is someone else here,' said Olaf, when he had opened his eyes. His nose was pinched and salt was crusted in his beard. 'He is watching us. He is waiting for me to die.'

'Let him wait,' I said and pressed some dried fish into his mouth. 'In the meantime, you can rest.' I bundled him in his cape and placed a roll of spare sail cloth under his head for a pillow. He was too weak to protest.

From then on, I was sailing the ship by myself, which proved difficult but not impossible, as I had thought it would be.

Twice I tried to remove the arrow head from Olaf's back, using the tip of my sword blade since I had no shorter knife. I felt like a butcher. Olaf cursed and beat his fists against the deck and finally, when his strength had given out, he wept.

With the tips of my fingers, I could feel past the broken arrow shaft to the tip, but could not grip it strongly enough to remove the point. The pitching of the boat and Olaf's cries for me to stop caused me to give up each attempt.

Eight days now. Ten. Was it ten? I had lost count.

My thoughts folded back upon themselves, plodding up and down the same worn paths like fever dreams. My sleep was not sleep but some other land I had begun to inhabit, which was as real as our drenched and pitching days out on this boat.

That night, as I sat with my head resting on the rope bindings of the steerboard arm, my thoughts began to race across the ocean as if following the moonlight on the water. I wandered through the streets of Altvik, peering in windows like the ghost of Sasser Greycloak. All the while, the storm pushed us further and further out to sea. I understood now why Cabal had called this wind alive. It seemed to be toying with the ship, defying us to turn against it.

On what I guessed to be the fourteenth day, I glimpsed sun like a waterfall in the distance, cascading out of the clouds. I could not help but steer towards it, even though I knew from the rippling light that it was just another world of tumbling waves. When at last we reached that raft of sunlight, it swam around us like a thousand tiny fish.

Olaf's eyes flickered open, as the warmth of the sun's fire touched his face. Since my last effort to remove the arrowhead, he had been drifting in and out of consciousness.

I checked the bearing dial, but we were so far south of where we had been the last time I'd checked it that it was useless to us now.

Then the clouds rolled past and the sea blinked back into grey, and we sailed on across the tumbling waves.

Panic closed around me. Every moment passed in a blindness of fear. I existed only in the shallow-breathing suddenness of waiting to die. In the past, the dangers I faced had never lasted long. When I was actually in danger, I had never been afraid. It was only afterwards that the terrors would come trampling through my skull and I would begin to shake. But this storm had dragged on for so long that that the fear caused by things that had happened in the past collided with dangers I was facing now. I could no longer keep them separate. They formed into one twitching mass inside me, crabbing its way through my veins and clogging my heart.

I prayed, while rain poured off my mumbling lips and dripped from my straggly hair. The only sound that came back to me was of wind moaning through the eye-sockets of the old walrus skull, and the sucking gasp of the bow as it ploughed through the storm.

I prayed all the time. I prayed until I was angry.

Why won't you answer?

Why won't you help us?

I begged for an answer, for thundering voices to set out on the wind towards me, like huge and unstoppable ships, carrying the message that we had not been forgotten.

'Are they listening to you?' Olaf blinked at me from the cocoon of his cape. The skin around his eyes was dark and his lips were white and creased with bloody cracks.

'I don't know,' I replied. As I said the words, a vast loneliness filled my head with shapeless, nameless horrors.

Slowly, Olaf crawled out from his cape. 'I will help,' he said.

On our knees, heads pressed together and hugging each other's shoulders, we prayed, while all around us, the sea washed into the sky like dye from cloth and the northern sky still grumbled with distant thunder, flickering with the struck-flint sparks of lightning.

That night, I discovered that our waterbarrels had salt in them. The waves must have seeped through the lids. We could still drink it, but the water was brackish and made us gag if we drank more than a few sips at a time.

I decided that we should eat the few remaining pieces of dried fish. White speckles of mould had already spread across the crumpled amber surface. From the days when my mother and I had hung and smoked the fish my father caught, I knew that this mould ruined the taste of the meat but that the fish would still be edible. But if we waited any longer, it would be too far gone. I washed the fish and tried to dry it in the wind by hanging it from the masthead. Then I gnawed on the hard, leathery meat until my spit ran red with blood from bruised gums. Some of this, I gave to Olaf, since he was too weak to chew it himself. I used the rest of the rotten fish to bait hooks, keeping five lines in the water, but never had a bite.

Then the last of the food was gone.

My breath tasted sweet and my tongue swelled up in my throat. I grew so weak I had to crawl around the deck, too tired even to scratch the itching salt-water boils which festered on my grotesquely swollen knees and elbows.

In the middle of the night, I ate my shoes.

Olaf said he wanted to sit up, so I propped him beside the steerboard and sat next to him. Hour after hour, we stared at the unchanging sea.

The strain on the boat was beginning to tell. These last few days, I had been bailing more and more frequently. The sail was fraying and the walrus-leather lines had stretched beyond their usefulness. Stress cracks appeared in the mast, spiralling up from its base, and there was no telling how deep they went.

Olaf began talking to people who he said were standing in front of him.

'Who are they?' I asked.

'I don't know,' he replied, 'but they say that they know me.'

Throughout the day, he raged at every thought which twisted in his brain. 'I was not the one who killed our friendship!' he shouted at me. 'I tried to preserve it. More than you know! All

258

I ever wanted was to see what you can see! Do you know what it is like to spend your life in doubt?'

I held up the black hammer, which still hung around my neck. 'This is not the key you think it is. It will not take away your doubts.'

Olaf drew back the flap of his cloak and held out a hand, fingertips chapped with bloody cracks deep in the skin. 'Then give it to me.'

I tossed it over over to him. I did not care anymore.

Slowly, he put the cord round his neck and tucked the black hammer under his shirt. 'This was always mine,' he said. 'It never did belong to you.'

We stared at each other, eyes filled with hate.

When Olaf fell asleep, I went and stood looking down at him. Watery blue light filled the air. For a long time, I watched him, steeling my mind for what I had to do. Then I reached down, grabbed Olaf by his shirt and shoved him over the side. His body seemed to weigh nothing at all. Olaf hit the water with a splash and disappeared, then bobbed up again, spluttering salt water from his lungs. He waved and called out my name.

It was only when I heard the fear in Olaf's voice that I realised the blindness of my anger, and the terrible mistake I had just made. 'Olaf!' I called. 'I will turn the boat around! Olaf! I am coming back for you!' I tugged at the steerboard, but it was roped in place. The knots which held the ropes had swollen tight, and while I pulled them loose I kept calling to Olaf. Meanwhile, the boat sailed on and he disappeared behind the waves. 'Olaf!' I screamed. 'Olaf, I am sorry!'

Then someone else was shouting. I blinked and saw Olaf, right in front of my face. I was lying down and he was shaking me 'What is the matter with you?' he asked. 'What are you sorry about?'

I struggled to my feet and looked in the wake of our boat, where I had seen him fall. Then I looked down at Olaf, who had crawled across the deck to wake me from my sleep.

'Why did you call out my name?' he asked.

'It was a dream,' I said.

'What was it about?' he asked.

I shook my head. 'Nothing. It was nothing.'

Olaf returned to his place beside the tiller and pulled the dirty cloak around his shoulders.

I knew then that I could not kill him. What we had lived through since we set sail on this journey had changed everything between us, and I would have died of loneliness if he had not been there.

At night a huge creature, outlined with flickering green sparks, slid under the boat. We watched it trailing away into the dark, like a path of fire falling from the sky.

'It is one of the monsters,' said Olaf, 'who live at the end of the world.' As the boat ploughed onwards, pitching over the white crests of the waves, we were seized by a fear that we had sailed past the limits of the ocean and were falling now through the abyss. Then we felt the surge of the Drakkar riding up the next wave, and the terror left us for a while.

Again the grey dawn showed us no horizon.

Time came unbuckled. Everything was slowing down. My thoughts. My body. Even the movement of the waves.

In the moment that the sun rose above the waves, Olaf cried out in a wordless, high-pitched shriek which drilled into my ears and sent me crawling to his side. But he was asleep, his grey face composed and calm. Nor could I wake him. Olaf seemed to be caught in some place between the living and the dead.

I woke that night to find Halfdan on the boat. It did not surprise me to see him. Not in this place. Not now. He was watching me, smiling a pitying smile as he stood on the prow, just as the bearcloaked Dane had done. But he was not holding onto anything. He just perched there, defying all possibilities of balance in the pitching of the waves.

'You should have killed Olaf while you had the chance,' he said.

I closed my eyes, but when I opened them again he was still there. 'What do you want?' I asked.

'I have come here to tell you to stop struggling,' said Half-dan. The words echoed around us, as if each one had come to life and fluttered around him like insects.

'Why?' I grunted.

'Because you are already dead.'

I shook my head. 'You do not frighten me with your lies.'

'It is no lie. You are already gone. You and your friend. Only the dead can travel to this place. Our gods cannot protect you here.' The longer he stood there, the less he seemed to be con-structed from the gauzy fabric of my thoughts. The boat charged on through the waves, smashing over one foam-crested hill and down into the valley of the next.

For a long time, we only stared at each other, until at last he spoke again. 'You must leave behind the ones you love,' he said, 'just as they are leaving you.'

I stood up, the pain of any sudden movement sharp in the joints of my knees and my hips and in the boils which bubbled on my skin. 'Look at me!' I howled at him. 'I am still alive!'

'I am looking at you,' he replied calmly, 'and what I see is a dead man, clinging only to the memory of his life.'

I lunged forward to grab him but had forgotten to tie up the tiller, which turned in the water, jibing the boat. The sail swung back and the sideways motion knocked me off balance. I saw the grey-white sheet of the sail, filling my vision as it rushed towards me.

The next thing I remember is feeling water all around me and being surprised that it was not as cold as I would have expected. At first, I thought I had been washed overboard. Then I sat up, just as a wave tipped onto the deck. The boat was nearly swamped. With a shout, I clambered to my feet.

Olaf was lying between the rowing benches. His eyes were closed. Water washed over him.

I realise that the boom must have hit me in the head and knocked me out. Pain thumped across my temples and down the back of my neck, but at least I knew for certain I was still alive. I lashed the steerboard in place, hauled Olaf up onto one of the benches, then grabbed one of the buckets and began to bail. I kept bailing, long after my muscles had ceased to shriek. My elbows locked and I could no longer feel my grip on the sides of the bucket. The endless stooping and straightening of my back traced lines of agony around each segment of my spine. Once, as I raised my head, an arc of water sliding from the bucket past my face and back into the waves, I looked towards the bow, expecting to see Halfdan there, but he was gone. I kept bailing until the bucket scraped against the wooden deck. At last the boat rode higher in the waves.

Now that the danger had passed, I was overwhelmed with anger. I raged at the living storm, barking obscenities until my throat was raw, while the storm mocked me with its serpent's hiss. Then suddenly I was myself again, afraid and so weak I could barely stand.

Olaf still lay unconscious on the rowing bench.

I pressed my ear against his naked chest and heard the wheezy rattle of his breathing.

With tears in my eyes, I begged him to wake and talk to me, but he just lay there in my arms.

All the while, Halfdan's voice chanted in my skull: 'You will never see your home again. No one can hear your prayers. You are already dead.'

The air was not as cold as it had been before. For several days now, I had only worn my cloak at night.

In the night, after a brief lull, the storm seemed to grow worse. I sat up bleary-eyed from where I had been sleeping with my head against the steerboard arm.

Thunder pounded all around and lightning flickered silvery in the air. In my mind, I counted off the things we had to do – shorten sail, lash the water barrels shut, check the steerboard. But then I noticed that the water was calm. I could see the stars. That was not thunder. It was a kind of drumming. Something flashed in front of my eyes. Some kind of bird. It flew straight into the sail. There were birds all over the deck. They were thin and had long wings. As I stood, I vaguely saw a ruffle in the water and then something struck me so hard in the chest that I fell over, gasping the air back into my lungs. As I rolled on my side to get up, I realised that the birds were not birds at all but fish with such long fins that they appeared to have wings. I stared at them for a moment, then without thinking, I grabbed one of the fish, picked it up and bit into it, flooding my mouth with the taste of salt and blood.

I ate the whole fish, sucking the fluid from the spine and swallowing the eyes. I ate the fins and spat out the flimsy bones. In the stomach, I found some minnows, which I rinsed and ate as well.

Again I tried to wake Olaf, but he remained asleep, breathing only faintly.

It began to rain, so I took the lids off the rain barrels to let them fill.

With fish blood dripping from the tips of my fingers, I held my wooden mug under the end of the sail's boom, where the water trickled off in a steady stream.

I drank until I thought my stomach would burst.

My strength was returning. I felt it as a prickling sensation spreading from a bowl of warmth inside my stomach. My sluggish thoughts began to race. I found myself laughing for no reason, suddenly falling silent at the eerie cackle of my voice, then laughing again a moment later.

At first light, I gathered up the rest of the fish, cut the meat from their bodies and threaded the pieces on a line between the bow and the sail to dry.

By late morning, the wind had slackened for the first time in as long as I could remember. Now that the boat was riding more smoothly in the water, I brought out my sword and rinsed it in the waves, watching the blade flash as it cut through the green water. Then I took the clothes from around Olaf's back and this time cut away enough of the skin around the arrow head that I could grip the piece of flint with my thumb and first two fingers and at last pull it free from the bone. Through all of this, Olaf remained asleep, but the sweat beaded up on his face and his breathing grew shallow and hoarse. There was a lot of blood, which I staunched with a bundled-up piece of my cloak. Then I fashioned a bandage from strips torn off my shirt. There was nothing to do now but keep the wound clean and hope that he recovered.

That night, the sky was so riddled with stars that I could barely make out familiar patterns.

At dawn of the next day, I noticed a few strands of seaweed drifting past. I knew this must mean we were close to land, but as hard as I looked, shading my eyes with salt-chapped hands, I saw no trace of mountains or the flattened clouds that gather above ground.

After a long time of staring, I began to see a brown haze above the water. At first, I was convinced that it had to be an island, but when I looked again a few moments later, the haze was gone and all I could see was water. And yet, something was out there. I felt it, even if I could not see it. I gave up looking for the shore and used the blade of my axe to hook up some of the weeds. As I brought them up, tiny flea-shaped shrimp jumped on the deck. I pinched their wriggling bodies and popped them in my mouth like tiny berries. I tried to feed some to Olaf, but still he would not wake.

The following morning, I went forward to the bow. The morning mist had just began to clear. Everywhere, clusters of weed dimpled the water. It was not long before the progress of the boat was slowed by this tangled forest.

Cormorants and seagulls scudded amongst the brown sinews. There were fish the same nut-brown colour as the weeds, with uneven growths jutting from their sides, looking so much like the weeds themselves that in this place the boundaries between plant and animal seemed to have come undone.

I set out lines baited with the scraps of meat, which sent tiny rainbows of oil to the surface as they sank. The dappled shadows of the weeds stretched down into the bottomless green below. It was not long before I had fish on the lines. They had the same shape as mackerel and put up the same kind of fight, and even had the same strong-tasting flesh, but instead of green and black stripes on their backs, they were the colour of new iron.

When I had caught enough to last us for a while, I slipped over the side and swam around the boat, picking off and eating the long-necked barnacles which were growing on the hull. I was shocked to see that the pine-tar used to plate the overlapping boards had almost worn away, which explained why I had been bailing so often.

Afterwards, I rested on the deck. At first, it was good to feel the sun on my bare back, but by afternoon, I had badly burned my face and hands and the tops of my feet. For shelter, I rigged a canopy of spare sail cloth which I stretched across the bow. Then I dragged Olaf in beside me. I kept up a one-sided conversation while I tried to make him comfortable in the cramped space, afraid that he would never wake from his death-like sleep.

At last, just as I was beginning to give up hope, Olaf spoke to me in a croaking, barely human voice. 'Why are we not moving?'

I smiled and patted his grey cheek. 'I thought you were not coming back,' I said.

'Have we reached land?' he asked.

'Not exactly,' I replied. Hooking my hands under his arms, I moved him gently out from under the canopy. His eyes were crusted shut and I had to moisten them with sea water before they would open. When I showed Olaf the weeds, which stretched as far as we could see towards the west, he seemed to wake completely from the blur in which he had spent these past few days. All he wanted to do then was look at the weeds, so I built him a chair out of our empty food boxes. He sat like the king of this watery world, while I brought him fish to eat and cups of rain water to drink.

Olaf was surprised when I told him I had removed the arrow head. He asked to see it, and for a long time just stared at the sharp little point, as it lay in the palm of his hand. 'You would not think something this small could cause such suffering,' he said. Then he flicked it over the side and slapped his hands together.

I had to help him move around the deck, but slowly Olaf was becoming his old self again. The scar, at first an angry poppy red, turned gradually to purple as it healed. Painfully, Olaf regained the use of his arm, clenching and unclenching his crab-clawed fist, until his fingers moved freely again. By now, in the sun, his blonde hair had turned almost white. His blue eyes glowed in his sunburnt face.

My own skin was darker now than it had ever been in Miklagard. Under the canopy, with my shirt removed, I was startled at how sinewy my arms had become. The bones of my elbows stuck out sharply under the skin.

Days passed. I could not say how long. We lived in an absence of time, speaking neither of the past or of where we might go on from here.

By the heat of the afternoon, we lived in the milky light under the canopy. Sun shone like the yolk of an egg through the sailcloth. The boat's gentle rocking and the smell of the weeds, thick and earthy in our lungs, lulled us into peaceful waking dreams. At night, when it grew cooler, we fished by the light of the stars.

'We could stay here forever,' said Olaf, 'and I would not regret it.'

Once I woke to find that he had moved himself out onto his food box throne. He sat there with a calm expression on his face, hands resting in his lap, and there was a seagull sitting on his head. It was a big old gull, with watery eyes and scaly legs.

'If I move,' he whispered, 'it pecks me.'

Then, as if to punish him for disturbing the silence, the seagull jabbed him in the ear with its yellowy beak.

For a long time, Olaf sat there with a seagull for a hat. Eventually, the bird flew over to the bow and sat on the walrus skull, which it pecked with a dry clacking sound, as if somehow the walrus had displeased it, too.

It was now too hot to wear our heavy woollen cloaks even after dark, so we made shirts from old pieces of sailcloth, which we stitched together using iron needles and leather cord.

Late one night, Olaf shook me awake.

I sat up. 'What is it?' I asked.

'Out there,' he whispered, and pointed across the water.

In the light of a sickle-blade moon, the calm surface of the water was ruffled by the vast plain of weeds.

'What is the matter?' I asked again. 'I do not hear anything.'

'Exactly,' he whispered.

And then I understood. It was as if the silence itself had come to life. All the weeds and birds and fish, each alive by themselves, had somehow merged to form a single living thing that watched us with a thousand unblinking eyes and did not want us here. We had become trespassers, as suddenly and clearly as if a voice had spoken to us from the black heart of this weed-choked sea, telling us to leave.

As quietly as we could, afraid of disturbing this angry still-ness, we rowed our boat out to the open sea, raised the sail and caught the wind once more.

With the water sliding past our hull again, we looked back at the island of weeds but it had disappeared. We felt as if we had woken from a dream, which might have folded us forever in its gently choking arms.

We discussed the possibility of heading north, but even if Olaf and I could have taken the strain, we felt sure the boat could not.

'What we must to do,' said Olaf, 'is put in some place, careen the boat on a beach and refit the hull. The way it is now, we have no choice except to let the wind carry us on until we reach land.'

I did not answer, because we both knew that there might be no land ahead, and that this boat might sail on long after we had died, cruising out under the cold light of the moon, which would shine on our wind-polished bones.

I woke up slumped over the steerboard with a crick in my neck. Opening my gluey eyes, I watched the sun climb ragged-edged from the sea, casting weak and coppery light over the waves.

Olaf lay sleeping on one of the rowing benches, hands folded across his chest.

Just then, something caught my eye. I stared past Olaf towards the horizon. At first, I thought it was a mirage, but the more I looked at it, the more certain I became that it was land.

It was well behind us and to the east. We must have sailed past it in the night.

I woke Olaf. He looked out into the glare, shielding his eyes. 'No mistake!' he shouted. 'That is an island!'

My heart jumped into my throat.

I prepared to swing the steerboard and jibe the boat.

'Wait!' shouted Olaf, holding up his hands. 'The wind is too strong. The cracks in our mast are too deep. If we lose the mast, we will not be able to steer over these waves. It is not worth the risk, and there may be more land ahead.'

In silence, we watched the island disappear beneath the waves. Even though we had missed landing there, the sight of land was enough to give us hope.

All day, a stiff breeze pushed us on. I was so restless that I could not sit still, and stared at the horizon until I no longer trusted my eyes. Blood-warm air swam around me, running its fingers through my long and tangled hair.

Olaf paced the boat like a cat, sniffing the wind for the smell of land, but there was only the lung-hollowing salt air of the sea.

That evening a large black bird appeared over the boat. It had long, pointed wings, sharply jointed in the middle, and seemed to hang in the air, more like the shadow of a bird than the bird itself.

When the bird turned away to the west, following the path of the wind, we set our course towards it.

Thunder.

It was the middle of the night.

I had been asleep. I lifted my arm from across my face and saw Olaf sitting on his whale bone seat, thoughtfully scratching powdered salt from his beard and eyebrows.

He glanced at me. 'Sounds like another storm,' he said, with resignation in his voice.

The wind had dropped. The dew-soaked sail hung empty.

Thunder. There it was again.

I sat up and craned my neck around, searching for the bank of dingy clouds which marked the storm. If we could catch the wind right, we might yet steer clear of the fire-hawking chaos that it seemed to promise. The noise came again but this time it did not sound like thunder.

I stood and stared into the dark. My eyes had been narrowed so long now against the sun and wind that when I opened them wide, salt dust crumbled from the creases in my skin.

Olaf, too, had noticed that something was not right.

We searched for some pattern in the moonlit clouds that might have tricked our eyes.

Slowly, the truth dawned on us that the sound we heard was not thunder, but the crash of surf against a windward shore.

'There!' said Olaf, and his arm pointed towards the west.

Against the star-flecked darkness of the night sky, we glimpsed a white band of breakers, stretching as far as I could see to the north and south. Beyond the breakers, we could just make out low-lying ground, which seemed to float on a bone-white strip of beach.

Fighting against the urge to run the boat straight at the land, not caring if we wrecked it on the reefs which probably lay between us and the shore, we convinced ourselves to wait until daybreak, when we could find safe passage through.

We rode in a little closer. Then, because the wind was gentle, we risked a jibing of the boat and sailed along the coastline. The breeze carried the dry and heavy scent of land. Here and there, the long-leafed silhouette of a palm tree stood out against the night sky.

I had seen palms before, on the coast of Africa, but we had been sailing south and west and were nowhere near Africa now.

'I do not care where we are,' said Olaf, 'as long as it is land.'

After sailing a long while without finding a break in the reef or any light from fires, we jibed the boat again and tacked back up the coast.

For both of us, it seemed the longest night we had ever spent.

At daybreak, Olaf went to the bow and began looking for a passage between the breakers. The sun rose behind our backs, making the sand glow pink. The ocean was a brilliant blue, diving into darker colours as the water grew deeper. Big, long-beaked birds flew just above the level of the waves. They made almost no movement with their wings, as they glided on the currents of air.

It was mid-morning before Olaf found what looked like a gap. I lined up the boat, while Olaf held the sail lines ready, studying the water. Under his breath, I heard him counting out the sets to mark the seventh wave.

The gentle colours of the morning disappeared. Now the white sand raked our eyes with its glare and the sun weighed heavy on our backs.

On the fifth wave of the next set, Olaf pulled hard on the sail line, pocketing the wind. The boat surged forward. By the time the seventh wave slid under our bow, I had the old walrus skull aimed at the gap. The boat seemed to gasp as it rose up in the water, carried by the force of the waves. From the corner of my eye, I glimpsed jagged rock the colour of rusted iron just beneath the churned white surf. Then we were past it, into the brighter blue of shallow water. I rode the wave until it scattered into foam. Then I turned the boat broadside a few hundred paces from shore and Olaf heaved the anchor stone over the side. The rope slithered over the side and then grew slack as the anchor reached the bottom.

The rustling of leaves reached our ears.

'That is the most beautiful sound I have ever heard,' said Olaf.

On the beach, trees with short, tangled branches and round leaves as big as my outstretched hand grew almost to the edge of the water. Only a few of the taller palms grew here, unlike the dense groves I had seen in Africa. Bundles of green nuts the size of a man's head bunched beneath the leaves and some of these had fallen on the sand, sprouting bright green shoots.

After untying the rowboat from its place just forward of the mast, we heaved it in the water. Then we loaded the bailing bucket and two empty water barrels, as well as our weapons.

While Olaf rowed us to shore, I looked over the side and saw fish darting about in the shadow of our hull. Once the bow of the boat ground up against the sand, we jumped out and hauled it clear of the waves. Grains of the white grit clung to our wet legs, and the unfamiliar effort of dragging the rowboat painted our faces with sweat.

Reaching the shade of the trees, we turned to look out at the Drakkar.

It was in even worse condition than we had thought.

The warped hullboards had grown a fur of weeds. A stubble of barnacles clustered on the steerboard. The sail was tattered almost into uselessness.

Olaf shook his head. 'New mast, new steerboard, tar for the hull. And we have no tools for the job.' Then he looked at me. 'Wherever we are, this may be our home from now on.'

With the handle of my axe, I traced a ring in the sand. Then Olaf and I knelt inside it and gave thanks for being alive. But even as I prayed, I felt as if we had strayed too far beyond the boundaries of our world for our voices to be heard.

Searching for signs of people, Olaf walked in one direction down the beach while I walked in the other. We both returned without having found anything more than bird tracks on the sand.

Then we took the bailing buckets and headed into the jungle in search of water, marking tree trunks with our axes as we went. The further in we travelled, the denser the undergrowth became. We took off our shirts and tied them around our waists. It was hard work struggling through the vines which thatched the sandy earth. A short distance inland, the ground turned muddy and we came across a small but deep pond filled with bluish water, sunk into the pale and crumbling rock.

Crouching at the edge, I reached my hand into the water and then tasted it off the tips of my fingers. 'It is sweet,' I said.

Olaf dropped to his knees and we both lapped up the water like dogs.

273

Back and forth through the jungle we carried the buckets, until we had filled one rain barrel.

Slumping down against a palm tree to rest, we watched the Drakkar roll sluggishly in the surf. The long-beaked birds glided silently over our heads, the tips of their wing-feathers spread like human fingers.

I picked up one of the green palm nuts which lay in the sand beside me and shook it, hearing the juice slosh inside.

Olaf cut off the top of one and gulped the sweet and salty milk.

Soon, we were surrounded by green nuts with their tops chopped off, and our stomachs gurgled happily. For a long time we just lay there, feeling the motion of the waves still rocking in our heads.

Olaf lifted the black stone hammer from his chest and let it fall again. 'A lot of good this has done me so far.'

'I tried to tell you,' I said.

When I received no reply, I looked over and saw that he had fallen asleep. I untied the shirt from my waist, rolled it up and stuffed it under his head for a pillow.

I had no memory of falling asleep myself, but when I opened my eyes, the sun was setting.

Olaf stood down by the water, staring out to sea in the rose-coloured light which filled the air. Ghost-pale crabs skittered back and forth across the beach behind him.

I walked down and stood beside him. As I watched the tired sun crumbling into the waves, I wondered how many people were out there, stranded on nameless islands, who would never see their homes again. Perhaps we were among them now.

When the sky turned purple with the closing in of night, we remembered our hunger and sharpened long driftwood sticks into spears to do some fishing. At first, we had no luck. Small fish nibbled on our toes, but the larger fish kept their distance.

Knowing they would have to be drawn in, I set the tip of the spear on the top of my foot and pressed down, gritting my teeth, until I felt the metal cut my skin. When I looked down at the water, I could see a silky thread of blood seep from the wound.

Soon the larger fish were coming to inspect.

The first one I struck, nailing it to the sandy floor with the point of the spear, was red along its back and as long as my forearm. I set it out on the sand and returned to the water, sand sticking to the wound in my foot.

By then, Olaf had also speared a fish. He held it up, grinning. 'Better get a cooking fire started,' he said.

I dug a hole in the sand and lined it with dead leaves and strips of clothy bark from around the base of the trees. I was just turning to Olaf, to ask if he had brought the flint and iron striker from the boat, when I heard him cry out in pain.

He stood in the surf, his arms and chest draped with what looked like pieces of black string. He had dropped the spear, at the end of which a small a fish was thrashing. Olaf's eyes were closed and his teeth clenched. Staggering forward, he dropped to his knees.

I ran to his side, grabbing at the wet black strings that laced his skin. The moment I touched them, pain ripped through my hands, tearing across my stomach, over my back and down my chest. I screamed, back arching, and tumbled into the surf. Waves boiled around me, filling my hair and eyes with sand. A strand of black weed clung to my arm but when I went to sweep it away, fresh pain jolted the length of my arms. I looked down and saw some of the dark strands across my legs. The pain seemed to be coming even from inside me now, glowing and pulsing like embers. I could not understand what was happening. I rolled in the surf, trying to esape the black threads.

Olaf had crawled as far as the trees, but then he collapsed, face down in the sand.

With nausea climbing into my throat, I used a twig to lift the remaining strands from Olaf's body and then from my own.

Pain blotted out my vision and slammed it back into my eyes, glittering with brassy sparks. Now I was struggling for air.

Olaf's mouth opened and closed, like the fish he had left dying on the beach.

The burning swayed through me. Darkness flooded my eyes. I felt myself falling, as if from a great height, out among the melting frost of stars.

A man stood over me, blotting out the sun, his outline rimmed with fire. I could not be sure if he was really there or if this was one of Halfdan's friends, conjured from the pain which still encased my body.

The man did not move.

I wondered how long I had been unconscious. I raised one hand to my face and tried to sweep away the grit that had collected in my eyelashes. It had blown up against my legs in tiny dunes. On my arm, I could see where the strands had draped across my skin. Neat lines of tiny brown dots marked my flesh, as if I had been methodically burned with the tip of a red-hot knife.

Olaf was lying beside me, eyes closed, his hair and beard filled with sand.

I could not tell if he was alive or dead.

I heaved myself up into a sitting position. The strands still lay in the sand beside me, and in the daylight I saw that they were not black. Some were blue, others dark red. I kicked out feebly, trying to bury them in the sand, then my gaze returned to the man. Only now was I thinking clearly enough to be afraid of him.

He was short and broad-shouldered, with a wide face, almond-shaped eyes and dark skin. His shiny black hair had been cut in a straight line across his brow and over his ears. The only thing he wore was a cloth tied around his middle and another piece of the same material draped like a cloak across one shoulder. In his right hand, he carried a short spear tipped with black stone.

I had never set eyes on anyone who looked like this man, not even in the slave markets of Baghdad, where I had seen men and women stolen from tribes so remote that the names of their people were not only unknown but unpronounceable to us.

From the look on this man's face, he had never seen anyone like Olaf and me either. He seemed to be deciding whether or not to kill us.

I was in so much pain I hardly cared what he did. I would have lacked the strength to pick up my axe even if he had handed it to me. My head slumped forward. I waited for him to make up his mind.

The man jabbed his spear into the sand. Then he squatted down, pointed at the brown scars on my arm and said a word I didn't understand.

I sighed and shook my head, to tell him of the pain, then watched in amazement as he lifted up his loin cloth, set his legs apart, and pissed on me.

I felt a flash of anger that he would insult me like this before finishing me off, but then the pain suddenly began to melt away. I was so relieved that I actually held up my arm to make it easier for him.

Then he pissed on Olaf, splashing his chest and his legs.

Olaf's eyes flickered open and he groaned.

When the man had finished his business, he brushed the loin cloth back in place and began to talk in a strange and stuttering language. He pointed at the boat, then out beyond the breaking waves towards the horizon, all the while looking at us.

Olaf raised himself up on one arm. 'Who is he?' he asked me, his voice a croaking whisper.

'I do not know.' Lying next to me, I saw the fish I had been about to cook the night before. Its scales were puckered and dry, the eyes filmed with sand.

'What happened to us?'

I shook my head. 'I do not know that, either.'

Slowly, Olaf and I climbed to our feet.

The man also stood. He stepped back and watched us, the spear in his hand once again.

I said a few words of Latin and Greek and a few of Arabic, but they meant nothing to him.

With one clawed hand, Olaf scratched the grit from his hair.

The man was staring at him. 'Kukulkan?' he asked, screwing up his eyes.

Now we realised he was looking at Olaf's hair.

For a long time, he regarded Olaf, as if waiting for him to do something. Then slowly the man reached out and touched the black stone hammer which hung around Olaf's neck. 'Kukulkan,' he said again, but this time there was no questioning in his voice.

He motioned that we should go with him, and immediately he set off along the beach.

We plodded after him on stiffened legs.

The pain still echoed deep inside my body.

The man walked ahead, turning every now and then to see if we were still there. 'Kohosh!' he shouted, then walked back, took Olaf by the arm and helped him along.

I was left to hobble on by myself. 'He seems to like you,' I said.

Olaf glanced back. 'Maybe he thinks I will taste better.'

I wished we had remembered our weapons, but it would have made no difference. We were too weak to use them.

After a while we came to an opening in the jungle, which turned into a path.

I grew increasingly nervous about our distance from the boat.

A short way from the beach we reached a clearing in which tall green plants with thick and floppy leaves were growing. In one corner was a crude wooden carving of a man with a broad forehead and deep-set eyes. He crouched on his haunches with his hands resting on his knees. It looked exactly like the wooden statue I had seen on Godfred's boat.

'Chac,' said the man, when he saw me looking at the statue. He pointed to the sky and wiggled his fingers.

I nodded, to show I understood that it was a statue of the god who brought the rain.

He smiled then, and in that moment I realised he was not going to kill us. If he had wanted to, he would have done it by now.

We continued down the path until we came to another clearing, in the centre of which stood a house. Its walls were made of narrow tree limbs bound together with vines. A dense mat of interwoven leaves formed the roof. The house had no door, only an opening, through which I saw a bed made from lengths of braided vines like a giant bird's nest stretched between the walls. A small fire was burning behind the back of the house. In the still air, serpents of sweet-smelling smoke twisted lazily into the sky.

The man shouted, 'Oh! Oh!' When he received no reply, he went into the house and came back out a moment later looking confused. He called into the jungle. Then he called again, hands cupped to his mouth. He looked at us and shook his head, then vanished off down another path, bare feet padding on the ground.

I leaned against a tree, weak and dizzy in the heat.

With movements like an old man, Olaf lowered himself until he was sitting on the dusty ground.

When the man reappeared, he was herding a woman and two small children in front of him. They had obviously fled before we entered the clearing. The woman gasped when she saw us and clutched at the boy and girl, both of whom were naked.

The man was explaining something to her in a loud voice, using broad sweeps of his arm and the occasional stamp of his foot.

He went over to Olaf and gently pulled him to his feet, saying the word 'Kukulkan' several times.

Slowly, the woman put down her children, who came straight over to us.

I kneeled down so as not to frighten them.

The children pointed at our eyes and then pointed at the sky to show the colour was the same. Their own eyes were so dark I could not see the pupils. The children tugged at my beard and giggled.

But the man would not let them touch Olaf. He shooed the children away, then turned to Olaf with a serious face. He slapped the flats of his hands against his chest and then held out his arms, taking in everything around him. After this, he pointed back towards the beach.

'What is he saying?' asked Olaf.

'Maybe he is giving us the choice of staying here or going back to the boat.'

'What do you think?'

'That woman does not like the look of us,' I said.

She had retrieved her children and held them to her body while they squirmed and giggled. She peered at us suspiciously over their heads of fine black hair.

Olaf gestured that we would go back to the beach.

The man gave a short nod, then went into his hut and fetched a bag made from the rough grey skin of a fish. It was filled with small yellow beans. 'Khana,' he said, and shook the bag, rattling the beans. Then he handed the bag to me, pointed to Olaf and raised his hand to his mouth.

The man walked us to the edge of the clearing and signed that he would come by to see us later.

I tried to ask him if they were the only people here, in case they might have been stranded as Olaf and I were stranded now, but he did not understand. He gave a quick wave of his hand and headed back into the jungle.

Once we reached the beach again, Olaf and I had to lean on each other to move across the sand.

'That man thinks my name is Kukulkan,' said Olaf.

'And he has got it in his head that this Kukulkan travels with a servant.'

'Which happens to be you,' said Olaf, managing a feeble smile.

I held up the bag of food. 'He wants me to cook you a meal.'

Olaf wheezed out a laugh. 'I would not want you for a servant.'

'No more than I would want you for a master,' I replied.

We joked to make ourselves brave, but the truth was that we were as frightened by what had happened to us the night before as we were of what might happen to us in the days to come.

Not trusting that the silver would be safe aboard our boat, we waited until after dark, brought the chest ashore and buried it in the jungle. It used up every bit of strength we had left, but the silver was too important to risk losing.

Then we returned to the boat and slept with our weapons beside us.

Several times, when the waves slid unevenly beneath the timbers of the Drakkar, I woke with a start and reached for my sword, watching the blackness of the jungle for any sign of movement. Then I lay down again and stared at the star-crowded sky, certain that the man who had helped us must also be awake, eyes fixed on the shadows, listening to every rustle of wind through the leaves and fearing us as much as we feared him.

My eyes snapped open. It was morning. A shadow slipped over my face. Only an arm's length above me, one of the sombre long-beaked birds flashed by. I noticed the soft cream and brown feathers of its underbelly, and its long beak jutting like the upward-lifted chin of a proud man. When I sat up, I saw that there were several of these birds, some of which had already flown past me. They glided through the curls of breaking waves. One of them pitched into the water and emerged a moment later with a fish in its beak.

Looking over the side of the boat, I watched a thing drift past that looked like some small animal turned inside out. It was a bright, deep purple, and blown up like a bladder. Behind this creature trailed purple, black and red strands, the same kind which had wrapped themselves around my legs.

I heard a noise on shore and looked up to see the man appearing from the jungle. This time he had brought along a friend.

I guessed they were not stranded, after all. 'We have company,' I said, as I nudged Olaf awake.

The second man was more ornately dressed, with a cape that stretched almost to his ankles. Tassles hanging from the hem dragged in the sand when he walked. He wore a crude but brightly-coloured hat, made from feathers which stuck straight up around his head. The men had been talking in hushed voices, but now that we had seen them, they fell silent.

We waved and they waved back. They did not move their hands from side to side, only raised and lowered them again.

Now we saw other people gathered further down the beach, half-hidden by the jungle. When they knew we had spotted them, they stepped back into the shadows of the big green leaves.

'We could haul up the anchor,' I said quietly.

Olaf shook his head. 'We would not get far in this boat. Our best chance is to hope that these people have the tools we need to make our repairs.'

Reluctantly leaving our weapons behind, we climbed into the rowboat and went ashore.

The feathered man did not smile at us, nor did he look like a person who ever did much smiling. He turned to Olaf and began speaking in a slow and expressionless voice. He touched one finger against the black hammer, then gestured to the ship and towards the sea beyond the reef. Again we heard the word 'Kukulkan'. When he had finished talking, he got down on one knee and bowed his head forward.

'How do I tell them,' said Olaf, 'that I am not who they think I am?'

'For now,' I replied, 'I think you should let them believe whatever they want. Whoever this Kukulkan is, he seems to be someone important.'

The feathered man remained on one knee for a long time, then cleared his throat and stood again.

I sensed a greater gulf between these people and ourselves than any common language could have fixed. I wondered who this Kukulkan could be. Perhaps he had been another blonde-haired traveller, blown by storms across the sea to this same place.

Over the next few days, we received many visitors who stayed only long enough to leave us gifts before vanishing back into the jungle. They brought fish and fruit and more yellow beans, as well as feathered headdresses, ornaments of jade and the skins of large and spotted cats. They even left us gold, fashioned into a half-moon crescent, with a gold-linked chain for fastening it across the chest. Everything we could not eat, we stored away in a food trunk under the rowing bench.

These people would appear only when we were out on the boat. When we came ashore to fetch more drinking water, we sometimes heard them moving in the jungle, but they would not come out to meet us.

The only one who did not seem afraid was the man who had first found us on the beach. We sat with him in the shade of the trees, sharing the food we had been given. We learned that his name was Choll and that this land was called Mayalum. His people were called the Maya, and there were many of them, scattered up and down this rocky coast.

Choll continued to treat Olaf with great respect. He would not even look Olaf in the eye or speak to him unless Olaf spoke first. Nor would he take anything directly from Olaf's hand. Olaf first had to put it down on the ground before Choll would pick it up. With me, Choll was more familiar, bordering on disrespectful. He ordered me with short, impatient waves of his hand to fetch more water or to kindle a fire.

Olaf played along with this, as he and I had agreed. I even feigned gestures of respect, bowing slightly when he spoke to me, and replying in a low and reverential tone. But the things I said to him were far from respectful, and afterwards, when Choll had gone, we would laugh about it.

When Olaf tried to explain that our boat needed repairs, Choll told us that there was a village just down the coast called Yochac, where we might find help. He prmised to take us there soon.

The next day, Choll brought his family to see us. The children were not allowed to come near Olaf, but Choll let the boy and girl wrestle with me and pull my beard. I would bring my face very close to theirs, until our eye lashes almost touched, then they would go squealing off down the beach. Choll's wife was named Vamukshell, and at first she would come no closer to me than a nearby tree, where she sat in the shade and glowered. But, after a while, I caught her laughing at some of the games I played with the children.

We learned a few Mayan words. The human-sounding bird that woke me every morning was called Chachalaka. Another type of bird, like a big starling, which hopped around on the beach making sarcastic-sounding noises, was called Izyalchamil.

The next morning, the feathered man returned to the beach. This time he brought others like himself who dressed in the same long cloaks and carried short, thick sticks decorated with bright feathers and the teeth of animals. He repeated the name of Kukulkan several times, rested his finger on the black stone hammer around Olaf's neck, and motioned that Olaf should go with them.

Olaf and I glanced at each other.

There was a hostility in the manner of these men which unnerved us. We knew it might not be long before the real Kukulkan appeared, or before the Mayans asked something of us which we could not give them, all in the name of this blonde-haired, blue-eyed stranger, for whom Olaf had been mistaken.

'I am not going anywhere with these bird-men,' said Olaf, 'especially not on my own.'

'Then you had better tell them the truth,' I said, 'before we find ourselves in trouble.'

When Olaf tried to explain that Kukulkan was not his name, they indicated to him with solemn expressions and hands swept in front of their faces, that he was mistaken. It was as if, in our long voyage over the ocean, Olaf had somehow forgotten his true identity, just as I, as his servant, had forgotten mine. What the men seemed to be saying was that there had been many Kukulkans in the history of their world. He was a kind of spirit, wandering in and out of human hearts. The manner of our arrival, and of our appearance, told them all that they wanted to know. In their eyes, Olaf was some kind of messenger, although what message he brought was as much a mystery to us as it was to these strange men.

'They do not think you are a man,' I said to Olaf. 'They think you are some kind of god.'

None of Olaf's protests could convince them otherwise, and when I stepped forward to add my voice to his, one of them silenced me with an angry click of the tongue.

The Mayans gave up trying to persuade Olaf to accompany them, but they were not happy about it, and indicated that they would return before long.

Afterwards, Choll explained with drawings in the sand that these men were powerful priests called Nacom and that the sticks they carried were called Calvac, with which they had the power to send people to Chibolba. We could not understand from Choll whether this Chibolba was a real place or an imaginary one, but clearly it was not a place in which he wanted to end up.

Olaf tried again to explain to Choll that he was not Kukulkan, and that I was not his servant.

I could not tell if he believed Olaf, but it seemed that from then on he looked at us with pity in his eyes, and particularly at me, as if whatever role I played in this was worse than I had yet imagined. Perhaps he grasped now that we were just two men who had lost our way out on the ocean. Even if Choll did not know where we had come from, or who we were, he could tell from the condition of our ship that we had travelled a long way and that we would be lucky if we reached our home again.

Later that same day, Choll guided us to the village of Yochac. He explained that we had nothing to fear. There were no Nacom in the village, as they lived further inland. But then he rested his hand against Olaf's chest and repeated the name of Kukulkan. Then he pointed down the coast towards Yochac, and gestured at the boat. From this, we understood that if we wanted help from the people in Yochac, it would be better if they believed that Olaf was indeed Kukulkan, and I his servant.

While Olaf handled the sail, I worked the steerboard. Choll sat beside me on the deck, laughing nervously at the speed of our boat over the waves. The walrus skull made him anxious. We had trouble persuading him that it was dead.

Yochac lay a short distance down the coast, set back in a shallow bay. All the buildings in the village were made of stick structures like Choll's house, except for one large stone pyramid, painted rosy pink and turquoise blue. It stood at the far end of the little bay, which was filled with silty green-white water. The bay was protected from the ocean side by several small islands made up entirely of tangled trees and roots. Large black birds, the same kind as the one who had appeared over the boat when we were out to sea, nested in the branches. They clacked their beaks when we sailed past and showed their baggy red throats.

By the time Olaf had hauled down the sail and dropped anchor, the whole village had turned out on the beach to watch. There were about a dozen families, with more than twenty children among them.

The harbour at Yochac became our home for now. In the days that followed we grew used to the daily life of the Maya.

They slept whenever they wanted and often stayed awake all night talking. They drank a potion made from water with mashed, soaked beans, and for food they ate small pieces of flat bread cooked over driftwood fires and a kind of fish called Uzcay, which they speared in the lagoon. The jungle was filled with lizards the length of my arm, fearsome to look at but easy to catch. Children knocked them on their heads with springy sticks, then cut their throats with the sharp edges of broken sea shells.

Olaf was given his own home, which was set up on a foundation of stone, unlike any of the others. I was provided with a lean-to shack, connected to the house by a door made of deer hide stretched across a wooden frame. Food was delivered to me, which I was expected to prepare for Olaf whenever he asked for it.

No sooner had we arrived than a wooden chair draped with the skins of some large spotted cat was placed in the shade of Olaf's new house. Olaf was made to sit there while children were brought before him, to be touched on their bowed heads. Then the old and sick were ushered in, and offerings of food for Olaf piled up around my shed.

While Olaf was busy holding court, I ran the boat aground and, with the help of several of the men, used logs as rollers to get it up above the tide line. Then I set to work scraping barnacles and weeds off the hull. Choll showed me how to prepare a thick, tar-like substance from the bark of a tree, which he and I and several of his friends painted on the boards with palm-frond brushes to re-seal them. Some of the planks had worm-holes in them and these we replaced, carefully saving the nails since the Maya had no iron. For blades, they used pieces of flint, which they carefully flaked until it was sharper, although more brittle, than any kind of steel.

That night, when I brought Olaf his food, I found him staring at the ceiling deep in thought, lying on a bed with his hands tucked behind his head.

In a hushed voice, I told him about my success at resealing the hull boards.

He listened for a while and then told me I had better go.

'Go where?' I asked.

He jerked his chin back at towards my lean-to. 'We do not want to make them suspicious.'

I stared at him for a moment, fighting back my irritation, then went down to the water and walked along the beach until I found a secluded spot. Lying on the sand, I prayed, with that same hollow feeling inside me that the words I was speaking were just words in this place. My thoughts raced from one end of my brain to another, like a school of fish caught in a net.

After a night of being mauled by insects in my lean-to, I returned to the boat, where Choll had arranged for some of the Mayan women to help me reinforce the sail. In places where the cloth had worn thin, they stitched patches of animal skin and rawhide lacing.

Again that night, when I brought him his food, Olaf listened impatiently for a while and then told me to go. 'Do not forget what these people think you are,' he said.

Early next morning, Choll and I walked back into the jungle, gathering vines to replace the leather cables which had stretched thin. Although we kept an eye out for a tree that would serve as a mast, we found none that was suitable. Most of the tall trees had either been weakened by beetles gnawing deep inside them, or had a milky white sap, which Choll said burned the skin.

That night, carrying a clay bowl of cooked beans flavoured with hot peppers, I tried to open the door which connected my lean-to and Olaf's house, but found it was blocked by the fur-draped chair on which he spent his days, receiving the people of the village. 'Olaf,' I whispered. 'Olaf!'

I pressed my ear to the door and heard him laughing softly,

followed by the sound of a woman tittering. I stood back, and let the bowl fall with a dull crash onto the floor. Another burst of laughter came from Olaf's darkened house. I returned to my shack, and listened to dogs fighting at the edges of the jungle.

In the days that followed, Choll and I travelled further afield, using his dug-out canoe to cross the wide and pea-green lagoon which opened out behind the village. The water was shallow, and we could have walked across it, but we kept to the canoe because of crocodiles. We had to be off the lake before sunset, as that was when the crocodiles came out to hunt. I had seen crocodiles before, basking in mud along the river Nile, and did not argue with Choll about taking our chances among them after dark.

The Maya called to each other across these marshes by blowing into large spiral shells, whose sound carried far across the water. Often, the quiet of the afternoon would be broken by the sad wail of a shell horn, followed by the distant, moaning reply.

By now Choll and I had learned to communicate well, in a mixture of Mayan, Norse and hand gestures. He told me that the people who lived here now were the remnants of a much larger population. Choll said that years of drought and storms had ruined the crops. Many people moved inland, where there was more fertile land to farm. The edges of the jungle were lined with abandoned stone buildings and some large roads, which the Maya called Sacbe. These had been reclaimed by the relentless creeping vines, leaving only narrow footpaths to snake among the dusty trees. The arrival of Kukulkan had been foretold by the Nacom as the beginning of a new age for the Maya, a time of plentiful crops and prosperity. Only when Choll had explained that to me did I understand the full measure of the danger we were in.

Choll was worried, too, as much for himself as for us. He

feared that the Nacom would punish him for helping to repair the ship, since it was clear that the Nacom did not want us to leave.

I offered to take him with us, but he shook his head. Alive or dead, his place was in this world and not in mine.

That night, finding Olaf's door blocked again, I went in through the front of his house.

He was in bed with a woman, who jabbered at Olaf when I appeared, pointing at me and then at the doorway.

'You cannot come in that way,' said Olaf.

'The other way is blocked.'

'I am not hungry,' he yawned. 'I have been eating all day.'

'Tell her to leave,' I said.

'I cannot do that. She is the daughter of the village elder. He gave her to me, you know.'

I pointed at the woman, who was running her hands through Olaf's hair. Her own black hair shined blue in the light of a palm bark fire, which burned in the middle of the stone floor. 'You,' I said.

She looked at me.

'Get out,' I told her quietly.

She turned to Olaf.

Olaf glared at me, then sighed and waved her away.

She gathered up her clothes and walked past me, bare feet padding on the stone.

'What do you think you are doing?' asked Olaf. 'We agreed to play along with this. I am only doing what is expected of me.'

'The deeper you tangle us into this dream of being Kukulkan, the harder it will be to get out. I cannot find us a new mast. Until I do that, we are not leaving. In the meantime, what are you going to tell the Nacom when they return?'

'Perhaps they won't come back,' he said.

Then I told him what Choll had explained to me about the new age the Nacom believed was coming, and how it began with the appearance of Kukulkan. 'They will come back,' I said. 'You can be sure of it. And if they find out that we are not who they think we are, it will be easier for them to kill us than to come up with another explanation for our being here. Do you not see?'

'Keep your voice down.'

I walked closer to him. 'The Nacom will have to answer to these people for their mistake. I have no doubt that some of them will answer with their lives, but not before they have taken ours as well.'

He rose up until he was on his knees on the bed. 'What if they are right?' he asked.

'Right about what?'

He shrugged. 'About who I am.'

'You are Olaf,' I snapped. 'That much I know for certain.'

He shook his head, as if I had misunderstood. 'It does not matter what you know.' Then he raised his hands and let them fall again. 'It does not even matter what I know!' he laughed. 'You understood what they said. Kukulkan is a messenger.'

'But you do not have a message, you fool!' I shoved him backwards.

He sat up and for a moment it looked as if he was going to lash out. But when he spoke, it was with a calm voice. 'The message that he brings is kept a secret even from himself. Perhaps my presence here is all the message they are looking for.'

'Are you honestly prepared to take that risk?'

He breathed out sharply through his nose. 'How much less of a risk is it to sail that boat across the ocean, hoping we can find our way home again?' He climbed off the bed and took hold of my arm, drawing me towards the doorway. 'I do not even think we are in the same world anymore. Whatever special treatment you received from the gods is over now. I see you shuffling off down the beach to pray, and look how much good it has done you.' We stood now at the entrance to his home.

In the doorways of the little houses, people had gathered to see what the noise was about. Their faces were lit by the soft light of their cooking fires, which filled the air with fragrant smoke.

'Know your place among these people,' Olaf murmured in my ear. Then, with a jerk of his arm, he shoved me off the stone foundation and sent me sprawling in the dirt.

By the time I got to my feet, he had disappeared inside his house.

There was another group besides the Nacom, who seemed equally certain that Olaf was Kukulkan. These were the slaves, of which there were four in the village. They had been given to certain people in the village by the Nacom, but why they had been given or where these slaves had come from, I did not know. These slaves lived in sheds beside the cooking houses of their owners, much as I did. There were three men and one woman, and they spent most of their time washing clothes.

The next evening, from behind the door of my lean-to, I watched as one of the slaves came crawling across Olaf's floor on his hands and knees until he reached where Olaf sat eating his meal of roasted fish. The slave was thin and sickly, with scabs on his legs and dirty hair that stuck up in tufts. He told Olaf his name was Achel. He clasped his hands in front of his face and begged to be set free.

Before Olaf had time to answer, a group of villagers arrived in the doorway and dragged the slave outside. They chased him to the edge of the jungle and beat him senseless with the same sticks used for catching lizards.

I saw that the life of a slave here meant as little as it had in

Miklagard. I could not bear the thought of being a servant again, even if the man I served was not my master.

All night, the high-pitched sound of Achel's wailing echoed through the jungle.

After another day of paddling through the labyrinth of shallow channels which connected the lakes behind Yochac, Choll made it clear to me that it was hopeless to continue our search for a mast. He explained that sometimes trees drifted up onto the beach which might have served the purpose, but he did not know where they came from. He said that the word had spread about the arrival of Kukulkan and that a great gathering was being planned by the Nacom at a sacred place inland. Mayans would be coming from all over the country. People had been awaiting this day for a long time.

Choll and I sat there, in the middle of the lake, water lapping at the sides of his dug-out canoe. Late-afternoon sun beat down on our backs. With a casting motion of his arm, Choll showed that he knew how far I had to travel if I ever wanted to reach my home again. Then he looked at me and shook his head, as if to say that no one could go that far, not even the dead on their voyage to another world.

That night, I waited until after dark, when most of the village was asleep. Then I went to the blocked door and whispered Olaf's name. I called to him until my voice went hoarse, but finally he answered.

'What do you want? You woke me up.'

'There is no hope of finding a mast,' I explained. 'It is only a matter of time before the Nacom return.' I told him about the gathering they had planned. 'We have to leave now and take our chances out on the water. The next time they ask you to go with them, they will not take no for an answer. I will start provisioning the boat tomorrow. Choll will help me with fresh water and food. Then you and I can sail down the coast and dig up the silver before heading out to sea.'

'You can do as you please,' said Olaf. 'I am staying here.'

'Olaf!' I shook the door, trying to wrench it open, but he had tied it shut with vines. 'Think straight! We have to get away.'

'I am not stopping you.'

'And how far do you think I could sail that boat by myself?' He laughed softly.

I heard him getting out of his bed and the sound of his bare feet walking across the stone floor.

Now he stood on the other side of the door. He had thrown away his old clothes and now dressed like the other Mayan men, with only a cloth around his waist.

I could not see his face, only his hands and his legs, on which the old salt-water boils had healed, leaving purple smudges on his skin.

'You must learn to accept the way things are now,' he said, 'just as I learned to accept what I did not want to believe, back in the place where we came from.'

'Olaf, do you not want to see your home again?'

'What if we are already home?' he asked. 'What if we have at last found the gateway into the other world that we searched for back when we were children? Perhaps, somewhere out on the ocean, we passed through without even knowing it. And now we are on the other side. Maybe, even now, we might be in Altvik. Kari might be standing right beside you. But of course you cannot see her, and she might sense that you are there, just as we sensed the other world but could not see it. I believe I have found what I have been looking for all my life.'

I slumped down onto my knees. 'But Olaf, even if you were right, this is not your world. We are travellers and we are lost.'

'If I am lost,' he said, 'it is because I choose to be lost, which means I am not lost at all.'

'We do not belong here, Olaf. We belong in that other place.'

'You belong there, my old friend. Go home, if you can. The temple is your responsibility now.'

It was hopeless to try and persuade him. I could not convince Olaf, because I no longer even knew myself what the truth was, or if there was more than one truth. Perhaps there were a thousand truths, partitioned in their own realities but inhabiting the same space, in which those who held one truth above another lived and died without ever knowing the others existed.

Olaf walked away without another word.

I stayed on my knees, breathing in the still, hot air of Mayan night and longing for the glacier chill of a breeze off the Grimsvoss mountains.

That night, Choll woke me from a dead sleep. He was excited about something, talking so quickly that I could not pick up any of the words.

My first thought was that the Nacom had returned, and I felt a jolt of panic arc across my chest. When I said the word, Choll laughed and swept his hand in front of his face to show I was mistaken.

He brought me down to the water's edge. A vast yellow moon balanced almost full on the rooftop of the jungle. It was so bright that I could even see the pale green colour of the waves as they rose and crumbled on the ghost-white sand.

Choll led me to his group of friends, who were gathered around a stone-lined hole they had dug in the ground. The stones had been heated and the hole was filled with the tar-like substance we had used to re-caulk the hull. The men carried the tarring brushes we had made for the job and now that I had arrived, they began to paint the mast with tar, filling in the cracks which spiralled up the wood.

Now I understood. They had figured it out. I grabbed a brush and began to paint alongside them. We were laughing as we worked in the moonlight, slapping each other on the back, because it was so simple, and so obvious, and we knew it would work.

I tried not to think about the difficulties of sailing the boat alone. I even considered bringing Olaf away by force but realised that it would do no good. I could not make a prisoner of him and expect his help sailing the ship anywhere but back to this same place.

By morning, the tar had hardened, sealing the cracks. It would hold now. It would be even stronger than before.

I decided to speak once more to Olaf, and try to sway his mind. If he refused, I knew I had no choice but to leave as soon as I could, before the Nacom returned. It was morning before Choll and his friends and I managed to refloat the boat, hauling it over log rollers. As soon as the stern had passed beyond a log, one of us dragged the log down to the bow and kept things moving. The boat was sealed up tight and bobbed high in the water. I anchored it in the lagoon and used the rowboat to ferry out green palm nuts, bags of yellow grain, and dried fish, which I laced along the boom so that they hung like tassles, twisting in the breeze. I even tied a hanging bed between two of the old oar-ports, since I had grown used to sleeping that way since my arrival among the Maya.

I discovered that, in my haste to seal the hull, I had forgotten to recaulk the waterbarrels. Now they were leaking badly. I had no choice but to heat up some more tar and paint it on. It would be late afternoon before the tar dried and I wanted to get out beyond the reef before sunset, as I could not cross it in the dark.

I went to find Olaf, running over in my head the words that I would say to shake him from his trance.

When I arrived at Olaf's, my heart jumped when I saw a large group of Nacom gathered outside. Their feathered cloaks glinted with deep blues and reds and greens. Among them stood men without capes, who were armed with short bows, arrows held in lizard-skin quivers and heavy, stone-tipped spears.

Olaf stood above them on the stone foundation of his house.

The sight of the Nacom and their guards had sent women and children back into their houses and left the men sitting uneasily in the shadows of the trees, repairing their fishing nets and glancing up to see what might happen next.

The Nacom were speaking to Olaf, gesturing towards the white-dusted Sacbe road along which they had come.

Olaf nodded and stood.

I pushed my way through the Nacom, despite their clicking tongues of disapproval. At the base of the stone foundation was a chair, built on two narrow poles, with two men standing at each end, ready to carry Olaf away. Over the top of the chair hung a canopy of interwoven leaves to block the sun.

I stood before Olaf, squinting up at him, because the sun's glare was in my eyes.

'You should not have come here,' he said.

'The boat is ready,' I explained. 'These men –'

'The men are taking me inland to the great celebration, which they have been planning for many days. Thousands of people will be there.'

'Come with me.'

He laughed. 'And what would I tell them? That I cared nothing for the hardships they have endured? That I would deny them the new age of prosperity which my arrival has assured?'

I shook my head. 'In your heart, you know that is a lie.'

Now he strode down the steps. 'You cannot bear to see that my luck has changed. What you do not know is that your own luck would never have come to you if it had not been for me.'

'Olaf, what are you saying?'

'How do you think it felt,' he shouted, 'to watch Ingolf, and then you and Kari walk home and leave me up there alone in the fields? I thought if I could persuade you that we were close to discovering something, we might go back to the way things were before, with all of us together as friends. But it went wrong.'

'What went wrong?' I asked.

He folded his arms, the way the Nacom did when they were speaking to someone of lower rank. 'All this time, you thought it was Greycloak who called you out into the storm that night. But it was me.' Then he spoke my name in that rasping, guttural whisper I had heard on the night I ran out into the storm.

'That was you?' I stammered.

He shrugged, to show how easy it had been. 'I put on Tostig's cloak and waited until the middle of the night. I was going to lead you up towards the hills and then hide until you went home again. It would have worked. It would have been so simple.'

'But why?' I asked, my voice cracking with disbelief. 'Why invent a lie when what held us together as friends was our searching for the truth?'

'To make you believe,' he shouted, 'until we really found what we were looking for. So that you who were my friends would not lose faith in me.' He paused. 'And now it is the faith of these people that matters, not yours.' Olaf pointed at the ship, riding at anchor in the jade green water. 'Go, and if you find your home again, tell them that Olaf no longer exists. Now there is only Kukulkan.'

He tried to step past me, but I held out my hands to stop him. 'Olaf, I am telling the truth.'

'Whose truth?' he demanded.

'The only one that matters to me,' I replied, still refusing to get out of his way, 'is the one that will keep you alive.'

The next thing I remember, I was lying on the ground. The left side of my head was burning, and branches of pain spread like long fingers beneath my skin, reaching along the line of my jaw and down my neck. I tried to sit up but fell back again. When my head hit the dirt, chips of light flickered in front of my eyes. I could feel blood trickling down the back of my throat. Olaf's face appeared over mine. He was talking to me, but his voice seemed to come from far away, and I could not hear the words.

Then I was hoisted to my feet by two of the guards, and my hands were tied behind my back with vines.

The Nacom and their guards set off down the white road. Olaf was carried in his chair, swaying gently with the motion of his bearers.

I stumbled along behind, pushed by the tip of a spear. The blood still dripped from my nose where Olaf had struck me. I felt the dryness in my lips and the greasiness in my joints which always came with fear. I thought about running, but knew it would be useless. Before the village was swallowed up by the jungle, I looked back and saw a small group of people watching. Choll was among them. From the expressions on his face, I realised he did not expect to see me again.

The route took us through the jungle along roads paved with the same crushed white stone. Vines and interlocking branches grew so densely on either side that I wondered how these paths could ever have been cleared, especially in this heat, which never seemed to fade from the moment the sun rose above the horizon until well after dark.

Now and then, the procession would pause to rest, and I would be given water to drink from one of the gourds, which all the Maya carried with them. The guards neither looked me in the eye nor spoke to me throughout the day, only pushing me impatiently onwards when I lagged behind.

Once, I saw that Olaf had turned in his chair to look back at me. I tried to read the expression on his face, but there was sweat in my eyes, and all I could make out was a blur.

We camped that night beside a sink-hole where the rocky ground had fallen in upon itself to make an underground pond. The roots of trees had wormed their way through the rock and dangled into the bright blue water. The guards climbed down these roots and went fishing with their spears, while the Nacom set up a triangle of stones around where Olaf sat, still in his chair. They brought out dried leaves, placed them upon each of the stones and set them alight. Then they sat around the triangle and began to chant in a low guttural murmur. I heard the word 'Ekchua' repeated over and over. The leaves burned peppery and sweet. When the Nacom had finished praying, they kicked over the stones and scattered the ashes.

I was brought to the edge of the clearing, made to sit at the base of a tree and tied to its trunk. After giving me a drink of water, they left me alone.

The guards caught some fish in the pond, which they cooked whole and offered to Olaf on a broad green leaf. When Olaf had finished eating, the rest of the fish were divided among the Nacom and their guards. Olaf left his chair and walked over to me.

'Do you see what trouble you have got yourself into?' he asked.

'We are both in trouble,' I said, refusing to look at him.

'These people do not seem to think so,' he said, and gestured towards the Maya sitting around their smouldering fires.

'Not yet,' I told him.

He laughed softly and shook his head. 'Good night, my old friend,' he said and went back to his chair, beside which a bed of fresh palm leaves had been made for him.

Colours bled together in the glow of twilight. Smoke hung in the still evening air. I was so exhausted that despite my fear, sleep overtook me.

Deep in the night, I woke to find strangers in our camp. The Nacom were speaking in hushed voices to a group passing by on the trail. Armed men stood about, but I could not tell if they were from our group or the other. Night birds sang in the depths of the jungle. It seemed to me I could also hear muffled weeping, but it was so faint that I felt sure I was imagining it or that it was the call of those human-voiced Chachalaka birds. The sky drifted back and forth above the trees, as if the black of night was a heavy liquid churned with the silver bubbles of the stars. Sleep shrouded me again and I dreamed of snow falling on the jungle, filling the air with the great silence of the northern winter night.

Butterflies. I opened my eyes and saw butterflies. Hundreds of them. Thousands. They were as large as my palm, black with pale greenish-blue patches and a single red spot on each wing. They fluttered from tree to tree, as if bounced at the end of invisible strings, and clustered on the ground around fallen leaves in which the dew had collected.

Three butterflies were standing on one guard's head, slowly flexing their wings. One was balanced on the tip of his spear.

The guard saw my puzzled face. He looked up at the sky and shrugged, as if these butterflies were only a compression of light, and might disappear as suddenly and inexplicably as they had appeared.

Sun rose bloody from the black silhouettes of the jungle.

We began to move again and soon passed a few small villages, palm-frond roofs dusted white. The path became broader and more travelled. Our procession drew many stares. As the sun climbed higher, even the Maya began to feel the heat of the day. No one had given me any water for a long time and my head was spinning. I stumbled on roots which rose like veins out of the earth and criss-crossed the ground. The leaves of trees lining the pathway were thin and sharp-looking, like the blades of little spears. Everything looked as if it might crumble to dust at any moment. I wondered how these plants could survive. I imagined their roots tunnelling to underground rivers, which swirled in total darkness, down and down to quench the burning belly of the earth.

Through the sweat that stung my eyes, I saw the path converging in the middle distance, clenched in the tiny dagger teeth of these sharp-leaved trees, while all around the air was speckled with the drunken wanderings of butterflies.

We reached a stone archway and, beyond that, a large empty clearing. In the centre of this clearing stood a huge grey pyramid, the sight of which shocked me, as I had never guessed that such a thing existed here, so deep within the jungle. Hundreds of narrow steps led steeply to a small stone house, which was painted bright pinks and blues like the one in Yochac. A chest-high wall separated the pyramid from the jungle and the scattered buildings that lay beyond it.

Olaf was carried into the clearing, followed by the Nacom.

The guards brought me around the outside of the wall to the back of the pyramid. Here, I was put inside a small cage made of sturdy branches bound with vines and left alone. Although the cage was sheltered by the trees, I had no food or water, and the space was too small for me to do anything but sit or lie down.

Throughout the day, I heard the sounds of many people gathering, but I could not see them because my view was obstructed by the wall. Sometimes there was chanting, and I caught the word 'Chulau', which someone at the top of the pyramid would shout, to have it echoed by the people down below.

I never stopped being afraid, remembering what the Emperor had said to me on my last day among the Varangian, that I would find myself one day at the end of the world, far from my friends and those who understood me. I would wake from my honey-coloured dream and find it was too late. It seemed to me then that those words had come true after all.

Some time in the afternoon, one of the guards reappeared and pushed a piece of fruit into my cage. It was oval in shape, with a leathery yellow skin. Since my hands were still tied, I had to press the fruit to the ground and tear at it with my teeth until it opened. The insides were bright orange and sweet, with strands that stuck between my teeth. By the time I had finished, my face was smeared with sticky juice.

Now the chanting of the crowd became constant, and it seemed to me that there were hundreds of people on the other side of the pyramid.

A large, spotted cat appeared from the jungle, moving easily and without sound among the impossible tangle of vines. Its eyes were bright green and I recognised its skin as the same kind which padded Olaf's chair. For a long time, the cat stared at me, not moving. Then suddenly it bolted back into the jungle.

A moment later, the guards arrived. They opened the door to my cage and motioned for me to come out, but my legs were so cramped that they had to drag me into the open. In the heat, their expressionless faces weaved in front of my eyes. The guards motioned for me to climb the pyramid steps.

I began to move hand over hand up the steep slope. Once, I turned around to see how far I had come and immediately felt sick from the angle at which I was climbing.

The guards moved behind me, jabbing the backs of my legs with the tips of their spears to hurry me along.

Beyond the clearing the jungle stretched as far as I could see, cleaved by white roads which shimmered in the haze. At the top of the stairs, I staggered to my feet and the guards took hold of my arms to steady me.

The Nacom priests gathered on the top of the pyramid, looking down at a huge sea of people below. There must have been thousands, many more than I had imagined. Bright flecks of coloured clothing showed amongst the reddish brown of their skin. The murmur of voices hummed like a giant beehive.

One figure stood at the edge of the platform, dressed in a cape of feathers so long it trailed onto the ground and a feathered hat shaped to look like a horn growing out of his head. He spread his arms, like a giant bird about to fly, and the crowd below sucked in its breath. Then the figure turned, and I saw that it was Olaf, his face painted with the same bright reds and greens as the feathers of his cape. He looked at me but did not speak, and no longer seemed to know who I was.

The rest of the Nacom had gathered around a narrow stone chair, which was shaped like a man lying on his back and resting on his elbows with his knees drawn up.

Butterflies perched on the chair. They crowded on the roof of the small house, tilting their wings, as if they meant to carry it up to the sky. They began to settle on me, too, drawn by the smell of the juice on my face. They rested on my head and shoulders and even on my fingertips.

I was pushed against the wall of the house, its red-painted stones hot against my back. One guard stood on either side of me, each carrying a spear.

At that moment, a man was led out of the stone house, guided by two Nacom who I realised were twins. With his back to me, I did not recognise the man, but when he turned, I saw it was Choll. He looked at me through eyes half closed with swollen bruises. The bridge of his nose was broken. His lips had been split by a punch to the face. I couldn't understand how he had come to be here, but then I realised that the crying I had heard in the jungle the night before must have come from him. They had set out later but had overtaken us in the dark.

There were so many butterflies now that the air seemed to shudder with the movement of their trembling wings. The Nacom watched with growing amazement as butterflies flooded out of the jungle, floating up over the rough stone steps to the top of the pyramid.

The twins brought Choll to the chair and made him lie down on it with his legs straddling the drawn-up knees of the human shape. He looked dazed as his head tilted forward and his chin was pushed into his chest.

Olaf was motioned to stand at the head of the chair. He strode across the platform and took his place, then looked around in dignified confusion, waiting to see what happened next.

The heat was stronger than before. The colours of the feathered cloaks flashed in front of my eyes. I could barely stay on my feet. In this delirium I watched one of the Nacom throw back the folds of his cape, revealing his bare chest. Around his throat hung a necklace made of human jawbones, laced together end to end so that they ringed his body like the blunted outline of a star. From a leather pouch he pulled a knife made from the same black stone as the Thor's hammer I had given Olaf. The man moved very quickly, and I shouted as he raised the knife and slammed it into Choll's ribs. The force of the blow buried the Nacom's hand in his victim's flesh. Choll's eyes were closed. His jaw locked open. He let out a scream, spraying droplets of blood into the face of the priest. The Nacom gritted his teeth and the muscles flexed in his arm as he twisted his

306

hand inside Choll's chest. Choll's legs thrashed but his arms hung useless by his side, blood runnning down them, pooling in his palms and running out between his fingers. Now the chest was cut wide open. The clothes and chair and the men who stood nearby were all splashed with Choll's blood. The Nacom hauled out his hand and in it, he held a knot of flesh and blood. He shouted at the sky, 'Chulau! Chulau!', then held his hand to Olaf. Choll's heart was clenched in his fist.

The opened chest glistened in the blinding sun. The blood which had rained onto the feathered men was already drying on the dusty stone of the pyramid. The Nacom were all looking at Olaf, as if he would know what to do.

But the horror on Olaf's face was clear to see. He stared like a man caught in a waking nightmare at the ragged clump of the dead man's heart, which dripped its thickening paint down the Nacom's arm and over the body of the corpse.

A bowl was brought from the stone house. The priest placed the heart in this bowl and handed it to Olaf, who took it in his hands and looked from face to wide-eyed face, as if to see the meaning in this butchery.

The smell of blood hung all around. I could feel my consciousness slipping in and out, as if pulled by powerful tides far beyond the jungle and the wave-crushing reefs.

The dead man was dragged from the seat. His head cracked on the stone floor and with this jolt his eyes, which had been shut, popped open. The body was carried to the edge of the pyramid and swung out into the air. Choll fell against the steps and tumbled to the bottom, patching the stones with his blood. 'Chulau!' the people shouted. 'Chulau! Chulau!'

The butterflies seethed around me, clinging to my chest and my legs, colours pulsing as they moved and making the light flicker just as it had done in that moment before the lightning struck.

The guards had begun to step away from me, overwhelmed by the sight of what appeared to them no longer a person but a swarm of tiny creatures massing as a human shape.

Olaf still held out the bowl, paralysed with fear.

Now, the Nacom signalled to the men who had been guarding me. At first, they did not want to move but then the priest with the jawbone necklace shouted out one word, which shook them from their hesitation. When this man opened his mouth to speak, I saw that his teeth had been filed down to points, like the teeth of a cat. The guards cut the vines which bound my hands, but they kept my arms twisted behind me. The men shoved me forward and when I struggled, the butterflies rose in a single mass, as if my body was scattering into the air. The insects whirled around me in a blur of black and blue and red. I tried to back away from the chair. 'No!' I was shouting. 'No! No!' Then the Nacom with the knife stepped forward and, with one swipe, cut me across my chest. The blade was so sharp, I barely felt the wound. The guards pinned me down upon the stone chair, slippery with Choll's blood against my back.

A rising scream climbed from my throat, scattering the birds from their leafy hiding places. The hot stale air of the jungle trailed out of me and when I gasped to fill my lungs again, it was like drinking smoke. I howled at the Nacom, asking them what kind of god could be satisfied by such a slaughter, but even as the words formed in my mouth, I remembered the names of gods I called my own and the lives which had been ended to appease them. In the blink of an eye the world around was bathed in red. It was not only Choll's blood but Cabal's as well and the gore of every sacrfice that I had ever seen, pouring like a river down the steps of this stone pyramid.

I felt as if my bones and everything which fastened me to life were falling away into an emptiness inside. And with them fell the rulers of the sacred world, like the rotten shutters of a house collapsing in upon itself. What remained had seemed unthinkable to me until this moment – that the world of the gods, and even the gods themselves, held no more substance than the dreams and fears of men.

The Nacom priest moved closer.

At that moment, Olaf raised the stone bowl above his head and smashed it down onto the stones. With a deafening crash, shards clattered away over the precipice of steps, leaving Choll's heart crusted with dirt at the feet of the Nacom. Olaf pressed his hands to the side of his head and turned away.

Everything stopped.

The Nacom stumbled backwards. Some of them dropped to their knees.

The two guards glanced at each other nervously but continued to pin me down.

The priest who had killed Choll stepped forward, offering the black knife to Olaf.

Olaf took the weapon from him.

'Olaf, no!' I shouted.

Then, with all his strength, Olaf hurled the knife out into the jungle. He tore off his feathered cap and flung the huge feathered cape out into the air, where it wafted down onto the steps of the pyramid.

The Nacom priest stared at Olaf, hands held out in a gesture of disbelief. Then he stepped back, and his arms dropped to his sides.

The guards released me, as if their strength had suddenly left them.

Olaf stood in a daze at the edge of the pyramid, the colours on his painted face streaked with sweat.

I rose to my feet and took Olaf by the arm. Then I began to lead him down the steps.

Nobody stopped us. Nobody spoke. The thousands of people who had gathered in the clearing stood motionless and silent.

When we reached the ground, I turned to look up at the Nacom. They had gathered at the edge of the precipice, but there they stayed, staring down at us. The hot breeze ruffled the feathers of their capes.

Olaf and I began to make our way through the crowd, which swept apart like a receding tide to let us pass.

We reached the stone arch at the entrance to the clearing, passed beneath it and kept going down the vine-ridged road. On and on. No one following. We began to run and kept running, feet pounding the dusty road, pausing only rarely to catch our breath. Sometimes I looked back and saw only the white path dissolving in heat haze. Olaf wiped the paint from his face and smeared it on the tree trunks as we passed.

We moved in silence all through the day, never stopping. Ribbons of shadow, cast down through the leaves, slithered like snakes over our skin. We marched on into the darkness, under the rafts of stars, the black air cleaved by bats and streaks of fire falling from the sky.

That night, in the distance, we heard the mournful sound of the shell horns but met no one along the trail. The darkened houses that we passed seemed empty of all life.

We did not speak.

It was dawn when we arrived back at Yochac. The village was still sleeping. The sound of waves and the rustle of palm tree leaves echoed among the huts.

At the water's edge, I found the rowboat just where I had left it. Olaf and I dragged it down into the surf and made our way out to the Drakkar.

Without a word, we hauled up the anchor and raised the sail. Soon we were heading towards the reef.

When I looked back, I saw one man standing on the beach. It

was Achel, the slave who had knelt before Olaf, begging for his freedom. Behind him, butterflies danced in the morning sunlight. He raised one hand to say goodbye.

We rode out over the breakers through the gap in the reef. The jagged rocks slid by beneath us. Soon we reached the deeper water and the pale green sea turned dark beneath our hull. It was only then that we remembered the silver, which we had left buried in the jungle. But it was too late to turn back. Before long, the low-lying coast had sunk from view. Then we were alone again out on the ocean, waves racing past as we steered across the endless field of blue.

It was months before we saw our home again.

For days, Olaf raged like a man caught in a never-ending fever. He did not eat or drink except what I forced down his throat, nor did he seem to know me or even where he was. One night, to stop him jumping overboard, I tied him to the mast, where he howled out his madness to the unanswering moon. By the following morning, he was himself once more, as much as he or I would ever be ourselves again. We were both changed forever from the men who had set sail to the west, already lifetimes ago.

At last, we reached the wreck-strewn coast of Africa. From there, with the help of the bearing dial, we travelled north. By then, the scar across my chest had healed into a pale and jagged line, like the shadow of a lightning bolt.

The Drakkar became so frail that when we rounded the windswept tip of northern Denmark, the boat was taking on water as fast as we could bail it out. We pulled into Hedeby to make repairs, noticing as we rode the Drakkar up onto the sand that the great crucifix which had stood on the headland was no longer there. We were even more surprised to see that the church in the centre of Hedeby was being used now as a covered market place. The platforms were empty now, where priests and would-be priests had once harangued all passers-by with threats of hell and promises of salvation. It was within the canvas-walls of the alehouse that we learned what had happened while we were gone. King Trygvasson was dead, killed at the battle of Rugen, when he jumped from his warship into the sea, still wearing the weight of his armour, rather than be taken prisoner. Without the backing of the king, the Christian priests had lost their footing in the country. Most of the churches had never been built, and all new taxes imposed by Trygvasson were cancelled, at least for now.

At Hedeby, we ran across the Bulgar, as he prepared to head down the Dnieper with another load of goods. We showed him the gifts we had been given by the Maya, the feathered head-dresses, the ornaments of jade and heavy half-moon scapula of gold. He bought them all, but would not believe us when we told him where they came from. 'It is no concern of mine,' he said. 'Jade is jade and gold is gold. That is all I care about.' When he bit down on the gold to test its worth, his front tooth broke in half. 'Very pure,' he said, and lisped as he counted out the silver bars he used for payment. Then he put a feathered hat upon his head and set sail for Starya Ladoga.

Olaf and I left Hedeby with a new mast, new tar on our hull, and 140 pounds of silver.

The closer we came to Altvik, the more nervous we became, not knowing whether we would find our homes intact. If Arne-son had returned to collect his money before the death of Tryg-vasson, we knew he would have kept his promise and left only ruins behind.

It was after dark when we rounded the point and came into the bay. The village was still there, slumbering beneath the first snow of winter, which had just begun to fall. Blue smoke drifted from the rooftops. There was no sound but water running in the streams and the slap of gently breaking waves.

Quietly we rowed ashore. Our bow ground up onto the sand.

Even before I went to find Kari, to share with her the news of Cabal's death, Olaf and I made our way through the empty streets and up the hill to the temple.

Out on the ocean, we had made a promise to each other which we now intended to keep.

We swung open the doors and walked inside, then started a fire in the hearth, using wood from the log pile I had built before I left.

As the glow of flames lit the room, we saw that it had not been used in a long time, probably not since we left. Dust had settled on the benches and the jaws of the pillars were grey with cobwebs.

Olaf looked around. 'This place made enemies of us,' he said.

With those words, we threw more logs on the fire. Smoke began to swirl around the room. As we piled on wood, flames spilled out over the ring of stones and reached above our heads. Soon the roar was deafening. The roof beams caught fire. Over the tops of the flames, I saw the faces of the pillars, mouths open as if crying out in pain.

One of the rafters fell to the ground, scattering sparks across the benches, which had also begun to burn.

The smoke forced us outside.

We staggered into the clean air, and for a while we could do nothing but choke the ashes from our lungs.

Flames jumped through the opening in the roof and set the turf ablaze. The thundering howl of the inferno pushed us back.

From around his neck, Olaf took the black stone hammer. For a moment, he weighed it in his hand, then threw it into the fire.

The roof collapsed in upon itself in a crash of breaking timbers. Wall stones scattered across the ground. Only the pillars
were still standing. Bright flames, like manes of orange hair,
streamed from their heads. Then slowly, they too began to fall,
first one and then the other, crumbling from below so that they
seemed to disappear into the ground. They vanished into the
blazing rubble of the temple, sending up a geyser of black
smoke and sparks.

We heard a noise behind us and turned.

There, in the firelight, stood Kari. She had been running and
was out of breath.

I stepped forward to embrace her.

'Cabal is not with you,' she said, before I reached her.

I stopped. Slowly, I lowered my hands. 'No,' I said quietly,
'he is not here.'

'Is he dead?' she asked, her voice without expression.

I nodded.

'You are sure? There could be no mistake?'

'No mistake.'

I embraced her as the tears came to our eyes, and was surprised to feel the curve and hardness of her belly pressed
against my stomach. I looked at her and did not have to ask.

She sniffed and tried to smile.

'He is with you still,' I said.

She glanced at the ruins of the temple and the black banner
of smoke which had unfurled across the sky. Kari did not ask
us why. She had known long ago what needed to be done.

Despite the late hour news of our arrival spread from door to
door. Soon the whole village had gathered in the alehouse to
hear about our journey.

Ingolf stared at us in shock, unable to grasp that we were
home. He kept coming over and hugging us, as if to reassure
himself that we were really there.

Olaf laid out the silver, just as we had promised. We said it belonged to us all.

Then even Tola uncrinkled her scowl-lined face, which made her look more like a new-born baby than an old woman.

It was almost morning before the story of our travels was all told. Whether Olaf and I were believed, or simply pitied as men whose minds had not returned from the voyage we described, I did not know or care.

The day after the fire, Guthrun and I went to the place where the temple had stood. I dug down through the ashes and showed him the black rock that lay beneath.

For a long time, he said nothing, smoothing his hands over the glassy surface of the rock. Then slowly he rose to his feet. 'Let it stay hidden,' he said. 'It has already cost enough lives. I would rather that its secret died with us than take the blame for all the blood that would be shed because of it in years to come.'

Now I have lived here many years, in my house on the top of the hill.

The Christians come and go. They give out food and promise us a better place, but we like where we are now and tell them so. They shake their heads and set sail for other towns.

These days, I run a fishing boat, just as my father did before me. Like him, I feel it in my blood when the fish come to the bay.

I still help Olaf with his summer trading run. We sail north in his boat, which is so patched it is more patches than boat. He trades with Grim and with the Lapps, who still love him for his luck. Then we head south to Hedeby, stopping in at every port along the way. Olaf is known in those places as a teller of tall tales, and I am known as the only one who believes them, but he and I both know that the tallest of his tales is true.

Kari looks after her son, whom she named after his father.

She also mends the broken health of everyone in town and tends a garden planted with seeds gathered from the farthest reaches of my friend's wandering days. Inside the ruins of the temple walls Kari's neatly planted flowers shelter from the wind.

Most days I go walking through the fields. In the shadow of these hills, I feel it still, the great vibration of the earth and the sacredness of everything around me. Often the boy comes with me. He has the gentleness by which his father is remembered in this town, and his mother's eye for finding treasures others overlook. Watching him, it seems to me as if my old companion did not die but has grown young again.

Through the purple twilight, I bring the young boy home, letting him ride on my shoulders. I seldom need persuading to stay for the evening meal. Afterwards, I rest in a chair before the fire, listening to Kari sing her child to sleep.

As his eyes close, I close my own and dream of no world but this world. No life but this life. No judgement on me but my own.

Author's Note

The presence of the Vikings in the New World was first docu-
mented in the twelfth-century Icelandic 'Vinland' Saga, but it
was not until 1961, when Helge and Anne Ingstad excavated
the indisputably Viking settlement at L'Anse aux Meduse on
the coast of Newfoundland in northern Canada, that the story
behind the Vinland Saga was established as fact.

Over the years, other clues have surfaced which point
towards the arrival of the Norse on the American continent.
These place the arrival of Norsemen all the way from Canada
to Central America. In the 1970s, for example, a coin from the
reign of the eleventh-century Norse king Olaf Kyrri was discovered in the grave of an American Indian in the state of
Maine. Further south, in Newport, Rhode Island, the remains
were found of a stone grain silo said to have been built by
Vikings.

Apart from the site at L'Anse aux Meduse, none of the
physical evidence to support these other stories has proved
conclusive. Some, like the 'discovery' in 1898 of an ancient
rune-carved stone in Minnesota or a map purchased by Yale
University's Beineke Library and apparently showing a
Viking-period chart of the Canadian/American coastline,
have turned out to be forgeries.

One of the most curious and controversial of these unproved legends is that of the Aztec god Quetzalcoatl, known to the Maya as Kukulkan. According to Spanish clerics who accompanied the Conquistador Hernan Cortez to the coast of Mexico in 1519, Cortez was perceived by the Maya to be the god Quetzalcoatl, returning from the east after five hundred years of exile as he had promised to do.

There are many contradictory myths surrounding the god/man Quetzalcoatl. This leads hisotrians to believe that there was in fact more than one Quetzalcoatl and that, in these separate incarnations, Quetzalcoatl was the name of both a man, most notably a twelfth-century Toltec ruler, and perhaps other men too, as well as the name of a god.

It is also possible that the Spanish cleircs reinterpreted what they knew of the legend of Quetzalcoatl in order to convince the Maya, and later the Aztec, that Spanish rule over South America was a foregone conclusion even in their own mythology.

> ' . . . and they held for certain that in coming times were to come from the sea towards the rising sun white men with beards like him . . . and in this way the Indians awaited the fulfillment of this prophecy and when they saw the Christians they called them Gods and the brothers of Quetzacoatl.'
> – Fray Olmos, one of the first Catholic priests in the New World

> ' . . . This was held as very certain that he was of good disposition . . . bearded . . . also said that it was a blonde beard.'
> – Fray Juan de Torquemada on the subject of Quetzacoatl

Torquemada went on to describe that Quetzacoatl had refused to allow human sacrifices to be made in his name and asked for butterflies to be sacrificed instead:

> 'You shall sacrifice before him only butterflies.'
> – The Florentine Codex

If the legend transcribed by these clerics did come from the Maya themselves, then it seems almost impossible that the Maya would have been able to conjure from thin air a description of a blonde-haired, bearded, white-skinned man, a genetic type previously unknown to them. Equally unlikely is the pure invention of European-type clothing, which was also prophesied. In addition to this, a story is still told along the Yucatan coastline of Mexico that, in the lagoon of Yochac, not far from the village of Tulum, a ghost ship with a pointed bow and stern is sometimes seen to rise from the water and head out to sea.

The Vikings represent the only culture who fit in with these legends and could have reached the Maya long before Cortez. Several replicas of Norse ships have sailed across the Atlantic, the first in 1893 when a Viking ship sailed from Bergen to Newfoundland in time for the Chicago World's Fair. More recently, another replica, the *Saga Siglar*, circumnavigated the globe. The Vikings could have rached Central America, in which case their arrival may well have become the stuff of myth by the time Cortez arrived.

Until the Ingstads excavated L'Anse aux Meduse, the Vinland Saga was thought by many to be nothing more than a fable. Of the other sites associated with Norse people in the New World, Gwyn Jones, in his definitive history of the Vikings, wrote: *'A single reliable archaeological discovery in any one of them could change the picture overnight.'*

This book is for W.D.

With thanks to C.R.W., C.B., G.P.-T. and D.R.